# Bones and Whispers

by

## Catherine G. Gault

**Grosvenor House
Publishing Limited**

This book is published by
Grosvenor House Publishing Ltd
28-30 High Street, Guildford, Surrey, GU1 3EL.
www.grosvenorhousepublishing.co.uk

A CIP record for this book
is available from the British Library

ISBN 978-1-78148-826-3

The author lives in Edinburgh. This is her first novel. She enjoys walking the city and (sometimes) reading Booker Prize winners.

# Prologue

The wind whipped him, licking at his face, making his eyes water. It was coming straight off the river tonight. You could almost taste the salt in it. It carried the voices to him. The kids were back.

"Fuck aff, ya wee bastards." He chased them half-heartedly, leaving off when they reached the perimeter fence. The old warehouse had been their meeting place and, even though it had been pulled down, they still hung around. Night like this you'd think they'd want to be somewhere warm. He looked back and got a finger for his bother. "Wee bastards," he muttered.

He headed back to the Portakabin, stopping at his van to pick up his fish supper and his half-bottle. In the 'kabin he settled himself in the ancient swivel chair, fish and chips unwrapped on his lap, the first of his whisky in a chipped cup on the desk beside him. Warmth from the calor gas heater crept drowsily up his body.

The scream shocked him upright and propelled him to the door before he was properly awake. He wrenched it open. Icy rain pattered his face.

The scream came again.

"Aw, shite." He pulled on a yellow waterproof, grabbed a torch and stumbled into the darkness, cursing an accompaniment to the rain now drumming on his hunched shoulders.

The torchlight showed him a route to avoid puddles before picking out two boys standing at the edge of a deep trench. They squinted up at him, flinching as the needles of rain pierced their thin hooded tops.

"He fell in. We cannae get him out," one of them said.

"Stand back from there." The man was surprised to see them obey. He directed the light down into the trench. The stranded boy huddled, shivering, in a corner. "Have you hurt yourself?" the man called.

"I want my mammy," a tearful voice shouted back.

Aye, don't we all. He crouched at the edge of the trench. "If I lean down, can you reach up and catch my hand?"

"It's watching me." The voice trembled.

"What are you talking about?"

The boy nodded towards the opposite end of the trench, eyes averted. "That."

The man shone his torch in the direction the boy indicated. It took him a while to realise what he was seeing. It lounged as if it had been propped there. The long bones of the legs gleamed in the torchlight. Mesmerised, he let the light drift into the cave of the pelvis; settled it briefly on the ribcage where the damp earth had filled the small gaps between the ribs; watched it slide over the sternum and finally come to rest on the glistening skull with its toothy grin and black holes where its eyes had been.

A raindrop slipped from his sodden hair and made a small splash on his hand. He dropped the torch.

The children screamed.

# Monday

## 1

It had been fine till she'd reached Canonmills. She loved Edinburgh. She really did. But on mornings like this... and she was well on her way to being late for her meeting. The one she'd spent most of her weekend preparing for. The one that just might set her off on a new career path. She glanced at the driver in the black GTI alongside. He smiled at her, his indicators flashing his intention to cut in. Bloody queue-jumper. And sunglasses. Rain pissing down and he's wearing sunglasses. The lights changed to green and she moved forward a couple of car lengths, ignoring the GTI and the obscene gesture from its driver now visible in her rear-view mirror.

She should have skipped her swim, that would have bought her a bit more time but it had become too much of a ritual. She missed the rhythm of the stroke, the soft buoyancy of the water, the newly acquired elegance of her tumble-turns, the underwater silence.

Her smile was already fading when her mobile phone disrupted her reverie. "Kate McKinnery," she announced, fiddling with her earpiece. She heard only crackles in reply and glanced down at the 'phone. The screen flickered and died. "Bugger," she muttered.

An angry honk from the car behind made her jump. She fumbled into first and swept round to her left closely followed by her new friend in the GTI. He had either fallen madly in love with her or was deeply into a fit of road rage judging by the way he drove halfway up her backside. Approaching a pelican crossing at amber she braked sharply and watched with satisfaction as the GTI driver almost hit his windscreen. Then they were off again like Siamese twins joined at the bumper. This was getting stupid.

She made her right turn into McDonald Road, the GTI close behind, the driver still gesticulating. Was he following her? At the lights at Leith Walk she squeezed through on the last of the amber. The GTI followed.

She slowed to give way to a bus that was pulling out of the bus lane. The bus had no sooner set off when it stopped again. Out of the corner of her eye, Kate saw a little girl standing on the pavement, arms outstretched, tears streaming down her face. A woman about her own age jumped from the bus, ran towards the little girl and hugged the child tightly to her.

"Ya stupid bitch. You want to learn to fucking drive."

Kate turned to see the GTI driver, his face distorted in anger, give her a one-fingered salute before he roared off down Leith Walk. When she looked back, the woman and little girl were gone.

She tucked her Yaris in behind the bus and indicated left. In the car park she reversed into a space and switched off the engine. Her heart was thumping. Bubbles of panic fluttered up from her diaphragm. She forced herself to breathe deeply focussing only on the air in and out, in and out. Calmer now, she pulled an envelope from her bag and took out the photograph she'd been carrying around since she found out. It was her favourite photo. The original was in a frame on her dressing table. Her mum was in her red coat. Kate wore her cut-down child's version, her blonde hair in pigtails,

2

each tied off with a red ribbon. They were smiling and waving at somebody. She didn't know who. In the photo she'd be about four, her mum twenty-nine. She carried it about now like a talisman, evidence of a happy time. Proof that there had been a happy time. She slid the photo back into the envelope, returned it to her bag and got out of the car. She gathered up her briefcase and was reaching into the back seat to get the laptop when she heard a voice behind her.

"This you just getting in?"

She turned to see her boss, Nick Johnson, grinning at her. "No," she replied, "I'll be here in about half an hour."

"Bit pre-menstrual today are we?"

"Well, I'm not," she snapped.

"That's what I like about you, Kate. You don't take prisoners. Even better, you don't take offence."

What's put him in such a good mood? Somebody must have died.

Nick headed for the entrance. "By the way," he shouted back, "I tried to phone you. The meeting's cancelled."

"Bugger." She grabbed the car door ready to slam it but at the last minute she changed her mind and closed it with a gentle push.

When she went into the building she noticed, not without satisfaction, that Nick had been cornered by a middle-aged woman in a grey pinstripe suit. The 'mother-in-law problem', she'd become known as. Kate moved quickly to the stairs ignoring Nick's fleeting attempt to catch her eye. He caught up with her at her office door.

She turned to him. "No, Nick. I don't do elderly. You know that."

He shook his head. "I just want you to check somebody on your system. Her name's Jessie Turner."

She nodded her agreement and watched Nick bustle off along the corridor wondering who he'd try to land Jesse Turner on, determined it would not be her. In her office, she dropped her briefcase on the floor beside her desk and lowered her laptop onto the table. The cancellation of her meeting left her feeling deflated whilst the excess adrenaline fuelled the merry-go-round of questions that crowded once again into her brain. She'd thought about starting a life-story book as a way of sorting out memory from imaginings. It was a well-tried social work method she'd used successfully with children who'd been taken into care but she wasn't sure it would work for her. She was wary of giving credence and authority to memories that might not be real by writing them down.

She shrugged off her coat, letting it flop over the back of a chair. Coffee. Kettle and mugs sat atop a two-drawer filing cabinet under the window. She switched the kettle on. The room looked onto Leith Walk. On a clear day, if she craned her neck, she could just see the hunkered shape of Arthur's Seat, one of Edinburgh's extinct volcanoes. No chance today. The rain was coming down in sheets, with that great shushing sound only really heavy rain can make. Through the blur she saw Nick, clutching his diary, make a dash for the front door from the shelter of the car park. He'd no sooner set off when he was confronted by a large, black and extremely agitated umbrella. Pinstripe suit. Got to be. Kate smiled. You had to admire the neatness of the move. Nick was trapped midway between the door and the car park getting absolutely drenched. And there was no way he was getting under the umbrella. By the time the woman had said all she wanted to say the rain was easing off but Nick was soaked, his sky blue shirt darkened to navy, his red, springy hair flattened against his scalp.

Still smiling, Kate turned from the window, powered up her computer and logged on to the new 'service user' data system. 'The Project', as it had come to be called, was now seen by many of her social work colleagues as her baby. She'd progressed from the token social work presence on the development team to being a crucial player in the system's implementation. Question was did she want to build a career on it.

There was a knock on the door and Nick came in. He'd borrowed a jumper from somebody, Noel Edmonds by the look of it. His round belly, encased in multi-coloured wool, bulged over his low-slung trouser belt. His hair stood in static-charged curls.

"Christ, see that woman," he began. "I told her I'd see her as soon as I could. Do you know what she did?"

"She didn't trap you in the rain and get you soaked whilst she laid into you?"

"Were you watching from your window?"

"I think everybody was watching from their windows."

"I couldn't get away without knocking her over and she was jabbing her finger at me." Nick stopped for breath. "She wouldn't even let me under her umbrella."

Kate couldn't stop the howl of laughter at Nick's heart-sorry-for-himself look.

"It's not funny," he said huffily. "I could get pneumonia or something." He pulled a chair alongside Kate's and sat down. "What have you got for me?" he said still frowning.

She tapped the computer screen. "Jessie Turner left sheltered housing at Leapark Terrace to live with her son and daughter-in-law." She turned to Nick. "I take it that was the daughter-in-law."

"Jessie's driving her up the wall. They want her back in sheltered housing."

"Why did she move out in the first place?"

"She says one of the women was bullying her."

"They're all in their seventies."

"But you know what the root of the problem is?" Nick paused to affect a look of horror. "Some of the flats are rented out to council tenants."

"No hope of keeping out the riff-raff." Kate fell in with Nick's pantomime. "So, Leapark Terrace." She tapped a few keys and up came a list of residents.

"Ah," they said in unison, "Maggie Keenan."

"There's a blast from the past," Nick said.

"My auntie Jean's just moved in there."

Outside the hee-haw of a siren interspersed with high-pitched whoops heralded the passing of a fire engine. Hard to imagine any fire getting hold in this rain.

"Why did she want to move to sheltered housing?" Nick asked.

"Fell off a ladder when she was trying to change a light bulb."

"She break anything?"

"Just the light bulb."

"Oh, haw, haw." Nick gazed at the screen. "So, Maggie Keenan, eh."

"The Intimidator."

"Not half."

"That sounds as if you've had personal experience."

Nick hesitated. "During my early days in Fife I was sent out to follow up a report about a wee lassie staying with Maggie. The wee lassie was fine but Maggie was quite something, wanted to know who had reported her."

"I take it you didn't tell her."

"I didn't have to, she found out herself. The woman had to move."

"Maggie obviously made an impression." Kate was enjoying watching Nick's remembered discomfiture.

"I'll need to find somewhere else for this woman. Can you do that on your new system?"

She called up the sheltered housing complexes, printed out those with vacancies and handed the list to Nick.

"I'll see what Mrs Pinstripe makes of this." He headed for the door. "I wouldn't worry about your auntie, Kate. If she's anything like you, Maggie Keenan doesn't stand a chance."

After Nick left, Kate sat considering the implications of this latest piece of information. Nick was right in his blunderbuss way: Jean was unlikely to interest Maggie Keenan. In her younger days Maggie had been suspected of being involved in a number of low-level criminal activities including dealing in stolen goods and money lending, with a bit of blackmail and intimidation on the side. Rumour had it that she'd wound her operations down as she got older, settling for living off what she'd already made. Sounded like she might have changed her mind, if Maggie really was behind Jessie Turner's abrupt departure from Leapark.

She got up, dropped a coffee bag into a mug and poured water over it. Whilst waiting for the coffee to brew, she picked up her coat and draped it on the hanger behind the door. At the table, she opened the laptop bag, extracted the USB key that held the presentation she'd been working on at the weekend and stuck it into one of the desktop's sockets. Leapark was an offshoot of what she'd come to think of as the 'Jean situation'. They'd been fairly close for the past twelve years since Kate had moved from Greenock to go to Edinburgh University, had grown closer when her grandmother, Jean's mother, had died, leaving the two of them the only surviving family members, as far as she knew. Then Jean dropped her bombshell about Kate's mother.

She fished the coffee bag out with a teaspoon, squished it against the side of the mug and eased it into the silver sachet it had come from before dropping it into the bin. Finally, she settled back in her chair and took a blissful sip watching computer- generated waves lapping a moonlit shore.

When she was growing up her grandmother had always told her that her mother had been happy. She wanted to believe that her grandmother had been telling her the truth. But if so, how come on a cold, dark November morning a few days after her own and her daughter's birthdays, this apparently happy woman decided to chuck herself in the River Clyde and inhale enough water to sink the Titanic?

## 2

"Hello, Mrs Post. Are you in there?" A woman's voice called.

Jean stopped. She'd just moved in at the weekend but the place was already getting on her nerves. She had to get out. So she'd put on her dark green coat, picked up her key and purse and went down the stairs outside her flat. The door at the bottom was a Fire Exit warning that it was alarmed. Always ready with a joke, her mother would have wondered what had alarmed it. Jean had almost smiled as she set off along the corridor towards the front door. Now she stood outside the door of the flat the voice had come from, looking down at the corridor's dark blue stain-resistant carpet, listening.

"Mrs Post?" The voice came again, the note of anxiety creeping up. "Harriet?"

She hesitated. Should she offer to help? She was still dithering when the door of the flat opened and a short, chubby woman in a green and yellow home help overall appeared.

"Oh," the woman gasped and jumped back. A plastic badge pinned to her chest identified her as Shona Wilson.

"Is something wrong?" Jean asked.

"It's Mrs Post. I think she's in the bathroom but she's not answering and the door's locked." Shona Wilson looked at Jean with wide, worried eyes. "I only started last week. Do you think I should call the warden?"

Jean sighed. She could see that, as in her own flat, the lock on the bathroom door was attached by a large screw that also turned the bolt. She rummaged in her purse then held out a two-pence piece.

The home help stared uncomprehendingly at the coin.

"Turn the screw," Jean said, nodding at the lock.

"Oh, aye." Shona turned to the bathroom door and fiddled with the makeshift screwdriver, fitting it into the groove of the screw at the third attempt. She followed the door as it swung inward. There was a sharp intake of breath then, "Oh my god."

The door drifted back to its closed position.

Jean stood where she was, waiting for the home help to reappear. The bathroom door remained resolutely shut. "Is everything all right?" she called.

No answer.

She stepped into the hall and knocked on the door then, hesitantly, pushed it open and looked into the bathroom. Shona was in a heap on the floor. Alongside her lay an elderly woman Jean took to be Harriet Post. She was on her side, knees drawn up, back against the pillar that supported the wash-hand basin. Her head, wedged under the radiator, rested in a pool of congealed blood, her legs in a puddle of urine. A thin, white forearm poked from the sleeve of her nightdress.

Jean squeezed into the small room, pulling her coat tighter. She gave Shona's ample backside a soft kick, wanting her to wake up, to take charge of this but only succeeded in pushing the home help's knees into the urine puddle. Sighing, she lowered herself onto the toilet seat. From there she got down on one knee and, gingerly, touched the back of her left hand to Harriet Post's bare forearm. The skin felt cold, lifeless. The eyes gazed unseeing at the toilet bowl.

Jean continued to kneel there for a moment, hugging her coat round her, purse and key clutched in her right hand tucked into her armpit. She became aware of the whirring of the ventilator; noted the lack of a window; looked up at the light bulb beaming under its lantern-style shade; turned again to Harriet Post. Her ankles were neatly crossed. She had small feet, still wearing pink, ballet- style slippers. The nightdress, white dotted about with rosebuds, primly covered her knees.

Jean got up, leaning on the toilet seat for support, and went into the sitting room. She was aware of feeling unnaturally calm and wondered if she was in shock. She stood looking at the phone. Should she dial 999?

Which service should she ask for? Did you call an ambulance for a dead person? The intercom swam into focus. Leave the decision to someone else, she thought, and pressed the red button that would connect her with the warden's office.

"Kirsten here."

"This is Jean Markham. Um, I'm in Harriet Post's flat. You'd better come right away."

There was a pause then, "I'm on my way."

She waited in the corridor for Kirsten. She felt she should check on Shona. It had seemed callous to leave her there with only Harriet Post's body for company but Jean had no desire to re-enter the bathroom. The scene reminded her too much of herself curled up on the floor of her sitting room in her old flat, scared to move, terrified she'd broken her hip or worse. What had finally shifted her was the thought that if she lay any longer she'd wet herself.

Despite their strained relationship, Kate had come when called. She'd seen the ladder and the broken light bulb and reached her own conclusions. What Jean didn't say was that she had no memory of falling: one minute she'd been halfway up the ladder reaching for the light socket, next thing she knew, she woke up on the floor.

"Are you all right, Mrs Markham?"

Jean jumped at hearing her name. "Yes, thanks."

Kirsten was already heading for the bathroom, led there by groans from Shona. She manhandled the home help into the sitting room before phoning for the doctor.

Jean followed her in but once there felt suddenly claustrophobic. She noticed a door leading from the flat to the outside. "Do you mind if I go out for a minute?"

She followed a pathway into the park. The sodden ground squelched under her feet. It smelled of dampness, as if the rain had penetrated to its core and it would never be properly dry again. She sat on a bench under a tree, needing to work out when and how to tell Kate about this. Their relationship was shaky enough as it was. She didn't want Kate thinking that she'd taken to mucking about with dead bodies to get attention.

She huddled deeper into her coat, pulling up the collar. Weak sunlight glistened on the blades of wet grass clustered round her shoes. The sheltered flat had been Kate's idea. The blond, brick building sat at the bottom of a quiet, residential street in Corstorphine. It formed three sides of a rectangle enclosing a small landscaped garden that was separated from the adjoining park by a railing with a gate in the centre. The flat Jean had eventually bought was in what she thought of as the backside corner overlooking the park. Later it occurred to her who benefited from it. Sheltered housing: wardens, emergency cords, help on call. If anything happened Kate wouldn't have to get involved. A sharp splash on the top of her head made Jean look up thinking even the birds had taken against her but it was just the rain starting up again.

Back in the building she stood in the entrance hall. Kirsten sat behind the small reception window, head down, concentrating on whatever she was writing. She looked to be in her thirties, a bit older than Kate. She was shorter than Kate too, and chunky with hair much darker than Kate's blonde. She had small, neat features, eyes a bit too small maybe, complexion a bit too pale. Jean did find herself comparing any young woman she met with Kate and one way or another they all fell short.

Wasn't this how mothers were supposed to feel about their children? Jean was still pondering this when Kirsten looked up.

"Mrs Markham, are you feeling better?"

Jean nodded and walked over to the window. "I wondered if there was any news on Mrs Post."

"The police may want to talk to you about finding the body."

"The police?" Jean thought Kirsten looked at her a bit intently.

"Apparently the doctor found some bruising and informed the police. It's standard practice." Kirsten's tone was reassuring but ineffectual.

"So this wasn't the first time you've had to deal with a death?"

Kirsten shrugged. "I used to work in nursing homes."

"I see." Jean turned away and headed for the stairs.

In her flat she debated calling Kate, rehearsing what she would say, how she would say it. She wanted to sound calm and in control, not needy, certainly not plaintive. She settled on the settee with the phone, took a deep breath and pressed the button for Kate's mobile number.

The familiar voice answered. "Jean, how are you doing?"

"There's been an incident here."

"What do you mean, an incident?"

"A woman died."

"Oh, right."

She could hear the puzzled impatience in Kate's response. "She was found lying in her bathroom by one of the home helps," she hesitated, "and me. They think she might have been attacked."

"What was the woman's name?"

"Post, Harriet Post." Jean had an image of Kate tapping into the computer to see what it knew about Harriet Post.

"Are you all right?"

"I'm fine."

A pause then Kate asked, "Do you want me to come out to see you?"

"You're welcome anytime, Kate, but you don't have to."

"Right. Well ring me if you get worried about anything."

The line went dead. So she was on her own. Nothing new in that but she'd really wanted Kate to come, or at least to have had to work harder to dissuade her. She laid the phone on the coffee table next to a shiny, pink, plastic folder. She could see through the transparent cover to the top sheet. It seemed to mock her, its multi-coloured lettering telling of the fun to be had in Leapark Terrace.

She wandered over to the window. The rain still pounded down and now the wind had got up and was rooting about in the trees. Across the park sat another sheltered housing complex. The city was full of them. She was scared. She didn't want to end her life dribbling dementedly in a home, like those where Kirsten had become inured to dealing with death. Kate had seemed to offer some security against that, Jean wasn't sure why, and it was academic now. Kate wasn't offering anything anymore.

It was fair enough. What had she ever given Kate? Belated birthday cards and the odd phone call. She hadn't visited often, Christmas and New Year and not always then. But Kate had been happy with her granny and that was what Alan, Kate's father, had wanted. Jean had learned that life was a lot easier if she went along with what her little brother wanted, even agreeing not to tell Kate about the suicide.

She reached into the pocket of her grey cardigan for a tissue. It was that bloody dream. Kate had been so upset by it. She'd got it into her head that she'd somehow been responsible for her mother falling in the river. Jean couldn't have let her go on thinking that.

"Kate, listen to me. It wasn't your fault. It couldn't have been," she'd said. They'd been in her sitting room in her old flat, Kate prowling, Jean trying to soothe her.

"You can't know that, Jean. You weren't there."

"Neither were you."

"I must have been. That's why I keep having the dream. I pulled away from her. I let go of her hand and she fell into the water." Kate shook her head at Jean's incipient denial. "It's so clear, Jean. That's why my dad left me. Why he couldn't bring himself to come back and see me. It all fits."

"It doesn't. Believe me, it doesn't." She grasped Kate's arms, wanting her to stop talking like this.

"I know you think you're helping but you're not. I'd rather know the truth."

She looked at this new distraught version of her niece. "Oh, Kate," she hesitated.

"What?"

Still Jean hesitated.

"What?" Kate almost screamed.

Jean removed her hands from Kate's arms and clasped them in front of her. She took a deep breath. "Your mother killed herself."

Kate stared at her, open-mouthed, blinked once, twice, three times. Her lips moved as if trying out what words might fit then softly, "What?"

"Your mother killed herself, Kate. You weren't there. Nobody was."

Kate still stared but ice was forming in those deep blue eyes. "How do you know that?"

"Your father told me." Jean waited, myriad, small muscle trembles causing her to shiver intermittently.

"How long have you known?" The tone was menacingly soft, the stare unrelenting.

Jean opened her mouth but the words wouldn't come. She wanted to be anywhere but here, she wanted to be as far away from here as she could get. Kate stood implacably in front of her, waiting for the answer, every cold, hard inch her father's daughter. Jean's hands moved to cover her mouth. She forced herself to meet Kate's eyes then lifted her chin clear of her restraining hands.

"Since the funeral," she barely whispered.

Kate didn't say a word, just turned away, picked up her coat and her bag and walked out the door, leaving Jean's pleas of "Kate..." trailing hopelessly behind her.

### 3

It was still early enough for the bars and restaurants on Queensferry Street to be busy. The lights from their windows contrasted with the darkness of the newsagents and sandwich shops but Kate had had enough. There was only so much to be said about I.T. systems and she'd heard it all. She'd dropped her bags off at her flat in Comely Bank Avenue, even found a parking space for her car, before walking along to Ryan's Bar. Now she was headed in the opposite direction. She'd thought a drink with her potential colleagues might clear her mind. Failing that, she turned to the walk home, the night's chill, but none of it was working. Her brain insisted on turning over the 'phone conversation with Jean earlier in the day. She'd known that Jean had wanted her to visit, and maybe she should have, but the move to Leapark was supposed to have brought closure, a good old social work term, to the rift with Jean: a fresh start if on a different footing. And what happens? First Maggie Keenan turns out to be one of Jean's neighbours then Jean gets herself involved in a suspicious death.

She stood for a moment on Dean Bridge listening. A hundred feet below, in pitch black immune to the streetlights, the Water of Leith gushed. Suffused by the morning's rain, it would foam through Stockbridge and Leith itself to the River Forth and the North Sea. At a lull in the traffic, she could just hear the water but could see nothing. Here, in the heart of the New Town, beneath the elegant Georgian edifices, was a bit of the wilderness, a dark underbelly that, in Edinburgh, was never far away.

"Long way doon, hen." An elderly man nodded and smiled at her as he passed. "A long way doon." The repetition drifted back to her.

Behind her, a brightly-lit double-decker bus rushed by leaving a small whirlwind in its wake shaking her out of her fanciful mood. A long way doon right enough. She turned from the water and resumed her walk home.

She was at the door into her stair when she saw the man get out of the car. The streetlight showed him to be tall, wide-shouldered, thick brown hair, sexy mouth. A couple of strides and he was standing in front of her.

"What are you doing here?" she said.

"Nice to see you too." Detective Inspector John Nelson smiled at her.

"Sorry. It's been a trying day." She couldn't help smiling back.

"That's why I'm here. Leapark Terrace."

"Right. Do you want to come up?"

She unlocked the stair door and he followed her into the close and up the two flights of stairs to her flat. As they entered, she caught a glimpse of her cat, Lucy, disappearing into the front bedroom. She led John into the kitchen.

"Coffee or tea?" she asked him.

"Whatever you're having." He pulled out a chair and sat at her scrubbed pine table. "You've been missed at the liaison meetings. Are you still seconded to that computer project?"

"For another couple of months." Kate topped up the kettle and switched it on then selected two mugs from the rack. She dropped a tea bag in each and turned to John. "I thought you'd moved on from those."

"I have now that someone's been appointed to head the Child Protection team."

"So, Leapark Terrace." She leant back against the worktop and looked at him expectantly.

"I wanted to let you know we're still investigating."

"So it wasn't just a fall?" The kettle bubbled to a climax and switched itself off.

"It's possible she was pushed. There was some bruising on her chest."

"A break-in?"

"We're considering that. Her flat had a door that opened directly to the outside but it wasn't locked."

"Anybody could've got in," Kate said dismissively and turned to busy herself with her tea-making, finally taking a carton of milk from the fridge and pouring some into each mug.

"You know Maggie Keenan has a flat there?"

"You think Maggie had something to do with it?" She carried the mugs of tea to the table, set one in front of John and sat opposite him. "I thought she'd retired from that sort of thing."

"So did we but we can't ignore her as a suspect."

"Are you in charge of the investigation?" she asked.

"It's Steve's case. I'm covering whilst he's caught up in court. He'll be showing up at Leapark at some point." He paused. "Is that a problem?"

"Not for me." She waited, wondering what was really behind his visit.

John held her gaze for a moment then dipped his head and lifted the pale blue mug to his lips, eyes down, long, dark lashes almost touching his cheek. His dark red tie hung slightly askew against his white shirt. His left hand, minus the wedding ring, rested on the table.

She became aware of him looking at her.

"Jean was unsettled by this, especially being fingerprinted," he said.

"Fingerprinted?"

"She'd touched various things in the flat. She seemed..." he searched for the right word, "depressed? And, aye, I know she'd just found a body but I got the impression it was more than that." He shrugged.

Kate nodded.

John drained his mug and stood. "Thanks for the tea."

As they walked into the hall Lucy poked her head round the bedroom door only to quickly pull back.

"Have I done something to upset your cat?"

"Don't take it personally. It's men in general she doesn't like."

He smiled at her. "Hope she gets over it. Bye, Kate."

She closed and locked the door and put the chain on, though if anyone could get through the locks the chain would be a doddle. She dropped her keys into their bluebell patterned dish on the hall table and stood gazing at the tiny blue flowers. What was all that about? Passing on a concern about Jean? Maybe. Wanting to let her know about Steve? Mmm. Or testing the water for himself. But why now? He would know that she and Steve had broken up three months ago. Of course, given his complicated love life, John may not have been available then. She wasn't sure that she was available now. She had enough on her plate without adding a new relationship to it. Yet there'd always been a ... frisson, yes, a frisson with John. A maybe, if she hadn't started seeing Steve. She turned to see a tabby face peering up at her.

"All clear, Luce." She scooped the cat up and carried her into the kitchen. Lucy leapt onto the worktop. Kate took a small carton of single cream from the fridge and dribbled some into a saucer. Whilst Lucy lapped up the cream, Kate stroked the cat's soft fur. "Ghosts, baby, everywhere ghosts," she said.

She collected the mugs from the table, rinsed them under the hot tap and put them on the draining board then stood at her window looking out across the back gardens. Through her reflection she could see the lights showing from the windows of similar flats. She walked to the door and switched off her own light, giving Lucy a reassuring stroke as she returned to the window. Now she could make out the shapes of the trees, their branches almost bare of the leaves that still carpeted the grass beneath them. A watcher in the dark. It was something she used to do as a child in Greenock, only then she looked out on the River Clyde. She could still see the image in her mind's eye, the shapes and shadows reaching down to the river and, from the other side, the lights of Helensburgh glinting and glimmering in the dark water.

Lucy jumped to the floor. Kate took the licked-clean saucer, put it in the sink and went into her bedroom. She sat at her dressing table looking at her reflection in the mirror: clear-eyed, clear-sighted, assured, the only flaw a small scar below the curve of her bottom lip. 'Good-looking and knows it', someone had once said of her. Fine, she'd thought, make the most of it. Strange, though, John turning up like that. She'd always been more attracted to him than she'd been to Steve.

"Ghosts," she said again.

Smiling she turned to a silver framed photo beside the mirror. Her gran smiled back at her. 'You don't want a picture of an old thing like me,' Gran had said, secretly pleased nonetheless. She shifted her gaze from her gran's photo to its similarly framed neighbour. Her thumb traced the outline of the small figure, blonde hair in pigtails, face creased in an open-mouthed smile, babyfat hand waving. She extended her fingers and let them trail gently down the tall, slender, red-coated woman alongside.

She'd been five the day her mum died. Her gran had met her from school. She often did that. Her dad was there when they got home. That was unusual.

'Have you told her?' her dad said.

'You know I wouldn't tell her a thing like that,' Gran replied.

Kate had stood there smiling, full of her day at school, excited about this secret that her gran couldn't tell her. She'd started to take her blazer off when her dad looked at her and said, 'There's been an accident, Katie. Your mum's dead.'

She'd dropped her blazer on the floor and ran to her dad crying. He lifted her onto his knee and held her tight against him. She'd been aware of her gran picking up the blazer. She could still see her now, standing in the middle of the floor, tears starting from her eyes, looking at Kate and her dad, her arms wrapped around the blazer.

That was the last time her father held her.

# Tuesday

## 4

Jean blinked. The brown carpet felt rough and scratchy against her cheek. She opened her eyes and raised her head warily. The room stayed still. She lay for a moment, trying to work out if she was sore anywhere. She thought she had crumpled rather than crashed down but reckoned she was unconscious when she landed. At least she could remember starting to fall, that was an improvement on the last time.

She pushed herself to a sitting position. The room didn't spin. She reached for the arm of the sofa and pulled herself up to her knees. If anyone walked in they'd wonder what she was doing apparently praying to a picture of a giant green crane with Scott-Lithgow on the spar. The crane had been a famous Port Glasgow landmark: a remnant from the shipbuilding glory days of her home town. Kate had given her the picture a few Christmases ago before Jean started having dizzy spells; before she'd all but destroyed her relationship with Kate; and well before she found herself in a sheltered flat.

She got her backside onto the sofa and slumped against the cushions. She'd have to go back on the medication. But it made her so dopey; it was like going about in a fog. She'd got it from her G.P. before she moved to Leapark. He'd settled on a diagnosis of 'positional vertigo', said it was probably an age thing. But he'd been thorough, sending her to the Royal Infirmary for various tests and scans. When nothing of note showed up he'd talked about depression, suggested counselling. She'd liked the sound of that, counselling: having someone to focus on her for a change, someone to talk to who would have to listen to her. When she'd tuned back in her doctor was talking about a nine-month wait for an appointment and offered her Prozac in the interim. First time she took it, it sent her sky-high. She went charging along Princes Street smiling at everybody. Got home with bags of stuff that was no use to her. After that she kept to what she thought of as her 'vertigo' pills though they'd actually been prescribed to 'assuage her anxiety' and help her adjust to the Prozac.

She went into the kitchen and took one washed down with water. She fancied coffee but decided to have tea instead. Cut down on the caffeine, her G.P. had said. It would make her jittery and could be affecting her balance. And avoid stress: like finding dead bodies?

She'd not told Kate any of this, didn't want Kate to see her as a problem, something to be solved then put aside. The tea was making her feel nauseous. She sighed and poured it away, tears beginning to build. She went into the hall, picked up her key and walked out. Sometimes the old-fashioned ways were best: a change of air and a bit of exercise. Take her out of herself. This time she walked along to the front stairs avoiding Harriet Post's flat on the ground floor. At the foot of the stairs a woman in a wheelchair suddenly appeared in front of her.

"For goodness' sake," the woman said as Jean careened into her.

"Ooh." Jean felt her right shin connect with one of the metal footplates. She pushed herself up off the woman to see a large, angry face, framed by grey-blonde curls, looking up at her. The woman had a build similar to Jean's own: 'big-boned' Jean's mother had called it though this woman had considerably more flesh on her big bones than Jean had ever had.

"Can you not look where you're going?"

"I'm very sorry but I didn't see you coming." She bent down to rub her shin. The floor tilted so that she rested her hand on the wall to steady herself.

"Have you hurt yourself?" The wheelchair woman caught Jean's arm. "You shouldn't walk so fast if you're not steady on your feet." The voice was firm in that refined Edinburgh accent that brooked no argument.

Jean was trying to think of a smart retort when the woman seemed to relent.

"You'd better come in for a minute." She spun her chair round. Jean limped after her.

"My name's Marjorie Collins," the woman said when they were in her sitting room. "Sit there. I'll get you a glass of water." She disappeared into the kitchen.

Jean lowered herself onto the settee and looked round the room. It was larger than her own sitting room but still too small for the furniture, big and heavy like its owner. A straight-backed, Paisley-patterned armchair sat near the window. The view was of the small front gardens and the two-storey terraced houses opposite, flats really, upper and lower with bay-windowed sitting rooms, like the ones she'd hankered after in her younger days. She turned to find Marjorie Collins holding a glass of water out to her.

"Do you do that often?"

"My doctor says it's positional vertigo." She tried to make it not sound like an apology.

"Doesn't tell you anything." Marjorie's mouth pursed in disapproval.

"I'm Jean Markham, by the way." She sipped her water.

"Ah…"

The doorbell rang and Marjorie wheeled herself off to answer it. She returned followed by a small, bird-like woman with beady, little eyes.

"This is Betty Smyth," Marjorie said.

Jean grimaced as the reek of perfume hit her. She pressed a tissue to her nose to block the vinegary smell.

"With a 'Y'," the little woman added.

Jean nodded then said, "What?"

"Are you the one who found the body?"

"Betty!" Marjorie's eyes narrowed. "You'd better not be here on one of Maggie Keenan's errands."

"Maggie Keenan?" Jean said.

"Do you know her?" Betty asked.

Jean shook her head.

"You'll see her at the lunch club," Marjorie said then turned to Betty Smyth. "You can tell Maggie Keenan that you've met the woman who found Harriet Post's body." She ushered Betty out of the flat.

Jean was struggling to follow the seemingly multifarious threads of the conversation. "What errands does Betty do for Maggie Keenan?" she asked.

"She's a tell-tale."

All the tables in the dining room were occupied when Jean went in apart from one by the window. As she started to move towards it a sharp voice called her name. Jean turned to see Marjorie Collins glaring at her. She wanted to ignore the command in Marjorie's voice and continue to the sunlit table but her feet turned back.

"That one's taken," Marjorie said as Jean sat next to her.

The wall where the 'taken' table sat consisted mostly of windows with a door in the centre, all looking onto the garden area and the park beyond. Unusually for Leapark the other three walls of the room were a creamy sunshine yellow, same colour as in Kate's kitchen.

"This is a nice room, isn't it?" Jean said. She was about to continue that at least it wasn't magnolia when she remembered that Marjorie's sitting room was painted magnolia. "Colourful," she finished, nodding.

Kate had offered to paint Jean's flat for her but Jean had said she'd wait till she'd been in a while. So Kate had cleaned it instead. Washed down all the walls, shampooed the carpets, the lot. She'd got a few of her friends to help: a few of her many friends. Jean pulled a tissue from her sleeve and dabbed at her eyes.

"Are you feeling ill again?" Marjorie Collins was speaking to her in that accusing way she seemed to have.

Jean squeezed out an embarrassed smile. "Something in my eye."

The door swung wide and a big woman strode in. Her dress was bright red, hair a startling black, the pageboy style a one-off in Leapark: 'land of the curly perm' according to Kate. At the table by the window the woman pulled out a chair and sat, back against the yellow wall, with a view of the gardens, the dining room and everyone in it.

"Maggie Keenan."

Jean turned to catch Marjorie's whisper. When she turned back Betty Smyth had slipped into the chair on Maggie Keenan's right, back to the window, view of the room. A fat woman sat next to Betty, eyes magnified behind thick, round glasses.

"Rose Toner," Marjorie said.

Where Maggie Keenan looked solid, Rose Toner was fleshy, folds of fat rucking her pink jumper. Her head was covered in lots of grey curls like the fluff-balls you find in dark recesses that haven't been dusted for a while but these were firmer, more like steel wool.

"Hello, Mrs Collins, Mrs Markham, what would you like?" Kirsten Cormack seemed to have come from nowhere.

Jean jumped drawing a suspicious look from Marjorie. "I'll just have the soup, thanks," she said.

Marjorie looked up from her menu. "Steak pie?"

"Courtesy of Frances."

"She's not on duty today."

"Thought she'd look in." Kirsten's reply sounded like it had to force its way out through gritted teeth.

"You can't always wait for the police to sort things," Maggie Keenan was proclaiming in a voice loud enough to encompass everyone in the room. "We had one of them bloody 'pee-the-beds' when I lived in Dunfermline. Always in and out of people's houses. The police might have needed evidence but we didn't. We got rid of him all right."

Jean turned to Marjorie. "Pee-the-bed?"

"Maggie Keenan's corruption, if that's not too ironic, of paedophile. She likes to pretend long words aren't her forte but it doesn't do to underestimate her."

Their conversation was interrupted as a heavy-set woman arrived at the table with a steaming tray. "Now then, who's having the soup?" she asked.

"That's me," Jean said.

"You must be Mrs Markham." The woman smiled brightly. "I'm the warden, Frances Wordsworth." She lifted the plate of soup from the tray and set it in front of Jean. A look of concern replaced the smile. "I hope you've recovered from the shock."

"The shock?" Jean's mouth hung open. "Oh, yes, thanks," she said.

"That's good. It must have been awful for you finding poor Mrs Post like that." Frances turned her attention to Marjorie. "And how are you, Mrs Collins? Not having soup today?"

"The steak pie will be adequate."

"Well, enjoy." Frances whipped the tray away with a fair old flourish.

"Humph, professional carers," Marjorie said.

"Yes," Jean replied distractedly, dipping her spoon into her soup. Maggie Keenan hadn't changed that much but even if she had, the hair would have clinched it. It was the same style she had over twenty years ago when Jean had first met her.

## 5

"You're a bunch of interfering, fucking bastards the lot of you."

The words carried to the meeting room where Kate had spent the morning preparing her colleagues in the Corstorphine office for the implementation of the final stage of the new I.T. system. She walked through the open-plan admin area and opened the door to the reception. Dawn Farrell stood centre-stage. A bottle-blonde touching forty she turned, face puckering in an angry frown, as Kate approached her. The scent of alcohol wafted from her like a perfume.

"It's Kate McKinnery, Dawn." She moved closer, taking advantage of Dawn's confusion. "C'mon in here." She opened the door of one of the small interview rooms off the reception area, signalling to Linda, the receptionist, for some water.

Dawn tottered in and slumped onto one of the wipe-clean chairs. She shrugged off her black, padded coat, large breasts jiggling in the low-cut pink top.

Kate sat opposite her. "I take it this morning's Hearing didn't go well."

There was a knock on the door and one of the clerical staff came in and placed two polystyrene cups of water on the coffee table. Kate nodded her thanks.

Dawn frowned at the water. "You no got a wee coffee?" She picked up one of the cups and drank thirstily. "I just want my wee Natasha back." She gave something between a gulp and a sob and turned a pleading gaze on Kate. "Why will they not give her back to me?"

"You know why," Kate said. Dawn looked away. "I heard you were doing well. Staying off the booze."

"I was that frightened about going to the Hearing by myself. I needed a wee drink to steady my nerves." She sniffed.

"Your mother not go with you?"

"I'm not speaking to her." She scowled at the table.

Kate waited for Dawn to make eye contact. "You'll only get Natasha back if you're in a fit state to look after her."

"What happened with Eddie wasn't my fault."

"That's my point, Dawn. You were too drunk to see what was happening." Or care, Kate thought to herself.

Dawn picked at the cup leaving a chip of purple nail polish on its broken rim. "Will they still let me see her?" she said.

The rumble of an engine heralded the arrival of a delivery lorry bumping half its weight onto the pavement outside the window. The vertical blinds fluttered as if in panic.

Kate got up and closed the window. "What did your solicitor say?"

"She says I'll still get supervised visits but I'll not be allowed to take her out."

"Is that what Natasha's worker recommended?"

Dawn shrugged.

"I'll have a look at the report." A curtain of two-tone hair fell across Dawn's face but not before Kate caught a gleam of triumph on it. She did some calculations in her head. "When did Eddie get out?"

Dawn's head shot up. "How would I know that?"

"That's why your mother wouldn't go to the Hearing with you. She's seen Eddie hanging around."

"You're a fucking bitch, McKinnery. My Eddie never touched Natasha. It's me he loves." She was on her feet now, face a match for her nail polish. She wrenched the door of the interview room open and charged out.

"You're going to pay for this," she shouted back at Kate. "You're all going to fucking pay." This to the world in general before she stormed out the front door.

Kate looked at Linda. "That went well," she said.

Tom Urquhart was waiting for her in the meeting room. "Not lost your touch, I see." He smiled, showing straight, white teeth.

Tom had been her supervisor when she was a student and later when she was a newly qualified 'baby' social worker. He still had a tendency to treat her as his protégé.

"Sort of thing that really sets you up for the day. I can't believe Dawn would get back with that bastard,

Ranford." She looked at Tom. "All right, I can believe it. I just don't want to."

"Got time for a coffee?"

Tom led the way up the stairs to his office. Ever colour-coordinated, today's theme was brown. Brown shoes, dark brown chinos, khaki shirt, light brown hair sitting neatly above the collar. She'd take a bet on beige socks.

"I listened in to your presentation," he said, fussing with his filter machine. "You're really enthusiastic about this system aren't you?"

She dropped her bags on the floor and sat in a small, green, faux-leather armchair under the window. "I wouldn't be doing this if I didn't think it was worth it." She knew what was coming next.

"When are you going to get back to what you're really good at?"

The coffee started dripping into the jug.

"If you mean frontline social work, I don't know. This project still has at least two months to run and I intend to see that through."

"That takes us up to Christmas when you could be starting in the new Team Manager job." Tom poured coffee into two earthenware mugs and handed one to Kate. "A specialised Child Protection unit with a city-wide remit. It's tailor-made for you."

She sniffed the aroma from her steaming mug and raised her eyebrows questioningly at Tom.

"Old Java. Strong but great flavour." He took a sip. "Mmm. Just right." He placed his mug on a cork coaster. "So, will you apply?"

"I haven't decided."

"But you are tempted."

"I said I'd think about it." She looked at him. "I'm thinking about it."

"You can't save them all, Kate."

"I know. Yet there's always that 'but', isn't there?"

"Natasha Farrell might be getting regularly raped by Eddie Ranford now if it wasn't for you. Even the police were impressed."

"I appreciate what you're saying, Tom, but I need to make up my own mind."

"Fine, I'll just say one last thing. Taking a break from frontline work is fair enough especially with the sorts of cases you were dealing with. But don't stay away too long." His phone rang and he reached to answer it.

Kate sat back sipping her coffee. Tom's wife smiled at her from a photograph on his desk. Sharp voices drifted in from the car park followed by the slam of a car door and the over-revving of an engine. The sub-text of Tom's 'can't save them all' referred to the Woodlands case. He'd assumed that had been the reason for her sideways move to the 'Project'. And he was partly right.

The first and only time she'd met the Woodlands was at Emily's school. It had been obvious that Emily's mother, Caroline, didn't like the idea of having anything to do with a local authority social worker. It didn't fit with the lifestyle of a detached house in Corstorphine and a successful businessman for a husband. Even so Kate had done everything she was required to do. She carried out all the checks when she'd got back to the office. She did everything right and still Emily died. Shortly afterwards Kate's childhood dream returned. The dream that had eventually led to Jean telling her of her mother's suicide.

"Sorry about that," Tom was saying as he replaced the receiver. "You still okay for duty on Friday?"

"As long as you're clear that it's only one session."

"I'm just happy to have got cover." He paused. "Nick all right about it?"

"Why wouldn't he be?"

"As long as he doesn't think I'm trying to poach you."

"I'm not a bloody salmon."

"You know what I mean." Tom smiled. "How's your aunt Jean? I heard she found a body."

"I'm keeping an eye on her."

"If you ever want to talk, Kate, I'm here."

She looked at her watch. "I need to get back." She gathered up her laptop and briefcase.

Tom walked to the door with her. "You'll let me know what you decide? About the job, I mean."

"I'll let you know." She smiled briefly at him and headed for the stairs.

In the car park she loaded her bags into her car and debated going to see Jean. Leapark was only five minutes' walk away and they hadn't spoken since Jean's phone call the previous day. She sighed. She needed to get back to the office; she had a training session this afternoon. She was seeing Jules tonight. Tomorrow then, maybe. She got into her car and drove out of the car park. As she turned onto Saughton Road she saw Dawn Farrell weaving along the path through the churchyard. A man walked ahead of her, an angry set to his narrow shoulders, Dawn struggling to keep up. It was Eddie Ranford.

## 6

Jean sat in her armchair waiting for the room to stop spinning. The lunch had seemed to go on forever.

Marjorie had complained about one thing or another throughout. Jean had kept sending surreptitious glances in Maggie Keenan's direction. One time she thought Maggie Keenan was looking at her as if sizing her up but she couldn't be sure. Avoid stress? Some hope.

She stood up and was heading for her kitchen when the knock came. Three raps: loud, firm, irresistible. Jean stood where she was, clutching the doorframe. The knock came again same as before.

"Mrs Markham?" a voice called. "It's Mrs Wordsworth, may I come in?"

Jean hurried to open the door. Frances Wordsworth swished in, the pleats of her black tunic swirling round her legs as she turned to Jean.

"I wanted to introduce myself properly and make sure you were settling in all right." That smile again.

"Everything's fine."

"Have you managed to have a look through our information pack?" Frances nodded at the pink folder lying on the coffee table. "As well as social events in the complex there's information on church services. You didn't indicate your religion on your application form." She looked at Jean expectantly.

"I'm not really a religious person. Not a churchgoer, that's what I mean."

"I see. Well, if you change your mind, the church I belong to always welcomes new members."

Jean nodded and began to move towards the door.

"And do call us if you need anything."

"Thank you." She put her hand on the door handle.

Frances finally took the hint. Jean closed and locked the door behind her trying to soothe her agitation. She went into the kitchen wondering if it was too soon to take another tablet and what Frances meant by that 'I see' when Jean said she wasn't a churchgoer? What did she see? And what business was it of hers whether Jean went to church? She wished now she hadn't answered so meekly. Kate would have told Frances to mind her own business. The knock came as she reached for the kettle. Three firm raps. Jean sighed and walked into the hall. She fixed her smile and opened the door.

"Hello, Jean," Maggie Keenan said. "Long time no see." She stalked past Jean into the sitting room. Rose Toner followed in her wake. The door closed of its own accord.

"You've got some nice wee knick-knacks." Maggie Keenan looked round the room. "Hasn't she, Rose?"

"Very nice," Rose Toner agreed in a deep monotone.

Jean stood in the sitting room doorway trying to control the rising panic.

"Nice picture." Maggie Keenan nodded at the painting of the crane. She picked up a framed photograph from the sideboard. "Who's this?"

"My niece."

"Nice-looking lassie. Neat wee frame, eh, Rose?"

"It is," Rose Toner said, big, round eyes taking it all in.

"No photos of the boy?" Maggie Keenan said looking round again. "Well, we'll not keep you, Jean. Just wanted to welcome you to your new home."

They moved to the hallway like a small tidal wave, Jean washed aside as they passed. Maggie Keenan looked at her. "Nice wee place you've got here, Jean."

"Very nice," Rose Toner echoed.

"We'll be seeing you again. Soon." Maggie Keenan gave a smile like a shark might smile at its prey before closing its jaws around it then she opened the door and they left.

Jean staggered to the kitchen. She filled a glass with water and took two of her pills, clutching the stainless steel edge of the sink, waiting for her heart to slow its terrified beating.

## 7

The tailback almost reached the Grassmarket. Conscience pricking irritably all the way, Kate had trailed out to Corstorphine to see Jean only to find the flat in darkness and Jean in bed, apparently asleep, at half-past six. Yet even at that time the rest of the building had been quiet. She had a sense of residents getting ready for a night in front of the telly. Though not Jean it would seem.

She'd taken a route through Stenhouse to avoid a traffic jam on Corstorphine Road, coming back into the city centre via the West Approach Road, only to end up stuck on the Cowgate. Started life as a ravine, apparently. It wasn't difficult to imagine even now with the buildings, some of them eight or ten storeys high, soaring up on either side.

She rolled to a stop outside Bannerman's, a pub haunt from her student days. They'd start with a meal in Black Bo's, a nod to Jules' vegetarianism, then wander along to Bannerman's, finally stagger home across the Meadows to their rented flat in Marchmont, giggling up the stairs with the effort of being quiet. There were five of them in the flat – neighbours from hell. She wouldn't put up with it now.

The brake lights of the van in front went off and she moved forward again, close enough to see the police car and the remnants of a collision between a yellow baby Fiat and a black 4x4 the size of a small tank. Not surprisingly the Fiat had come off worst and was now perched on the edge of a hole in the road gazing down at the barrier that had been guarding the hole. A police officer waved them through and she accelerated past thinking the barrier would have the company of a few inebriated bodies by the morning. At the lights, she turned onto St. Mary Street and pulled into a space halfway up. She got out of the car and stood for a while adjusting her thoughts to the meal with Jules. The night was cold and clear, allowing a silvery, gibbous moon to show itself off amongst the few stars that glowed softly in the dark blue sky. She flicked her mindset-switch to 'friend, close friend' and crossed the street to David Bann's restaurant.

The waitress greeted her like the regular she was and showed her to a table for two then waited as Kate took her coat off and pushed her scarf into one of the pockets before handing it over. When the waitress returned Kate ordered two glasses of purple grape juice and garlic bread with houmus. She sat facing the entrance and the windows onto the street seeing a blend of outside and in, reality and reflection. The restaurant was getting busy. She glanced up as a group of women hurried in from the street shivering, relieved to be out of the cold. One of them smiled at her and Kate nodded a response trying to remember where she knew her from: most likely a face in the audience at one of her child protection sessions. Not social work though, the university maybe or one of the voluntary organisations. Her speaking skills were in increasing demand from councillors to police officers, teachers and health workers as well as the usual students and social workers.

Jules arrived at the same time as the grape juice. "Sorry I'm late. Meeting ran on." She reached for the tall glass and took a sip looking flushed and flustered.

"Is that the top you got in Markies?" Kate said. "You really suit that colour."

Jules smiled an acknowledgement of the compliment. The top was a deep plum colour that set off her dark brown hair and pale skin. That glossy hair had been the first thing Kate had noticed about Jules, just before the English accent. They'd met at university and she'd been ready to write Jules off as yet another product of privilege. But not this time. Even in that first meeting she'd sensed a connection.

The scent of garlic heralded the arrival of their starter. After she'd set it out the waitress stood with her pad poised to take the orders for their main course: aromatic vegetable curry for Kate, baked portabello mushroom with fennel for Jules.

"So what's the latest from Leapark?" Jules asked after the waitress had gone.

Kate picked up a slice of garlic bread and smothered it with houmus before answering. "You know Jean found the body?"

"You don't sound too sympathetic."

"It hadn't been a great day. I could have done without it." She was aware of just how unsympathetic she sounded. How much it reflected the way she felt.

"I imagine Jean felt the same." There was a hint of sharpness in Jules' tone. "Don't be too hard on her, Kate. It can't have been easy for her to tell you about your mother."

"Hearing about it wasn't exactly a bundle of laughs." She swallowed a mouthful of food and washed it down with some grape juice. "I know this hasn't been an easy time for Jean but every time I look at her I think of all those years she kept something like that from me."

Jules reached for a slice of the garlic bread. "The suspicious death: do you know who the investigating officer is?"

"Steve Oakley," Kate said, grateful for the change of subject, knowing they'd return to their original topic soon enough.

"Have you seen him?"

Kate shook her head. "Nor thought about him since we broke up. And I doubt that he's had thoughts about me, or not very pleasant ones, anyway." She took a long swallow of grape juice. "I have seen John Nelson. He was waiting for me last night when I got home." She finally met Jules' eyes. "Wanted to bring me up to date on Leapark."

"And?"

"And he brought me up to date."

The arrival of the waitress cut off Jules' response. They sat back whilst she removed the used plates and returned to set out their main courses. Jules had met John and Steve when she was considering extending her degree to incorporate forensic psychology. Kate had organised a foursome to give Jules an insight into the police perspective.

"I still think you should be keeping a journal of some sort," Jules said cutting a piece of her mushroom. "You don't have to think of it as a life-story book, just a way to sort through your thoughts."

"Maybe." Kate took a forkful of her curry. "Mmm, lovely. Have some of this."

"Want some of my fennel?"

They concentrated on swapping bits of food, letting the conversation drift onto work and long-winded colleagues who caused meetings to over-run. Although they were in different professions, the child protection network was a small one and they had many contacts in common.

"Sometimes I feel I've tapped a stream of memories," Kate said. "Unfortunately it's usually in the early hours of the morning. When I wake up later I wonder if they really are memories or just what someone else told me."

Jules studied her. "So don't label them," she said in her soft, therapist's tone. "Write down whatever occurs to you and let it lie, set it aside as dealt with, for now. Come back to it when you feel clearer and calmer. Take charge of the process, Kate, and take your time."

"But my life is based on a lie." She set her fork down and wiped her mouth with her napkin, trying in vain to match her voice to Jules' calming note. "I thought I was a poor wee soul whose mum died in a drowning accident and whose father had to go away to work. Turns out I was a sad wee bastard whose mother killed herself and whose father buggered off and left her. There's quite a bit of difference there."

Jules reached out and touched Kate's hand. "Your grandmother was lovely. 'She loved you to bits' is how you put it and I could see that when she came to visit you." She paused. "You know how important that is."

Kate gazed at the window focussing on the reflections of the room: the soft lighting, the flickering candles, faces smiling, frowning. Her gran's love had saved her, had made her feel so special that she could do anything she chose. She shifted her gaze back to the table, picked up her fork and stabbed at a piece of aubergine. "I need to know why my mother killed herself. What if it was something genetic and I've inherited it? I'm nearly the age my mother was when she threw herself in the Clyde. How can I be sure I'm not going to go the same way?"

"Kate, you're one of the strongest people I know."

"Because of who I thought I was. But I never was that person. Do you not see that?"

Jules sighed. "I see you pinning everything on finding out what really happened. As if it's going to clear away all the feelings and let you move on. Have you thought that you might find knowing harder than not knowing?"

"Knowing has got to be better than this wondering." She looked at Jules. "Hasn't it?

She replayed bits of the conversation as she drove home. She was amazed now at her gullibility in believing the story that her father had to go away to get work. Yes, the shipyards were closing but there was other work to be had. I.B.M. was rapidly becoming the area's major employer. So what other reason would there be for her father to disappear from her life, the cards on her birthday and at Christmas the only evidence of his continued existence? Was that what Jules meant when she said that knowing might be harder than not knowing?

At the lights on Waverley Bridge a group of under-dressed teenage girls staggered across in front of her. She automatically checked to see if she recognised any of them as clients or runaways. As they reached the pavement one of the girls threw up, her pals squealing as the vomit hit their shoes. An older couple hurried by, heads shaking their disapproval.

The lights changed and she negotiated her way past the latest round of tram works: yet more holes in the road. She did know how lucky she was to have had her grandmother to bring her up; to be one of the few kids in her street whose childhood wasn't blighted by alcohol. But she'd created a persona of someone who'd succeeded against the odds. Now she was haunted by the image of herself as a reject that neither mother nor father wanted to stay with. Yet worse even than that was the question that kept rolling round in her brain: why hadn't she been enough for her mother to go on living? Why hadn't she been enough?

By this time she was on Queen Street waiting to turn right down towards Stockbridge. As she swung round she became aware of a car close behind her that narrowly missed being sideswiped by a van coming in the opposite direction. It was still there three sets of traffic lights later as she crossed the bridge over the Water of Leith. Only when she reached the bay-windowed terraces of Dean Park Crescent did the lights disappear from her rear-view mirror.

She turned onto her avenue and let the car rumble down, bouncing gently over the cobbles, or maybe they were setts. Only way to tell, apparently, was to dig them up. She finally found a parking space on Learmonth Gardens. The gardens themselves consisted of trees and grass surrounded by a hedge and stretched from Comely Bank Avenue to South Learmonth Avenue three streets away. Another incursion of nature but this was a civilised version, manicured and trimmed, any hint of wildness quickly erased. She walked to the junction with her avenue and, shielded by the hedge of the gardens, stood listening for the sound of a car engine. Nothing. She hurried across the road. At the door into her stair she turned. The street was quiet, the only sound the whispered rustle of the wind in the trees, their branches waving gently in the gardens opposite.

# Wednesday

## 8

Jean stood looking in the shop window. The face of a child stared back at her: a little boy, black with big, brown eyes. She'd already bought a picture of a kitten in the cancer research shop. Her father had died of the disease when she was ten. She told herself the purchase was in his memory but underneath was a daft notion that she was protecting herself from the same end. Now she pondered Oxfam's shop window. Not much chance of her dying of starvation. Even so. The door pinged as she opened it. Not keen on second-hand clothes she drifted towards the books and the music. She finally chose Ian Rankin's 'A Question of Blood' for Kate and a book of 'Miss Marple' short stories for herself. Her concentration didn't have the stamina for novels these days. At the till she turned back and picked out a C.D. from the music section.

She wandered along St John's Road with her purchases, giving only the smallest of jumps when the pelican crossing began its insistent beeping. She resisted the temptation of a Poundstretcher, the windows kitted out with witches and broomsticks for Hallowe'en, knowing she'd buy something that, at the time, seemed essential then spent its life at the back of a drawer unused. Woolworth's used to offer that sort of temptation. Never thought she would outlast them. In the shop at the corner of Leapark Terrace she bought a newspaper and a pint of milk or half a litre as it was now. What she'd come out for in the first place. She was looking forward to some fresh coffee to go with the chocolate éclairs she'd bought in the baker's. To hell with positional bloody vertigo, and Maggie Keenan.

She stood for a moment in the park. A smell of dampness lingered but the grass looked greener, refreshed by the recent heavy rain. She'd give Kate the picture of the kitten as well as the book. Make up for last night. She'd just lain down when she heard the door open and Kate's whispered 'Jean'. She'd feigned sleep telling herself it was tiredness but knowing she'd wanted to punish Kate for not coming on Monday, regretting it as soon as she heard the door close and Kate's key turn in the lock. Later she'd taken two of her pills hoping they'd help her sleep. And for once it worked.

At Leapark she looked through the toughened glass of the door's side panels to see Kirsten cross the entrance hall and disappear in the direction of the kitchen. She let herself in and stood savouring the silent solitude. The pastel colours of the A4 pages on the notice board drew her towards them: pink for events within the complex, sky blue for jaunts beyond it, pale green for general information. A sky blue sheet described an outing to the German Christmas Market that sat next to Princes Street Gardens from the beginning of December. She'd gone with Kate and Jules last year, bought some Christmas ornaments for her flat and a music box for Kate: a teddy bear skating to the tune of 'Jingle Bells'. She'd let Kate and Jules persuade her onto the big wheel but decided she was too old for the galloping horses. Then it was back to Kate's flat for the evening: eating, drinking, talking, laughing. She shared a taxi home with Jules, Jean dropped off first and seen safely into her stair. Smiling, she picked up the pen that dangled on the end of a string of silver tinsel and aimed it at the sheet of paper listing those who wanted to go. She stopped, pen poised. Maggie Keenan's name topped the list followed by Rose Toner and Betty Smyth. Jean stepped back. The pen fell, swinging on its glittering thread.

Somewhere to her right a door closed. Ill-fitting shoes flapped along the corridor in her direction. Her move to the stairs was halted by chattering voices coming towards her. She turned and scurried into a small lounge off the entrance hall. Two young women in nurses' uniforms came down the stairs, still chatting, and went out the front door. Moments later Shona flapped into the entrance hall, crossed towards the reception office and disappeared into a corridor.

Jean was back at the foot of the stairs when she heard the muffled wail. She stopped. The wailing continued. She listened for the sound of an alarm, footsteps running towards her. Nothing. She turned, heavy-footed, in the direction Shona had taken minutes earlier. At the door of the first flat she came to she called 'hello' then, warily, pushed it open.

Shona stood in a doorway at the end of the narrow hall whimpers squeezing their way out past her fists. Jean edged along the wall towards the home help, tensing as the front door clicked shut behind her. She could smell it now.

The sitting room looked like a tornado had hit it. At its centre lay Maggie Keenan in a silky, pink nightdress. She was on her stomach, face turned towards the door, sightless eyes wide open. Rivulets of blood had formed like red ribbons on her face and on her neck. Behind the left ear, the unnaturally black hair was a sticky mess. Her bladder and bowels had unloaded contents not even the deep pile of the cream carpet could absorb. It was a reeking cocktail of human waste. Jean could feel the nausea rising yet she struggled to drag her eyes from the bloody tableau. She found herself focussing on Maggie Keenan's legs. The pink nightdress had flipped up exposing pads of thick, white fat on the backs of the knees and a knotted, blue network of varicose veins on the calves.

Jean shook herself and started to turn away from the room pulling Shona with her.

"Aaah!" Shona reared back.

"What? What is it?"

"Over there," Shona shouted, pointing at an overturned armchair.

"Where?" What the hell was the woman talking about?

"There!"

"Stop this, Shona." Jean wanted to shake her. Should she slap her?

Shona looked at Jean, eyes wide and terrified. "It's the angel, the angel!" She pulled away and ran from the flat.

Jean ran after her but not fast enough to stop the front door from closing behind her. She fought to open it, fear rendering her fingers as useful as a pound of sausages. She caught up with the home help in the entrance hall. "What did you see?"

Shona turned to her. "Mrs Post's angel. It's lying on the floor. In there."

## 9

Jean tried a smile directed at John Nelson as she entered the dining room. They'd met when Kate had enlisted his help to collect a storage unit Jean had bought at Ikea.

Why John Nelson rather than Steve had been something to do with favours and roof racks though it was as well that Steve didn't see how much the pair of them seemed to enjoy putting the unit together.

John Nelson led her to a table and pulled out a chair for her then sat opposite. "This won't take long. You know me and this is Detective Constable Heather Mair." He waved towards the dark-haired young woman sitting at the top of the table, laptop, like Kate's, in front of her. Heather Mair nodded unsmiling at Jean. "D.C. Mair will make a note of what you tell us then we'll ask you to read and sign it."

"You mean like a statement?" Jean asked.

"Aye, like a statement. Okay?" He didn't wait for an answer. "Just tell us in your own words about finding Mrs Keenan's body."

Jean described hearing the scream and how she'd gone into Maggie Keenan's flat. "Mrs Keenan was lying on the floor and there was blood on the side of her face and neck." She swallowed. "I tried to get Shona out of the flat."

"Did you touch anything?" This was from Heather Mair. The sharpness in her tone was unsettling.

Jean looked at her. "Of course not."

"You didn't check if Mrs Keenan was dead?"

"Well, no. I could see her eyes were open and she just looked dead. It didn't occur to me that she might be alive." Jean turned to John Nelson. "She wasn't still alive, was she?"

"She'd been dead for a while." He threw a warning glance at Heather Mair then looked encouragingly at Jean. "So you were trying to get the home help, Mrs Wilson, out of the room," he reminded her.

"Yes." Jean struggled to concentrate, needing to keep her wits about her. She took a tissue from the pocket of her navy blue cardigan and dabbed at her nose. "I pulled at her arm but she screamed and started shouting about an angel."

"What did you think she meant by that?"

"To be honest I thought her mind had snapped. Then she said it was Mrs Post's angel."

"Did you see this angel?"

"We were in the entrance hall by this time. I didn't want to go back and look in the room again."

"Okay, Jean, you're doing fine." John Nelson smiled at her.

Jean found herself returning the smile like a child who's pleased her parents.

"What did you do then?"

"I went to the office to call the warden..." Jean began.

"Why didn't you pull one of the emergency cords when you were in the flat?" Heather Mair interjected.

Jean looked at her. Hard-faced wee madam. "I wanted to get out of that flat." She turned back to John Nelson. "As I was saying, I went to the office to call the warden then I realised what I'd seen and dialled 999."

"That's great, Jean. A few more questions then we'll let you go." He smiled again.

God, he was good at this, Jean thought. It was like being bathed in warm milk.

"Was this the first time you'd seen Mrs Keenan?"

Jean's eyes strayed to the 'taken' table by the window. "I saw her at the lunch club yesterday."

"Did you speak to her?"

"She was at a different table."

There was a pause whilst Jean had another dab at her nose with the tissue.

"Did you know Mrs Keenan before you moved in here?" John Nelson asked her.

Jean sat up a bit straighter in her chair. "No," she shook her head, "no, I didn't."

"You were there when Mrs Post's body was found. Did you know her?" This was Heather Mair again.

"No, I did not and I would rather not have been there when either body was found, thank you very much." Jumped-up wee bully.

"Okay, Jean. Would you read and sign the statement?" John Nelson passed the sheet of paper printed by D.C. Mair to Jean.

She had to give the young woman her due, it was an accurate record of everything she'd said. She signed it and slid it across the table to John Nelson.

"Thanks for your help," he said. "We'd appreciate it if you didn't talk to anybody about what you saw."

Jean nodded. "Can I go now?"

"Sure."

John Nelson escorted her to the door and held it open for her. "Are you sure you're all right?" he asked her.

He was smiling at her again in that reassuring way he had but there was something else going on behind it. The policeman in him was watching her and he was no fool.

"Yes, thanks."

As soon as she got back to her flat she collapsed onto the settee. Her legs wouldn't have held her for much longer. Her hands were still shaking. Stupid, stupid old woman. Look where keeping secrets got her with Kate. Now she was keeping secrets from the police. Oh, the chickens were coming home to roost right enough. Or what was it they said on those American cop shows? Payback time. That was it. Payback time.

## 10

Kate was mentally composing her C.V. when a mobile phone burst into life. Everyone in the meeting room started checking pockets and bags, hoping for a reason to get out of the rest of the session. The meeting had already passed the productive stage. All that would be achieved by it had been. The information had been imparted, questions asked and answered, coffee and biscuits come and gone. The systems analyst was 'recapping the salient points', otherwise known as the idiot-proof section: saying it all again for those too dim to grasp it first time round.

She had already done her bit, her presentation well received. Nick was basking in her reflected glory, beaming at everyone as if the whole thing had been his idea.

"Sorry, I'd better take this," she said wondering why John Nelson was calling her. A few minutes later she was packing her papers into her briefcase and heading for the door. She mouthed a 'sorry' to the speaker then nodded to Nick who followed her out.

"What is it, Kate?" Nick asked.

"Jean's found a body."

"Again?"

"It's Maggie Keenan and this time it is murder. I need to go and see Jean, try to find out what's going on. I'll give you a ring later."

"Aye, keep me up to date," Nick said distractedly. "Christ that's going to put the cat among the pigeons, isn't it?"

"As long as Jean isn't one of the pigeons."

She stopped off at her office to collect her bag and laptop and let her secretary know how to contact her. Then she was on her way. At this time of the morning the worst of the rush hour traffic would be gone but she still chose to avoid the city centre, cutting through the northern fringes of the New Town to Ravelston Dykes.

The sun glinted through the branches of the trees that lined the road. This was what she thought of as Edinburgh's lottery land or one of them. Ravelston with its large detached houses, followed by Murrayfield's three-storey semis, leading to the neat bungalows of prim and proper Corstorphine. A twenty minute journey and you'd struggle to find a two-bedroom flat that would sell for less than £200,000. A banker's bonus and a bit of luck and you'd have a fair few properties to choose from.

At Leapark Terrace she noticed John's Audi alongside the panda car in the small car park. There was something about the way the cars had been almost thrown into the parking spaces that marked them out. Normal rules no longer applied.

In the building the entrance hall was dotted about with furniture. She was manoeuvring around it when she heard grunting and saw a woman struggling to get a small, rectangular dining table into one of the flats.

"Do you want a hand with that?" Kate asked.

The woman looked at her. Sweat shone on her brow, her cheeks glowed red. A corner of her white blouse had worked loose from the waistband of her black skirt. "I've got to get this ready for the police," she said.

Kate put her bags into the office and grabbed one end of the table. Between them they manhandled it into the small room. The small pink room. Even the white ceiling emitted a pale pink glow. Only the windows had escaped though there was a pink tinge to the vertical blinds. "What's this room used for?"

"It's a guest room for visiting relatives to stay over if they want to."

"But not for too long."

The woman smiled. "I've to set it out like an interview room."

"So it's just the chairs to go in now?" Kate headed back to the entrance hall noting the police tape across the door of the flat opposite the reception office. "I take it that's Maggie Keenan's flat."

"It was. I'm Kirsten Cormack by the way. I'm the deputy warden."

"Kate McKinnery. Jean Markham's my auntie."

"She'll be glad to see you."

"Have you seen her this morning?"

"No but the police have spoken to her."

Kate deposited two of the chairs at the table. "Do you need a hand with the rest of this stuff?"

"I'll stick it in the cupboard." Kirsten smiled. "Thanks for that."

"What are you doing here?" Jean ushered Kate into the sitting room.

"That's a nice welcome."

"I wasn't expecting you. That's all I meant."

"John Nelson phoned me." Kate dropped her bags onto a chair. "What's going on, Jean?" It came out like an accusation.

"I wish I knew." Jean sank onto the settee, pale and panda-eyed.

"Sorry. I didn't mean that the way it sounded." She bent down and squeezed Jean's hands. "Let's start again."

"It was Shona's reaction. Kept going on about an angel. I didn't know what she was talking about."

Kate hesitated, responsibility resting its heavy hand on her shoulder. "Do you want to move in with me for a while?"

"Do you not think I should try to settle here?"

The response was too bright, a delaying tactic, Jean not wanting to seem too keen, waiting for a bit of persuasion. Fortunately, the intercom broke in with an announcement of a meeting in the dining room to be attended by the police.

"Let's go and see what they've got to say." Kate walked to the door and waited as Jean tucked a fresh tissue into her pocket and picked up her key. In the corridor she watched Jean fumbling to fit the key into the lock. The usually short grey hair straggled over the neckband of her long, navy blue cardigan. Her grey trousers hung loosely from her hips. She looked old and vulnerable. Kate was tempted to reiterate her offer for Jean to move in with her but she could still feel the relief when Jean had let her off the hook.

"Awful fiddly." Jean straightened and turned.

"You'll get used to it." Kate smiled and tucked her arm through Jean's.

In the dining room it looked as if most of the thirty or so residents had turned up. Kate wrinkled her nose. The hum of conversation carried an undertone of freshly sprinkled talcum powder on old bodies and eye-wateringly fierce perfume. She and Jean settled at a table near the door.

"Do you know many of them?" Kate asked.

"That woman in the wheelchair is Marjorie Collins."

"The big one with the jewellery?"

"Aye, and the wee woman sitting with her is Betty Smyth. With a Y, she made a point of telling me."

"Not just any old Smith then." Kate smiled as Jean had hoped she would.

"She was a friend of Maggie Keenan. Marjorie called her a tell-tale." Jean looked at Kate, hoping for some enlightenment as to what this might mean in a sheltered housing building rather than a school playground.

"Who's the fat woman with them?"

"Rose Toner. She was sitting with Maggie Keenan and Betty Smyth at the lunch club yesterday."

Kate waved to a woman at the next but one table.

"Who's that?" Jean asked.

"Annie Hargreaves. She's a friend of mine."

Jean wondered how a woman her own age could be a friend of Kate's but said nothing.

The entrance of the police officers drew everyone's attention. Even old, rheumy eyes brightened as the tall, athletic figure of John Nelson strode into the room followed by the cheeky young female, Mair, as Jean now thought of her.

Frances Wordsworth stood as they entered and addressed the gathering. "Well now, I'm sure you all know why this meeting's been called."

She faltered as a voice asked in hushed tones. "Is Maggie really dead?"

"Yes, Mrs Smyth, I'm afraid so."

Betty Smyth burst into tears. A chorus of tutting and murmuring echoed round the room.

John Nelson stepped forward. "It's a distressing time for everyone but the priority is to find whoever did this and we need your help to do that." The room quietened apart from the occasional hiccupping sob from Betty

Smyth. "I'm Detective Inspector Nelson. I'm in charge of the investigation into the death of Mrs Keenan. This is Detective Constable Heather Mair. She'll be speaking to those of you who knew Mrs Keenan to arrange for you to be interviewed."

"What's being done about security in here?" Marjorie Collins asked.

"A uniformed police officer will be patrolling the outside of the building at all times. I understand the owners of the building will extend the intruder alarm system to all doors and windows that could give access from the outside." John Nelson looked at Frances as he said this.

"That is correct," she said. "This will be at no cost to the residents."

"I should hope not," Marjorie said.

"I'm going to have a word with John," Kate said when the meeting was declared over.

Jean thought John Nelson had the look of a lion eyeing up its next meal as he turned to find Kate walking towards him and wondered whether he was the reason Kate and Steve broke up.

As Kate approached she noted the glare she got from the young detective constable with John. Heather Mair was short, not more than 5'3". Her dark hair was also short, shorn even. She had small, sharp features and looked trim and fit in a neat, black trouser suit, and almost certainly on the up.

"Could I have a word, John?"

"Sure, Kate." He gave her a half-smile then turned to Heather. "You know what you're doing?"

"Yes, sir," Heather replied. She shot a narrow-eyed glance at Kate as she walked away.

"Watched 'The Killing' once too often," John said nodding at Heather. "What can I do for you?"

"I'm concerned about Jean. Harriet Post was one thing but anyone who'd murder Maggie Keenan has got to be a threat."

"There's not a lot I can tell you. Harriet Post's death could've been an accident. The post mortem shows she died from the head wound. But did she fall or was she pushed?" He shrugged.

"Did Maggie Keenan have a door to the garden?"

"Yes, and it was unlocked."

"So she might have been expecting someone?"

"Or somebody's found a way to pick the locks and is going into ground floor flats."

"Maggie's not a likely target for a burglar."

"That's assuming whoever it was knew Maggie lived there. But we're not taking that too seriously at the moment partly because there doesn't seem to be anything missing from Maggie's flat. Rather the opposite."

"What do you mean?"

"Maggie had quite a collection of stuff, mostly ornaments and jewellery, locked in one of the bedrooms. It'd be interesting to find out how much originally belonged to her."

"Jean said something about an angel. Only to me," she finished hurriedly when she saw the look on John's face.

"As long as it stays that way." He looked around ensuring no one was within earshot. "The murder weapon was a bronze angel that apparently belonged to Harriet Post. We're waiting for the daughter to confirm it. Ellen Post listed the angel as something missing from her mother's flat along with a small ceramic clown."

"You think Maggie was blackmailing Harriet Post?"

"It's one possibility. The pathologist found some bruising on Post's upper arms and thighs."

"She wasn't raped?"

"Wasn't that sort of pattern. More like the result of an occasional punch."

"Maggie throwing her weight around?"

"We're cross-checking to see whether either woman was in the other's flat."

"And it's just you and Sarah Lund?" Kate nodded in Heather's direction.

John smiled. "There's another detective constable, Gordon Donald. He's away telling Maggie's sons about her death and I've got a team looking into Maggie's activities elsewhere."

"Maggie's sons: that's Scott and Fraser?"

"Do you know them?"

"I saw Scott around when I worked in Leith. Built like his mother. I don't know Fraser." Kate paused giving John an opportunity to tell her more but he didn't take it. "What about the newspapers? I don't want them getting wind of Jean's role in this."

"They won't get it from us, Kate. But this place is a hotbed of gossip." John stopped as Heather returned.

"Thanks, John," Kate said, aware of Heather frowning at her.

When she went back to the table there was an elderly man sitting with Jean. He wore a cream shirt and a yellow tie with a gold tiepin attached to it. It was a sickly combination but his tan and his age let him just about get away with it. He and Jean were sucking on sweeties from a bag lying on the table.

"This is Kate, my niece," Jean said.

The man stood. "Sam MacEwen," he held out his hand.

Kate shook it, noting the appraising glance. "I'm going to have a word with Annie," she said to Jean and walked away.

11

"Right, Heather, let's see what we've got." John Nelson closed the door of the guest room and filled a mug with some of the coffee from the flask supplied by Frances Wordsworth.

Heather Mair handed him a list of names. "The first ones are those who had most contact with Keenan."

Betty Smyth topped the list followed by Rose Toner and Annie Hargreaves. The next grouping was of those who might be able to assist the investigation because they knew or heard something. This consisted of Frances Wordsworth, who'd been on duty when Maggie Keenan was killed, and Marjorie Collins who was the nearest ground floor occupant though still some distance away. The guest room had been unoccupied and the flat above was vacant.

"Uniform have already spoken to Wordsworth and Collins," Heather went on. "Both claim not to have heard anything. I'm still waiting for the typed statements."

"Who else was living in the flat?"

"Tracy Spencer. Apparently she was Keenan's carer. She was visiting family in Dunfermline for a couple of days which is why she wasn't in the flat last night."

"Has that been confirmed?"

"By her sister. Tracy was looking after her niece and nephew while her sister recovered from having another baby."

They turned as the door opened and a young man entered. He was small and slim with pale, freckled skin and fine, fair hair.

"Gordon, how did it go with the Keenan boys?" John asked.

"Interesting, once they'd passed the grief-stricken stage. To quote Scott 'it was that wee shite Cormack. She never liked my ma. When I get my hands on her...' I warned him not to make threats, to leave it to us to find the culprit at which point he clammed up. Wouldn't elaborate on what went on between Maggie and Kirsten Cormack."

"How did Fraser react?"

"Quiet, leaving big brother to do the talking."

"Find Cormack and let her know we'll want to talk to her before she leaves. Then get your report written up." He turned to Heather. "Let's you and me go see Mrs Smyth."

Betty Smyth opened her door almost before John Nelson knocked. Bedecked in baby blue, there was a sickly smell of perfume wafting from her. Her face looked like she'd been attacked by a demented powder puff.

"Come in." She led them into the sitting room then disappeared into the kitchen.

The two police officers looked at each other, sinking deeper into the plush cream carpet, twin to the one in Maggie Keenan's flat. Betty reappeared with a heavily laden tray and almost dropped it onto the glass coffee table. John sat on the pale blue leather sofa. Heather joined him. Betty perched on a matching armchair opposite them.

They wasted a good ten minutes whilst Betty fussed, laying out the cups and saucers, making sure they had tea, milk, sugar, biscuits, and, once they'd settled down, kept wiping away invisible crumbs.

"You've come to talk about Maggie, haven't you?" Betty asked looking at the two police officers in turn. She took a white hankie from the sleeve of her blue jumper. "There are things I could tell you about some of the people in here. That Harriet Post wasn't all she cracked up to be and…"

"Mrs Smyth," John interjected before Betty could get up a head of steam. "We do want to hear anything that could help us find out who killed Mrs Keenan but we'd like to start with some specific information." He tried to make eye contact but Betty's eyes wouldn't stay still long enough.

"You're not drinking your tea." Betty began to fuss and flutter again. "Let me warm it up a bit for you." She reached for the teapot.

"Mrs Smyth, it would really help us if you could answer some questions."

"All right," Betty said, eyes still darting about. She wiped away some more crumbs only she could see. Then, as if aware how oddly she was behaving, sat back in her chair, hands clamped round her hankie.

"How long had you known Mrs Keenan?" John began.

"I only met Maggie when I moved in here. That was, um, a wee while ago. I can't remember the date."

"You mentioned Mrs Post. Was she a friend of Mrs Keenan?"

"She was not. Thought she was too good for Maggie but Maggie put her in her place."

"How did she do that?"

"We found out about the daughter." Betty leant forward. "She's not normal."

"In what way?" John asked.

"She's got a girlfriend. You know what I mean?" She nodded, eyes like saucers.

"And Harriet Post didn't want anyone to know?"

"She did not but she wasn't so high and mighty after Maggie let on that we knew and then there was that Kirsten Cormack, no better than she should be, and that boy..."

"What boy is that, Mrs Smyth?" John asked.

"That paper-boy. Been in all sorts of trouble. It's not natural, him and that Sam MacEwen. And that new woman, Maggie knew about her too..."

"Sam MacEwen?" John interrupted Betty's flow whilst Heather searched her list of residents.

"He lives in the flat opposite mine. He tried to tell Maggie off about that paper-boy but Maggie put him in his place. Having a young boy like that in his flat." Indignation had Betty almost bouncing off her chair.

"What was the nature of the relationship between Mrs Keenan and the other residents?" Heather asked.

Betty stopped dead and stared at Heather as if she'd spoken in ancient Greek. She turned to John as if for a translation.

"Mrs Keenan seems to have had some items that might not have originally belonged to her. Do you know why that should be?"

"People gave Maggie things for helping them. Maggie could be very good that way. I don't know what I'm going to do without her." She tailed off, head shaking, tears streaming from her eyes. The hankie remained unused in her clenched fists.

John sighed. "Thanks for your help, Mrs Smyth. We'll talk to you again when you're feeling better." They moved to the front door. "Is there anyone we can call for you?"

Betty waved vaguely in the direction of the next-door flat. "Rose'll come in," she said tearfully.

As if on cue Rose Toner opened her door and looked out.

"Oh, Rose," Betty wailed.

## 12

Gordon Donald was leaning back in his chair drinking a mug of tea and munching his way through a Tunnock's caramel wafer. Sunlight streamed in through the half-open blinds. He sat up as the door opened and John Nelson and Heather Mair came in.

"I've got Kirsten Cormack waiting in the dining room, sir," he said swallowing then nodded at the packets of chocolate biscuits on the table. "One of the elderly ladies handed these in for us."

"Get them out of sight. I don't want this looking like a picnic." John turned to Heather. "Get Cormack."

"Anything useful from Mrs Smyth, sir," Gordon asked.

"Coherence wasn't her strong point."

The door opened and Kirsten Cormack followed Heather Mair into the room. She tugged at her jumper and smoothed her skirt before sitting in the proffered chair, vacated a few minutes earlier by Gordon Donald, then laid her hands in her lap and gazed across the table at John Nelson. Heather Mair settled herself in the chair at the top of the table, laptop at the ready. A small, smug smile wafted across her face. Gordon Donald leaned against the wall, just beyond Kirsten Cormack's peripheral vision.

"Ms Cormack," John said, "there's a couple of points we want to check with you. Detective Constable Mair will take notes. Okay?"

Kirsten Cormack nodded.

"How well do you know Scott Keenan?"

"I don't, other than as Mrs Keenan's son."

"Why would he say you didn't like his mother?"

"I don't know." She shrugged then, under pressure of the silence, offered, "Maybe it's because I wouldn't let him into his mother's flat when she wasn't there."

"You wouldn't let him into his mother's flat and now he's accusing you of murdering her."

Kirsten sat up. "What has he said? I've got a right to know."

"What I need to know is the truth about your relationship with Maggie Keenan."

"I've told you the truth. My relationship with Maggie was the same as with all the other residents."

"She couldn't have been the easiest person to deal with," Gordon commented.

Kirsten hesitated, looking down at her hands. "We did have a sort of disagreement once." She looked up. "But it was months ago. It was over and done with."

"What was this disagreement about?" John asked.

"I'd rather not say."

"This is a murder investigation. You don't have a choice."

A flash of light at the window made them turn.

"Gordon." John nodded at the door but Gordon was already on his way. "Close the blinds, Heather." He turned back to Kirsten. "The disagreement?"

"They better not have taken my photo. I don't want to be all over the papers."

"You're trying my patience, Ms Cormack."

She took a deep breath. "I told Maggie that one of the residents had complained about her."

"What's so sensitive about that?"

Kirsten waited whilst Heather fought with the blinds.

John drummed his fingers on the table. "When you're ready, Heather."

"Sorry, sir." Heather switched on the light before resettling herself at the computer.

"Ms Cormack," John said, fingers still drumming.

She glanced up at him. "The woman moved away not long after that. Her daughter-in-law threatened to make a formal complaint. I was worried that I would get blamed for telling Maggie the woman's name. I hadn't been in the job that long. I didn't want to lose it."

"Did the daughter-in-law complain?"

"Not that I know of. I didn't want to say anything to you about it in case it all got stirred up again."

There was a pause as Gordon entered the room. John Nelson looked questioningly at him.

"Sorted," he said.

"What was her name, this woman who moved away?" John asked.

"Jessie Turner. But I don't know where she moved to."

"That's all right. We can find that out." John Nelson waited for Kirsten to make eye contact. "Something else you want to tell us?"

She hesitated. "When I wouldn't let Scott Keenan into Maggie's flat he started shouting. Mrs Collins intervened. I can't be sure but I think Maggie might have gone to see her."

"How did Scott Keenan react to Mrs Collins' intervention?"

"He left. Mrs Collins asked if I was all right then she went back to her flat."

John sat back letting the silence stretch out.

Kirsten's gaze wandered over the table before being drawn back to John Nelson. "That's all." She gave an apologetic shrug.

John reached for the statement Heather had printed. "Read and, if you agree that it's an accurate statement, sign it."

Kirsten glanced down the sheet of paper then picked up the pen Heather passed to her. She looked up at John. "You'll not let them print my photo? I don't want people thinking I'm a suspect."

"I'll decide who's a suspect."

She signed the statement then stood and turned towards the door.

"We may want to talk to you again but we've got your address so we'll know where to find you," John said.

Kirsten ignored him and walked out.

"Got your summary for Inspector Oakley, Heather," John Nelson asked. They were back in the incident room at police headquarters on Fettes Avenue. It was a non-descript modern building in upmarket Comely Bank not unlike the high school opposite and the

Waitrose supermarket alongside. History and tradition were represented by Fettes College across Carrington Road to the north. Looking like something out of Harry Potter, it sat on a site larger than that occupied by all three of its more mundane neighbours.

"Maggie Keenan, apparently bludgeoned to death, found in her sitting room at 9.05 by her home help, Shona Wilson, who'd gone in to make Keenan's breakfast, and Jean Markham, a resident, who was passing at the time. Markham called us. Murder weapon seems to have been a bronze angel belonging to Harriet Post. It was lying on the floor, bloodied, and could have made the wound to the side of Keenan's head." She looked up at him. "We'll know more when we get the pathologist's report.

"Nobody else had a key to Harriet Post's flat. There's a daughter, Ellen, who lives in Fife. She couldn't tell us when she had last seen the angel, only that she hadn't noticed that it was missing till after her mother's death. But she didn't visit that often."

"Check out the paper-boy that Betty Smyth mentioned and see what you can find out about what went on between Maggie Keenan and Jessie Turner. I take it we've nothing on Sam MacEwen."

"Nothing, sir."

"You're with Steve in the morning, aren't you?" He didn't wait for an answer. "I'll take Gordon and talk to the rest of the women on this list. In the afternoon, I'll go and see Scott Keenan with D.I. Martin from Leith. Got that?"

Heather nodded.

"Good," John said and left.

## 13

Kate went back to Jean's flat with her after the meeting. She'd picked up some snippets of information from Annie Hargreaves. They'd first met when she'd done a report on Annie's grandson for a Children's Hearing. Annie had reminded Kate of her gran. It wasn't just the physical resemblance in Annie's small, compact figure but her warmth and her sense of fun. So she'd kept in touch. And when Annie's arthritis had led her to seek sheltered housing, Kate had helped her through the maze of forms and assessments. Annie had likened Maggie to a puppet-master tugging at strings to punish, intimidate, humiliate.

"Do you want a cup of tea?" Jean asked.

"I'll get it." Kate went into the kitchen. When she returned with the tea, Jean had dozed off on the sofa. She looked troubled and every one of her seventy years. Kate left the mug of tea on the coffee table. She dug her mobile phone from her bag and went back into the kitchen to phone Nick.

"How's your auntie?" He sounded pleased to hear from her.

"She's pretty shaken up."

"Tell me all about it."

Kate had an image of Nick settling back in his chair, eager for a good gossip. "Somebody murdered Maggie Keenan," she said.

"I know that bit." Nick couldn't keep the excitement from his voice. "What about Maggie's sons, how are they taking it?"

"I'm not exactly in the police's confidence, you know."

"You used to be."

Nick, the diplomat. "Do Maggie's sons still live in Leith?"

"Far as I know. What are you asking that for?" The note of disappointment was clear.

"Just curious. I want to spend some more time with Jean, make sure she's okay."

"What about your implementation report for next week's Directorate meeting?"

"I can work on it here."

"You'd not get this much flexibility if you were a team manager."

Kate remained silent. She'd wondered when Nick would bring that up.

"Hang on a minute, Kate."

She could hear Nick's muffled voice talking to someone but couldn't make out what he was saying. She wandered over to look out the window. The kitchen was a long narrow room with the units along one wall. The window was at the side of the building overlooking the park where it met the street. A railing marked the border between them, a threadbare hedge leaning against it. She hated these interludes, hanging on the end of a phone, waiting. It created a vacuum that was all too easily filled with the stuff she wanted a respite from. She could feel it now, her focus dropping away, the sense of confusion rising, the questions surfacing – 'Why? Why? Why?'

"I'm back," Nick announced.

She jumped. "I'm overcome," she said, relieved to revert to some sense of normality.

"Cut the sarcasm. You know there's talk of your secondment being extended?"

"So I heard."

"I'm arguing for the post to be upgraded but keep that under your hat for now. And keep me posted on any developments. Right?"

"And I'll let you know how the report goes as well."

"You look after your auntie."

"Bye, Nick."

What it was to be in demand though there was more chance of Scotland winning the World Cup than there was of her current post being upgraded. Question was how much Nick knew about the offer from the I.T. company. Edinburgh was to be the showcase for their records system. Then came the roll-out to other local authorities with Kate as their social work expert. If she wanted to be. A big 'if'.

"Oh, there you are." Jean appeared at the door. "Are you staying for your tea? I've got enough eggs to make us an omelette."

"I'll make it." Jean's omelettes had the consistency of a rubber door-mat.

"Who was that on the phone?"

"Work." Kate opened the cupboard under the sink and took out the frying pan. "What was your admirer saying in the dining room?"

Jean opened the fridge. "He's not my admirer. I've only just met the man." She set the eggs on the worktop and reached up to the wall cupboard for her Pyrex bowl.

"Bit overdressed though, especially the tiepin." Kate put the frying pan on the cooker, setting a hotplate to medium. "Butter?"

Jean turned back to the fridge. "I thought he looked quite smart. And the tiepin was a present from his late wife." She put the butter beside the eggs. "Leave me some for the morning."

Kate cut a rectangle of butter and dropped it into the pan then broke four eggs into the bowl and began whisking them. "Did he know Maggie well?"

"He said he didn't have much to do with her." Jean's fingers played with the butter's silver wrapping. "Do you think I'm in danger here?"

Kate poured the eggs into the pan, moving and flicking the mix before it could harden. She was good at omelettes. The key was cooking them just enough so that they were still soft on the inside.

"Don't make mine too runny."

She folded and turned the egg mix now officially an omelette. "You heard John say there'd be a police officer patrolling the building." She removed the pan from the heat and switched off the hotplate, ignoring Jean's tutting. "Plates?"

"They're there."

The phone put a stop to any further conversation. Jean went to answer it.

Kate divided the omelette in half and slid each onto a plate. She searched for something to go with them but there was nothing, not even a bit of limp lettuce. She put the plates on a tray, added knives and forks and carried the lot to the sitting room.

"I thought we could eat in here. I want to watch the news." She set the tray on the coffee table and turned to Jean. "Is that okay?"

Jean was standing pale-faced fingering a tissue.

"What is it?"

"That was the police. They want to interview me tomorrow morning. They're coming to see me at nine o'clock."

"About Maggie Keenan?"

"I don't know. I never thought to ask. I was so taken aback."

"Why?" Kate was watching Jean closely now.

"I know I'm being stupid. It's just the way she said it."

"The way who said what?"

"It was that wee Constable Mair."

"What did she say?"

"She said something about new information they want to ask me about. What does that mean?"

"I imagine it means they've got some new information they want to ask you about."

"That's a big help, Kate."

"How should I know what they want to ask you about? You're the one with all the secrets." The words came out sharper than she'd intended.

Jean shook her head. "When I was interviewed this morning, Mair was acting as if I had something to do with the two deaths. Kept asking if I knew either of them, did I check that Maggie Keenan was dead. Things like that."

"In all honesty, Jean, I can't see the police trying to fit you up for two murders." The guilt kicked in. "But if you're that worried, I'll sit in with you."

"Would you? I'd feel a lot better if you were there. But I don't want you putting yourself to a lot of trouble. I know you're busy at work."

"I'll manage." She watched Jean relax a bit.

"I just wish I knew what they were going to ask me about." The tissue was in shreds now.

"I'll give John Nelson a ring later." Kate walked over to the television. "Let's see if we're on the telly." She was smiling as she turned back to Jean who looked as if she might snap in two if she moved too quickly.

## 14

The bar was half empty. The after-work drinkers had gone home and the night revellers were yet to appear. John was at a corner seat sipping his pint when she arrived. She unbuttoned her coat as she approached the table enjoying the appreciative look her denim skirt and close-fitting, red, cashmere v-neck jumper earned. The skirt was short enough to show off her long, swim-toned legs in opaque black tights. She had it so why not flaunt it. She enjoyed a bit of flaunting now and again,

"White wine?" John asked.

"Thanks." She unravelled her scarf, took off her coat and sat down whilst John went to the bar. His bomber jacket lay on the cushioned bench next to her. The soft black leather felt new. She looked over at the bar. John had already paid for the wine but the woman serving him was lingering over giving him his change, she'd already had the benefit of the charm offensive. The eyes had it: long-lashed brown, crinkling at the sides when he smiled.

She had phoned John on her way home from Leapark. He hadn't seemed to know about the intention to interview Jean but said he'd find out what he could. She wondered if it was a ruse to invite her for a drink but she'd agreed anyway. She wanted to be as prepared as possible for Jean's interview. And an evening in one of her local pubs with John Nelson was no great hardship.

She watched him as he headed in her direction with her glass of wine: snug, black jeans, light blue jumper, a faint whiff of aftershave as he shifted his jacket and settled beside her.

"Cheers, Kate." He lifted his pint and took a sip then licked the foam off his top lip and set the glass down on the table. "Jean's interview was arranged after I left."

"She said it was Heather Mair who phoned her."

"I suspect Heather thought I was a bit too easy on Jean."

"What was she hoping for, a bit of water boarding?"

John smiled. "Heather works on the principle that everybody's got something to hide and it's her job to wheedle it out of them."

"Is she playing you and Steve off against one another?"

"Steve's responsible for the Leapark end of the investigation. Heather's part of his team." He took another mouthful of beer, seemingly oblivious of the appraising glances from a besuited, dark-haired woman nearby.

"Will Steve be there tomorrow?"

"Very likely."

Kate sipped her wine waiting for him to say more. When he didn't she said, "You must be getting desperate if Heather's targeting Jean as a potential suspect."

"Forensics were useless. People were in and out of the flats all the time, including the wardens and home helps."

"Was the angel the murder weapon?"

He nodded.

"So how did Maggie come to have it?"

"Blackmail. Ellen Post's gay."

"And Harriet Post wouldn't have wanted anybody to know?"

"Seemingly she was a bit strait-laced."

The door opened and a bulky, forty-something man in a grey double-breasted suit bustled in. He looked round the bar then walked quickly to the dark-haired woman, shaking his head. The woman looked relieved as she raised her face to meet his kiss.

Kate twirled the stem of the wine glass in her fingers. "Who was the last person to see Maggie alive?"

"She spent most of the evening in Rose Toner's flat. Went back to her own flat about half-past nine." John shook his head. "There's probably any number of people in Leapark who wanted to kill Maggie but it's hard to see any of them actually doing it. She was a big woman; it was a powerful blow that killed her."

"What about her sons?" She pushed her luck, making the most of his forthcoming mood.

"We're keeping an open mind about Scott, still digging on Fraser."

"Is Scott really a suspect?"

"There's a rumour that he was doing a bit of drug dealing and Maggie didn't like it."

"I like the jacket, by the way." She stroked the leather. "Feels new."

He gave an embarrassed shrug. "Birthday present from my mother."

"She's got good taste. Or is that Maureen?"

"You know the routine: my mum pays, Maureen chooses."

She smiled at his continuing embarrassment. It didn't suit his image to have his mother buying him clothes even if it was his sister who chose them. She reverted to a more comfortable topic.

"Who's on your interview list tomorrow?"

"Marjorie Collins first then an Annie Hargreaves."

"Marjorie Collins didn't look like an easy target."

"Maybe she wasn't." John was concentrating on positioning his glass in the centre of the beer mat.

"I know Annie. That should be an interesting interview."

He looked at her. "What does that mean?"

"She's a bit lively, likes a laugh." She smiled, wanting to lighten the mood, not sure why it had dipped. "She'll enjoy having a good-looking police officer to talk to."

He turned away and lifted his glass to his lips again. When he put the glass down, she dug him gently in the ribs. "Just bat your eyelashes at her."

He gave her a sideways glance, his expression softening. "Let's leave my eyelashes out of this."

She smiled and sipped her wine.

The suited couple faced each other across the table. The woman shook her head, turned away, made a glancing eye contact with Kate then grabbed her bag and hurried out. The man threw up his hands, as if in exasperation, and went to the bar. Not so suited after all.

Kate turned her attention back to John. "I saw Dawn Farrell yesterday."

"Was she drunk?"

"Is the Pope a Catholic? Guess who she was with."

He looked at her. "Tell me it wasn't Eddie Ranford."

She stayed silent.

"Did Ranford see you?"

"Don't think so. I spoke to Dawn in the Corstorphine office. I didn't see Eddie Ranford until I was leaving. He didn't seem too pleased. Probably been counting on Dawn getting Natasha back."

"Where are they living now?"

"Dawn was re-housed in Ratho when Ranford was sent down but her mother still lives in Corstorphine. I think she twigged that he was back in the picture. That's why she wouldn't go to the Hearing with Dawn."

"Right." John thought for a moment. "I suppose he would be out by now."

"We were lucky he got prison in the first place. It was no thanks to Dawn."

"It was mostly down to you: your report and your testimony. How is Natasha?"

"She's doing well. Misses her mum but her foster parents are good. Any sign of Ranford, they'll call the police."

"Make sure you do the same. Eddie Ranford's an evil bastard and he blames you for getting him sent to prison."

"I'm not a six-year old, John."

"Ranford might be on the scrawny side but he's strong enough to keep Dawn in line." He raised his hands to stall her objection. "I know you can look after yourself but for once in your life take the easy option. If Ranford comes anywhere near you, phone me. I'd love an excuse to beat the shit out of him."

"But where would you find a phone box to change in?"

"I'm serious, Kate. Okay?"

"Okay, Batman." She checked her watch. "I need to go, John. I've got some work to do and I want to get to Leapark early tomorrow." She swallowed the last of her wine and stood up.

"I'll walk back with you."

She looked at him.

He shrugged. "My car's parked over that way. You know what parking's like round here." They walked towards the door. "Oh, and it's Superman," he said.

"What is?"

"The one that changed in the phone box."

He smiled as she aimed a punch at him.

Later, alone in bed, she thought about the couple in the pub. Were they having an affair? Both had worn wedding rings but there'd been a sense of the illicit in their behaviour. Ending an affair maybe: the man late again, the woman having had enough. It was something she'd steered away from – affairs with married men. Female solidarity had been the original reason though, apart from a brief dalliance with one of her lecturers, there'd never been enough temptation to test it. Until she met John. Yet even when his marriage was in its 'off' phases she'd avoided him. Got involved with Steve instead, if you could call it that.

Lucy jumped up beside her and pawed at the duvet. Kate lifted it let her to crawl underneath. Now there was no Steve but there was still that 'maybe' with John. She'd misjudged things turning their conversation to his family. It was supposed to be a reminder of earlier confidences, a way of encouraging more about the investigation but it hadn't worked that way. It seemed to distance him from her. He'd probably known she was playing him. Yet, as usual with John, she wasn't sure what she did want from him. The 'frisson' was still there though. She'd felt it as he'd walked with her to her stair door. And she couldn't deny the small stab of disappointment when he'd said goodnight there and walked off in the direction of his car. Under the duvet, Lucy shifted onto her side. Kate did likewise, curling round the small, warm body for sleep.

# Thursday

## 15

Kate pulled into a space at the top of Leapark Terrace and watched a taxicab edge its way towards the sheltered housing building. The media were making their presence felt, gathering in the street, double-parking, upsetting the neighbours. The police were keeping them out of the car park but there was still a gauntlet to run to reach it.

It bothered her that Jean should be so anxious about this interview. She'd skipped her swim to make sure she had time to talk to her before the police arrived but the weather and a broken traffic light had scuppered that. First drop of rain, most of the population got their cars out. Add an Edinburgh wind and pedestrians lost all sense of sight and sound. The wind in Edinburgh was a thing of wonder. It had a way of shifting and swirling about that felt almost personal. She'd just about flattened a man who was making a mad dash across Corstorphine Road. He got stranded halfway, battling with the wind for control of his umbrella as a gust threatened to rip it from his grasp. Lucky for him the wind won with a sudden change of direction that propelled him and his now shredded umbrella beyond the reach of her fast approaching car.

She picked up her bag and got out. An elderly woman was being given a police escort from Leapark to the taxi. Kate turned and walked back to the park gates. She followed a path parallel to the street that led to Leapark's gardens. The railings that ringed the area were more boundary marker than security. She undid the latch on the gate in the centre and walked towards the building. On her right, police tape marked out the door to Maggie Keenan's flat. Odd that, after Harriet Post, Maggie would be so careless about locking her door. Unless she'd felt she was untouchable; or she'd known more about Harriet Post's death than the police had as yet uncovered.

There were a number of other doors leading to communal areas. With a bit of luck her key would work on at least one of them. She was drawn to a lilac glow emanating from a room in the centre section of the building. The door opened onto a small lounge trying to pass for a conservatory. Apart from the lilac walls. A rattan sofa with beige cushions sat looking out at the garden whilst a couple of pink, high-backed chairs faced each other across the laminate floor. The room had an air of all dressed up with nowhere to go. The sun wouldn't arrive till the afternoon, if then.

At Jean's flat Kate knocked before going in.

"That's a nice dress," Jean said, looking her up and down.

She'd decided on her blue, Hobbs' fitted dress, styled to show curves. Her sexy, professional look as she liked to think of it or maybe just more flaunting.

Jean was again dressed in grey trousers but they were topped off with the soft blue-green cashmere jumper that Kate had bought her for her birthday. "Do you want a cup of coffee?" she asked. "I've just brewed some fresh."

"Thanks."

Jean went into the kitchen. Kate set about reorganising the furniture. She positioned the two armchairs side by side opposite the sofa, setting one slightly at an angle to the other: close enough to touch Jean but also to watch her reactions. The two police officers would have to take the sofa.

"You've moved the chairs," Jean said when she returned with the coffee.

"We'll sit in the armchairs, that way I can see both police officers."

"Will there be two of them?"

"There's always two of them."

Jean was still standing with a mug of coffee in each hand.

Why are you in such a state? Kate wondered. But there wasn't time to get into that now. She didn't want Jean any more wound up. She took the mugs of coffee and set them on the coffee table then guided Jean to one of the armchairs. She would take the one nearest the door so that she could deal with the entrances and exits and the coffee if they chose to have it. With that in mind, she went into the kitchen and set out another two mugs and the percolator on a tray then added milk in a jug and a bowl of sugar. Steve took neither but she didn't know about Mair. When she turned Jean was standing at the kitchen door.

"I'd have done that."

"Will you sit down, Jean." She looked so jumpy moving about.

The doorbell rang as Kate set the tray on the coffee table. Jean jumped. Kate went into the hall and looked through the peephole: Steve Oakley and Heather Mair. She took a deep breath and opened the door. Steve held onto his composed look but not before a modicum of surprise had leaked out. Did he really think she'd leave her auntie to his not so tender interrogative mercies? He still looked good though: tall, blond, fit. Mair stood straight-backed not as proficient as Steve in controlling her expression. She was looking to boost her reputation with this one.

"Come in." Kate held the door open and directed the two police officers to the sitting room.

Jean stood when she saw them, surprise at Steve's presence written on her face. Kate was concerned to see relief there as well. If Jean thought she'd get an easy ride from Steve she didn't know him.

Kate walked to her chair. "Have a seat," she said, indicating the sofa.

Mair sat opposite Jean. Steve paused to twitch up the trousers of his grey wool suit to avoid the 'saggy knee' effect before sitting next to her. He settled back on the sofa, one leg draped over the other, more observer then participant.

"Would you like some coffee?" Jean offered. "It's just made." She smiled from one to the other.

"No thanks." The police officers remained straight-faced.

Jean's smile faded.

"We'll have a top-up," Kate said. She took her time topping-up the mugs, adding half a teaspoon of sugar to Jean's, a dribble of milk to her own.

"D.C. Mair has a few more questions for you, Mrs Markham," Steve said.

Kate heard the touch of impatience in his voice and felt Jean's tension increase at his formal tone. She looked into Jean's face so that their eyes met.

"Is that all right for you, Jean?" She held out the mug of coffee, the rich smell making her mouth water. Her omelettes might be rubbish but Jean knew her coffee.

Jean nodded and took the mug, looking down into its black depths. Kate sat back and crossed her legs allowing the dress to ride up just a bit. Steve flicked a glance in her direction.

"Mrs Markham," Mair said.

Jean's head jerked up.

Mair gave a hint of a closed-mouth smile. "Where were you going when you found Harriet Post's body?"

"I was going for a walk."

"In the rain?"

Jean turned to Kate. "It wasn't raining then, was it?"

"It's all right, Jean, last time I checked, going out in the rain was legal." Kate looked at Mair. "My aunt had just moved in at the weekend as you already know. She was finding it hard to settle."

Mair glared at her before turning to Jean. "So, Mrs Markham, you were going for a walk in the rain just as the home help found Harriet Post's body?"

Jean went over her story again, taking a few sips of her coffee when she'd finished.

"You've missed a bit haven't you?"

"I don't think so," Jean said.

"Mrs Wilson said the bathroom door was locked and you showed her how to unlock it." Mair sounded a bit too smug for comfort.

"The locks are all the same." Jean sounded mystified.

"So you'd know how to lock the door from the outside as well."

"It's hardly rocket science," Kate said concerned about where this seemed to be heading.

"I was asking Mrs Markham."

"And I was answering for her."

There was a pause as they glared at one another. Mair blinked first. Kate glanced at Steve sitting back on the settee letting Mair play tough cop. She leant forward to reach for her coffee then sat back, smoothing the dress from hip to thigh, fingers gently tapping her knee.

"Why did you call the warden?" Mair persisted, focussing a hard stare on Jean.

"I didn't know who else to call for. I wasn't sure if you called an ambulance for a dead person."

"What about the police?"

Jean looked blank.

"Why would she think of calling the police?" Kate asked for her.

"She'd just found a body."

"In Jean's shoes I'd have called the warden. I bet if you asked the other residents in here they would too."

Mair made a show of checking her notes. "Why did you leave Harriet Post's flat by the door to the garden?"

"I was upset." Jean turned again to Kate. "I've already told all this."

"Let's move on," Steve said.

Jean smiled at him and sat back, nursing her mug of coffee.

"Where were you going when you were involved in finding Mrs Keenan's body?"

"I was going back to my flat. I'd been out for a walk again." Jean paused. "And the sun was shining at the time."

Kate smiled. Good for you, Jean.

"You said you heard a scream. How did you know it came from Mrs Keenan's flat?"

"I didn't know. It was the nearest, so I thought I'd check there first."

"Why did you call the police that time?"

"Because it looked like somebody had hit her over the head." Jean's voice went up a couple of notches. She set her mug on the table. "I can't do right for doing wrong here."

Kate put her hand on Jean's forearm. "You're doing fine."

Steve cleared his throat.

Mair paused or was it a hesitation? "You told Inspector Nelson you didn't know Mrs Keenan before you moved in here," she said.

"That's right."

"So how would she have known you?"

Kate felt Jean's arm tighten. She pressed her palm lightly against the jumper's soft wool and looked at Mair. "Are you suggesting Jean's lying about knowing Maggie Keenan?" She turned to Steve. "Is that what this is about?"

Steve fixed his gaze on Jean. "We've had information that suggests Mrs Keenan might have known something about Mrs Markham," he said.

"What sort of something?"

"We don't have any detail."

"Maggie Keenan died before she could tell anyone," Mair chipped in.

"Are you saying Jean's a suspect?"

"No," Steve said, silencing Mair. He leaned forward. "We need to confirm that Mrs Markham didn't know Mrs Keenan before she moved in here."

"I've already said I didn't."

Kate stood. "You've had your confirmation. So if there's nothing else..."

"Well..." Mair began.

Steve stood up. "I'm sorry if you've found this upsetting, Mrs Markham, but we have to check these things."

"It's all right," Jean said meekly.

"No, it isn't all right," Kate said. She looked at Mair. "If you want to make a name for yourself don't do it by badgering a 70-year old woman who's still recovering from seeing two bloodied, dead bodies." She turned to Steve. "If the police feel the need to interrogate Jean again we don't want her doing it and I want to be present. Right, Jean?"

Jean nodded.

"It'll be noted." Steve looked at Kate for a moment then turned and walked into the hall. Mair had no choice but to gather up her notebook and handbag and follow him. At the front door he paused as if about to say something then he opened the door and walked out, Mair hurrying after him.

When Kate went back into the sitting room Jean was putting the mugs on the tray.

"I'll take that." She left the tray in the kitchen. In the sitting room, Jean was moving the chairs. Kate stood at the sofa.

"Come and sit down and tell me what's going on."

"What do you mean?" Jean tried, still fiddling with the chairs.

"Jean," Jean turned to her, "come and sit down."

## 16

Marjorie Collins scrutinised the police officers' I.D. cards before leading them into her sitting room. She manoeuvred her wheelchair alongside a high-back, paisley-patterned armchair by the window. John Nelson sat on the matching settee. Gordon Donald perched on the edge of the seat alongside, notebook in hand.

They'd already established that she'd moved into Leapark nine months earlier. The reasons given for the move were arthritis and a heart condition. She was described as 'intermittently ambulant.'

"We're questioning anyone who had a disagreement with Mrs Keenan," John Nelson said.

"That should keep you busy." The sharpness of the reply took him by surprise.

"Did you know Mrs Keenan before you moved here?"

"We didn't move in the same social circles and, before you ask, I kept her at a distance in here. The disagreement, as you call it, came about because I remonstrated with her older son for causing a disturbance in the entrance hall."

"This was the disturbance that involved Kirsten Cormack?" Gordon Donald asked.

Marjorie Collins looked at him as if surprised to hear him speak. She turned back to John Nelson. "As far as I could ascertain Kirsten had refused to let him into his mother's flat. He began swearing at her." She paused. "He'd been drinking of course."

"Do you recall what Scott Keenan was saying to Ms Cormack?"

"I didn't listen. There were too many expletives."

"How did he react to your intervention?"

"He went away."

"Just like that?"

"He seemed surprised that I had intervened." Marjorie Collins paused as if waiting for the next question.

John let her wait, puzzled and mildly irritated by her attitude. Her stern expression reminded him of his mother when she was giving him a telling off but without the soft underbelly. He wondered what was going on beneath that cold, disapproving formality.

"Maggie Keenan came to see me the following day, ostensibly to apologise for her son."

"What do you think was behind her visit?"

"She wanted to know whether I had heard what he said."

"And you hadn't?" Gordon asked.

The question earned him a hard stare. "I have already answered that."

"We believe Mrs Keenan was killed on Tuesday night sometime after ten p.m." John added an edge to his voice, matching Collins' formality. "Did you hear anything suspicious?"

"I go to bed at ten o'clock."

He waited. Sunlight squeezed through the slatted blinds creating stripes on the diamond pattern of the Axminster carpet. The silence hung heavy.

Marjorie Collins shifted her position. "I didn't hear anything."

"Thanks, Mrs Collins." John Nelson stood.

"There's something else you should know." She looked up at him.

"What's that?"

"Mrs Smyth has told me that yesterday she took medication not prescribed for her. I believe Rose Toner gave it to her." She lowered her gaze. "That's all I have to say."

"How well do you know Mrs Smyth?"

"I've known her for many years." She began to wheel her chair towards the hall.

"How did you feel about her friendship with Mrs Keenan?"

Marjorie Collins stopped at the sitting room door, her back to the police officers. "I didn't consider it to be my business," she said.

The reason for Annie Hargreaves' admission to Leapark three years earlier was confirmed in her gnarled, misshapen hands. She led the two police officers into a bright, cluttered sitting room. Another elderly woman stood smiling at them.

"Get the tea, Renie," Annie Hargreaves said to her. "Renie doesn't live here but she met Maggie a few times. Sit yourselves down." She ushered the police officers towards two plump, pale green armchairs.

Renie set a tray on the coffee table. At its centre sat a plate of cream doughnuts surrounded by four mugs of tea, a milk jug and a sugar bowl.

"Renie'll do the honours," Annie said. "Arthur's playing up today." She settled on the settee.

"Arthur?" Gordon looked around.

"Arthur Itis." Annie laughed, waving her hands. "Did you think I meant my fancy man?"

Gordon blushed.

"Mrs Hargreaves," John Nelson began.

"Call me Annie. We don't stand on ceremony here."

"How long had you known Mrs Keenan?"

"Eh, be about three years. Since I moved in here."

"Just milk," Gordon said in response to Renie's questioning look.

Renie added milk to the mugs and set them in front of the two men.

"You didn't know her before that?" John persevered.

"No, though we're both Leithers. Maggie lived in the Banana flats for a while, she told me, then her mother moved to Waverley Tower when it was built. I lived in South Fort Street before I moved in here." Annie looked at Gordon who was taking what notes he could. "You're not eating, son. Have a cream doughnut." She held the plate out to him.

"Thanks, Mrs Hargreaves, I mean Annie." Gordon smiled, juggling cake in one hand, notebook in the other.

"Give the boy a plate, Renie," Annie commanded. "You'd never think she comes from Morningside, would you?" She smiled at John. "What were you saying, son?"

"Were you and Mrs Keenan friends?" He struggled to control his impatience mindful of Kate's comments from last night.

"You mean because I'm not bubbling into a hankie?" Annie shook her head. "Maggie didn't 'do' friends, as my grandson would say. She was all right with me but I'd no illusions about her."

"Did she 'do' enemies?"

"Touche." Annie laughed. "Though I don't know that I would call them enemies but she had run-ins with a lot of people."

"Could you give us some names?"

Annie sat back balancing her mug of tea in her lap. "There was the Post woman, as I liked to call her, but she's dead so that's no much use. Ehm, there was Betty's pal, Marjorie, her and Maggie had what Betty called a wee countertemps."

Renie spluttered into her tea then, at a frown from John Nelson, offered, "There was that bust up with wee Kirsten."

"That got sorted out," Annie said dismissively. "Maggie liked wee Kirsten."

"Did wee Kirsten, I mean Ms Cormack, like Maggie?" John asked.

"Oh aye, Kirsten doesn't bother you. Not like the sainted Frances, eh Renie?"

"Daffodil," Renie rejoined and both women collapsed against one another in a fit of giggles.

John sighed. Gordon bit into his doughnut. A dod of raspberry jam dripped onto his open notebook.

"We call her daffodil because of her name," Annie explained wiping her eyes.

"Frances?" Gordon asked wiping his notebook.

"No, son, Wordsworth. Renie here's a bit literary."

"Why sainted?" John said, patience wearing thin in spite of Kate.

"She's always going on about her Christian duty. Thinks she's Leapark's answer to Mother Teresa. What does that say about us? That's what I'd like to know."

John decided to cut his losses. "I think we'll leave it there." He stood up. "Thanks for your help."

"Are you away?" Annie said. "Well if you want to talk to us again, you know where we are." She picked up one of the cream doughnuts. "Here, son," she called to Gordon. "You take that with you. Get him a wee bag, Renie."

"It's all right, Mrs Hargreaves," Gordon demurred but the bag was pushed into his hands regardless as they were ushered out the door.

"Fucking hell," John said when they were outwith earshot. "And what is it about you, Gordon, that women keep giving you food?"

"Must be my underfed look, sir."

"Well take your doughnut and your underfed look back to Fettes and see if there are any reports waiting for us."

"Are we not going to interview Frances Wordsworth?"

"Heather should be here. I'll use her."

Gordon looked disappointed.

"This is Steve's case. It's better if Heather can report back directly to him rather than second-hand."

They were at the front door now. "And chase up any links Cormack might have with Scott Keenan."

"Right, sir."

## 17

"How come you knew Maggie Keenan?"

Jean looked at her, denial hovering on her lips. "Was it that obvious?"

"Only to me I think." Kate waited. "Jean?"

Jean sighed. "I borrowed money from her."

"That doesn't sound like you."

"It was a long time ago." She took a tissue from her sleeve and seemed to come to a decision. "You know I was married to an American sailor?"

"Aye, my gran told me."

"We met at the Cragburn. The sailors used to come over to Gourock for the dancing." Jean was smiling down at her tissue. "We got married here and I went back to America with him."

She'd been fourteen when her gran had told her the story. She'd struggled to match it to the auntie Jean she knew. She couldn't encompass the idea of Jean dancing with sailors, American or otherwise, let alone marrying one and going off to the States with him.

Jean was frowning. "But it didn't work out."

"What happened?"

"He had a big family all living in the same town. The naval base was nearby and just about everybody in the town worked there. And, being in the navy, he was away a lot so I was left with his family." Jean looked at her. "I stuck it out for over two years but I felt like I was suffocating." She turned away. "So I came back to Greenock."

"On your own?"

Jean nodded, fiddling with her tissue. "I'd been back a month when I realised I was pregnant."

"Pregnant?" It came out wrong – disbelief with a hint of bewilderment though she wasn't sure how she meant it to sound anyway. It had been the first thing she'd thought of when her gran told her the story but not a pregnancy two years on.

"I didn't know what to do. I was living with your gran. I didn't have a job."

Kate rested a guilty hand on Jean's shoulder. She followed Jean's gaze to the photos on the sideboard, herself and her gran smiling back at them, and thought about the cousin she might have had. "What did you do?"

"I had the baby. Wasn't much choice in those days." Jean smiled wistfully to herself. "A wee boy."

"What happened to him?" Kate asked gently, kneading Jean's shoulder, trying to ease the increasing tension there.

"He was adopted."

"Adopted?"

"What else could I do?" Jean looked at her, pleading for her to understand. "Your gran wanted me to keep him but we couldn't afford it. This was in 1964. There wasn't the help you would get now. You were lucky to get anything."

"What about your husband? Could he not have helped?"

Jean plucked at the cuff of her jumper, focussing on her hands in her lap. Rain tapped at the window. "I didn't tell him I was pregnant."

"Why not?" She couldn't conceal the hint of anger in her voice.

"I didn't want to go back to America."

"Preferred Greenock, did you?"

"I couldn't go back, Kate."

"Why?"

"My in-laws made my life a misery."

"How?"

"They just did, all right?"

They paused. Jean stared into the abyss her life would become were Kate to walk out of it.

Kate forced herself to flick the switch that would shift her perspective from niece to social worker. She needed the detachment, the distance that would give her to listen to the rest of Jean's story. She rubbed her forehead aware of the desperation in Jean's expression. "How does Maggie Keenan fit into this?"

"My son came to see me when he was twenty-one. Andrew, his name was. He said he wanted to know about his father." She shrugged. "I told him what I could and offered to help him if he wanted to go to America. I had a bit put aside but it was quite expensive so I borrowed £200 from a woman in Leith I'd heard about – Maggie Keenan. But Andrew didn't come back for it. I never saw him again."

"You don't know where he is?" she asked, softly now, feeling Jean's loss.

"No," Jean said quietly.

She stroked Jean's cheek, feeling she wasn't getting the whole story but unwilling to push it. "Tell me what happened with Maggie Keenan."

"I took the money back. I had to leave it with her mother. Maggie was living in Fife at the time. She did her Edinburgh business, as her mother put it, out of the Leith flat. About a week later she came looking for what she called her profit margin. She had her reputation to think about, she said." Jean was looking down, folding and unfolding her tissue. "She took a locket that had belonged to my granny. It wasn't worth a lot of money but it had a wee picture of Andrew in one side and a lock of his hair in the other." She turned to Kate, tears glistening on her cheeks. "I couldn't stop her."

"It's okay." She patted Jean's shoulder.

"I'm sorry I told lies to the police, especially with you there, Kate, but I couldn't have told them all this."

"I can see that."

"And I'm sorry I didn't tell you about your mum. I'm really sorry about that."

There was a flicker of fear in Jean's eyes. Kate gave her a brisk hug and felt her release her breath in a juddering sigh. "That's over and done," she lied.

"I'd like to lie down for a wee while." Jean looked at her hesitantly. "Will you be staying for your tea?"

She nodded and offered Jean a supporting arm. In the bedroom, she pulled back the quilted bedspread. Jean slipped off her shoes and lay down on her side. Kate covered her then pulled the curtains. When she turned back to the bed Jean's eyes were closed.

The mess just seemed to get bigger. Now she might have a cousin somewhere. Assuming Jean was telling her the truth, the whole truth rather than just enough to gain her sympathy. She stood at the bedroom door and looked at Jean lying on the bed. She saw a seventy-year-old woman who'd buggered up her life and was scared she was heading for a lonely old age. Could Jean have killed Maggie Keenan? The motive was there. Was this what Steve was referring to? She shook herself. Get a grip, Kate. Problem was she didn't know what to hang onto any more. She'd lost all her bearings.

## 18

Frances Wordsworth sat upright in the chair, hands relaxed in her lap. Her calf-length black dress with its white collar seemed to echo Annie Hargreaves' 'Mother Teresa' comment. She smiled across at John Nelson and at Heather Mair once again ensconced at the top of the table with her laptop.

"Mrs Wordsworth, we'd like to check a few points in the statement you gave to the P.C." John Nelson returned her smile. "You've worked here for five years?"

"Since the complex opened."

"How did you get on with Mrs Keenan?"

"I get on with all my residents."

"Some of them seem to have found Mrs Keenan intimidating. Were you aware of that?"

Frances shifted in her chair. "She could be a bit loud but I don't think there was any harm in it."

"Were you aware that your colleague, Ms Cormack, had some difficulties with Mrs Keenan?"

"She probably mishandled the situation. This is not an easy job. You need to be patient and flexible."

"Flexible?"

Frances nodded. "Yes. It's not part of my remit but I occasionally assist residents if they're unwell for example, with medication and suchlike."

"Did you ever assist Mrs Keenan?"

"Ms Spencer, Mrs Keenan's carer, would do whatever was necessary."

"Was her absence on Tuesday night planned?"

"She had arranged to be away from Monday morning until Wednesday afternoon. Mrs Keenan was offered replacement care but she refused." Frances shrugged. "If she'd accepted perhaps she'd be alive now."

John Nelson paused. Frances Wordsworth's look of pleasant expectation didn't waver.

"Did her sons cause you any problems?"

"Mrs Keenan wouldn't have allowed that. They didn't like to upset her."

"How well did you know Harriet Post?" Heather asked.

Frances seemed caught on the hop by the sudden change in topic and questioner as if she'd forgotten Heather was there, the only reminder being the soft tapping of the computer keys.

"Um Harriet Post? She liked to keep to herself. I know there was a daughter but I don't think she visited very often."

"Did she have any friends in Leapark?"

"She'd not been here that long when she died."

John picked up a pen and tapped it lightly on the table. "How many keys do the residents get?"

Frances turned back to him. "Two. One for the resident and a spare in case they want a relative to have one. And, of course, we have the master key."

"Thanks, Mrs Wordsworth. That's all for now. We may want to speak to you again." John threw down the pen and stood up.

Frances looked surprised it was over. "Goodbye then," she said smiling and went out.

"Is it possible there were two Maggie Keenans and we're investigating the wrong one's murder?" John said.

Heather shrugged. "Maybe she'd changed her ways."

"And Harriet Post gave her the angel as a reward?"

"Is there a problem with keys to the flats, sir?"

"So far we've only found one key to Maggie's flat and one to Harriet Post's flat. And, no, Maggie's sons don't have one." He walked to the window and looked out at the gardens. Nothing moved. The wind and rain of the morning had gone. Pale grey cloud kept the sun at bay. A nothing day going nowhere. He turned to Heather. "Is there anything I need to know from the interviews you did with Steve?"

There was a pause as Heather pulled her notes towards her. Steve had decided to re-interview Betty Smyth himself with a vague suggestion that John had let her off the hook.

"Smyth said that Scott Keenan had done some 'little jobs' for her."

"What sort of jobs?"

"Putting up shelves, fixing a cupboard door."

"Did she pay him?"

"She said she gave him 'something for himself'. She also admitted that she'd taken one of Rose Toner's anti-depressants yesterday and she thought Toner had given Tracy Spencer a couple too."

"Did Scott Keenan know about that?"

"Toner was a bit vague. She admitted giving Spencer the pills once, 'to cheer her up'. She didn't know whether Scott Keenan knew about it. Said he'd offered to fix the lock on her jewellery box but she didn't take him up on it." Heather frowned as she looked through the remainder of her notes. "That's all, sir."

## 19

Dave Martin finally appeared at the door of Leith police station. He had been John's D.I. when John had first joined C.I.D. The most valuable lesson John learned from him was how not to run an investigation. He was grinning as he trotted to the car.

"Brief me on the way," John said, buckling himself into the driving seat.

"You were always in such a fucking hurry, John." Martin manoeuvred his paunch into the passenger seat. "I like the car. Still an Audi man, eh." He sprayed breath freshener in his mouth. "You still shagging that D.I?"

"The Keenans?" John turned onto Constitution Street.

Dave Martin laughed and pulled out his notebook. "Maggie Keenan – the Fife years," he announced. "'74, Maggie marries Jacky Keenan and moves to Dunfermline. Scott was three at the time. If anything looked like falling off the back of a lorry Jacky would be there to pick it up. Maggie took the opportunity to expand her money-lending business, helping people buy the stuff Jacky was selling." Martin chuckled. "Quite a team, eh.

"Fraser was born in '79. Jacky died five years later. Shortly after that Scott started getting into bother. When he was sixteen he was fingered for a spate of break-ins but when it came to the bit, nobody would testify."

"That down to Maggie?" He'd done his homework so already knew most of this but Martin was good at bringing it to life and putting up with him was easier if they kept to work.

"She was well in with Mark McNaughtan by then. Nobody was going to go up against him."

"How much do we know about McNaughtan?"

"He's a Fifer. Owns a security business and some bars and clubs in Dunfermline. Rumour is his son's trying to get into Edinburgh."

At the lights at Bernard Street an articulated lorry aiming for the docks was struggling to correct an erroneous attempt at a right turn. John reversed to give the driver more room.

"Stupid bastard," Martin muttered.

A considerate bus driver held up the oncoming traffic long enough for the lorry driver to manoeuvre his vehicle onto the bridge leading to Commercial Street. John followed, accelerating past the lorry when the road widened only to get stuck at the next set of lights.

"How did Scott get his record?"

"Tried going into the drugs business for himself. Fife got a tip-off and got him on possession, class A, so he got sent down."

"Sounds a bit neat."

"Rumour was that he was stepping on Mark McNaughtan's toes. Being Maggie's son saved his kneecaps but the price was prison. And Maggie wasn't too cut up about it. Kept the police away from her door."

They sat in the inside lane. A single-decker bus alongside waited to turn down towards Ocean Terminal with its shopping centre, upmarket flats and the Royal Yacht Britannia, this last a favourite with his son, Michael. It was Michael's birth that had brought him up short: as if his life had been tossed in the air and come down in a different shape. He'd even tried to make his unworkable marriage work. Went a bit wild when it didn't. D.I. Susan Taylor had been the latest in a long line.

The lights changed and John moved off. "How old was Scott when this happened?"

Martin looked down at his notebook using his hand as a shade against the sun now streaming through the windscreen. He hadn't worn well. Booze, fags and two ex-wives had taken their toll.

"Twenty-six. Served two years. His wife had moved while he was inside, wanted nothing to do with him, so it was back to Maggie."

John turned left, away from the river just as it hove into view sparkling in the sun, so different from the grey mass he saw this morning from Arthur's Seat. He'd run himself hard up the slope, battling against the near gale-force wind, and stood on the top watching the city come to life, wondering what he really wanted.

He became aware of Martin watching him. "Is Scott still into drugs?"

"Small-time stuff. Seen anything of that social worker Oakley was shagging?" Martin leered. "Great arse on her."

John swung the car to the left and pulled over outside a row of small, terraced houses. "We'll leave the car here." He unfastened his seatbelt and got out.

Martin followed his example, laughing. "Touched a nerve, have I?"

John strode off towards a tower block. "What do you know about Tracy Spencer?"

"If you slow down I'll tell you."

He stopped and waited for Martin to catch up. "Keeping up a problem these days, Dave?"

"Only with golden boy bastards like you."

"Tracy Spencer?" John repeated his question as they set off at a slightly slower pace.

"Maggie used her in her scams, mainly blackmail. Brought her with her when she moved back to Leith,"

Martin said, huffs and puffs punctuating his sentences. "Scott tried to muscle in. Maggie put a stop to it. After that Scott added pimping to his C.V. Lot of his customers were on the game. Took a commission off them. Cash or kind."

"But not Tracy?"

"Maggie would have killed him."

A trio of teenage boys crowded the doorway to the tower block; behind them an elderly man waited to exit. When he saw the two men the biggest of the boys tried a challenging stare. John didn't break his stride. The boy stood his ground until it became clear he could move or be mown down. He shuffled aside as casually as he could. John held the door to let the old man out before entering, aware of a grinning Dave Martin behind him. Inside he headed for the door to the stairs.

"Fuck's sake," Martin said.

John turned back towards the lift. "Just kidding, Dave. Just kidding," he said smiling.

Scott Keenan was dressed in a baggy T-shirt and jogging bottoms when he opened the door. He didn't look pleased to see John Nelson and a still sulking Dave Martin on his doorstep.

"Have you found out who killed my ma yet?" he asked.

"The investigation is ongoing," John replied. "There are a few questions you can help us with." He stepped forward.

Scott turned and moved ahead of them, leading them into the sitting room.

Their feet sank into the deep pile carpet. It was cream, like the leather sofa on which Scott now lounged. Its twin sat at right angles to it, back against the wall.

Scott faced the window and the view across the Forth to Fife but his attention was focussed on the widescreen T.V. in the corner. He pressed the remote to put the T.V. on standby and looked at the two policemen who had settled on the sofa to his left.

"So," he said, "what are these questions?" Then, "Tracy," he called.

A young woman appeared in the doorway.

"Get me a beer," Scott ordered.

The woman complied silently. She opened the can and handed it to Scott before disappearing to wherever she'd come from.

"You had a disagreement with Kirsten Cormack a few months ago. What was it about?" John said.

"What are you asking me that for? It's got nothing to do with this." Scott scowled. "Thought she was better than us. My ma put her in her place."

"Hardly a reason for killing her."

"I didn't say she killed her," Scott shouted.

John raised his eyebrows.

"I was in shock. I didn't know what I was saying."

"The disagreement?"

"I wanted in my ma's house and she wouldn't open the door."

"Your mother wasn't pleased about it."

Scott swallowed a mouthful of beer. "Who told you that? My ma was fine about it. She told that bitch Cormack off."

"Or told you off for disturbing her neighbours."

"My ma didn't tell me off about nothing. I'm no a wee boy."

"All right, Scott." Dave Martin sidled into the conversation. "We've got to check out what we're told.

You know that. We're just trying to get a picture of how things were for were for your ma in her new place."

Scott shrugged and reached for his beer, his gaze shifting to the blank screen of the television.

"She seemed to have made some friends there," Martin continued in his soothing tone. "They mentioned you helped them out now and again."

"I might have done but only if my ma asked me."

"Was Rose Toner one of them?" John asked.

"I don't remember their names. These old bitches all look the same to me."

"Maybe Tracy would remember her."

"What's Tracy got to do with it?" Scott's scowl was back.

"She helped some of the residents out too, didn't she?"

"She was there to look after my ma."

"Rose Toner was one of your mother's new friends."

"What do you keep going on about her for?"

"She was a wee bit free with her medication," Dave Martin contributed. "Tracy seemed to find it helpful."

"Then your mother put a stop to it. Told you to back off, didn't she?"

"My ma didn't tell me what to do." He turned back to the television, fingers playing with the buttons on the remote control. "Anyway, I've got better things to do than worry about what some old bitch does with her medicine."

"What sort of things would they be, Scott?" Dave Martin asked.

"Nothing to do with you." He directed his glare to John Nelson. "When am I going to get my ma buried?"

"When we let you." John looked steadily at Scott who turned away and went back to fiddling with the remote control.

## 20

Kate saw the little woman in the blue dress through the glass panel. She watched her listen at the door then peer through the letterbox. The woman was about to ring the bell when Kate pushed the stair door open.

"Oh." Betty Smyth jumped.

"It's not working."

"You're the niece, aren't you?"

Kate stared at her.

"Um, I was wondering how your aunt was."

"How thoughtful."

Betty smiled hesitantly. "I can see she's being well looked after." She nodded at the supermarket carrier bags Kate was holding. "Well, I'll not keep you."

Kate let her get halfway along the corridor. "Mrs Smyth."

She turned.

"I'll pass on your interest to my aunt."

Betty gave a weak smile and hurried off.

Kate let herself into Jean's flat. She left the carrier bags in the kitchen and went to the bedroom door. Jean seemed to be asleep. Kate returned to the kitchen and unpacked the shopping. Eggs and butter to replace that used for their omelettes; a pack of chicken breasts and some fresh vegetables if Jean felt like cooking, ready-made meals for one if she didn't; a small loaf in the bread bin, another in the freezer; tinned soup and baked beans for her store cupboard. Should keep Jean going for a while.

In the sitting room she replaced the note saying she'd gone to the supermarket with one saying she'd be back in half an hour. Jean would wonder where she was but that was nothing new.

Betty Smyth opened the door after the first ring of the bell. Kate smiled at her look of puzzlement.

"Come in." Betty stepped back. "It's the niece," she called and ushered Kate into the sitting room.

Rose Toner looked up at her from a pale blue leather sofa. She was dressed in a pink jumper and white skirt. A widescreen television at the window proclaimed itself to be 'HD Ready'. Kate waded through the deep-pile carpet to the armchair opposite, thinking how much Rose Toner looked like a giant blob of the coconut ice her gran used to love. Betty sat on the sofa, eyes like neon-lit buttons.

Kate waited. She got a strained smile from Betty, a steady stare from Rose Toner. "What did you want to speak to my aunt about?"

"We were just wondering how she was," Betty said. She turned to Toner. "Weren't we, dear?"

"She's fine."

"It can't have been easy for her. Just moved in and finding two people dead. Especially Maggie." Betty's words tumbled out breathlessly.

"Why especially Maggie?" Kate kept her expression blank, aware of Betty's search for a reaction.

Betty hesitated. Rose Toner shifted closer to her. "Do you not know?" Betty said.

"Know what?"

"Maggie knew your aunt."

"Maggie knew a lot of people."

"But she knew something about your aunt."

"What was that?" She searched their faces. She was pretty sure that Betty was fishing. There was a hungry look about her like an addict in need of a fix. Rose Toner was impossible to read, she gave nothing away. She gave nothing at all except that stare. Kate concentrated on Betty. "You don't get something for nothing, Mrs Smyth."

"I don't know what you mean."

"Fine." Kate stood.

Betty's leg twitched. "What do you want to know?" she asked.

Kate sat down. "Tell me about Sam MacEwen."

Betty glanced at Toner. "He's a pervert." She paused. "That boy goes into his flat nearly every morning."

"What boy?"

Toner moved slightly.

"The paper boy," Betty said hurriedly. "He's been in trouble before." She shot a shrewd look at Kate. "But you'd know about that, you being a social worker."

"Is that something Maggie did tell you?"

Betty shrugged, looking pleased with herself.

"What about Harriet Post?"

"Thought she was too good for Maggie. She even…" Betty winced.

Kate looked at Toner. Not so much as a blink. "So why would she give Maggie presents?"

"I don't know anything about that."

Kate made as if to stand.

"Maggie was very helpful," Betty blurted. "She'd get Tracy to do things for people." The hungry look was still there but it had been joined by a note of panic.

"Tracy?"

"Maggie's carer."

Kate swallowed her disbelief. "What sort of things did Tracy do?"

"Tidying." A glance at Toner. "What about your aunt Jean?"

"Tidying?"

"Mm. Cleaning, polishing." Betty's eyes darted sideways to Toner then back to Kate. The fear was almost palpable. "Helping out," she pleaded.

Kate couldn't take any more. If it was an act it was a good one. "I need to get back to my aunt." She stood up.

Betty reached out a restraining hand. "But you've not told us anything,"

"I'm sorry, Mrs Smyth," she said, meaning it. She walked into the hall and opened the door. It closed behind her on a whimper from Betty.

## 21

The clear sky and an increasing chill in the air threatened a frost later. Kate turned into a side street and pulled into a space under a solitary streetlight. It was a while since she'd been in this part of Leith. A few of her clients had lived here, some between stints in secure units and Saughton prison.

Before leaving Leapark she'd phoned a friend in the Housing Department then coaxed Jean out of bed long enough to eat a microwaved chicken casserole. At home she fed Lucy before swapping her dress for jeans and her black trainers. She'd topped this off with a black jumper and her close-fitting black leather jacket then added her rainbow-coloured scarf. She could almost feel her gran's fingers tucking the scarf in, pulling up the collar of her jacket. 'That's better now, isn't it?' Gran would say. Kate would nod her agreement then, once outside, loosen it all off. But not before she heard her gran's soft prayer to St Anthony to watch over her.

Waverley Tower was set back from the street onto which it fronted. With its sixteen floors it dwarfed the two-storey terraces on the other side. If your flat was high enough up, you could have a view of the Forth or the Castle. She was headed for the main entrance when a man appeared ahead of her. He turned to face her and she mentally revised his age downwards to teenage boy: big teenage boy, hard-muscled, hard stare, weight itching to be thrown about. He stood in her path. She veered to her left. He stepped to his right. She stopped, unwilling to get involved in a poor imitation of a Scottish country dance that would only leave her at more of a disadvantage.

The boy closed the gap between them giving her a better look at him: shaved head, face pitted with acne scars. A silver stud glinted in his left earlobe. "No seen you around here before," he said.

"I'm looking for Scott Keenan." She kept her voice steady.

"Big Scott? What do you want him for?"

"That's between me and him." Her stomach was heaving at the smell from his breath: rotted food and a sickly-sweet undertone.

"Lucky Scott."

Two other boys, their faces shrouded under hoods, shuffled towards them threatening to surround her. The door to the block of flats was only a few yards away. All she had to do was force her way through. Wouldn't be the first time. Instead she shifted her bag so that it covered her crotch.

The boy with the acne scars smiled. He reached out to finger the fringes of her scarf letting the back of his hand press lightly against her left breast.

She stepped back, bumping against one of the boys now behind her. He leaned closer. In her peripheral vision, she glimpsed tendrils of dark, curly hair under a pale grey hood. His breath felt warm on the nape of her neck. His lips brushed against her ear.

"Is that blonde hair natural?" he whispered.

Nearby a door closed followed by footsteps going away from her. Somewhere a car started up. Her brain screamed at her to move but her body wouldn't obey. With each breath she felt the pressure of acne boy's hand against her breast. Behind her, fingers traced a path down her back, curved under the hem of her jacket and hovered there. Her hands clutched uselessly at her bag, the buckle of the strap digging into her palm. She couldn't control this.

She looked up at the lighted windows that dotted the tower block knowing it was one more sign of weakness.

Acne boy's smile spread smugly across his face but his eyes, on a level with hers, were hard, unblinking, challenging.

"Don't worry nobody's going to bother us." He lifted his left hand and caressed her cheek with his nails, stopping just short of scratching her. "Got plenty of time." His fingers moved towards her nipple. She tried to pull back and was surprised to feel the pressure behind her give way. The hand was removed from her jacket. Acne boy flicked a glance at his cohorts.

"All right, boys?" a voice said.

Kate shifted her gaze to the good-looking, smartly-dressed man standing at the door of the tower block. He was slender and no taller than she was.

Acne boy continued to stare at her but his bravado was crumbling. He dropped his hands and turned to the man behind him, nodding almost imperceptibly before standing aside to let Kate pass.

"Are you going in?" The man smiled at her, holding the door open.

"Thanks." She returned the smile.

Inside she turned and watched through the glass panel as the man, his back to her, spoke to the boys, their heads drooping lower the longer he spoke. In the lift she pressed the button for the twelfth floor and released her breath unaware that she'd been holding it.

As the lift quietly hummed its way upwards she leant back against the wall and closed her eyes. Maybe this hadn't been such a good idea. The lift stopped and she stepped out. The lighting was dim but the narrow hallway, like the lift, was unusually clean and recently painted in a cheery yellow. She walked along to the door of Scott Keenan's flat: a river view from this one. Before the doubt had time to harden she rang the bell. Silence. Question was whether the bell was broken or one of those that only rang inside the flat. She waited, wondering whether to ring again. Or maybe just take the opportunity to go away. She was still debating with herself when the door opened.

Scott Keenan's mouth gaped before forming itself into a smile. Then suspicion narrowed his mean, little eyes, buried in a puffy, lardy face. "What do you want?" he said.

"Kate McKinnery." She held out her hand, every nerve ending recoiling at the thought of Scott Keenan's touch. "I'd like to talk to you about your mother's death."

Scott took the proffered hand limply, still peering at her. "Are you from the papers?"

The opportunity was too good to miss. "I'm carrying out an investigation into how the police deal with the families of murder victims, Mr Keenan. We wondered if you would agree to be interviewed. We will of course cover any expenses you incur in giving us your time."

Scott stepped back. "You better come in."

She'd prepared herself for the flat to reflect its resident so the sitting room surprised her. It could have been cloned from Betty Smyth's flat and was just as clean. Someone had done a thorough job especially on the deep-pile carpet and Scott didn't strike her as the cleaning type. But it was the view across the river that impressed her, the lights of Fife softly reflected in the water. "You've got a lovely view, Mr Keenan." She turned to find Scott close behind her.

"Aye, I have," he replied grinning.

He shuffled to the sofa facing the window, hitched up his joggers and sat down. He used the remote control to mute the enormous television burbling away in the corner then patted the cushion next to his. In your dreams, she thought, and sat on the other sofa, ensuring she had a straight run to the front door. She pulled a small notebook from her handbag and smiled at him.

"Can you give me a bit of background on how things were for your mother in Leapark, Mr Keenan?"

"Call me Scott." He smiled back, showing stained teeth. "Do you want a beer?" He handed her the last can from a four-pack on the coffee table. "A lot of stuck-up old bitches in that place. Didn't like my ma being in there. But she sorted them out. Even old sour-face in the wheelchair."

"Sour-face?"

"Collins her name is. Thought she could threaten us. Her and that wee shite, Cormack. 'Scuse my French.

There are things I could tell you about her. She wouldn't be in the bloody job if it wasn't for us, she'd be in the jail."

"What sort of things, Mr Keenan?"

"I'm not a grass." He took a slurp from his beer can. "Now they're trying to say I was dealing drugs. Just because some daft old bitch handed hers out like sweeties."

"What was the woman's name?" The television was giving her a headache. The actors on the giant screen seemed to be in the room with them.

"What do you want to know that for?" Scott's suspicious frown was back.

"Um, we may want to interview her."

"Her name's Toner. But she's not the full shilling if you know what I mean." He continued to frown at her. "Anyway, I thought it was the police you wanted to talk about. That big bastard, Nelson, was here earlier. He's always had it in for me."

Kate had a small panic that she might bump into John Nelson on her way out. If he thought she was carrying out her own investigation he'd cut her out of the loop completely. "Can I check some details with you, Mr Keenan? There's just you and your brother now, is that right?"

"Aye, me and wee Fraser, and young Tracy of course. Me and my ma kept an eye on them. Now it'll be just me." He shook his head sadly but the effect was somewhat spoiled by the leer he gave Kate in the process.

"Tracy was your mother's carer?"

"Aye. We took her in when we lived in Fife. She looks up to me." He preened and took another slurp of beer.

"Why did your mother need a carer?"

He glared at her, his suspicion returning. "What's it to you?"

She wondered how much he'd had to drink and decided she'd pushed her luck far enough for one day. She made a show of checking her watch. "Thanks very much, Mr Keenan." She stood. "You've certainly given me a lot to think about."

Scott hauled himself off the settee and moved toward the door, blocking it. "And now we can talk about what I get."

She tried a professional smile. "You'll be entitled to any expenses or losses you've incurred in talking to us." She shouldered her bag. "I'll get the form sent out to you as soon as I get back to the office."

"You've not even touched your drink."

"I'm driving, Mr Keenan." She made a move to the door but Scott stayed put.

"I told you to call me Scott." His voice and stare hardened. "Do I not know you from somewhere?"

She swallowed then looked again at her watch. "I'm meeting a colleague in five minutes, Mr Keenan, so I really must go." She forced a note of authority into her voice whilst she felt in her bag for her car key, the closest thing to a weapon she had.

He scowled at her but stepped back from the doorway. "What paper did you say you were from anyway?"

"I'm freelance." She hurried down the hallway. "Thanks again, Mr Keenan," she flung back as she let the door close behind her.

She took the stairs rather than wait for the lift in case Scott Keenan followed her out. How could he have swallowed all that? Or was he just pretending he did in the hope that there might be a reward in it for him. Her stomach gave a lurch at the thought of rewarding Scott Keenan in the way he'd hoped.

On the ground floor she looked through the main door's glass panel once again checking her escape route was clear. There was no one in sight, the only movement a blue plastic carrier bag that skittered across the concourse and billowed up before settling softly on a grass verge. She took her car key from her bag and walked quickly from the building, rounding the small terraces that cowered in the tower block's shadow.

The street where she'd parked was darker than it should have been, lit only by borrowed light from the tower block. She ran to her car, using the remote to unlock the doors. Pieces of glass from the streetlight were strewn across the bonnet.

"Fuck." She slammed into the car, activating the central locking before starting the engine. She roared off, hoping the glass would be dispersed by the movement and the paintwork survive intact. She headed through upmarket Trinity to Ferry Road turning off at Goldenacre, named after either the yellow wildflowers that may once have grown there or a rampaging corn-destroying weed. Take your pick. Now it was pricey tenements and a rugby ground.

On Raeburn Place she pulled over at the chip shop and bought a fish supper and a single fish. She felt safer now, more her professional self, in Stockbridge with its cafes and its neat little shops, a butcher, a baker, no candlestickmaker... 'Rub-a-dub-dub'.

At home she pulled the batter from the single fish and put the white flesh in a saucer for Lucy then stuck a C.D. in the hi-fi. She poured herself a glass of the wine she'd bought with Jean's shopping and carried it to her kitchen table to concentrate on her fish supper, wishing she had some white bread to make a piece with the chips. It wasn't the same with brown bread and her ciabatta rolls would probably self-destruct at the very idea. She smiled to herself and went to make tea. It always went better with a fish supper than wine.

Back at the table she thought about what she'd learned from Scott Keenan. There was Rose Toner and her drugs 'habit'. John hadn't mentioned that. Did that mean he didn't know or did he just not want her to know? She chewed thoughtfully on a chip. What could Scott and Maggie have known that could not just lose Kirsten Cormack her job but put her in jail? It was certainly a motive for killing Maggie but not if Scott was left alive. And what about the stuff in Maggie's flat that John doubted belonged to her. Was that really payment for favours done, or secrets kept?

When in doubt, make a list. She booted up her laptop.

Betty Smyth and Rose Toner – the two surviving members of the not-so-holy trinity. Rose Toner was an unlikely drug dealer, but she was sharper than Scott Keenan seemed to think. And vicious with it. And how much had Maggie told them about Jean? Not enough, it seemed.

Kirsten Cormack – threatened with jail by Maggie and Scott, if Scott was to be believed. But for what?

Sam MacEwen – was he a paedophile? Even if he wasn't his relationship with the paper-boy could be enough for Maggie to have a hold over him.

Marjorie Collins – was 'sorted out' by Maggie and didn't look the type to appreciate it.

Frances Wordsworth – for good measure.

Scott Keenan – was Maggie cramping his style enough for him to kill her? Assuming he had a style to cramp.

Fraser Keenan – the unknown quantity.

Tracy Spencer – was she really just Maggie's carer?

Was Maggie blackmailing any of them or just keeping them in line? Making them dance to her tune. Kate shook her head. Would that be enough to drive someone to murder her?

How to find out more:-

Annie Hargreaves would be a reliable source – arrange to see her tomorrow.

Social work records would give background on the residents – pull the files tomorrow morning at the Corstorphine office. Her conscience gave a sharp prick at that one but she chose to ignore it.

Could she find a way to check personnel records for Kirsten and Frances?

And what about Fraser? Though if he really needed Scott to look out for him he wasn't the most likely candidate on her list of suspects.

Leapark itself seemed an oddity in the sheltered housing market. According to her friend in Housing it was owned by a private company, A.F. Holdings, and marketed as an exclusive development. Potential buyers were vetted and had to meet certain medical criteria but the Council had nomination rights on five of the twenty-five flats. It was hard to see how that enhanced the exclusivity tag, especially if people like Maggie were nominated.

She pushed the remains of her meal to one side and sat back, sipping at the wine. Lucy settled on her fleece-lined cushion under the radiator, smacking her wee chops, savouring every last morsel of fish. 'Wouldn't call the

Queen her auntie,' Gran would have said. On the hi-fi, Tom Waits still searched for the heart of Saturday night, a legacy from a schoolteacher who'd taught English in her fifth year. Their relationship had teetered towards something more but never got beyond an uneasy friendship. He'd used music to catch the imagination of the more reluctant students, usually boys, extolling the virtues of vinyl. So occasionally they'd spend a lesson deconstructing albums by the Stones, Tom Waits or, her favourite, Springsteen. She'd searched out female artists from the same era looking for someone he hadn't heard of, found Carole King, Janis Ian and scored a hit with Dory Previn. He'd devoted a whole lesson to 'Reflections in a Mud Puddle' though it was the flipside, unusually with its own title, that they'd focussed on: 'Taps, Tremors and Timesteps (One Last Dance for my Father)'.

She crushed the polystyrene container and aimed it at the bin. It clattered in through the swing lid, the noise earning her a sleepy glare from the cat.

"Sorry, Luce." She carried her dishes to the sink and turned to study her Joan Eardley print on the wall above her table – 'Catterline in Winter'. It showed a precariously perched row of cottages at Catterline in north-east Scotland with a full moon above them in a cold, grey sky. She'd fallen in love with Eardley's work when the National Gallery held an exhibition a few years ago and had bought numerous prints of her landscapes as well as her street kids, currently represented on a sitting room wall by one from the 'Children and Chalked Wall' series which showed two girls, one with an arm round the other's shoulders. Best pals, like she and Jules would have been had they grown up together.

She shook her head. As a child she'd learned to show strength not weakness. Be tough and save her tears for when she got home where her gran would comfort her with hugs and sticking plaster. Like the time she stopped two girls tormenting Josie. She'd been ten at the time; Josie, small, pale, wraith-like, was six. The bigger girl had wanted to make a fight of it but her pal had pulled her away. Kate had earned a reputation as somebody not to be messed with. So why had she let herself be so intimidated by the three boys? She knew how kids like that operated; she'd dealt with situations like that before. They sniffed out uncertainty, vulnerability. Had she changed or had boys got more aggressive? What would have happened if that man hadn't intervened? Maybe nothing much, bored kids having a bit of fun at some woman's expense yet it hadn't felt like that. And even if it had, she didn't like being the woman. It wasn't how she saw herself. Or it hadn't been. Finding out about her mother's suicide had let her childhood doubt and uncertainty creep up on her, leaving her at the mercy of tough-guy kids wanting to throw their weight about. She couldn't have that. She really couldn't have that.

# Friday

## 22

"No more sign of Dawn?" Kate asked.

The receptionist shook her head and swallowed a mouthful of coffee before speaking. "She's phoned a couple of times to speak to Natasha's worker. All please and thank you."

"Long may it continue." Kate headed for the duty office. She'd take a bet that Eddie Ranford was behind the improvement in Dawn's behaviour. Working her like a ventriloquist's dummy. One aim – get Natasha back. Dawn doing what she was told because she knew, whatever she wanted to believe, that without Natasha she had no hope of hanging onto Ranford and Dawn would always need someone. Though not, it would seem, her children. The two older ones, now in their teens, had been adopted and it looked like Natasha would be going down the same route. Yet she did wonder why Ranford hadn't moved on to some other unsuspecting single mother. Maybe it was getting harder to find any that would take him on. Or maybe it was finding one with his particular type, a little girl with dark curls and big blue eyes like Natasha. She made a mental note to find out who his criminal justice worker was and have a word. If Ranford was back with Dawn he could be in breach of his conditions of release.

The somewhat grandly named 'duty office' was really a screened off cubbyhole in the admin area on the ground floor. Its one advantage was proximity to the small kitchen and the willingness of the clerical staff to bring the occupant coffee whenever they went for their own. Thus armed with her first mug of the day Kate began allocating the morning's tasks, brain settling into its social work groove. There were three office appointments and two home visits, one a bit tricky. Two workers: Sheila, experienced and competent and Simon, recently qualified and too cocky. She decided to keep Simon for the office appointments and follow-ups from yesterday's session. She'd send Sheila on the home visits but have a word with her about the tricky one involving a child custody dispute. She would deal with the overspill and any emergencies herself. As she'd expected, Simon tried to persuade her to let him do the home visits. With his dark hair and green eyes he was used to getting his way. Kate found the manipulation too obvious and disliked the arrogance and the whiff of contempt that underlay it. She returned his smiles, let him wheedle, let him think she was about to change her mind. Then "Nice try, Simon," she said checking her watch. "Your first appointment's at 9.30."

He stomped off, huffing and puffing like a school kid. Kate pulled her haul of data towards her and settled down to read. She'd arrived early and had extracted and copied the family and social histories from the files. Computer systems were all very well but every enquiry left a trace. Paper files didn't. She started with Maggie Keenan. Maggie had spent much of her adult life in Dunfermline, had moved there in '74 when she married Jacky Keenan, Fraser's father. There was no information about Scott's father. Maggie had returned to live with her mother in the council flat in Leith in 1998 bringing Tracy with her. Scott followed at some point. It wasn't clear whether Fraser did. The tenancy transferred to Maggie when her mother died then to Scott when Maggie moved to Leapark in 2007. Why Scott? What about Fraser? And where did Tracy fit into this?

Heart disease was cited as the reason for Maggie's application for sheltered housing; mobility problems justified the ground floor flat, all supported by her G.P. Kate suspected it was as much to do with getting Maggie off his list as anything else but she made a note to check with John on the results of Maggie's post mortem. Assuming he'd tell her. And here comes Tracy again, this time as Maggie's 'carer'. If Tracy had been living full-time with Maggie in Leapark she was now homeless. So was she back in Leith with Scott, and Fraser? The cleanliness of Scott's flat yesterday could be down to Tracy. More questions than answers right enough.

She moved onto Betty Smyth: asthmatic, moved to Leapark in November, 2009. She'd lived near Marjorie Collins before that. Marjorie had arthritis and angina, hence her move. That was just over a year after Betty. Both were widows, both childless.

There was little more to work on in Rose Toner's file. She'd lived in Corstorphine all her life and with her parents by the look of it. She'd never married, never had a job. What had she done? Looked after her parents when they were too old to care for themselves? They'd died within months of each other. A couple of years later, Toner moved to Leapark. That was just before Christmas 2008. 'Depression' was the primary reason given with 'social isolation' as a back-up. Or maybe nobody to beat up.

Prior to moving to Leapark, all three had owned two or three-bed houses in Corstorphine. As had Sam MacEwen. He was a widower with a daughter living in

London. Angina was the reason given for the move to Leapark. He'd been self-employed.

She sat back sipping her second mug of coffee. Assuming, as was likely, that there was no mortgage on their respective houses and allowing for the cost of their sheltered flats, they'd now collectively be worth not far short of £1million, at least. The phone rang as she was wondering about the significance, if any, of this.

"I've had a call from the police at Corstorphine. They need someone to accompany a young person at an interview," the receptionist explained. "The boy's name is Jake Harrison. I've sent the file along to you."

The file arrived courtesy of Simon. "I could do this one."

"Write-ups all done? Phone calls to the Reporter's office all made?"

His head drooped. "Kate," he stretched her name out, giving her his best pleading look.

"What's your mantra?"

He sighed and fixed his gaze beyond her right shoulder. "Follow-through good, procrastination bad."

She waved him away and turned her attention to the file. She already knew about Jake's time in foster care but the file showed that two years ago he had participated in an attempted break-in to an elderly woman's bungalow. He'd been referred to Children's Hearing and placed under the supervision of a social worker for a year. Put that with Jake being the paper-boy at Leapark Terrace and you could see why the police wanted to question him. Now that both duty workers were caught up in work it was legitimate for her to do the police interview. She arranged for Tom Urquhart to cover for her, picked up her bag and headed for the door, aware of Simon's resentful stare boring into her back.

## 23

John Nelson and Gordon Donald stood in the middle of the room until invited to sit. They chose the sofa. Sam MacEwen sat in the armchair. He'd looked surprised to find two police officers on his doorstep. There'd been a moment's hesitation before he stood back to admit them.

A widescreen television dominated the sitting room. It sat atop a smoked glass unit with a combined video and D.V.D. recorder on the shelf underneath. It was faced by the large, gold-coloured sofa and matching armchair. In a corner was a small desk on which sat a laptop computer.

"What can I do for you?" MacEwen asked.

"We're investigating the death of Maggie Keenan," John Nelson began. "There are a couple of things you might be able to clarify for us."

"I'll help if I can, of course, but I didn't know the lady particularly well." Sam MacEwen held onto his mildly disinterested expression.

"We've been told you had a disagreement with Mrs Keenan."

He shrugged. "It was a minor matter."

"Tell us about it."

"Maggie Keenan complained to the boy who delivers the newspapers about getting her order wrong. I spoke to her about it."

"Why?"

He looked puzzled. "The boy was upset."

"Why should that concern you?"

He hesitated. "I consider Jake a friend."

"Male company in short supply?"

"Look, Inspector…"

"How did this friendship start?"

"I bumped into him in the corridor one morning when he was on his paper round. He looked wet and miserable. I offered him a cup of tea."

"How long ago was this?"

"About three months."

"Do you still see him?"

"Most mornings." MacEwen's irritation was growing. "He comes in for a cup of tea and some toast before he goes to school. That's all." He emphasised the 'all', looking pointedly at John Nelson, who returned the look with interest. Sam MacEwen turned away, shaking his head.

"How many other residents knew about this?"

"I don't know. It wasn't something I talked about."

"Why was that?"

"I like my privacy." Indignant now.

As if to emphasise the point voices sounded in the corridor outside the flat then faded as a door closed.

"I'm not so naïve that I don't know how some people might have chosen to construe my friendship with Jake." MacEwen continued. "And I didn't want Jake to be hurt by any of it."

"Was it just Jake you were worried about?" Gordon asked.

"Primarily," he sighed. "I admit I was concerned about Maggie Keenan knowing about it but time went on and nothing more was said."

"What did you think of Maggie Keenan?"

MacEwen shrugged. "I didn't like her. She was a bully."

"Did she bully you?"

"She didn't try." He plucked at the piping on the arm of his chair. "From what I could see, she concentrated on women."

John Nelson walked to the window and stood looking out. "Are you married, Mr MacEwen?"

"I'm a widower."

"Any children?"

"A daughter. She lives in London."

"I see you have a computer, Mr MacEwen." Gordon Donald nodded at the laptop sitting on the small desk. "Do you use the internet much?"

"I used to work in finance. I like to monitor the value of my investments," he said irritably.

"Your window looks out onto the garden area, did you see anything unusual on Tuesday night?" John Nelson said.

"I rarely look out of my window other than when I close the blinds."

John could feel MacEwen's eyes boring into his back. He turned to look at him. "When you were closing the blinds on Tuesday night did you see anything out of the ordinary?"

Sam MacEwen stood up. "No, Inspector, I didn't."

John Nelson held MacEwen's gaze for a moment then said, "Thanks for your help, Mr MacEwen. We may want to talk to you again."

"I'll be here," Sam MacEwen said.

## 24

"How are you doing, Jake?" Kate said.

He was sitting at the table, head down. His fair hair stood up on his head 'Oor Wullie' style. In his oversized jacket he looked small and vulnerable despite his fourteen years. He'd looked up as Kate was shown in by a W.P.C., giving a nod of recognition. She sat beside him and gave him an encouraging smile.

The room was bright, painted in shades of blue and cream. The pale wood table looked new, as yet unscarred. The chairs were upholstered with cushioned backs and seats in the same colours as the walls whilst a curtained window looked out onto blocks of flats and a supermarket car park, all built round the site of an old piggery apparently.

The door opened and Steve Oakley came in. He gave Kate a long, hard look then walked to the table followed by Heather Mair. Once seated he nodded to Heather to begin. She confirmed with Jake that he was here voluntarily to answer some questions and advised him that he could leave at any time. She glanced at Kate before turning to her notes.

Thereafter it was downhill all the way as Steve pushed and prodded Jake about his past history and his relationship with Sam MacEwen until Kate put her hand on Jake's arm. "Inspector Oakley, I'm reminding you that Jake is a minor and should be treated as such," she said, matching Steve's cold stare with her own.

"Two women are dead."

"And if you consider Jake to be a suspect in that then he should have legal representation not just an appropriate adult."

He glared at her. "Fine," he said. "This interview is terminated." He stood, gathered his papers and left the room.

Kate looked at Heather who was trying to hide her puzzlement at Steve's behaviour. "I take it we can go now," she said.

"I'll show you out."

The sky darkened as they stepped outside. Jake hunched his shoulders against a vicious, little breeze and the gobs of icy rain spitting on them.

"C'mon, I'll give you a lift back to school." She beeped the remote and they got into the car. "How's your dad?" she asked when they'd set off.

Jake stared out through the windscreen. "We look out for each other." The barriers were up.

"Do you still have your life-story book?"

"I keep it with my mum's photos and stuff."

The windscreen wipers swished to and fro. "Did it help you?"

He shrugged. "I suppose." He turned to her. "What did you ask me that for?"

"Bit of research."

He nodded. "Sometimes if I'm trying to remember something about my mum, I find it in the book. My dad looks at it as well."

By the time they reached the school the rain was pelting down. Kate pulled up at the kerb. "Jake, you know you can contact a social worker if you're worried about anything," she said.

He released his seat belt and turned to open the car door. "Will the police want to talk to me again?" he said keeping his back to her.

"If they do we'll make sure you're properly represented."

He seemed to hesitate. "I don't want to leave my dad."

"Why would you have to leave your dad?"

He focussed his attention on a middle-aged woman being hurried along the street by a gust of wind. She was getting drenched, her umbrella held aloft like a banner, spokes pointing skyward.

"Jake?"

"Mr MacEwen's all right. I know what you're all thinking but he's not like that. And neither am I. I can look out for myself. I'm not stupid."

She wanted to tell him that it wasn't stupidity a paedophile looked for but vulnerability. Instead she handed him a business card. "If there is anything you want to talk about, give me a ring."

He flicked the card against his fingers and turned his head in her direction. "Can I go now?"

"Aye". She watched him sprint across the empty playground and into the school building before she started back to the office.

She'd been Jake's social worker when he was nine and having one of his spells in foster care. It had been that way since his mother had died and his father had made an intermittent descent into alcoholism. Jake had been in his running phase then: in the 'gotta get out of this place' sense rather than the sporty one. He always went back to the house he'd lived in when his mother had been alive, as if it still held a trace of her, a trail he could pick up. But not this time: three o'clock on Christmas Eve afternoon and no sign of him till Jake's father had told her about Jenner's.

Every Christmas Eve Jake's mum would take him to see Jenner's Christmas tree. And that was where Kate had found him. The tree reached up past three floors almost to the ceiling, dwarfing Jake's small figure. She'd stood beside him, his hand tucked into hers, tills and carols jingling whilst the last-minute Christmas shoppers surged round them. Sometimes that was the best you could offer kids like Jake: a quiet centre, a point of stillness in a world that seemed to be spinning wildly out of control, holding onto them until they found their own way through.

It had reminded her of something she saw on a trip to London. She was travelling on the underground, train full to bursting, station platforms heaving. The escalators seemed to creak with the weight of humanity they were forced to carry. In the midst of this swirling mass of people, rushing, pushing, driven, eyes glazing over at the relentlessness of it all she saw the poster: 'Be still and know that I am God'. And in that passing moment she felt its appeal. Atheist though she was, the message caught her attention. She'd played with it in her head. 'Be still and know', leave out the God bit. It had stayed with her. And now, when there was so much she wanted to know about her past, she sometimes thought that if she could be still for long enough she would remember.

## 25

Jean rummaged in her cupboard under the sink. When she stood the room tilted gently. She sighed. Maybe she could have put it better, got a bit more sympathy from Kate. But she was struggling with the memories it had resurrected, somehow made worse by giving voice to them. She sprayed the polish and gave the coffee table a vigorous rub with her yellow duster then turned her attention to the sideboard. She lifted the photographs, sprayed and polished, wiping the frames as she repositioned them.

She'd read somewhere that every thought causes a physical reaction, that emotional shocks can resonate in the body for years. Seeing Andrew again had felt like being punched in the stomach. She'd just got in from work when the doorbell rang. Her breath had left her body when she saw him standing there. For a moment it was as if her dream had come true. Tall and dark, he smiled, held out his hand.

"I'm Andrew," he said.

But all she could do was stare. Too long.

He lowered his hand before she could grasp it, his smile fading. "Your son," he said.

So like him. Mood turning on a sixpence.

Then, when it was already too late, she invited him in, offered tea, coffee. He refused, looked round her sitting room before settling on a dining chair next to the mahogany gateleg table. She'd stood in the centre of the room, hands clasped in front of her, not knowing what to say to him, where to begin. She saw the room through his eyes: the worn carpet, the second-hand furniture. She tried to smile, finally opened her mouth to speak.

"I want to know who my father is," Andrew had said abruptly.

She headed for the bedroom and started on the dressing table, moving her jar of Pond's moisturiser to one side. It wasn't a proper dressing table, more a chest of drawers with a mirror attached and a veneer you could almost see your face in now. She'd bought it years ago from a second-hand shop on Leith Walk, a job lot with the gateleg table and four chairs, celebrating her new job with the accountancy firm where Robert was a senior partner.

She would organise her evenings and weekends around when he could spend time with her. Sometimes it was planned, like when his wife went to her evening classes. Other times he'd phone and say he was on his way, having made an excuse about seeing someone on business. His wife never seemed to suspect anything and there'd never been any suggestion of him leaving her. Jean hadn't wanted to see herself as a home-wrecker.

She sat on the bed, polish in one hand, duster in the other. Robert had put her back together after the fiasco with Andrew. A soft, round man, he'd won her over with his kindness. Fifteen years of snatched moments, dinners in out of the way places, secret love. The first time she'd seen his wife was on a beautiful spring day at Robert's funeral. Jean had sat with her work colleagues, holding her grief to herself, had nursed it all through the summer.

The autumn had brought Kate bubbling over with energy and enthusiasm for her university course, for Edinburgh, for life. She buzzed round the city, couldn't get enough of it. Jean had always felt Edinburgh to be a cold, unfeeling place. Kate had seen that as part of its attraction. Disdainful, she called it, knowing its worth, wearing its history like a crown. They went to cafes, restaurants, cinemas, theatres. Trawled up and down the dank closes of the Old Town, dim even in the brightest sunshine. So easy to believe a Burke or Hare lurked in one of the dark corners. In the wide streets and Georgian terraces of the New Town it was Conan Doyle and Robert Louis Stevenson, even a visit to the Oxford Bar. Jean saw bits of Edinburgh she didn't know existed. Like the night Kate took her to Calton Hill, the whole city spread out below, all the colours of the rainbow.

She gave her bedside cabinet a perfunctory wipe, nudging the book aside with her tin of polish: 'The

Reverend I.M. Jolly', a present from Kate a couple of Christmases ago. It made a miserable bugger funny. Jean had wondered if there was a message aimed at her.

She dumped the duster, picked up her key and went out. The building was quiet. She hesitated at Sam MacEwen's flat wondering if she would seem too forward if she knocked on his door and invited him for coffee. He'd been attentive at the meeting on Wednesday, sympathising with her plight as body-finder-in-chief but she'd not seen him since. So she headed down to Marjorie Collins' flat instead. She was 'winging' it, as Kate would say, but the worst that could happen is that Marjorie would send her away. She took a deep breath and rang the bell.

"Jean." Marjorie stood foursquare in the doorway. "What do you want?"

"I wondered if you'd like to come up for a cup of coffee, or tea, if you prefer." Maybe this hadn't been such a good idea.

"Did you?" Marjorie studied her. "Right." She closed the door.

Jean wondered if Marjorie had misheard her. Then the door opened and Marjorie stepped out leaning on a walking stick.

"We'll take the lift," Marjorie said. She hooked the walking stick over her arm as she locked her door.

"You didn't mind me coming to see you?"

"Not today."

They made slow progress although Marjorie seemed to speed up the longer she walked. As they crossed the entrance hall, heading for the lift, Marjorie nodded at the reception window that showed the office to be empty.

"There should be someone in there," she said then waved her walking stick in the direction of the front door. "And those reporters should be sent away. It's like being under siege."

They moved into the corridor leading to the lift. The door to Maggie Keenan's flat was on their right, the blue and white police tape still stretched across the doorway.

The stick pointed at it. "That shouldn't still be there. We don't need reminding."

"I suppose they have to keep it there." Jean shrugged, unsure what to say next. She was relieved when the lift doors swished open. Her once bright idea for getting herself some company was starting to look tarnished.

In Jean's sitting room Marjorie stomped to the window.

"I would have preferred this end of the building, but only some of the ground floor flats are designed for wheelchairs and, unfortunately, there are times when I need to use one." She sat on one of the armchairs. "They'd no business giving Maggie Keenan that flat. We all knew it was a nonsense."

"Would you like tea or coffee, Marjorie?" Jean asked.

"Tea, thank you. Coffee doesn't agree with my medication."

Jean rolled her eyes as she went into the kitchen. She made the tea in her blue Spode teapot and set out her matching cups and saucers, a birthday present from Robert. The following year he'd presented her with a matching coffee pot and side plates whilst the Christmas brought four small, delicate silver teaspoons. She smiled to herself as she put her favourite chocolate ginger biscuits on one of the side plates and tucked a teaspoon onto each of the saucers. Apart from Kate, Marjorie was her first proper visitor. Not counting the police, of course. She waited until the percolator stopped burbling before pouring the coffee into the coffee pot, adding it to the tray and carrying it all out to the sitting room.

"Here we are."

"Very nice set," Marjorie said grudgingly, examining one of the cups.

Jean smiled as she waited for the cup to be returned to its saucer then poured tea for Marjorie, coffee for herself. "Do you take milk, Marjorie?"

"A soupcon, thank you." She looked round the room. "You've not made many changes."

"Sugar?"

Marjorie reacted like she'd been offered a dose of the plague. Jean smiled as she handed the cup and saucer over then added a soupcon of sugar to her coffee.

"My niece, Kate, offered to paint it for me but I thought I'd wait till I settled in." Jean sipped her coffee then reached for a biscuit, Marjorie watching her every move. "Would you like a chocolate biscuit, Marjorie?" She held the plate out.

"Thank you, no."

Jean allowed herself a smile with just a hint of smugness. "Did you know the woman who lived here before me?"

"Maggie Keenan drove her out of here," Marjorie said, eyeing the biscuits. "She went to live with her son and daughter-in-law."

"Was she a friend of yours?"

"We spoke occasionally." She sat back in her chair, cup and saucer in her hand. "Was your niece at the meeting on Wednesday? Tall with short blonde hair?"

"Mmm," Jean replied as best she could through a mouthful of biscuit crumbs and melting chocolate.

"Does she visit often?"

"She has recently with what's been going on. Do you have any family, Marjorie?"

"None to speak of."

Subject closed, thought Jean. "That's a lovely brooch." She nodded at the large gold oval pinned at the neck of Marjorie's beige jumper.

"My late husband dealt in jewellery." She sipped at the tea. "Have you heard any more about this murder business?"

Jean was taken aback by the abrupt change in topic. "Have you?"

"I've spoken to the police. I was concerned about Betty."

"Is she a close friend?" Jean swallowed the last of her biscuit and reached for another one.

"We belong to the same church." Marjorie glared at her. "Maggie Keenan manipulated her. I'm not sorry she's gone."

## 26

A removal van sat in the middle of the street outside the sheltered housing building, a police constable keeping the reporters at bay. Kate cut through the park and walked round to the back of the building, entering once again through the lilac lounge. As she did so, the door from the entrance hall opened and Frances Wordsworth stepped in.

"Can I help you?" she said.

Frances Wordsworth was a bit shorter than Kate but heavier with a well-upholstered bosom beneath her black, square-necked tunic. A thin, white polo-neck jumper completed the ensemble. Kate walked towards her, her hand extended. "I'm Kate McKinnery."

Frances clasped it, smiling, as if they were old friends who hadn't seen each other for a while. "Yes, Mrs Markham's niece."

She'd arranged the meeting ostensibly to talk about security hoping that Kirsten would be on duty but had to make do with Frances. All she'd learned about them so far were their middle names: Frances Sarah Wordsworth and Kirsten Mary Cormack. Wow. Don't give up the day job, Kate.

"Shall we?" Frances turned and led the way along the corridor, stopping at the dining room door to usher Kate in. "It's more pleasant here than in the office."

Kate chose a table by the window, sitting with her back against the wall, giving a view of the garden and the park beyond. Frances looked uncomfortable as she sat opposite.

"As I said earlier, we are careful about security but we can't force residents to lock their doors. It's not like in a home." Frances spread her hands nervously. "Of course I always check the doors from the communal areas are locked. As I'm sure Kirsten does. I have started to check the doors from the ground floor flats even though it's not part of my remit."

The spiel sounded practised but there was an air of tension in it. How many other relatives had heard it? "There's just you and Kirsten?"

"We share the warden duties although I am the senior member of staff. I've been here since it opened five years ago." Frances' hands continue to flap an accompaniment.

"How long has Kirsten been here?"

"About nine months. She worked for an agency as a care assistant and had a lot of experience in nursing homes, so she did seem well-suited to this job."

This sounded like a justification. Kate wondered how much pressure Frances was under and whether Kirsten was to be her sacrificial lamb. "Have you always done this type of work?"

"I like older people. I looked after an elderly aunt then my husband when he became ill. Both dead now." She nodded sadly. Her ringless hands had finally settled on the table.

"I'm sorry. I didn't realise you were a widow."

"Fingers got too fat." She smiled, waving the offending hand. "And death comes to us all. I like to think I eased the path for my aunt and my husband. Not in any sinister way, you understand." A nervous laugh. "Just helping them be reconciled with their fate and at one with the Lord. I find faith so helpful in difficult times don't you?"

Kate chose to treat the question as rhetorical. "Did you know Mrs Keenan well?"

"Mrs Keenan had her own carer so I didn't see that much of her. Perhaps if I had…" Frances shrugged.

"Did she have many friends here?"

"Miss Toner and Mrs Smyth were her closest friends. And I think she visited a few others now and again." Frances looked at her watch. "I'm sorry to hurry you, one of our residents is moving out and I want to say goodbye to her."

"Is she moving out because of the deaths?"

"I'm afraid so. I did try to reassure her but the family were adamant." Frances leaned forward as she stood. Something that looked like a wedding ring tumbled from the neck of her tunic to swing freely on its chain.

## 27

Annie Hargreaves' flat was on the second floor, directly above Jean's and with the same outlook to parkland on two sides. It felt light and airy and well above the hubbub of the ground floor with its entrance hall and communal rooms.

"Come in, hen." Annie held the door wide. "Kettle's just boiled."

Kate followed her into the small bright kitchen. "Do you want a hand?"

"Arthur's behaving himself today but you can bring the biscuits." Annie poured water from the kettle into the mugs and added milk. "I've not got any cakes left. My granddaughter was up earlier with the weans and they ate all my cakes."

In the sitting room Annie sat back in her armchair. "I take it it's Maggie you want to talk about."

"I'm concerned for my auntie. I persuaded her to move in here and within days she's found two bodies. Harriet Post could have been an accident but not Maggie. I need to be sure that Jean's not going to be next."

"You don't have to explain to me. I'm happy to talk to anybody as you know. Even had the police in to see me asking if Maggie had any enemies. Where would you start?" Annie paused for reflection. "Lovely looking man that, mind you."

Kate smiled and picked up her mug of tea. "How did Maggie get her information?"

"Tracy. Maggie would farm her out to do shopping, cleaning, even hairdos now and again. Anything Tracy found out was reported back to Maggie. It doesn't take long to have a quick look in a drawer when you're supposed to be cleaning the kitchen or dusting a sideboard. Maggie would use her 'contacts' for the rest."

"Did she try anything with you?"

"She hinted she knew about my grandson having been in trouble. That time he was up before that Children's Hearing thing. I made it clear I had nothing to hide. She never mentioned it again but there were others in here that paid up."

"Blackmail?"

Annie nodded. "Some of the owner-occupiers weren't pleased about Maggie having that flat so they set up a residents' committee and tried to get her thrown out. When that didn't work they tried sending her to that place in England, what do you call it?"

"Coventry," Kate supplied and picked up a chocolate chip cookie.

"Aye. That didn't work either. Timbuktu would have made no difference to Maggie."

Kate laughed. She felt comfortable here. Family photos bedecked the walls encompassing Annie's adult life from her marriage to her two great-grandchildren whose regular visits were marked by the small clutter of toys: a box of Lego under the window, a couple of toy cars on the windowsill and the tattered, bow-tied teddy tucked into a corner of an armchair. "Why did they have anything to do with Tracy?"

"They thought Maggie was trying to get in with them but once Tracy found something, it all changed. Maggie was no saint but I can't help thinking that if they'd left her alone in the first place none of this would have happened."

"Do you think Maggie was blackmailing Harriet Post?"

"Because of the angel?" Annie smiled at the look on Kate's face. "It's all right, hen, everybody in here knows about that. Shona came back to see us."

Kate shook her head. "I wouldn't let on to the police about that, Annie."

"You can't keep things like that a secret in here." Annie drank some of her tea. "What were we talking about? Oh blackmail, that was it. Maggie played on people's sense of shame, Kate. She could only take advantage of people who had something they wanted to hide. What surprised me is how many of them in here were like that. "

They sat silent for a moment. "She was some operator," Kate said.

"Oh, she was that alright."

"Was Scott involved in any of this?"

"I think he wanted to be. Then he upset big Marjorie. Maggie sorted it though she wasn't happy about it. But it all blew up over Rose. She gave Tracy some of her pills. Scott tried to get some for himself: to sell, I mean, not to take. When Maggie found out she went ballistic."

"Because it was drugs?"

"Because it was Rose. Don't ask me why but Maggie seemed to really take to Rose."

"Did Fraser visit much?"

"Only saw him once. Seemed nice enough."

"Did you like Maggie?"

Annie sighed. "She sounds a right bugger doesn't she? But she could be good company. She livened things up. And she didn't always bear grudges." She drained her mug. "Look at that thing with Kirsten."

"What thing?"

"Jessie Turner started it all. She told Kirsten Maggie was intimidating her. Kirsten and Maggie had a right shouting match about it but when it was done, it was done. Maggie let it go. And Jessie Turner went to stay with her son and his wife, which was what she wanted in the first place. So I suppose you could say everybody was happy."

Except Jessie's daughter-in-law, thought Kate.

"You could never be sure how Maggie would react to something."

"Like Rose," Kate said.

"Aye, like Rose."

## 28

'Will the real Maggie Keenan stand up?' Kate muttered to herself as she sauntered along to the entrance hall. The police tape still blocked any hope of access to Maggie Keenan's flat. She knocked on the door of the guest room and looked in. Heather Mair sat at the far end of the table tapping at the laptop in front of her. A half-eaten Tunnock's caramel wafer lay close by, its red and gold wrapping glinting in the tail-end of the sun that managed to squeeze through the vertical blinds.

"I was looking for Inspector Nelson," Kate said.

"As you can no doubt see he's not here." Heather re-wrapped the biscuit and tucked it into her bag, tongue matching her sharp wee face.

Kate smiled and wandered in forcing Heather to turn as she strolled past her to stand looking out at the gardens.

"Does the Council do the gardens? Or does A.F. Holdings make their own arrangements, do you think?" She walked round to the other side of the table.

Heather pulled the lid of the laptop down, shutting the screen away from Kate's prying eyes.

"Nice machines, aren't they?" Kate tapped the laptop as she passed. "Will the police be here much longer?"

"We'll be here as long as we need to be."

"The proverbial piece of string, eh?" She smiled at Heather's look of puzzlement.

"Was there something specific you wanted to speak to Inspector Nelson about?" Heather's face displayed irritation but she couldn't disguise the note of interest in her voice.

"It'll keep," Kate said and walked out.

She stepped into the entrance hall at the same time as John Nelson walked in the front door.

"I thought you'd have been here earlier," she said.

"I thought I'd have been here earlier." His dark grey suit looked crumpled; his navy tie hung loosely from the collar of his blue shirt. "Got stuck in traffic on the bridge." He sounded fed up.

"The bridge?"

"Aye, big concrete thing, makes it easier to get across the river."

"Ouch. So Heather's been holding the fort."

He narrowed his eyes at her. "Have you been winding her up?"

"I was looking for you."

He walked over to the notice board. "Are you planning on going to this?" He tapped a black-edged notice about Harriet Post's funeral.

"I thought I might take Jean."

"Why were you looking for me?" A frown darkened his brown eyes.

"Doesn't matter." She touched his arm. "Are you okay, John?"

"Fine." He turned and walked along to the guest room.

Kate stood watching his disappearing back, puzzling over his reaction. She seemed to have developed a knack for upsetting police officers. She left the building and walked back to the office via the churchyard. The morning's cloud had thinned and a filtered sunlight glinted off the gravestones, old and new. There was a fair assortment from the bog-standard uprights to crosses and angels, and tombs and tables. At one of the uprights, the reds and yellows of fresh flowers brightened the black marble where a recently carved name had been added to the list of the dead, longevity seemed to be a family trait. Some of the stones had been laid flat, or leant stiffly against the bases from which they'd been detached. The tabular ones looked to be the oldest. They sat astride their graves, their surfaces, stained by more than a century of bird droppings, pitted and worn to illegibility. In the summer she'd seen a workman sitting on one eating his lunch, his flask and sandwiches set out next to him like a picnic.

She was trying not to think about Steve's reaction to her intervention in Jake's interview. She thought he would have been past that stage by now. They'd broken up three months earlier, just before Steve's thirtieth birthday and shortly after she'd found out about her mother's suicide. Unusually, he'd seemed to sense something had gone wrong in her life and tried to get her to talk about it but that had only made her push him away even harder, convinced his interest was more to do with the power of information rather than a concern for her welfare.

She stopped in a patch of full sun and let the warmth seep into her body, feeling her shoulders soften, tensions slipping away. Somewhere above her, birds chirruped and twittered. Then, as if someone twisted the dimmer switch, the light faded taking the warmth with it. She looked up at the streak of dark cloud closing down the last of the sunshine. A strengthening breeze curved cold round her neck. She hurried from the graveyard and crossed the road to Westfield House and the argument to come with Tom Urquhart.

## 29

"I see they've still not identified that skeleton," Jean said. She was perched on the edge of the settee watching 'Reporting Scotland'.

Kate let the front door close behind her. "What skeleton?" she said.

"The one they found on that building site." Jean switched the television off and went into the kitchen. "Do you not read the papers?"

Kate stared at the blank screen for a moment then followed Jean into the kitchen.

She'd driven out to the Gyle shopping centre after leaving the office, needing to clear her head, to regroup after a tense 'debate', as Tom Urquhart called it, on utilising duty staff. 'How can they learn if they're not tested in the field', he'd argued. 'They need to be open to learning' was her riposte, 'Simon thinks he knows it all as it is.'

She'd wandered round Marks' food hall, her favourite source of comfort food, where she bought a pack of 'Eve's Puddings' to share with Jean and a couple of custard tarts at their use by date and reduced as a consequence. She'd eaten one of the tarts sitting in her car before setting off for Leapark, relishing the lovely soft custard dotted about with little bits of nutmeg nestled in the crumbly pastry, promising herself an extra long swim in the morning to make up for it.

"Broth, like your granny used to make it," Jean was saying. She lifted the lid from a pot on the cooker and gave the contents a stir. "And I've saved some grated carrot for you." She nodded at a plate with an upturned soup bowl on it.

The rich, orangey-red mound underneath the bowl acted like a time-machine sending Kate back to her gran's kitchen in Greenock. It had been their Sunday morning ritual: the 'Sunday Post' for Gran, 'The Broons' and 'Oor Wullie' pulled out for Kate. Then would come the making of the soup. Ham for lentil soup, beef for broth but always the moist, finely grated carrot, the plate on the table so that she could reach it. When the meat was removed to cool she would move from munching the carrot to picking at the meat. 'You'll burn your fingers,' her gran would say. But Kate had picked on, the slivers of meat all the more delicious for the pain of getting them.

"Thanks, Jean," she said, smiling at the memory, so vibrant and vivid, and wondered why she couldn't remember any meals her mother had made. It was as if her memories began when she was five.

She set the table. Jean dished up the soup. They sat.

"Have you just come from your work?" Jean asked.

"Mm." Kate nodded in the affirmative.

"Oh, I thought I saw you earlier," Jean said with a pretence at lightness. "You were walking up the street."

Kate hesitated. "I had a meeting with Frances Wordsworth."

Jean looked at her, spoon halfway to her mouth. Blood dotted a sticking plaster wrapped round her thumb. "About me?"

"Security, stuff like that."

"Oh," Jean said huffily and picked up a slice of bread.

"Soup's lovely," Kate said. She could almost see the hands of the clock in Jean's head marking the time she might have spent in the building somewhere other than with Jean. "I went back to the office for a while to finish off some work." Her argument with Tom Urquhart resurfaced. 'He needs to learn to deal with the mundane,' she'd said. 'Ditch the bids for glory. It's not his risk to take.' "Have you been out today?" She kept her tone light, ignoring Jean's mood.

"Marjorie came up for coffee."

"That's nice. Did Marjorie have much to do with Maggie Keenan?"

Jean looked up. "How would I know that?"

Kate shrugged and they finished the soup in silence. She'd felt virtuous in agreeing to have her tea with Jean but, as usual, it wasn't enough. It didn't help that she'd left the 'Eve's Puddings' in the car. "That was lovely, Jean. I couldn't take some with me?" Now she felt guilty at the beaming smile Jean gave her, a smile that wouldn't be there at all if Jean knew who the soup was really intended for.

"Of course you can." Jean got up and hunted in her cupboards for a container.

"Will you have enough for yourself?"

"Plenty," she said, ladling soup into a plastic bowl. "I'll make you some sandwiches with the beef as well. Use up some of that bread."

"Thanks." Kate carried the empty plates to the sink.

"Are you going now?" The plaintive note was unmistakable.

"I'll wash these up first." She ran hot water into the basin and added a squirt of washing-up liquid, aware of Jean hovering behind her. "I was thinking about going to Harriet Post's funeral tomorrow. Want to come with me?"

"Oh, I would like that," Jean said then shook her head. "I mean the two of us together, not the funeral. Och, you know what I mean."

"Aye, I know what you mean." She smiled. "Does that pot need washed?"

"No, I'll leave the soup in it. Just heat it up tomorrow." Jean wrapped the sandwiches in clingfilm then checked again that the lid of the bowl was secure. "Now what about a bag for them?"

"They're fine like that," she said, feeling like the fraud she was.

Jean turned to her. "We're all right now, aren't we?"

"We're fine," she said softly. "Come here." She hugged Jean feeling some of the anxiety seeping out of her. "I might see you later. I've got some papers to pick up at the office." It would have ruined her grand exit to have turned back for them. 'My duty session, my judgement,' had been her parting shot.

## 30

She balanced the sandwiches on the lid of the bowl and used her free hand to turn the door handle. John Nelson looked up as she entered the room. He was sitting at the table, bathed in a pink glow, a buff folder open in front of him.

"I've brought you some soup and sandwiches."

"I hope you're not trying to bribe me."

"Oh, aye, a bowl of soup and a beef sandwich and you're anybody's." She took the lid off the dish and set it in front of him.

"Smells good. Tell you what would be really handy though."

"What?"

"A spoon?"

She frowned. "I'll get you one from the kitchen."

"Couldn't get me a cup of tea when you're there?"

She came back with the spoon and tea for two and sat opposite him. His jacket was draped over the back of his chair, the sleeves of his shirt rolled halfway up his forearms where the remnants of a tan showed through the brown hairs. The folder he'd been working on was closed.

"I'd never have thought pink was your colour," she said.

He glanced at her then pushed the half-eaten sandwiches to one side and started on the soup. "This is nice. I take it you didn't make it?"

"Jean made it. And I'd have put bromide in it if I'd known you were going to be so bloody cutting."

He smiled at her. "It's Michael's sixth birthday tomorrow."

"Of course." She remembered a 'date' the previous summer when they spoke about little else than Michael starting school. Part of her unpaid child care advisor role. "Are you taking him out somewhere?"

"Dynamic Earth in the morning; he's got a party in the afternoon."

"How's he been about the divorce?"

"Better. Probably sees more of me now than he did when I was living with Carole. Your advice helped a lot. I appreciated it."

She nodded. Another child care advice session.

"Sandwiches are great by the way."

"You'll be pleased to know I didn't make them either." She looked across at the folder. "Have you had the post mortem report on Maggie Keenan yet?"

"Why would you be interested in that?"

"I'm curious about how Maggie managed to get herself a sheltered flat. She's supposed to have had heart disease."

He swallowed a mouthful of his beef sandwich. "There's nothing in the P.M. report to suggest that. She was overweight, arteries narrower than was healthy for her but no more than you would expect in a woman her age."

"Annie Hargreaves mentioned that Maggie and Scott had a bust-up."

"We're keeping an eye on him."

"Surveillance?"

He gave her a 'keep out' look and took another bite of his sandwich.

"How well do you know Scott?"

"I was based in Leith for a while. Scott liked to throw his weight about."

"You threw harder?"

"Something like that." He scrunched up the now empty cling film and pushed it aside.

She could imagine the confrontation: a younger, fitter Scott Keenan trying to play the hard man, John not giving a centimetre. "What about his brother?"

"Keeps a low profile. Might even be a legitimate businessman."

"The white sheep of the family, eh? How come Maggie's never been convicted of anything?"

"Could never get enough evidence." John shook his head. "Maggie covered her tracks well. There's nothing in her flat to suggest how she made her real money, just some 'gifts from grateful friends'."

"What about the Leith flat?"

"Nothing there either. Scott was very keen to let us search it. We know she must have made a packet but all we can find is a bank account with £40 in it."

"I can see the headlines now – 'Maggie's Missing Millions.'

He leaned forward. "We've got some information about a Jessie Turner. Apparently, she moved out of here to get away from Maggie. The family were a bit cagey." He looked at her expectantly.

"I heard the same story. Do you think there's more to it?"

"There was an accusation that Maggie had extorted money from Turner. It was retracted shortly after Turner moved out."

"I'll see what I can find out." She paused. "What do you make of Sam MacEwen?"

"Had an argument with Maggie about the paper-boy. Uses a laptop to keep tabs on his finances."

"And you wouldn't mind having a look at what else might be on it?"

John shrugged.

"I don't think there's anything unsavoury in his relationship with Jake Harrison. Not at the moment anyway."

"Do you know Jake Harrison in a professional capacity?"

"I was the appropriate adult at his interview this morning."

"Ah."

"What does that mean?"

"Steve was a bit grumpy at lunchtime."

"He wasn't exactly Mr Happy this morning."

John looked about to say something but instead he drained his mug and sat back. "That was excellent, Kate. I need to get on."

"I'll give you a hand if you like."

He smiled. "I appreciate the offer but I think I'll be quicker on my own."

"So much for bribery and corruption." She stood and picked up the bowl and their mugs. "Have you interviewed Rose Toner?"

"Steve and Heather did that one. Decided she had nothing useful to tell us. Why?"

"Wondered what you made of her."

"If you know something, Kate…"

"I don't, John. Enjoy your weekend." She turned to the door.

John got there before her and blocked her exit. She waited for him to open the door and when he didn't she looked up at him.

"Be careful, Kate," he said. Then he opened the door and let her go.

It had sounded more like a command than an expression of concern.

## 31

"Ooh." Jean plucked at the sticking plaster. Her thumb still looked raw where the grater had got it. She pulled the plaster off, folded it in on itself and put it in the bin. She wasn't even that keen on soup. She had envisaged Kate pleased and grateful at Jean's thoughtfulness, the two of them laughing at shared memories. What she hadn't envisaged was Kate gulping down the soup and rushing off god knows where. It wasn't like her to take food away with her. Sometimes Kate was a closed book to her. Sometimes life was a closed book to her.

She searched her cupboards for her box of sticking plasters. Where had she put it? Bathroom. No. Back in the kitchen she switched on the kettle. She'd make some tea for when Kate came back. 'I might see you later', she'd said. That would be after she left her office, before she went home. Did that mean she wasn't going out tonight? Kate didn't talk much to Jean about her social life and even less about boyfriends. Not since the argument about the car. Steve had offered to get Kate a smaller, less sporty version of the car he had through his father's garage. But Kate had gone off and bought the Yaris on her own. She could be so awkward at times. Thrawn, Jean's mother would have said. Only she wouldn't have, not about Kate. Kate had been the apple of her granny's eye.

She found her plasters in the sideboard drawer next to the things she'd bought in the charity shops on

Wednesday. She'd forgotten all about them. The kitten gazed up at her from its pale blue frame. Waste of money. Buying for the sake of something to do. She stuck a plaster on her thumb then put on her coat, picked up her key and went out, locking the door behind her.

In the entrance hall the small reception office was in darkness but a light showed under the door of the guest room the police had commandeered. She went out the front door and walked round to the small, brightly lit car park, shivering from the cold. There were a couple of cars in it, one of them red, but it wasn't Kate's and she wouldn't have taken her car to go to her office, it was as quick to walk. Unless she'd left her car at her office and had walked here but she was only picking up papers so she'd have been back by now. Jean checked the street, wandering halfway up in case Kate had parked the Yaris there. But no, Kate had gone.

Jean sighed, pulling her coat round her, and walked back to the front door. A middle-aged man she didn't recognise was blocking it.

"Do you live here?" the man asked her.

"Excuse me." She tried to go past him into the building but he didn't move.

"I just want a couple of quotes about Maggie Keenan. Did you know her?" He pulled out a notebook.

"Let me pass."

"Were you one of Maggie Keenan's victims? Is that why you don't want to talk to me? You're better telling me then I can make sure your name's kept out of my report. What is your name?"

"I don't have to tell you anything." She struggled with the reporter, trying to push past him.

"There's no need for that." He was smiling at her, mocking her panic. "You're not Jean Markham, by any chance."

The admission was written in her face.

He grabbed her arm. "I can get you a good deal for your story. Was Maggie Keenan blackmailing you? How did you feel when you saw she was dead? Were you relieved?"

Jean stood transfixed. How could he know all this?

"What's going on here?"

Jean turned to see a police constable walking towards them. A whimper started in her throat.

"Is this man bothering you?" the policeman asked.

"I want to go home." She hated the pathetic whinge in her voice.

"I'm just doing my job," the reporter complained.

"I'll do you, pal, if I see you here again."

The reporter backed away and Jean made her escape leaving the two men glaring at each other.

She hurried along the ground floor corridor wondering how the reporter knew her name and whether she would see it in the paper tomorrow. But what could he say? He hadn't known anything else. Had he? A pair of brown brogues appeared on the stairs ahead of her. She ducked into the darkened kitchen and hid behind the door, not sure why she was hiding at all. The soft tread of footsteps passed the doorway and she peered round to see Sam MacEwen's disappearing back. Had he been to her door? He'd been very pleasant on Wednesday though Kate seemed to find it suspicious. Probably thought seventy was too old to be interested in men, or for a man to be interested in her.

She walked over to the window, picking at her sticking plaster as she looked across the garden. Most of the windows showed a light. This time on a cold October night not too many people her age wanted to be anywhere than at home. Maggie Keenan's flat was in darkness. She wondered what the police had found there. Her locket, maybe, with its baby picture and the lock of hair. Could they test the hair for DNA? And trace it back to her? She'd have to tell them everything. Then the papers would get hold of it. The room began to spin. She put her hand out to steady herself and flinched when she felt the cold steel of the draining board. A noise behind her made her jump. She turned to see a large figure silhouetted in the doorway. She caught her breath. The fluorescent light flickered into life.

"Marjorie." She clapped a hand to her chest, trying to sound casual. "What a fright you gave me."

"What are you doing in here in the dark?" That accusing note again.

"Um, collecting this." She grabbed a plastic container from the draining board at the same time registering Marjorie's brown tweed coat and matching hat. "Are you going out?"

"I've just come in." Marjorie continued to study her. "I was at a church service."

"That's nice." Jean hugged the plastic bowl to her chest.

"I'll say goodnight then." Marjorie turned away with a disapproving shake of her head.

"Goodnight, Marjorie."

In her flat she left the lights off, preferring the dimness of the borrowed light from outside. She'd found herself hoping that Marjorie would suggest a cup of tea. How desperate was that? She went into the kitchen and switched the kettle off at the socket. Kate wouldn't be back tonight. Yet she had come back or maybe hadn't left when she said. A faded red and yellow Woolworth label on the plastic bowl identified it as the one the soup had been in. What had Kate been up to? The light under the guest room door – who'd been in there? Maybe Steve. She wanted it to be Steve and not John Nelson. If she'd just been a bit quicker on Wednesday none of this would have happened because she would have been sitting in Kate's flat now. Kate would be getting ready to go out, Jean would tell her how nice she looked, that of course she didn't mind being left on her own, Kate wasn't to worry about that. Then she'd settle on the big, blue sofa in the sitting room and watch the television, the cat lying in front of the fire, both of them waiting for Kate to come home.

She went to the sideboard and opened the drawer that held her purchases from Wednesday. She pushed the books aside and took out the C.D. She turned it over in her hands remembering the night Kate had taken her to see the show at the Playhouse, 'Les Miserables'. She'd sat there with tears streaming down her face, Kate holding her hand, whilst a woman she'd never seen before or since sang a song that seemed to sum up her life. A song of love and loss and longing. 'I Dreamed a Dream'. When she got home she'd cried as though her heart would break.

She replaced the disc and checked the time. Half-past eight, too early to go to bed. And the dreams meant sleep wasn't the refuge it used to be. Oddly, it was Harriet Post she dreamed about rather than Maggie Keenan. That thin, bare forearm seemed to float towards her, accusing. With Maggie Keenan it was the pink nightdress and the fat white knees that stuck in her memory. And now Andrew and those voices that had left her dream a tatter of shame. She shuddered, pressing her hand to her diaphragm. The sitting room glowed softly in the light from the streetlamps. She sat on the sofa and looked out at the deepening darkness.

## 32

At five past nine Scott Keenan's fat figure appeared at the entrance to the tower block. He stepped out into the cold, stopping to pull up the collar of his black padded jacket before waddling off in the direction of the car park at the back of the building. Minutes later a dark coloured Mondeo set off towards Great Junction Street. Kate waited a few minutes then picked up her bag, got out of her car and set off for Waverley Tower.

She'd parked in a small, well-lit cul-de-sac that gave her a clear view of the entrance to the tower block. She wanted to speak to Fraser but couldn't take the chance of bumping into Scott, or any police officers that might be 'keeping an eye on him'. And she needed to prove to herself that yesterday's unsettling confrontation had been an aberration. She was back in her jeans and trainers but had added a thick, grey, polo neck jumper and her long navy blue coat. And not just to keep out the cold.

She tensed as a thin, shivering figure in jeans and hooded sweatshirt came towards her.

"Got a light?"

She had to bend slightly to see the face under the hood of the sweatshirt. "Mikey?"

He squinted up at her. "Christ, Kate, what are you doing here?"

"Meeting Fraser Keenan."

"Here?" Mikey scanned his surroundings like a soldier expecting an ambush.

"Does he not live here?"

"Fraser Keenan? Live here?" He sniffed, shaking his head in disbelief.

"Do you know where I can find him?" She saw his hesitation. "It's a personal thing, Mikey, about Maggie." She looked around as she said this feeling a prickle of fear at the nape of her neck. Who was Mikey watching for?

"Might be in Cammie's." Mikey was saying, sniffing again and rubbing his hands together.

"Is that not a bit of a dive?"

"Tarted it up." Mikey did another scan, Kate following his gaze. "Need to watch yourself, Kate."

"I will, Mikey. How are you getting on?"

"Och, know me. Ducking and diving." He gave her a half-smile, struggling to mime a boxer's movements, his pallor intensified in the moonlight.

"You look after yourself, Mikey."

He nodded, holding onto his half-smile, then, with a last look round, jogged clumsily across the concourse.

He'd been one of her first clients. It was a family tradition, Mikey the latest in a long line. Born into a losing streak, he was the kid on the fringes, looking to find something to belong to. She'd liked him. He'd had a charm then, so eager to please. She'd thought she could make the difference he needed but it was all too late. He was already falling into that depressing progression that, for some kids, starts with the Children's Hearing system and ends in prison. He'd never recovered from that. Kate watched till he was out of sight then headed back to her car.

Ten minutes later she turned into the small car park behind Cammie's bar. If she hadn't worked in Leith, she wouldn't have known of Cammie's existence. It was tucked up a cobbled alleyway in a part of Leith too seedy for all but the most adventurous 'Trainspotting' tourist. She nosed her car into a space, her headlights picking out the bollard and the low narrow ditch between it and the back wall. She wondered how many cars had edged into the ditch before the bollards had been installed. Now they could hit the bollards instead. There were only two other cars there, one a year-old BMW. Not what she would have expected of a Cammie's patron.

She walked round to the front, tidied a stray hair behind her ear and opened the door. The smell rushed at her: a potent mix of beer, sweat and cigarette smoke. She stood for a moment, letting her senses come to terms with this assault on them, fighting the urge to cough. Cammie's was well beyond the reach of the smoking ban. Who'd complain? Who would care? She became aware of the silence. A surreptitious look round the room showed scarred tables; hard mahogany benches lined the walls. A spittoon wouldn't have been out of place. And this was tarted up? Suspicious, middle-aged male eyes stared back at her. The few females looked older, the years, like the make-up, settled heavily on their faces. She walked to the bar glad of the screening her long, loose coat afforded her.

The barman's face was a study in quiet hostility. He lifted his chin a millimetre and threw her a questioning look.

"Um, orange juice, please." She looked around the room again. "Is Fraser in tonight?"

"Who?"

"Fraser Keenan." She smiled at the barman. It occurred to her at this point that she wouldn't know Fraser Keenan if she fell over him.

The barman looked her up and down. "Who's asking?"

"My name's Kate McKinnery." She continued to smile brightly, inoffensive, unthreatening.

The barman nodded straight-faced and turned away. When he turned back, he placed a glass of an orange-coloured liquid in front of her. "£2," he said.

Kate dug into her bag for her purse, aware of the barman watching her. She handed hin the money. As he took it he shifted his gaze to a point behind her left ear. She turned.

The man she was looking at had the build of a bouncer and a face that had seen more than its fair share of disputes. He looked to be in his forties, not Fraser then.

"Come with me," he said.

She hesitated.

"Do you want to see him or not?"

The man led her along a narrow hallway to a half-glass door. He opened it and stood back for her to enter. She forced her shaking legs to keep moving, cursing herself for ever thinking she could do this.

The small room surprised her. Soft lighting reflected off burnished dark wood panelling; a fire burned in the grate. She managed not to jump as the door closed behind her. Her escort nodded in the direction of a booth in the corner by the fire where a man and woman sat watching her approach. She recognised the man. It was her saviour from Waverley Tower the day before. She revised her estimation upwards – considerably.

"I'm Kate McKinnery." She extended her hand and was relieved when Fraser shook it. The young woman sitting beside him was the personification of 'heroin chic', with her thin frame and a pinched, haunted look that was exacerbated by the lack of make-up. Only the designer labels were missing.

She seemed surprised to see Kate's hand held out to her but she brushed it with her own and said, "Tracy." Then she slid the hand under Fraser's arm and let it rest on the soft lemon wool of his jumper.

"So, Kate," Fraser said, "what do you want?"

She sat opposite him and slid her coat off her shoulders. She thought briefly about repeating the pretence she'd used on Scott but Fraser didn't look half so gullible.

"My auntie's Jean Markham," she said.

He blanked her, waiting for more.

"I'm trying to find out if she's in danger." It sounded weak even to her.

"Why do you think I can help you?"

"I don't know who else to ask," she floundered. "And you seem to be respected around here."

"Ah, flattery." Fraser took a sip of white wine. "Scott's wondering when he's going to get his money." He looked at her. "And that's not all he's waiting for."

She opened and closed her mouth trying to swallow a burgeoning anxiety. She sensed someone else in the room, coming towards her, stopping behind her. She swallowed again, waiting for Scott Keenan's fat hand to land on her shoulder, to demand his money and more.

Fraser was smiling. "What would you like to drink, Kate?"

"Um, lemonade and soda, thanks." She turned to see the man who'd shown her in standing where Scott Keenan was supposed to be. She didn't know whether to be angry or relieved.

"Lemonade and soda for the lady, Pete." He looked at Tracy. "Want a refill, darling?"

Tracy shook her head. "I'm fine, babe," she said.

Fraser nodded Pete away then turned his attention back to Kate. His smile was of the smug variety, knowing he'd put her firmly in her place. "Who told you where to find me?"

"Nobody in particular." She struggled to get her act together, to shake off that feeling of vulnerability. "I'm wondering whether your mother was killed because of something going on in Leapark."

"What do you think?"

Pete placed her lemonade and soda in front of her. She nodded her thanks at Fraser and took a tentative sip, praying the drink hadn't been doctored. "Had your mother..." she was about to say 'upset someone' but Maggie had probably upset most of them at one time or another, "...fallen out with anyone?" she finished lamely, irritated at her placatory tone.

"Like the snobs who thought she wasn't good enough for Leapark? Say what you mean, Kate."

"I can understand how that would upset your mother."

"You can understand it? You with your flat in Comely Bank." He sneered at her. "Don't try to patronise me."

She wasn't sure whether it was the shock of Fraser knowing where she lived or his questioning of her working class credentials. Either was enough to trigger her anger. "Don't you judge me because of where I live. The place I grew up in would give any of Edinburgh's deprived areas a run for their money."

Fraser held his hands up. "I take it back. I shouldn't have jumped to conclusions." He shook his head, laughing at her. "You've got some nerve, Kate." He took a card from his wallet and wrote something on the back of it. "You want to know more about what my mother was like," he said as he wrote. He handed her the card.

"Nellie Pearce?" Kate read, with an address in Dunfermline.

"Speak to Mrs Pearce. She can tell you about my mother. The unvarnished truth. That right, Tracy?"

Tracy nodded and reattached herself to Fraser's arm.

Kate thought she saw a glimmer of amusement in his eyes. Was he making fun of her? Or just enjoying Tracy's jealousy? She tucked the card into her jeans pocket.

"One more thing."

She looked at him: no sign of amusement now.

"Anything you find out or even think you've found out, you bring to me. Understood?" He held her eyes locked into his.

"Understood."

The lock held for a few more seconds then he nodded and she was free to go.

"Pete'll show you to your car."

She stood and shrugged her coat on.

"Remember, Kate. You come to me first."

"I'll remember." She turned to follow Pete, desperate to escape.

"Kate," Fraser said.

She turned back to him. He really was rubbing her nose in it.

"Be more careful in future. An attractive young woman like you shouldn't be wandering around these parts alone at night."

She nodded, withholding the glare she wanted to aim at him, knowing it was as much threat as warning.

Pete led her round behind the bar and down a narrow passageway till they came to a door marked as a Fire Exit. He pushed the bar up and the door opened onto the car park.

"Thanks," she said as the door slammed shut behind her. She got into her car thinking she'd have got more response for thanking the bollard for stopping the car going into the ditch.

### 33

She sped along Ferry Road muttering exhortations about being better prepared, doing the groundwork before rushing headlong into dodgy situations. She'd done that often enough in the past to know better by now. She'd got her assumptions all wrong. But so did he, based too much on her middle class address. Yet he'd checked enough to know where she lived. Because she was related to Jean? Or because Scott had reported her visit?

She turned onto East Fettes Avenue and drove past the tree-lined acres of Tony Blair's old school, dwarfing the local high school across the road. The dark expanse of Inverleith Park sat opposite. Beyond that were the botanics, or the Royal Botanic Gardens of Edinburgh to give them their Sunday name. She'd taken her gran there once with Jules. On that short visit, Gran had managed to lock herself in a toilet and get stabbed by a cactus. Kate was smiling at the memory when headlights came up fast behind her. At the last minute the car swerved round her Yaris and raced through the traffic lights as they went to red.

"Prat," she muttered as she waited for the green light to reappear. When it did she drove sedately through onto Comely Bank Avenue looking for a parking space. She spotted one near her stair and had just positioned her car to reverse into it when she heard an engine revving. Headlights on full beam hurtled towards her. She froze, waiting for the impact. Brakes squealed. A car door slammed. She reached blindly for the central locking button as a face appeared at her side window.

"I knew I recognised your wee nyaff car," the man blazed, wrenching at the door handle.

She was reaching for the horn when the man disappeared. The headlights went out and she saw him spread-eagled on the bonnet of his car, John Nelson standing over him. She released the door locks and got out.

"What the hell..." She saw her would-be assailant properly for the first time and recognised the angry face of the GTI driver who swore at her before roaring off down Leith Walk. "This is about Monday?"

"You made me late for fucking work."

"Shut it," John Nelson said. He looked at Kate. "You all right?"

She nodded, watching the approaching police car. The GTI driver started to complain but a look from John silenced him. When the uniformed officers got out of their car John let them take over. Kate shook her head when asked if she wanted to make a statement. She thought the driver had got enough of a fright that he wouldn't try anything like this again. And by the look on his face when he saw the breathalyser being produced he wouldn't get the opportunity for a while.

"I'll park your car if you want to go up to your flat." John held out his hand for the key.

"I'm capable of parking my own car." But she handed him the key anyway and headed for her stair wondering what had brought him here in the first place.

In her flat she went into the kitchen, dumped her bag on the floor and threw her coat over the back of a chair. She'd just fed Lucy when the entry-phone buzzed. She confirmed it was John and let him in putting her door on the latch for him. She was closing the blinds when he came into the kitchen. She registered his faded jeans and dark blue jumper under his leather jacket. His dark brown hair looked damp.

He put her car key on the worktop, his hand resting beside it. "What was all that about Monday?"

She briefly described what had happened with the GTI. "And that's it?"

She nodded. "Was he on something do you think?"

"Tonight? Almost certainly."

"How come you turned up when you did?"

"A call from the unit watching Fraser Keenan."

Kate's heart started to sink.

"Your car was noted entering the car park at a bar he owns. You were in the bar for nearly half an hour."

She shrugged and turned away from him, busying herself with filling the kettle, trying to buy some thinking time.

"I trusted you, Kate. I gave you information so that you would keep out of this."

"There's no law against me going into a bar and talking to somebody." She kept her voice level not wanting to get into a shouting match with him.

"You could be jeopardising a police investigation. Now back off." His voice had an edge to it.

She turned to him. "How is me talking to Fraser Keenan jeopardising your investigation, John?"

"You've always got to do things yourself. You can't trust anybody else to get it right."

Lucy paused in her mauling of her catnip mouse to watch them, furry head moving from one to the other like an umpire at Wimbledon.

"I'm sorry if getting called out like this has ruined your evening but I don't understand why you're so angry with me."

"You're putting yourself at risk. You're getting into situations you don't understand. If you're seen with Fraser Keenan again I can't intervene."

"I don't have any reason to be seen with him again."

She watched him relax and walked over to him. As she reached for a mug from the rack behind him she caught a scent of sandalwood, more like shower gel than cologne. Had he been in the shower when he got the phone call? She resisted the image that was trying to force its way into her brain. For a moment they stood very close. Her hand brushed his jumper, feeling the warmth from his body. Then he moved aside, shaking his head at her offer of tea.

"Did Fraser tell you anything useful?" he asked.

She stared at him. "That is rich. After you've just been lecturing me about messing up your investigation you want to know what I found out?"

"If you're going to play investigator I might as well make use of you." He smiled at her for the first time.

The reduction in tension came too late for Lucy. She'd already made her escape to her hiding place in the bedroom, abandoning her catnip mouse to its own devices.

"He gave me a name, Nellie Pearce, said she can tell me what Maggie was like. I didn't get anything he didn't want me to know. He was almost as hard to read as you are sometimes."

He ignored that. "And you're going to speak to this Nellie Pearce?"

"I don't see why not."

"Depends why Fraser told you about her." He leant back against the worktop and folded his arms.

"How come it was you they told that I'd been to see Fraser Keenan?"

"Bob Mackay picked up the call. You remember Bob?"

She abandoned her tea for a glass of wine. "Of course I remember Bob."

"He still talks about you and Eddie Ranford. Especially the bit where you told Ranford to butt out."

"I didn't say that."

"What was it now? 'Are you related to Natasha in any way? No? Then you have no say in the matter, Mr Ranford.'" He mimicked her west of Scotland accent.

She smiled in spite of herself.

"The way Bob tells it you and Ranford were eyeball to eyeball when he went in. Like you wanted him to try something."

And she had. She'd almost lost it in that claustrophobic flat: Ranford strutting, Dawn pie-eyed on the sofa. For a moment she was the street fighter of her childhood, convinced she could take Ranford, desperate for him to give her an excuse. Then Chief Inspector Bob Mackay turned up.

They'd found Natasha sitting on her grubby bed, told to stay there by Ranford 'while he sorted these interfering bitches out.'

"I was angry, John. We should have removed Natasha before that. Dawn was worse than useless and Ranford was so bloody sure of himself." Her expression softened.

"It's their confusion, that look of bewilderment. You know?"

"Aye, I know." He held her gaze. "But you take some risks, Kate."

"I got Natasha out of there."

"And you got Ranford charged and imprisoned. And maybe that time it took you to do it but not this time. Two women are dead: one of them a minor criminal but with major contacts. You're out of your depth. Leave it to us. At least we're paid to take risks." He straightened. "I have to go." He stood looking at her for a moment. "You really need to be more careful."

Another warning. They walked into the hall. At the front door he reached out and touched her face, letting his fingers trail down to her neck.

"Check your messages," he said softly. "Steve's been trying to contact you." Then he turned and walked out the door.

At the sound of the door closing Lucy appeared from the bedroom and sat looking up at her.

"What was all that about, Luce?" Kate said. She got the impression that, had it been physically possible, Lucy would have shrugged her shoulders and replied, 'search me.' Instead the cat set off for the kitchen, tail erect, looking back to make sure Kate was following her.

She dribbled cream into a saucer and put it on the floor next to Lucy's dish then stuck two slices of bread in the toaster and set the kettle to boil again. She needed comfort food and hot buttered toast always worked for her. It was what her gran had fed her on those early days after her mother's death when she'd been too upset to go to school. Gran had tucked her up on the sofa and kept up a supply of milky tea and hot buttered toast.

Kate wasn't sure whether it was overdosing on dairy but it certainly made her feel better.

She set her toast on the kitchen table with a mug of tea and tried to concentrate on her notes but her mind kept going back to Natasha Farrell and the anger that was so close to the surface. Ranford had been plausible at first though she could see the threat behind it that had deterred a previous worker hence the police presence. Dawn ranged from anger to tears with violence never far away. She had a record of fighting with neighbours: a bit of slapping and hair-pulling. Yet it was never directed towards Ranford, never used to protect her daughter.

She reached for a slice of toast and adjusted her thoughts to the present. Why did Fraser tell her about Nellie Pearce? Was he sending her on a wild goose chase? Was there something he wanted her to know that only Nellie Pearce could tell her? And where did Tracy fit in? Scott had suggested that Tracy was like a wee sister. She didn't look very sisterly with Fraser. And why did John tell her that Steve wanted to talk to her?

She munched on her toast savouring the buttery taste. She should have asked John to find out if the GTI driver had followed her on Tuesday night. But that would have led to more questions. Anyway it was much more likely that it was someone who happened to be going in the same direction as she was. Your paranoia's showing, Kate.

She reached for her mug and found it empty. She sipped her wine instead. She'd gathered a lot of information but had very little idea what to make of it. Maybe Harriet Post's funeral would shed a bit of light. Failing that there was always Nellie Pearce. Sleep on it.

She tidied her notes and put her plate and her mug into the sink then took a deep breath and dug out her phone. She switched it on to a cacophony of beeps. There were three messages from Steve asking her to call him. As she headed for her bedroom she turned to her landline handset and pressed the playback button.

"Kate, it's Steve. Look, I'm sorry about this morning. Can we talk? There's something really important I need to discuss with you. Call me...please."

She checked the time of the call – 9.43, whilst she was chatting up Fraser Keenan in Cammie's bar. If Steve knew that he might not be so keen to talk to her. She wasn't sure she wanted to talk to him but was intrigued by the 'really important' thing he needed to discuss with her, as he would expect her to be. It was too late to phone now. Sleep on it.

# Saturday

## 34

Kate dropped her towel into the wash basket and rinsed her swimsuit before settling down with her coffee and her online trawl of the news via the BBC website, another of the 'what if' questions in the independence debate. She was one of the 'undecideds','mibbees aye, mibbees naw', something to ponder when she was ploughing up and down the swimming pool. It had been empty when she'd got there, not unusual at that time on a Saturday morning. Two kilometres she'd set herself. She had to make up for the days she missed, not to mention the increasing tendency to stuff her face with cakes. She needed a regular swim or her stamina levels dropped. She lost her rhythm.

She always started with the front crawl, proper swimming as she still thought of it. It was the first stroke she'd mastered as a child. She'd jumped in and started moving her arms like she'd seen other swimmers do and she was off. So easy. This morning she did a few lengths of breaststroke, head down, stretching her arms and shoulders, powering through the water. She eased down with a leisurely backstroke, somersaulting into the final length to come up in the crawl position again. She'd leapt out of the pool, her body tingling all the way to the changing rooms.

She shut down her laptop and stretched her arms out to the side, flinging her head back, breathing deeply, luxuriating in the feel of toned muscles. Time to get ready. On her way to the bedroom she dropped to her knees to kiss Lucy curled up in her bed under the radiator and got a sleepy murmur in reply. Her black suit hung from the wardrobe door, a dark red polo neck showing under the jacket. The last funeral she'd been to was her grandmother's nearly eight years ago. She'd just started her social work course when she got the call. Her gran had been taken to hospital, she'd had a cerebral haemorrhage and wasn't expected to survive. When Kate arrived at the bedside her gran was in a coma. Her breathing was ragged, her body, under the bedcovers, small and inconsequential. Yet she looked peaceful, as if she'd just dozed off. Kate held her hand and spoke softly to her, stroking her face, hoping for some recognition, a final connection, even though the staff had told her there was too much brain damage. Just before the end, she thought she felt a light pressure from her gran's fingers, the gentlest of squeezes at the base of her thumb. 'Gran?' she'd whispered. Then a nurse came over. 'She's gone, dear.'

At the funeral she'd been surprised how upset she was. She'd assumed that being all grown up would somehow protect her from the confusion and devastation she'd felt after her mother's death. Jules had comforted her though in tears herself. Jean had seemed more sad than upset, giving the occasional shuddering sigh, but mostly tearless.

For weeks afterwards she had found herself crying for no apparent reason. She'd wake in the night, tears streaming down her face, convinced she'd felt that pressure at the base of her thumb. It was then that she'd become interested in ghosts and hauntings. She'd read about something called 'thin places' where the barrier between the natural world and the supernatural was at its most permeable. Edinburgh seemed to have more than most if its reputed hauntings were to be believed. She'd visited some of them including the underground streets of Mary King's Close. The Close was under the City Chambers. The story was that the street and its inhabitants had been walled up and left to die because of the plague. There was supposed to be the ghost of a little girl called Sarah in one of the rooms. Apparently the psychic who 'discovered' her thought she looked sad and brought her a doll and thus began a shrine to an imaginary child. Kate had trailed round, stumbling on the uneven stone floor, fingers trawling the rough surface of the walls, wanting to feel something, a 'presence', anything, but she might as well have been standing in the middle of Princes Street. She'd lost interest then. Had gradually adjusted to there being no one left with whom she could share her childhood memories.

She listened as the final strains of the intermezzo from 'Cavalleria Rusticana' died away. It had been one of her gran's favourites, along with Mario Lanza singing 'Ave Maria' and the Beatles' 'She Loves You.' Gran had been nothing if not eclectic in her musical tastes. Smiling, she switched off the hi-fi, gathered up her bag and her keys and headed out to collect Jean. On the way she phoned Steve and arranged to meet him at eight o'clock at a restaurant in Leith. He wouldn't say what he wanted to talk to her about.

She walked into the entrance hall at Leapark to the sound of excited chattering in the corridor. Frances Wordsworth appeared at the head of a small, black crocodile of residents, heeled shoes now tip-tapping on the stone tiles of the entrance hall floor. Frances smiled as she passed; her troupe of elderly ladies, black-hatted heads bobbing, some voluntary, some not, trailed after her: a pied piper in monochrome.

A coach awaited them. Given that Harriet Post was not the friendliest of women, a couple of taxis should have been more than adequate, but the funeral of a woman who might have been murdered was too good to miss. Not to mention the chance to get your picture in the papers or, better yet, on the television. And judging by the promise of 'shocking revelations to follow' it did seem that at least one of the journalists had an inside track to Leapark.

She found Jean in dithering mode. The funeral was to take place at Warriston Crematorium and Kate didn't want to get stuck behind the coach should the driver decide to go up Clermiston Road so she tried to hurry Jean up a bit. But Jean was not for hurrying, not this morning.

"Just let me do things my own way. Now where's my handbag?"

She handed Jean the bag and watched her check it for the third time for purse, keys, lipstick, kitchen sink. "C'mon, Jean," she urged.

"Was there anybody waiting at the front door when you came in?"

"No, just a bloody big coach and we're going to get stuck behind it if you don't get a move on."

"All right, Kate." Jean walked huffily to the door. She turned. "There was a reporter here last night…"

"Tell me about it in the car." She hustled Jean from the flat.

The coach still sat in the street and, by the way its occupants were faffing about, it would be lucky to see the crematorium this side of Christmas.

"So this reporter?" Kate said when they'd set off.

"He knew my name. Asked me if Maggie Keenan was blackmailing me. How could he know all that?"

"Stabs in the dark. If you didn't tell him anything, he's got nothing to write about."

"But what if Betty Smyth or Rose Toner told him about me?"

"They've nothing to tell."

"How do you know that?"

Kate hesitated. "I spoke to them on Thursday. They were fishing. So they couldn't have known." She was aware of Jean's glare.

"You might have told me."

"Sorry."

Jean was silent for the remainder of the journey. Kate concentrated on her driving. The Yaris went up Clermiston Road smoothly. Close to the top, the houses on the right gave way to the wilderness that was Corstorphine Hill. Civilisation was represented by Clermiston Tower, a monument to Sir Walter Scott, and a couple of communication pylons that could be seen from a range of vantage points in the city. Further on, a driveway started its long climb to Clerwood House, once a temporary social work H.Q. in the '80's whilst the Albany Street building was being renovated. Both had new owners and new lives, only Shrubhill House waited in limbo, a gutted canvas for local graffiti artists. The new corporate headquarters was firmly ensconced at New Street. Social Work no longer existed as a department, how much longer would it have as a profession? Maybe it was time to move on, take up the I.T. offer before it was too late.

The Forth came into view as they breasted the top of the slope, Fife's rolling hills obscured by the low-lying cloud. Ringed by villages, Edinburgh sat tucked between the River Forth to the north and the Pentlands Hills to the south, at its heart the twin volcanoes of Arthur's Seat and the Castle Rock.

At the foot of the hill she turned right onto Queensferry Road and from there down through the village of Davidson's Mains with its rough-stone cottages, cheek by jowl with Muirhouse and Pilton with their freshly renovated housing estates and their very own social work offices. And in all three were people getting on with their lives as best they could. She hated it when judgements were made according to where you lived. In her job she visited areas of the city many would rather stick hot needles in their eyes than go to. Urban myths grew up around them, most no more true than the 'fur coat and no knickers' view of Morningside. Though, even in these straitened times, if you stretched to buy a house in Morningside and wanted a fur coat as well, you probably would have to forego the knickers, and serve you right. She smiled to herself then glanced across at Jean staring straight ahead, face and shoulders set against life's injustices.

At Warriston they waited in the car park under an increasingly leaden sky as the only official funeral car arrived. Kate assumed the young woman emerging from it to be Harriet Post's daughter, Ellen. Had Betty spread the news that Ellen was gay?

"Do you smell something burning?" Jean whispered.

Kate looked at her. "Are you serious?"

"What do you mean?"

She waved her hand towards the crematorium a few feet away.

"Oh." Jean stifled a giggle.

Kate smiled. "That's the kind of thing my gran would have said."

"I must be more like her than I thought."

A half-hearted drizzle of cold rain began as the coach made its entrance into the car park and manoeuvred into a parking space. It was like a sightseeing tour. Black hats bobbed as the coach's occupants twisted and turned. Trying to catch a glimpse of the gay daughter? A black Ford Focus pulled into a space alongside and Heather Mair got out wearing her best officious frown. The coach finally disgorged its occupants and Frances shepherded them into the crematorium. Heather followed. Kate turned to Jean. The black coat was doing her no favours. 'Death warmed up' could have been coined for her.

"Are you all right?"

Jean nodded.

Inside the crematorium Kate noticed Heather trying to be unobtrusive in the back row. She shifted her gaze to pick up Betty Smyth sitting at the end of a row next to Rose Toner. Frances Wordsworth stood alongside. There was almost a stand-off as Frances waited for Betty to make room for her. Kate led Jean to the row behind them intrigued by Frances' choice of companions.

Betty gave a sideways glance at Frances sitting silent and straight beside her. "Sad, isn't it?" Betty said.

Frances nodded.

"Poor Ellen. Both her parents gone." Betty shook her head. "And only a child when she lost her father."

"I'm sure Ellen will have friends to help her through this."

"But they're not here, are they?" Betty leaned closer. "Not even one special friend." She sat back. "Of course

I daresay it's not the sort of thing they'd want to see in the newspapers." The tone was more matter-of-fact now with just a hint of disapproval.

Frances took the bait. "What do you mean?"

Betty turned round as if checking who might be listening. Kate earned a dirty look before Betty turned back to Frances. "It's not really for me to say but there's a rumour that Ellen has a 'girlfriend'." This last word was mouthed rather than spoken aloud and was accompanied by a knowing look and a nod of the head.

"That's none of our business." Frances looked straight ahead, her demeanour exuding disapproval.

Betty whispered something to Rose Toner nodding in Kate's direction. Toner turned to look at Kate before fixing Jean with a malignant stare. Only at the change of music signalling the entrance of the coffin did Toner release Jean and turn to the front.

Kate didn't recognise the hymn that accompanied the coffin down the aisle. She'd chosen Mario Lanza singing 'Ave Maria' for her gran's funeral. Gran would have been over the moon at the idea of being serenaded by Mario singing her favourite song. Kate tried not to smile as the bearers slid Harriet Post's coffin onto its platform. A noise from the back of the room made her turn to see Sam MacEwen slip in and sit in the row nearest the door: ready for a quick getaway, maybe.

## 35

Bowls of thick soup steamed on the tables in the dining room alongside platters of white bread sandwiches and plates loaded with cakes, scones and biscuits: comfort food with a vengeance. Frances and Kirsten moved smoothly amongst the occupants, topping up plates and cups, chatting briefly in muted voices, mindful of why they were there. In the centre of each table was a small, black doily on which sat a narrow vase with a single red rose, lest anyone forgot.

"There's a seat beside Renie, Jean. You come and sit here, hen." Annie Hargreaves grinned at Kate, shifting her chair to make room for her.

Jean gave a half-hearted smile as she sat next to Renie who mumbled a 'hello' through a mouthful of ham sandwich. She'd wanted to stay in her flat, pleading tiredness and fear of reporters but allowed herself to be persuaded otherwise, partly out of curiosity about the appeal for Kate of Annie Hargreaves.

Kirsten arrived and began placing plates of soup in front of Kate and Jean.

"Are you all right, hen? You're looking a bit pale," Annie said.

"Been talking to Ellen," Kirsten said softly.

"Will she be joining us?" Betty Smyth asked from across the room.

"Ears like a bat," Annie muttered.

"She wants a bit of time to herself." Kirsten looked pointedly at Betty before heading back to the kitchen.

Betty shook her head. She was sitting at the table by the window next to Rose Toner. Marjorie Collins sat opposite them. The chair against the wall was empty.

"So when's Maggie's funeral, Betty?" Annie asked.

"There's to be a service on Tuesday. Rose and I have been invited specially of course." Betty rested her hand on Rose Toner's fat fist.

Kate watched for Toner's reaction. She fancied she saw a tightening in the arm belonging to the hand still held by Betty but the face remained expressionless.

"Oh, aye. Best pals weren't you, Betty?" Annie continued.

"Yes, we were." Betty pulled a hankie from her sleeve and dabbed her eyes. A look passed between her and Toner. "I'm going to lie down for a while, Marjorie." She stood as she said this and walked, head down, from the room. Marjorie Collins watched her leave, caught Kate's eye briefly and turned away.

The room darkened and the rain that had been threatening all morning began an onslaught on the windows. Heads turned to watch as the water streamed down, puddling on the patio. Frances picked up a large teapot and went round the tables topping up cups and offering cakes. Chattering voices reasserted themselves, tutting at the vagaries of the weather.

Rose Toner reached for a fairy cake. Her fat fingers delicately picked the small, red jelly tot from the centre of the icing and placed it carefully in her mouth. She repeated the procedure with the icing then abandoned the sponge on the plate.

Jean shivered and wrapped her hands round the cup of hot comforting tea. The room was dominated by old women. The only two men sat at a table in a corner, neither of them Sam MacEwen.

"We think Betty wants to pick up where Maggie left off," Annie was saying, "but she's not got Maggie's presence. You couldn't imagine anybody being intimidated by Betty."

"What about Rose Toner?" Kate asked.

"That's even less likely than Betty."

"Are you sure, Annie?"

"Rose is a bit short of what you might call the old intellectual capacity. The light's always on, you're just never sure when there's anybody in."

Kate smiled. "Do you think it was Betty who spoke to the reporter?"

Annie and Renie looked at each other. "That might have been our fault," Annie said. "There was a reporter here yesterday trying to get us to dish the dirt. We sent him to Marjorie. Told him that she was lonely and loved talking to people and that she was a bit slow on the uptake so he should speak very clearly."

Kate looked across at Marjorie Collins. The jumper looked like cashmere, the jewellery real gold, the face closed, forbidding. "I can imagine the sort of reception the reporter got."

"We think it was after that he met Betty."

"And you said it took Maggie to liven things up."

"Couldn't resist it, Kate. That reporter was an obnoxious bugger, talking to us as if we were senile. We knew Marjorie would put him in his place." She giggled. "Straight for the jugular she went. You should have heard her."

"Where were you two?"

"Hiding in the kitchen."

"You're incorrigible, Annie."

"But it doesn't make me a bad person." All three were laughing now.

Jean smiled feeling more left out than ever. "Excuse me a minute," she said to Kate.

Marjorie's reply to Jean's smiled 'hello Marjorie' was clipped and cool. Jean strained to think of something to appease her, struggling under Rose Toner's blank stare.

"I wanted to ask you, Marjorie, about the church you go to." She hesitated. "Would you mind if I come with you tomorrow?"

Marjorie glanced at Toner who was in the process of wrapping the last of the scones in a napkin. "We meet in the entrance hall at half-past eight, sharp. You can share the taxi."

"Thanks, Marjorie."

Marjorie nodded and turned away. Jean went to rejoin Kate. Toner wet her index finger and dabbed at the crumbs lying on the plate. When it was cleared she stood and walked slowly from the room, the scone clutched in that fat fist.

Jean sat for a while nodding and smiling as if she was following the conversation but really giving Toner time to get along the corridor to the lift. She made a point of looking at her watch as if there was somewhere else she had to be though no one was paying her any attention anyway. She tapped Kate's arm. "I think I'll go up to my flat now. I'm a bit tired."

"Okay, Jean. I'll come up and see you before I go."

Jean walked away knowing Kate would already have turned back to Annie. She hurried along the corridor to the back stairs trying not to hear them start to laugh again. As she put her hand out to catch the banister she felt the floor come up to meet her.

## 36

Kate walked Annie back to her top floor flat but refused the offer of more tea. She was up to the eyeballs with the stuff and she needed time on her own before going to check on Jean; time to tune out the moods and the play-acting; time to try to establish a relationship that was less wearing on both of them. She strolled along to the front of the building wondering how John's day with his son was going then why he'd told her that Steve was trying to contact her, and that frisson when he'd stroked her face. She pushed the memory away. Her life was complicated enough.

She wondered yet again whether seeing Steve was such a good idea. It had been fun some of the time, like their picnic on Cramond Island. They'd left it late getting back and got caught out by the incoming tide, Steve fussing about his Nikes and his designer jeans and ending up in a huff because she laughed at him. She'd enjoyed teasing him out of it. But Cramond Island had different associations now. The deaths of Caroline and Emily Woodlands had seen to that.

The seating area above the entrance hall was empty. Through the rain-streaked window she saw puddles dotting the street below. Lights shone in some of the windows opposite in deference to the mid-afternoon gloom. A black cab drove slowly down the street and disappeared into the car park. Was this where Maggie had sat with her minions watching the comings and goings? Hatching her plans? The taxicab reappeared to pull up at the front door. A young woman emerged from the building and got in. Ellen Post.

Kate rested her head against the window. She'd been covering a duty session the day the call came in from the school. Emily's teacher thought Caroline had been drinking, and not for the first time, but she couldn't risk ignoring what Caroline was saying about Emily being 'in danger'.

Caroline had both sobered up and clammed up when she realised Kate was a social worker. Emily, on the other hand, proved to be a chatterbox. Kate was treated to tales of confident performances at various dancing classes, and a starring role in a school play attended by two sets of adoring grandparents as well as mummy and daddy. She got no sense of a child under pressure to keep inappropriate secrets. Throughout Emily's performance, Caroline stroked the child's long blonde hair, held back by a pink velvet hairband, seemingly in awe of her self-assured daughter. Nevertheless when Kate got back to the office she checked for any record of the Woodlands and found none. The family G.P. had no concerns: Emily was a healthy, happy little girl and Caroline an over-anxious mother with too much time on her hands. Kate wrote it all up and left it at that. She had too many other cases that needed her attention. Two weeks later the bodies of Caroline and Emily Woodlands were found on Cramond Island. Five-year-old Emily's freshly squeezed orange juice had contained enough sleeping tablets to fell a horse. Caroline had washed down her share with Chardonnay before lying down and taking her small daughter in her arms. The suicide note was tucked into the empty wine bottle resting beside them. 'This is the only way out for us. I don't know what else to do. I have to protect my daughter.'

She straightened. The investigation had cleared her of any wrongdoing and she knew Tom Urquhart was right. She couldn't save them all. And yet... She caught her breath at the sudden panic bubbling up from her diaphragm, tingling round her ribcage. She gripped the window sill and closed her eyes, forcing the breath from her lungs, seeing her gran leaning over the bed, holding her hands, 'Breathe out, darling. Blow the bad dreams away.' Calmer now she relaxed her grip and opened her eyes, took a few deep breaths. She adjusted her vision to focus on her rain-blurred reflection in the window. And saw the shadowy figure behind her, watching her. She swallowed and turned slowly.

Rose Toner stood staring at her, hands by her side. She didn't move, didn't seem aware of Kate's presence. Or was this a tactic, leaving Kate to ponder on how much Toner had seen? Toner continued to stare as if waiting for Kate to blink first. Light glinted off the thick glasses shielding her eyes from any examination.

"Could you help me?" Toner said.

Underneath the deep monotone there was the hint of a pleading note. It occurred to Kate that it was the first time she'd heard Rose Toner speak. You wouldn't forget that voice.

Toner turned towards the stairs. Kate wondered about offering to take her arm then realised that touching Rose Toner was the last thing she wanted to do but Toner seemed satisfied that Kate was following her and led the way back to her flat.

The sitting room was reminiscent of Scott Keenan's and Betty Smyth's with its deep pile carpet, pink this time, cream leather sofa and widescreen T.V. Maggie must have had a job lot.

Kate waited. Toner flicked the light switch. "It's not working."

"You should call the warden."

"She's not answering."

They were standing either side of a coffee table on which sat a small, blue teapot with gold trim and a matching cup and saucer. The pilfered fruit scone lay on a side plate, a bone-handled knife next to it. Alongside was what looked like a wooden jewellery box with its lid standing open.

"It needs a new bulb," Toner said holding one out to her.

Kate pulled a wooden chair from the kitchen, slipped off her shoes and climbed up to the light socket. She was aware of Toner standing beneath her and was oddly relieved that she was wearing trousers. She removed the old bulb and passed it into Toner's raised hand before inserting the fresh one. She stepped down and flicked the light switch. The room brightened. She replaced the chair in the kitchen and turned to look at the jewellery box.

Toner reached out and tapped the lid so that it closed with a snap. She used her foot to push Kate's shoes towards her. "How is your aunt?"

"Improving. How about you? Missing Maggie?"

Toner stared. "Does your aunt?" There was something like a sneer growing on her face.

Kate smiled at her. "Don't let your tea get cold," she said and walked out.

At times Rose Toner's behaviour bordered on the robotic, a touch of Annie's 'nobody in' syndrome. Maybe it was the medication she was on. Yet there was a glint of calculation in her eyes, something not quite hidden behind the round, distortion of the glasses. Scott Keenan did say Rose Toner wasn't the full shilling and Annie had suggested as much but Kate wasn't convinced. It could be a very effective way of keeping difficult questions at bay.

She was almost at the door of Jean's flat when it opened and Sam MacEwen came out.

"Are you sure you're all right now, Jean?" he was saying.

"I am, thanks, Sam."

They turned at Kate's approach, Jean looking caught out.

"Oh, Kate, you've met Sam, haven't you?"

"Briefly," Kate said waiting for an explanation.

Sam MacEwen nodded at her and walked away.

"What was all that about?" she asked when they were in Jean's sitting room.

"Um, he was just checking that that reporter wasn't hanging about. Are you staying for your tea?" Jean sounded quite bright.

"I'm eating out tonight."

The bright look faded.

"I could do with a bit of toast though. Keep me going."

"Toast it is." Jean went into the kitchen.

Whilst Kate nibbled at the toast Jean disappeared into the bedroom. She came back carrying a shoebox and laid it on the coffee table.

"If my gran was here she'd be telling you it's bad luck to put shoes on the table," Kate said.

"It's not shoes. It's family stuff. I thought you might want to have some of it."

Kate pushed her plate to one side and pulled the box towards her. She lifted the lid and looked inside. Stuff was a good description. There were photos, black and white as well as colour; letters, some enveloped, some not; and cards, Christmas and birthday. "Do you not want to keep this?" she asked, not sure she wanted any of it, afraid of what it might suggest, mindful of Jules' comment about better not knowing.

"It'll still be in the family." Jean sat smiling at her. "Take anything you think will help."

"Can I ask you something?"

"Anything you like. No more secrets."

"It's about my father," she said quickly.

Jean's face tightened. "I've told you all I know."

"How did he know my mum's death was suicide?" She hesitated before plunging in. "Was there a note?"

"Your dad didn't tell me that." Jean paused seeming more confident. "I'm sorry, Kate. I'd tell you if I knew."

"I know, Jean. It's all right." She reached across and squeezed Jean's hand, wondering whether to believe her yet relieved by her answer.

The dining room had been returned to its usual tidy state, the tables cleared, the floor swept. Nothing remained of the last goodbye to Harriet Post. Kate wandered in, shoebox under her arm, focussing on her impressions from the day. There were so many undercurrents: Jean and Marjorie, Kirsten and Frances, Marjorie and Betty, and, at the centre of it all, Rose Toner like some giant spider spinning her sticky web. Question was who was to be the next fly. 'Come into my parlour' right enough.

She wondered what had happened to brighten Jean up and whether Sam MacEwen had anything to do with it. Whatever it was, long may it last. She had enough going on without worrying about Jean's moods. Yet, when she said she had to go, there had a hint of feeling abandoned in the look Jean gave her. She'd tried to soften it by telling Jean about Steve and was now wishing she hadn't. Jean had always been blinkered where Steve was concerned.

The clink of glass on glass from the kitchen caught her attention. She walked to the door. A figure sat at the table in semi-darkness. Kate switched the light on.

"Christ, what a fright you gave me." Kirsten Cormack jumped, blinking in the sudden brightness.

"Sorry. You okay?"

"Not even close."

A half-empty wine bottle sat on the table. Next to it was a full tumbler, Kirsten's hands wrapped round it.

"Anything I can do to help?"

Kirsten knocked back some of the wine and looked at her. "You could shoot Scott fucking Keenan."

Kate pulled out a chair and sat down. "Why?"

"It doesn't matter now. Either way I'm going to lose my job."

"How come?"

"Scott Keenan says he'll get me the sack if I don't have sex with him."

Kate grimaced. "Can he do that? Get you sacked, I mean."

"He knows about something I did." She drank more wine then reached for the bottle and topped up the glass.

Was this what Scott was referring to when he said Kirsten could be in jail? "Did Maggie know?"

"It was Maggie stopped Scott from doing anything about it."

"Was what you did illegal?" She took Kirsten's silence for assent. "Wouldn't Scott be in bother if he told anyone about it?"

Kirsten shrugged. "He says he'd do it anonymously."

"Can't you put him off for a while, stall him?"

"How?"

"Tell him you're having your period or something."

"Then what? He's just going to keep coming back."

"He's probably going to do that anyway."

They sat staring at the table, Kate trying and failing to avoid the image of sex with Scott Keenan.

"Have you spoken to his brother?" she asked.

"Don't know him."

"I do."

Kirsten looked at her expectantly.

"You put Scott off. I'll speak to Fraser."

"Why would you do that for me?"

"I've met Scott Keenan. I wouldn't wish that on anybody."

Kirsten shrugged. "What have I got to lose?" she said and refilled her tumbler.

Kate took that as her cue to leave. It was only as she drove out of the car park that she remembered exactly what Kirsten had said. 'Either way I'm going to lose my job.' She hadn't said what the other way was.

## 37

Jean threw the half-eaten toast into the bin and rinsed the plate along with the cup and saucer from Sam MacEwen's visit. It had been a sop: 'keep Jean happy, let her make me some toast'. Did Kate think she was that sad? Still, she did feel pleased that Kate was seeing Steve again. Even if telling her had been another 'make Jean's day' moment.

They hadn't seen eye to eye about Steve. So he wasn't perfect but he was better than someone like John Nelson. She didn't trust him. It wasn't just his looks. If anything Steve was more handsome but there was something about John Nelson that would be hard to resist. Even at her age she could see it, could feel it when he was asking her about finding Maggie Keenan's body. It was those 'come to bed' eyes that drew you in and that smile.

If it hadn't been for Mair butting in Jean might well have told John Nelson everything. 'Trust me, I'll take care of you.' That's what they wanted you to believe men like that. Well, she'd been there, done that, bought the T-shirt. Bought the whole bloody wardrobe. Sometimes being seventy didn't seem so bad.

She dried her dishes and put them in the cupboard then wiped the draining board and stood squeezing the cloth. She'd been horrified when she'd come round to find Sam MacEwen bending over her. It had been embarrassing yet she'd felt a stirring of pleasure at the look of concern on his face. He'd been so solicitous, helping her up, escorting her back to her flat. He'd insisted on making her a cup of tea and had sat with her till she drank it. It had been nice being looked after like that, being cared for.

She wondered about going along to his flat to thank him and maybe to explain about Kate and not wanting her to know about the fainting. That sounded plausible. He wouldn't think she was chasing him would he? She wasn't, not in that way. Those days were long gone. Romance. That was what she wanted. A little romance. Someone to take her to the theatre or for a meal, make her feel a bit feminine now and again. Remind her she was still a woman. Like Robert had done.

She draped her dishcloth over the edge of the sink and went into her bedroom and studied herself in the mirror. Not one of her favourite pastimes. Her clothes were dull but she couldn't change them, that would make him suspicious. She settled for combing her hair and touching up her lipstick, the only make-up she wore these days, then picked up her key and went out.

In the corridor she looked out of the window that faced the gardens and the park beyond. The rain had stopped but everything looked dank and windblown. In her old flat this weather would have set her worrying about the roof. It was such a bother to get repairs done and, being on the top floor, she was the one suffering the leaks whilst trying to get everyone's agreement. Kate had organised it all the last time. Had probably bullied some of the owners into accepting the estimate though Kate would have called it cajoling. Jean had had neither the nerve nor the energy for either.

Yet she'd been a person in her own right there, living her life like everyone else. Here she was just another old woman. That was why she was here, too old to live unsupervised in case something happened to her. She'd moved because Kate had suggested it and she needed Kate. She couldn't contemplate a life completely alone with no one to remind her who she was, where she'd come from, ending up in some geriatric netherland of fantasy and confusion. Kate was her reference point, her buffer zone. The price was her privacy: always someone watching her coming and going, checking up on her, making sure she was safe. As if. Risk wasn't in her nature, not any more.

C'mon, Jean, she said to herself, beginning to lose momentum. She turned from the window and walked slowly along the corridor moving closer to the wall as she neared Rose Toner's flat. The door to Sam MacEwen's flat was round the corner, opposite Betty Smyth's. To get there she had to pass Rose Toner's door. She didn't want either woman to see her. The sound of footsteps coming towards her halted her progress. She half-turned, already trying to find an excuse for dawdling in the corridor. A doorbell rang – Betty Smyth's maybe. The door opened.

"Oh. You'd better come in," Betty said.

A murmured reply faded as the door closed.

Jean hesitated, wondering who the caller was. Betty hadn't sounded very enthusiastic about the visit but maybe that was just a ploy. Annie Hargreaves had said that Betty was trying to take on Maggie Keenan's mantle. Had the caller been one of Maggie Keenan's victims? Probably thought they were off the hook with Maggie's death and here it was starting all over again. Jean knew how that might feel. She sighed. It was no use. Her Sam MacEwen moment had passed. She turned and walked back to her flat.

### 38

The shoebox Jean had given her lay waiting to be examined on the kitchen table. On the hi-fi Janis Ian sang of the torment of life at seventeen. Kate slid into the warm, rose-scented bathwater and lay back still uncertain about the wisdom of accepting Steve's invitation. She'd always been more attracted to John. They'd first met over two years ago on the Natasha Farrell case, long before Steve, and the attraction had been mutual. But his personal life seemed permanently set to turbulent. At that time his marriage was very much an on-off affair and when it was off there seemed to be a never-ending supply of women. What tied him in knots and sustained the 'on' element of the marriage was his son, Michael.

She trickled water over her shoulders, trailing her fingers down her arms, breathing in the rose-scented air. Six months ago she'd spent an evening talking with John about all the hoops Michael might put him through on being told that his parents were finally going to divorce. It was the only time she'd ever seen John scared. As a police officer he dealt with everything the job could throw at him with the same controlled energy. Emotionally he seemed armour plated. Yet a five-year-old boy was capable of punching great gaping holes in it with no more than a look.

They'd chosen a pub on the southern outskirts of Edinburgh to minimise the risk of being seen together. She'd been seeing Steve at the time and preferred that he didn't know about her meeting with John. Police stations were like sweetie wives' conferences. And the meeting was purely platonic. She had agreed to give John the benefit of her professional expertise. But there was a moment after they left the pub, as they stood at her car, him shuffling his feet, thanking her, checking she would find her way back into the city okay, when she ached to put her arms around him. But she didn't and the moment passed as those moments do.

She climbed out of the bath, pulled the white towel from the radiator and wrapped its warmth around her. In the mirror above the wash-hand basin her face glowed pink. She took her cleanser from the cupboard and smoothed away the city's grime with a cotton wool pad. Her hair was damp but would be fine when it dried off. It always did its own thing anyway. The last of the bathwater gurgled down the plughole. She threw the towel over the side of the bath and put her bathrobe on, tying it loosely at her waist.

In the kitchen Janis was looking for 'Tea and Sympathy'. Kate switched the C.D. for one she'd made for her gran. As she carried a mug of coffee to the table, the Beatles launched into 'All My Loving'. She sat down and pulled the shoebox towards her. Amongst the photos was one of Kate as a baby, kitted out in pink. The others were mostly school photos. Gran never had mastered a camera. They had more photos of their feet than anything else. There was a clipping from the local newspaper about Kate winning a prize at school and another about the time she won a debating competition. There were letters written by her gran to Jean, mostly about Kate: warm, chatty letters telling Jean how well Kate was doing. When she read them she could hear her gran saying the words and feel the concern for Jean in Edinburgh on her own.

The batch of Christmas and birthday cards was at the bottom of the box. Again these were from her gran and herself to Jean, except one. It was a Christmas card from her father. Underneath was a photograph: a wedding photo. Her parents stood side by side. In her heeled shoes her mother was the taller of the two. She was wearing a cream suit and a small hat with a veil and was smiling at the camera, showing off her wedding ring. She looked happy. Her father was smiling too but looked uncomfortable. They were flanked by another man and woman. The woman looked to be in her thirties and was short with brown hair, the man the same height as her father but stocky and going bald. She didn't recognise either of them.

She put the photo on one side and picked up the Christmas card. It was a basic, run-of-the-mill job with a Christmas tree on the front covered in glitter. Inside her father had written a note. "We're even," it said. "Let the past lie." What did that mean, 'we're even'? And whose past was he talking about? Jean's? His own? Some joint secret? The card wasn't dated. She sat looking at it. She'd brought all her own Christmas and birthday cards with her when she moved to Edinburgh including some from her father. They'd stopped when she left university. She got up and went into her boxroom, found the ones she was looking for and took them into the kitchen. There wasn't much written in them, just 'Katie,' he'd always called her that, and 'happy birthday' or 'happy Christmas, all my love, Dad'.

She placed the card from her father to Jean next to one from her father to herself. She spotted the discrepancy immediately. She took one of the letters her gran had written to Jean and set it beside the two cards. Three sets of writing; two matched. Problem was it was the wrong two.

## 39

She parked her car on the bridge across the Water of Leith that linked Bernard Street with Commercial Street and headed for the restaurant. She'd spent nearly an hour deciding what to wear, reminding herself that it was only Steve and that it had been his idea. She finally settled for a loose, blue silk blouse and black trousers, her blue, knee-length 'Ness' coat on top.

She'd dawdled through Leith reliving memories. It was where she'd learned her trade, the Leith office being the one where she started out as a newly qualified social worker. It had been a good place to start, young families alongside a mainstay elderly population. She'd done a bit of research on its history. Discovered it had been a separate burgh until around 1920 when it reluctantly allowed itself to be absorbed by Edinburgh, though even now it still had the feel of its own identity. Its prime position on the Forth had made it the major port of Scotland, until the Clyde took over.

Steve was waiting at the door of the restaurant wearing a frown and his black leather Armani jacket. His blond hair looked soft and freshly washed. He nodded when he saw her then reached for her arm and leaned toward her, smelling fresh, clean and masculine. Her hand brushed against the soft grey wool of his jumper. She turned her head to the side to meet his kiss on her cheek.

"Good to see you, Kate. We've got a lot to talk about."

The waiter led them to a window table and took Kate's coat. He returned and handed them menus then produced a lighter from his trouser pocket and lit the tall, milky-white candle in the centre of the table. Kate smiled a thank you whilst Steve studied the wine menu. Her choice of a mushroom risotto with garlic bread earned her a sharp glance. Steve opted for lasagne with a green salad and settled on a Soave, one of her favourites, though not one of his.

"Just a glass for me, Steve. I'm driving," she said.

He ordered a bottle. "I'll help you drink it." He smiled at her, handing the menus to the waiter with an air of dismissal.

"How's the case going?" she asked warily. His behaviour was out of character given the way their last meeting had ended. He was being too accommodating. He was fussy about his wine and had considered her own tastes as bordering on plonk.

"A bugger." He slipped off his leather jacket and draped it carefully over the back of his chair. "John's got the juicy bit, chasing Keenan's money. I'm stuck with the rump. I'll be spending my time interviewing demented old women while he charges about Edinburgh and Fife doing real police work."

"Right." She'd forgotten how he could be when things weren't going his way, seeing conspiracies against him at every turn. And always at the centre of it was John Nelson. John was an inch taller, a month younger and had been promoted sooner than Steve: this last despite Steve being the fast-track graduate. Put the two of them in a room together and you could bottle the testosterone.

"But that's not what I want to talk about," Steve was saying.

The waiter returned and poured the wine for Steve to taste. He nodded his approval and the waiter topped up Steve's glass and filled Kate's.

"So what do you want to talk about?"

"I've been offered promotion." He leaned forward excited now. "It's in the uniform branch but in a couple of years I could be back in Edinburgh in C.I.D."

"Back in Edinburgh?"

"The post's in Inverness." He took her hand. "Come with me, Kate. I know things have been difficult between us recently but I want you with me. You're good for me. You can help me make this work."

She stared at him, at a loss for words, feeling as if she'd landed in a parallel universe. She was relieved when her garlic bread arrived. She removed her hand from Steve's grasp and sat back shaking her head. "I can't just up and leave Edinburgh, Steve. I don't want to."

"We could have a good life together."

"I don't know why you think that. When we broke up that last time I assumed we were finished." She looked at him. "And I wasn't broken-hearted about it."

Steve looked down at the table. "Is there someone else?"

"I don't base my decisions on whether there's a man in my life. Everything I've got is in Edinburgh. And that includes a job I love, that I'm good at. You're asking me to give all that up on a whim."

"I love you, Kate. That's not a whim. If you loved me, you'd do this."

She took a deep breath. "I don't love you, Steve. I'm not going to rip up my life here to go anywhere with you. I'm sorry."

He shook his head. "You're still angry with me, aren't you?"

She controlled the impulse to punch him. "Why would I be angry with you?"

"Those things I said when we broke up. I didn't mean them. I was hurting. I need you, Kate."

The waiter returned to check everything was satisfactory and to top up their glasses. Kate's head was spinning. Where was all this coming from? How had she missed it? "I can't do this." She reached for her bag.

"Okay." He caught her hand. "Relax, Kate. I didn't mean to put pressure on you." He smiled at her. "Let's just enjoy each other's company."

The garlic bread was cold, the butter congealed. She pushed it aside and nodded to the waiter to remove it when he brought her risotto. She took a mouthful, hardly tasting it. She needed to understand what was going on here, how much of it was her fault. There was such a gap in their understanding of the sort of relationship they'd had. Love had never been mentioned.

Steve kept topping up her glass alongside a flow of light conversation: memories of the fun they'd had, often at his expense. She kept reminding herself that she was driving. Then that she could get a taxi and pick up her car in the morning. By the time they left the restaurant all she wanted to do was lie down and go to sleep.

Steve's flat was only five minutes from the restaurant along the Water of Leith walkway. She agreed to go back with him on a promise of black coffee, ignoring the bit of her brain that was telling her not to be so bloody stupid. The chill of the night air woke her up but made her shiver. Steve used that as an excuse to put his arm around her. In the block that housed his flat she moved ahead of him into the lift, making herself less accessible by leaning back against the wall.

Once in his flat Steve went into the kitchen and started brewing up. The sitting room was warm. She threw her coat over the back of the brown leather sofa and sat down. What the hell was she doing here?

She jerked awake when she felt someone stroking her trousered leg. Steve placed a mug of coffee on the glass table then took her hand and drew her to her feet. He'd put some music on. She felt his arms around her, moving her slowly to the rhythm of k.d. lang singing 'Save me'.

"I remember when I first heard this," he said smiling at her.

"First time I invited you back to my flat." She returned his smile. "I thought you seemed a bit too sure of yourself."

"I'd been waiting for weeks for a chance at you. And just when I thought I'd finally made it: k.d. lang."

"You should have seen your face." She was laughing now. "I knew you'd think I was gay."

"You taught me how to be spontaneous, to loosen up." He pulled back to look into her face. "You were good for me, Kate. I've not been the same without you. And this case…" he shook his head, "if I don't get it right, it could spoil everything, including my promotion."

"I can't go with you, Steve. I don't want to."

"I hear you, Kate, but just stay with me tonight. I'm under so much pressure right now and you were always good at making me see things differently." He rested his head on hers. "Please, Kate, just stay tonight. That's all I'm asking."

She felt his arm tighten round her waist and let him raise her face to his and kiss her: gently at first then with more urgency. He broke off and led her towards the bedroom.

"This isn't a good idea, Steve. Nothing's changed."

"Just give me tonight, Kate. Please."

She thought of going home and the letters and cards lying in wait on her kitchen table. Then he was kissing her again and she gave up the fight.

# Sunday

## 40

Kate slid out of the bed and gathered up her clothes. In the bathroom she showered and dressed quickly then headed for the kitchen where she drank two glasses of water while waiting for the small 'Gaggia' to produce the coffee. The wall clock showed 7.04 and a thumping headache was developing just behind her eyes. She pictured Lucy stretching her chubby body before sauntering to her eating place and sniffing at her empty food dish. The coffee machine began to gurgle. She grabbed a jug and stuck it under the outlet just in time. The steaming, black liquid poured in, giving off that lovely coffee smell. She filled a wide-mouthed cup and went into the sitting room where she stood looking out at the Water of Leith glimmering in the lamplight.

The flat was in what had once been a bonded warehouse. All over Leith buildings like this one had been converted to flats, part of the 'gentrification' process. Lots of young upwardly mobiles moved in attracted by Leith's image of trendy but with a bit of an edge. Not that Steve would ever put himself in that category. Ambition he would admit to. Police work was a means to an end: as high as he could go on the promotion ladder in the fast-track graduate scheme. The bonus was the advantage it gave him over his better-paid contemporaries who'd opted for the insurance companies and law firms. None of them could employ the power and authority Steve could when in charge of an investigation.

A mobile phone sounded from the bedroom.

"Oakley." She heard Steve say, then, "I'll be there in twenty."

Steve came into the sitting room in his dressing gown. He frowned at her fully-dressed state.

"What is it?" she asked.

"Scott Keenan's been stabbed."

"Is he dead?"

"He's in the Royal Infirmary. Expected to recover. John's got Fraser Keenan and Tracy Spencer at Leith. I need to be in on the interviews."

"I thought the Keenans were John's bit of the case."

"Who told you that?" Steve said accusingly.

"Don't jump down my throat," she fired back.

"Sorry. I need to know if there's any link to Maggie Keenan's death." He turned towards the door. "Get me a coffee."

She sketched a mock curtsey behind his back and went into the kitchen, relieved that he had to be elsewhere, that there would be no long drawn out goodbyes and it could be finally over for both of them. She wondered now what she'd seen in him apart from his blond good looks. She'd been impressed by his determination to get her to go out with him; her ego had been flattered by the reports of the difference she'd made in him, but love had never entered into it, not for her. And the physical attraction hadn't lived up to her expectations. The packaging promised a lot more than it delivered.

Steve returned dressed and towelling his hair. He picked up his coffee and took two quick gulps.

"Take your time, Kate. We might manage lunch if I can leave this to John. I just want to be sure nothing's going to come back on me."

She stared at him. "I'm going home."

"Okay, I'll pick you up from there."

"I don't want you to pick me up from there. I told you last night. Whatever you decide to do, I won't be part of it."

An angry frown darkened his face as he finally seemed to hear what she'd been telling him. "What was that then," he said, waving in the direction of the bedroom, "a goodbye fuck? God, you're something else." He looked like he was about to cry.

She moved towards him. "I'm sorry."

He threw his hands up, warding her off. "I can't deal with this now. I've got an investigation to run. Great fucking sense of timing you've got."

"It's your choice of timing not mine." She softened her tone. "I shouldn't have stayed."

"So why did you?"

She shook her head. "I need to go."

He caught her arm. "There is somebody else isn't there? John Nelson's been sniffing around you for months now. It's him isn't it?"

"John's got nothing to do with this."

"What is it then? C'mon, Kate, I want to know." Steve's sneering face was centimetres from hers. "Just tell me."

"I felt sorry for you. Okay? Feel better now?" She jerked her arm free of his grip and headed for the door. She fiddled with the locks, fingers turning to thumbs before she got the door opened.

"You fucking bitch," followed her out.

She clattered down the stairwell, couldn't wait for the lift. Outside a blast of ice-cold air greeted her like a slap.

She ran along the walkway to the bridge, rummaging in her bag for the car key, hands still shaking. Inside the car she sat trying to calm herself, trying to rid herself of the look on his face when she'd told him. Regardless of whether love had driven his proposal he'd hate her now. But it was his own fault. He shouldn't have pushed it. She started the engine and drove off.

At home she fed and fussed over Lucy then went into the bedroom to change. Back in jeans and jumper, she gathered up her swimsuit and a towel and headed out again ignoring the cat's accusing stare. There was a cold rain falling so she drove to the swimming pool. She hadn't been able to find a parking place anyway, might have better luck when she got back.

The water's soft caress and the rhythmic stroking of the swim soothed her. She dived under the surface, pulling herself along the bottom of the pool. At the shallow end she came up for air, brushed the side then tumble-turned to head back up the pool. She dove below the surface again but swimming strongly now, kicking hard, arms pushing the water around and behind her, loving the rhythm, the buoyancy, the otherworldly feeling, that underwater silence. At the deep end, she arched her back and gave a powerful kick to break the surface in a burst of air and water then climbed out and strode to the changing rooms.

It was just after nine-thirty when she got home. There was a space right outside her stair. Things were looking up. She parked the car and went up to her flat. She stripped and went into the shower again to wash off any residue of chlorine. When she came out she wrapped herself in her towelling robe and thought about breakfast.

She felt ravenous. She took a ciabatta roll from the bread bin and put it in the oven to warm whilst she scrambled a couple of eggs with chopped tomatoes in a drizzle of olive oil. When it was ready she got the butter from the fridge and carried the lot to her dining table. Lucy dashed in and glared at her as if alarmed to see her there then snatched up her toy rabbit and shot out the door. Kate smiled as she pushed the contents of Jean's shoebox to one side and settled down to pamper herself. She was wiping the plate with the last of her ciabatta roll when the phone rang.

## 41

Jean stood in the entrance hall. Alongside her, Marjorie leant heavily on her sturdy walking stick. They were waiting for Betty Smyth and Rose Toner to join them. Marjorie kept looking at her watch. Jean kept wondering what she was doing. It was years since she'd been inside a church. She'd never been that interested in religion but if this was what it took to get a life of her own, well, she'd give it a go. She couldn't depend on Kate all the time.

Rose Toner came down the stairs saying she couldn't get Betty to answer the door. Marjorie looked over at the reception window.

"There's never anyone there when they're needed."

They turned as Frances Wordsworth came into the entrance hall from the corridor, heading for the office.

Marjorie stood in her way. "Betty's not come down to go to church and she's not answering her door."

Frances looked at her watch. "I should be off duty by now. I don't know what's happened to Kirsten."

Marjorie held her ground.

Frances sighed. "I'll go and check on her." She started up the stairs.

Rose Toner stumped after her.

"Betty's never late," Marjorie said.

Jean stood where she was, feeling at a loss, brain a bit foggy. She'd taken one of her pills earlier, afraid of keeling over in the church. She couldn't see Marjorie being as solicitous as Sam MacEwen had been. She smiled, hugging the memory to herself, then straightened her face when she saw Marjorie watching her.

Frances appeared on the stairs, looking down, avoiding the question in their eyes. She hurried to the office. Marjorie stalked after her, the walking stick thumping the floor with each step.

"Where is she? What's happened?" Under the demanding tone there was a catch in Marjorie's voice. "I have a right to know."

Frances came out of the office and looked at Marjorie. "I'm sorry, Mrs Collins…" she began.

"I knew it," Marjorie shouted. "Maggie Keenan should never have been allowed to live here."

"We mustn't jump to conclusions. I've called the doctor. Let's wait and see what he has to say." Frances tried to guide Marjorie into the small lounge off the entrance hall. She looked at Jean. "Maybe some tea?"

"Right." Jean turned and almost bumped into Rose Toner who had come up behind her.

"I'll sit with her," Rose Toner said nodding at Marjorie.

When Jean returned with the tea Frances was talking to a young man in the entrance hall. Rose Toner was nowhere to be seen. Jean continued on into the lounge. "I think the doctor's arrived," she said.

"Not before time," Marjorie said but some of the steam had gone out of her words.

The two women watched as Frances led the young man up the stairs. Jean sat next to Marjorie. "Do you want to try to drink some tea?"

Marjorie waved the mug away. "Not now."

A few minutes later Frances came down the stairs on her own and walked over to them. She lowered her head. "I'm sorry to have to tell you this. Mrs Smyth is dead." She held up a hand to forestall Marjorie's questions. "Because of what's been happening recently the doctor has contacted the police."

Marjorie threw her head back and let out a wail. "This should not have happened." She began to rock back and forth, fists clenched on her knees. Frances stood there neither use nor ornament. Jean put her arm round Marjorie's shoulders, rocking with her, wondering whether she should tell the police about Betty's visitor.

## 42

A sleety rain battered the window as John Nelson watched the coffee drip into the jug. He'd already interviewed Tracy Spencer, hoping for a useful revelation in the emotional aftermath of Scott Keenan's stabbing. The interview was recorded at the insistence of her solicitor but the tapes contained only the questions that were asked and Tracy's unsuccessful attempts at rational speech. It had all been too much for her, seeing Scott like that. This impression was reinforced by regular sniffs and dabbing at her eyes with a handkerchief reluctantly provided her solicitor. The only other response she'd offered was the acceptance of a cup of tea which she drank whilst twirling a packet of cigarettes round and round on the table.

He turned as the door opened and Steve entered.

"Ready to go?" Steve asked.

"Waiting for Fraser to have a word with his solicitor. Want some coffee?"

Steve shook his head. "How long is this going to take?"

He looked properly at Steve for the first time, noting the pallor, the angry frown. "You okay?"

"I'm fine. Why shouldn't I be?"

"Keep your hair on, Steve. I'm just asking."

Steve moved towards him. "Well don't fucking bother," he said.

There was a knock on the door and a young P.C. entered. "Fraser Keenan's ready to be interviewed, sir," he said to John.

"Right." He turned to Steve. "I don't know what your problem is but just remember, this is my case. You're only here for as long as I let you be." He walked out the door leaving Steve to decide whether to follow him.

Fraser Keenan turned from the window as the two police officers entered the room. Dressed in a soft, brown leather jacket and pale moleskin trousers, he was the image of the up and coming young businessman. Unlike Tracy, he showed no ill-effects from the events of the past night.

The solicitor lounging at the table could have been Fraser's clone. He stretched and straightened, making a show of wrinkling his nose, their combined colognes unable to overcome the room's scent of stale sweat with an undertone of urine.

The tape recorder was switched on. The date and time and the names of those present were noted as was that the interview was being recorded at Fraser's request. Fraser, now seated, looked pleased with himself.

"Where were you last night between midnight and two a.m.?" John said.

The solicitor rested his hand on Fraser's arm. "I want it noted that Mr Keenan is here of his own accord."

John glanced at the solicitor. "Noted. Fraser?"

Fraser reached for the jug of water, another request, and poured some into a plastic cup. "Tracy and I were at a private function at Edinburgh Quay till around midnight. There are numerous people who will confirm that. We dropped a couple of friends off on the way home and got back to the Leith flat about half-past twelve."

"Where was Scott?"

"Stayed at home. Something on television he wanted to watch."

"You got home at twelve-thirty. What then?"

"We went to our separate beds."

"Are you living in the Leith flat now?"

"Staying over." Fraser looked down. "It's not been easy for us since our mother was murdered." He let his gaze rest on Steve.

"Is Tracy living there too?" John asked.

"For the time being."

"And that doesn't bother you? Tracy living with Scott?" This was from Steve.

Fraser lifted the cup and sipped at the water. "As you know Tracy's not been allowed back to the Leapark flat since my mother's murder. The Leith flat has two spare bedrooms. Tracy has one of them."

"Does Scott see it that way?"

"Of course he does."

Fraser's solicitor scribbled on his yellow pad and sat back.

"Where was Scott when you got home?" John asked.

"In the sitting-room." Fraser glanced at the pad as he spoke. "At least I supposed that. The door was shut and I could hear voices but not what they were saying."

"How many voices?" John was making a point of getting his questions in quickly, stopping Steve from taking over, wondering if Kate had anything to do with the tension emanating from the man next to him.

"I'd be guessing."

"So guess."

"Two, maybe three."

"Male or female."

Fraser seemed to consider this. "Male, I think."

"What happened next?"

"I woke about two o'clock. Scott was shouting for me. I got up and found him on the floor in the kitchen." Fraser topped up his cup and took a sip. "There was a knife sticking out of his stomach."

"Did he say anything?"

"Just my name. He looked terrified. I grabbed a towel and shouted to Tracy to get more from the cupboard."

"Where was Tracy?"

"She was at the kitchen door by this time. I told her to phone for an ambulance."

John waited, Steve silent beside him.

"I tried to stop the bleeding," Fraser continued. "I was going to take the knife out but then I thought that might make things worse so I left it."

"Did you touch the knife?"

"I grabbed the handle."

"That's convenient isn't it, Fraser?" Steve said.

"You think finding my brother like that was convenient?"

"I think it was like this – you and Scott had an argument about Tracy. And you stabbed him."

The solicitor leaned forward gold-tipped pen tapping his yellow notepad.

Fraser held up his hand. "It's all right, Cal." He looked at Steve. "Scott and I are not rivals." He held Steve's glare for a moment then turned to John Nelson. "It happened the way I told you, Inspector."

"We know that Scott thought Maggie was holding him back," John said.

"Then you know more than I do."

"If Scott poking Tracy wasn't enough to push you over the edge killing Maggie certainly would be." Steve sneered. "We know how you loved your mother."

Fraser shook his head, nurturing a look of disappointment. He leaned forward. "A word of advice, Mr Oakley. It's never a good idea to mix the personal with the professional."

There was a knock at the door.

John reached across to switch off the tape, blocking Steve's incipient lunge at Fraser. "Interview suspended nine thirteen," he announced.

The P.C. reappeared beckoning to John. Steve followed him out.

"There's been a suspicious death at Leapark, sir." He held out a note.

Steve grabbed it, glowering at the young man. "That's my case," he said. "Find Heather Mair. Tell her to get her arse over to Leapark." He stomped off along the corridor.

The officer looked at John for confirmation.

"This death, who is it?" John asked him.

"Betty Smyth, sir. And there's a message for you from D.C. Donald." He held out another note.

John smiled as he read it. "Wait here," he said and went back into the interview room. "Sorry for keeping you waiting." He removed the tapes from the machine and handed one to Fraser. "We'll be in touch." He turned to the P.C. "Show Mr Keenan and his solicitor out then do as Inspector Oakley asked."

Fraser stood. "Thank you, Inspector. I appreciate your professionalism."

John smiled. "I'm truly gratified to hear that, Mr Keenan." He walked out to his car and set off for Corstorphine.

## 43

Jean was sitting with a calmer Marjorie when she saw the police arrive. Steve Oakley strode in first followed by Mair. Frances hurried from the office to greet them.

"The police are here, Marjorie." Jean could see that Steve wasn't pleased about something and whatever it was Frances was bearing the brunt of it.

"Why didn't you call the police as soon as you discovered the body?" Jean heard him say. He didn't wait for Frances to answer before telling her about the evidence she might have destroyed, the time lost to his investigation, how much more difficult she'd made his job. Jean began to feel sorry for Frances standing there, head hanging, whilst Steve harangued her. When he started towards the lounge Jean quickly turned back to Marjorie.

Steve planted himself in front of them, Mair beside him. "Mrs Markham, we need to talk to you about your involvement in the discovery of this third body," he announced.

Jean was trying to formulate a response when Marjorie erupted.

"How dare you refer to my friend as a 'third body'. If you had done your job properly this would never have happened." She struggled to her feet leaning on her walking stick. "You have nothing but contempt for us and I refuse to have anything more to do with you. Now get out of my way."

Marjorie seemed disorientated as she pushed unsteadily between the two police officers, walking stick poking the air in front of her. Mair was slow to react and was toppled into a nearby chair. Steve tried to catch a flailing arm heading in his direction.

"Don't touch me," Marjorie screamed. She turned quickly, heading for the door, and caught Steve a whack behind the knee with her walking stick. His leg buckled. The stick clattered to the floor leaving Marjorie tottering like a top nearing the end of its spin. In a final flourish, her fist connected with the side of Steve's face and she toppled forward across the coffee table, sending the mugs of tea flying. She came to rest half on the sofa, half on the coffee table, her fists still tightly clenched.

Jean became aware of someone behind her and turned to see John Nelson standing in the doorway, a look of disbelief on his face. She found herself wanting to giggle and avoided catching his eye. Instead she went over to where Marjorie lay.

"Get me up," Marjorie said.

John Nelson moved Jean out of his way and motioned to Steve to help. "Okay, Mrs Collins." He crouched beside her. "Can you put your arm around my neck?"

"Not him," Marjorie insisted as Steve moved to her other side.

Frances appeared with a wheelchair and quickly hurried to take Steve's place.

"Get me my walking stick."

This was done and, with John Nelson taking most of the weight, Marjorie was finally hauled upright then gently lowered into her wheelchair.

"Jean, take me to my flat, please."

"Shall I send the doctor in, Mrs Collins?" Frances asked Marjorie's disappearing back.

Jean looked back and mouthed a 'yes'.

"What the hell was all that about?" John said.

Steve turned, nodding at John to close the door of their makeshift office. "Tell me honestly have you been seeing Kate?"

"Only to keep her up to date with what's been going on in here."

"We've broken up, for good this time. She's been a right bitch about it."

"That's between you and Kate and right now I'd say it's the least of your worries. What happened in there?"

"I messed up, John." Steve sighed. "At this rate I can wave goodbye to any fucking promotion."

"Only if Marjorie Collins complains."

"It's not just her. I had a go at the warden as well."

"You're really making a day of it aren't you?" John shook his head. "You apologise to Wordsworth. I'll have a word with Collins."

"Why would you do that for me?"

"A complaint from here reflects on the pair of us even if you're the only one with the black eye."

Steve touched his face gingerly. "Christ, she packs some punch."

John smiled then started laughing. Steve couldn't resist joining in.

When Heather Mair knocked and entered they were still wiping the tears from their eyes.

"When do you want to do the interviews, sir?" She looked from one to the other, refusing to see the funny side of any of it.

"What are you doing here anyway, John?" Steve asked.

"Following a lead in the Scott Keenan stabbing." He was still smiling when he closed the door behind him. 'Inverness here he comes,' he muttered to himself.

## 44

Kate walked into the entrance hall at Leapark to meet John Nelson coming from the guest room. Charcoal suit, pale blue shirt, dark blue tie. He looked cheerful for a man investigating three deaths and a stabbing.

"Kate," he said smiling. "You all right?"

"I'm fine. Why shouldn't I be?"

"No reason. I take it you've heard about Betty Smyth."

"Frances Wordsworth phoned me, said it was being treated as a suspicious death."

"Not here, Kate. Can we go up to Jean's flat? She's likely to still be with Marjorie Collins."

"What's Marjorie Collins got to do with it?" She was aware she was sounding more petulant with each word but she'd seen Steve's car in the car park and had visions of him and John discussing the break-up: all boys together.

"Can we go up to Jean's flat?" John said.

In the flat Kate went into the kitchen and filled the kettle. John followed her and sat at the small kitchen table turning his chair round to face her, fingers drumming on the table.

"Coffee?" she asked him.

"Wouldn't mind."

Kate looked at the kettle then reached for the percolator, feeling the need for something to fiddle about with. "So what did happen?"

"Betty Smyth has been found dead. Looks like anaphylactic shock possibly brought on by an adverse drug reaction. Steve's investigating that. I'm investigating the Scott Keenan stabbing." He stopped until Kate turned to look at him. "I take it you know about that."

She nodded. "Frances also left me a message saying that Jean had been involved in some kind of bust-up with Steve."

"It didn't happen quite like that."

"So what did happen?"

"Jean was waiting in the entrance hall with Marjorie Collins. They were going to church."

"Church?" The percolator began to gurgle. She watched for its red light to come on indicating the coffee was ready.

"Betty Smyth didn't come down. Wordsworth went up to check on her."

Kate unplugged the percolator and put it on the table. She placed a mug in front of John and set another out for herself. "What was the bust-up with Steve about?" She began pouring the coffee.

John turned to face her. "Steve said something to Jean and Marjorie lost the plot." He smiled.

"What's funny about that?"

"I'm tempted to say 'you had to be there' but I don't want to be wearing that percolator. Marjorie charged into Steve and Heather. She knocked Heather over, spun round, punched Steve in the face and ended up lying across the coffee table."

"Marjorie Collins?" Kate could feel a giggle rising in her throat. John was still smiling at her. She could see he wanted her to see the funny side, to lighten up for Christ's sake but she couldn't get rid of the image of him and Steve discussing what a bitch she was and was annoyed that that should matter so much. She shook her head.

"Why did she do that?"

John shrugged. "Steve said something that upset her." He turned his attention to the coffee.

"Why is Betty Smyth's death suspicious?"

"She's allergic to penicillin. If that's what brought on the anaphylactic shock it's likely someone gave her the penicillin telling her it was something else. We'll know for sure after the post-mortem."

"So Jean wasn't involved in finding the body, that was just Frances?"

"Kate, I don't know why Steve decided he needed to talk to Jean, okay? He's not been in the best of moods this morning."

"That's not my fault."

"I'm not saying it is." He finished his coffee. "Are you planning on seeing Jean?"

"That's why I'm here," she said amazed at the speed he could eat and drink at times.

"I need to have a word with Marjorie Collins at some point. Would you or Jean let me know when would be a good time?"

"You don't think Marjorie Collins had anything to do with Scott Keenan being stabbed?"

He smiled. "I'd say that's unlikely. I want to talk to her about what happened this morning with Steve. Try to calm things down a bit."

"Stop her from complaining you mean?"

"That as well. Steve could do without that right now."

"What do you mean by that?"

He shook his head. "Christ, I should get a job with the U.N. I mean I wouldn't want Marjorie to scupper Steve's promotion and she might do that if she complains about his behaviour."

"Oh." She shrugged. "Do you want to come down now to see her?" She stood up leaving her coffee untouched.

"Why not?"

Jean answered Kate's knock on Marjorie Collins' door. "Come in. Marjorie's lying down just now."

"I'll leave you to it. Speak to her later." John walked away.

"Why does John Nelson want to speak to Marjorie?"

"He wants to persuade her not to complain about Steve." She touched Jean's arm. "What happened this morning?"

Jean gave a brief, straight-faced description.

"So why did Marjorie hit Steve?"

"She didn't mean to hit him, Kate," Jean said defensively. "She got upset with what he said. I felt really sorry for her." She paused. "She's taken Betty's death very hard."

"How did you come to be looking after her?"

"She asked me. That's not like Marjorie." Jean sounded almost proud.

"Does she not have any family?"

"Not to speak of."

"What does that mean?"

Jean shrugged. "Anyway it's me she asked." She smiled. "When Marjorie wakes up I'll speak to her about what happened with Steve."

Kate noted the expectant look Jean gave her thinking she was doing Kate a favour by getting Steve out of trouble.

"So you're all right?"

"I'm fine, Kate."

"You're not frightened?"

"That somebody's going to murder me?"

Kate nodded.

"This is all to do with Maggie Keenan and what she knew. I'm quite safe." She took Kate's hands in hers. "You don't have to worry about me. If you've got things to be getting on with you go ahead. I'll be here with Marjorie for a while yet."

"Right. Well, I'll give you a ring later?"

"If I don't answer you'll know I'm still down here." Jean smiled.

Kate smiled back as best she could and left, feeling dismissed. She walked through the entrance hall, thought briefly about knocking on the guest room door to see if John was there, decided not to in case Steve was.

In the car park she sat in her car pondering what to do next. She needed to be active, to stop the merry-go-round starting up again. She pulled out her phone. Five minutes later she set off for Morningside and Jules' flat.

## 45

Kirsten Cormack walked into the guest room and sat at the table. John Nelson faced her with Gordon

Donald alongside. Her clothes looked like she'd slept in them.

"I want to say something," she said.

"Carry on, Ms Cormack."

"I don't know what you've been told but I didn't kill Betty Smyth." She looked at the two policemen in turn as she said this. Their faces remained blank. "I admit I was angry with her. She upset Ellen. I'd had a bit to drink after the funeral yesterday and, well, I said things I shouldn't have but that's all. I didn't kill her." She sat back.

"How did she upset Ellen Post?" John Nelson asked.

"Ellen wanted some time on her own in her mum's flat but Betty went along there. It's sick. It's all because Ellen's gay. Anyway Ellen was in tears when I saw her because of what Betty had said to her. It made me angry. So I told Betty off." She shrugged. "But she was fine when I left her. She gave as good as she got, that one."

"You had an argument with Betty Smyth on Saturday afternoon?" John looked to Kirsten for confirmation.

She nodded tugging at the collar of her not-so-white blouse.

"What time was this?"

"Um, it would have been about half-past three."

"How well do you know Ellen Post?" Gordon asked.

"We were at school together for a while."

"And you didn't think to tell us that when Harriet Post was found dead?"

"I didn't know Harriet Post other than in here. Ellen wasn't a close friend at school. We were just in the same class for a while."

"Where were you last night between midnight and two a.m.?" John Nelson asked.

"I was in bed asleep with my boyfriend. I told you, I'd drunk a bit too much on Saturday. That's why I was late this morning." She paused, rubbing her forehead as if it was as close as she could get to massaging her brain. "Is that when she died?"

"Tell us about your relationship with Scott Keenan."

Kirsten frowned. "I haven't got a relationship with Scott Keenan."

"He certainly seems to like dropping you in it," Gordon contributed.

"You can't still think I murdered Maggie Keenan."

"You mentioned your boyfriend," John said. "That would be Billy Morris?"

"Aye," Kirsten said hesitantly. She shifted her position, trying to avoid the attentions of a rogue shaft of sunlight that was slanting in through the side window.

"The same Billy Morris who used to live in Waverley Tower, two floors below the Keenans?" John waited for the nod of confirmation. "Why didn't you tell us this before? And don't say it's because we didn't ask."

"Well you didn't. Anyway Billy lives with me now. He doesn't have anything to do with Scott Keenan."

"But he did have."

"That was over a year ago, before I met him." She rubbed her forehead again. "Can I have a drink of water?"

"Do you own your flat in Gorgie?" John asked.

"I've got a mortgage."

"A mortgage? They're not that easy to come by these days. Did well there."

"I work for my money."

"What's Billy's contribution?"

The shaft of sunlight hit Kirsten full in the face. "He works in a supermarket." She held up her hand, shading her eyes.

"Not exactly well paid, is it?"

"He does overtime. Can I have a drink of water?"

John nodded to Gordon who went to the window and closed the blinds then poured water from a lidded jug into a cup and set both in front of Kirsten. She drank the water in one go and poured some more.

"And what about you, Kirsten? Where did you work before you came here?"

"I worked for an agency."

"An agency that employed staff to provide cover in nursing homes?"

"Yes."

"That would be about the time there were a number of thefts of drugs from nursing homes?"

Kirsten coughed. "I – I don't remember," she said and sipped at the water.

"Did you know Billy when you worked for this agency?"

"He wasn't involved with Scott Keenan then. I wouldn't have let him."

"And he does what you tell him?"

"I got a good reference when I left the agency. That's how I got the job here. I'll let you see it if you don't believe me. Anyway why aren't you asking Scott Keenan about this if you think he's involved. It was nothing to do with me."

John leaned forward. "Scott Keenan's in hospital. He was attacked some time between midnight and two a.m. last night. He suggested we ask you about it."

"I never went near him. I wouldn't touch him with a bargepole."

"How about a knife?"

"This is all wrong. Why are you always picking on me?"

"Because your name keeps cropping up, Kirsten. And if you find Scott Keenan so loathsome what was he doing at your flat on Friday night?"

"You're a bastard. D'you know that?"

## 46

Everywhere you turned in Edinburgh someone with a claim to fame was waiting for you. She'd driven up by Craiglockhart past the old Hydropathic, now Napier University's Business School. It had been requisitioned as a hospital during the First World War for sufferers of shell-shock. Siegfried Sassoon and Wilfred Owen were treated there, their presence commemorated in the 'War Poets' Collection', a small exhibition of writings of the soldiers who had spent time there. The psychiatrist who treated them, W.H. Rivers, had a clinic at the local mental hospital named after him. At Holy Corner with its plethora of churches was the Eric Liddell Centre. Now she waited at the lights on the crown of Morningside Road. In the distance, the Pentlands huddled under a darkening sky. J.K. Rowling used to live a few streets away. Ian Rankin still did, neighbours with Alexander McCall Smith. And then there was 'Morningside Maisie', a kilted kitten born just up the road and currently adorning the number 5 bus.

She found a parking space next to the wheelie bin, its lid billowing up in the strong wind, and went up to Jules' flat.

"Red pepper quiche all right?"

"Great, Jules," Kate said. "You didn't have to do this."

"You sounded a bit down. And I would be having lunch anyway." Jules cut the large quiche into four triangles and slid one onto Kate's plate. She'd bought her flat in her last year at university with the help of her parents. Kate shared it until she bought her own flat. The kitchen had a similar layout to Kate's own but with the addition of a scullery that Jules used as a laundry room. The terracotta walls gave it a countrified feel, mirroring the kitchen at the family home in Oxford, only the Aga was missing.

"You're not seeing Ken today?"

"Tonight. So we've got plenty of time to talk. Help yourself to the salad and coleslaw."

"I don't know where to start." Kate scooped rocket lettuce and baby cherry tomatoes onto her plate and added a spoonful of coleslaw.

"You and Steve haven't got back together?" There was a note of dismay in Jules' voice.

"We went out for a meal last night." She gave a resume of the conversation.

"He proposed?"

"More or less."

"I take it you turned him down."

"After I picked myself up off the floor." She shook her head. "I still don't understand where it came from." She turned her attention to the food, cutting a piece of the quiche. "This is lovely." She knew Jules would see through it as the delaying tactic it was though the food was truly delicious, the sweet tang of the pepper livening the soft, moist egg. "I went back to his flat after we left the restaurant. Stayed the night."

"Oh, Kate." There was more than a hint of irritation in Jules' comment. She shook her head. "Just a wee touch of a mixed message there." The Scottish phraseology still sounded strange with the English accent. It was something they'd laughed about in the early days of their friendship especially when Jules inadvertently mimicked Kate's west of Scotland twang.

"I felt sorry for him. He was so excited about this promotion and he was talking like I was the love of his life." She paused to spear another cherry tomato with her fork. "These are bliss," she said then looked at Jules. "I'd drunk too much wine and, in his flat, it was the good old times, the pressure he was under, and one thing led to another."

"Same old, same old. And you fall for it every time."

"The sex was awful. I just wanted it to be over. You know that way? But he thought he was getting it right and that it changed everything. So you can imagine what Sunday morning was like."

"It's done now and nobody's died. Don't beat yourself up."

"Somebody has died, actually.

"What? Who?"

"Not Steve, someone at Leapark."

"Another murder?"

"It looks that way."

Kate told her the whole story, finishing with Marjorie Collins punching Steve. Jules sat open-mouthed then burst out laughing. Kate joined in until both were in tears.

"Did you see John Nelson?" Jules asked when they'd recovered.

"Briefly." She loaded her fork again. "You need to tell me how you make this quiche."

Jules smiled. "We were talking about John."

"He seemed more concerned about Steve missing out on promotion if Marjorie Collins complained."

"Kate, Steve's promotion takes him to Inverness, yes?"

She nodded.

"Work it out." Jules sent her a meaningful look.

"You think John wants Steve completely out of the picture? That presupposes he wants me in it. And I don't know if I want to be." She hesitated. "There's something else."

"You are putting yourself through the mill."

"You remember the cards I used to get from my father?"

Jules nodded.

"They weren't, from my father I mean. My gran wrote them." She was horrified to hear the hint of a sob edging into her voice.

Jules reached across the table to stroke Kate's hand. "How do you know?"

Kate told her. "I always wondered why the cards stopped when they did but I didn't make the connection with my gran dying."

They sat looking at one another. "Look, I can call Ken, put him off."

"Don't do that. I just needed to tell somebody who'd understand what it meant. I need time on my own to take it in. Decide what I'll do next."

"What do you mean?"

"I don't know how much more I want to find out about all this. Maybe you were right. Settle for what

I know I had." She paused. "Let the past lie," she gazed at her empty plate with its smears of mayonnaise and tomato juices, aware of echoing her father's warning to Jean.

"I know what you need," Jules said. She got up and went to a wall cupboard. "Coffee and," she turned to Kate, "chocolate". She held up the bar, smiling.

Kate gathered up their plates and carried them to the dishwasher. "Ooh," she said, "This isn't any old chocolate," they duetted in their best seductive tones, "This is Chocolate Tree Winter Spice blend."

The rest of the afternoon was spent on Jules' sofa in the sitting room eating chocolate and watching two of their favourite films, tissues at hand: 'Casablanca' with its re-united wartime lovers and old-fashioned nobility, followed by the restrained desire of 'Brief Encounter'.

"Brilliant," they sniffed in unison as Rachmaninov's Second Piano Concerto brought it all to an end.

From the hallway, Jules' grandmother clock chimed six times.

"I'll get off," Kate said as she stood. "Let you get ready for Ken and a night of passion."

Jules laughed. "A night's pushing it a bit. More like half an hour these days."

"Thanks, Jules." They hugged, holding onto each other, feeling the depth of their friendship and how much it meant to each of them.

## 47

The roads were quiet, only a couple of cars behind her as she drove back into the city. After she left Jules she'd headed west, driving down to the Calder Road and out to Ratho, another Edinburgh village, before turning round and heading home. She'd almost bought a house in Ratho: a three-bed semi. She'd been about to put in a bid when the Comely Bank flat came onto the market and she'd gone for that instead. It was partly because she wanted to live in the city proper, and partly because of the proximity to Inverleith Park and the Botanic Gardens; but mainly because she fell in love with the flat with its bay-windowed sitting room and large kitchen. It had needed a bit of work so the asking price was lower than it might have been but it was still a stretch for her financially. The deposit her mum's insurance money allowed her had made the mortgage affordable.

She squeezed her car into a space in Comely Bank Grove and strolled along Learmonth Gardens to her avenue, crunching and squelching through the leaves crowding the pavement, taking time to breathe in the scents from the still damp grass. The air felt cold and fresh; the only sound was the occasional breeze rustling through the leaves of the hedge that bordered the gardens. She was still puzzling over Steve's quasi-proposal. She'd thought their relationship had run its course. He'd become more controlling. She was having none of it. Things came to a head over the holiday. He'd booked it without telling her, a surprise, he'd said, furious when she refused to go. Later she discovered what was behind it. John had been selected over Steve to attend an anti-terrorist course in London. She'd met him a few days earlier outside the National Museum of Scotland. They didn't talk for long because Michael kept tugging at John's hand, saying, 'we going now, Dad?', eager to get to the museum, resenting Kate's intrusion on their day, wanting his dad to himself. She wondered now if a proposal was to have been part of the holiday. Steve's way of getting one over on John.

At her close, a brightly-lit pumpkin grinned at her from a ground floor window: the Americanisation of Halloween. When she was little, her gran would help her dress up to go out on 'galoshuns' as it was called. Now it was 'trick or treat' as if it was some new idea. The stair door was unlocked. A new neighbour had taken to going out without his key and leaving the door on the latch. He'd already found himself locked out a number of times and tonight, Kate decided, would be no different. Muttering self-righteously, she set the yale lock back on and closed the door, remembering an outfit from when she was about eight – poncho, chocolate cigar, low-slung gunbelt, only the mule was missing. She smiled as she turned towards the sound of footsteps.

Before she could react a hand clamped her mouth, an arm was wrapped round her waist and she was being hauled along the narrow corridor towards the stairs down to the back door. Her boots scrabbled uselessly on the stone floor. She grappled with her attacker to stop him shutting off her breathing. He slowed. Must be at the stairs. She felt him turn his head, his foot searching for the top step, still holding her tight against him. She had to stop him now. She pulled at the hand over her mouth. He started dragging her down the stairs. She grabbed his thumb and bent it back.

"Fucking bitch," he hissed. His fingers caught the flesh at her side and squeezed.

Her roar of pain was muffled by the hand over her mouth. She pulled harder at his thumb. Felt something give. His turn to roar.

He tried to lift her. She twisted and kicked off the wall, toppling them backwards onto the stone floor. She landed on top, rolled free and made for the stairs. Halfway up, she felt him catch her ankle pulling her back to him. She grabbed the stair railings and kicked at him with her free leg.

"What's going on down there?" a voice called out.

Her body was strung tight as a bowstring, hands clinging to the railings, ankle held tightly by her assailant. Her arms and shoulders screamed with the strain. But he had to maintain the tension. If he released it she'd be able to get her feet under her and run or fight.

"Help," she yelled. "Fire!"

There was a pounding on the stair door. The man let go of her ankle and ran up the stairs past her. She scrambled after him. The door flew open.

"Who locked the bloody door?" her new neighbour snarled.

"Call the police," Kate panted.

Eddie Ranford lay against the wall, blood streaming from his nose.

## 48

"You're not going to shout at me again?" Kate tried a smile as she said this.

"When did I shout at you?" John Nelson asked her.

"On Friday night, when you were telling me off for seeing Fraser Keenan."

"I don't think I shouted at you."

"It felt like shouting." They were standing in her hall, Kate trying to seem normal when she felt nothing like it.

"Come on." John led her to the sofa in the sitting room and sat her down. He turned on the gas fire then sat next to her. She'd given a statement about Eddie Ranford's attack on her. As had her new neighbour. John Nelson had turned up about ten minutes later. She knew he was reluctant to leave her on her own.

"You said you were coming to see me anyway. What about?" she asked him.

"To tell you that Betty Smyth's death looks like murder."

"So it was penicillin?"

He nodded. "Question is how she came to take it. It wouldn't have been prescribed for her. Her allergy to it was well documented. Most likely scenario is someone gave it to her without telling her what it was."

"Someone in Leapark?"

"We don't know yet, but it's not exactly scarce in there."

"What about Scott Keenan? Do you know who stabbed him?"

"We're still investigating."

"Right." She felt weird, disassociated, as if she was not wholly part of what was going on around her. She knew she wasn't reacting the way John expected.

"Is there anything I can do?" he said.

She looked at him. His lovely brown eyes were serious. She could see the small scar below his left eye, where, twelve years old and teased beyond endurance, he'd tried to cut his eyelashes. She wanted to kiss it better. Instead she went into the kitchen and returned with the letters and cards from her gran and her father and laid them out in front of him on the coffee table.

"Would you look at these for me and tell me which look to be written by the same person?"

He leaned forward, elbows on his knees, fingers spreading the papers on the table. He studied each in turn then separated her father's card to Jean from the rest.

"That's what I thought."

"Is that a problem?"

"It means that after my father left I never heard from him again. My grandmother wrote Christmas and birthday cards for me and pretended they were from my father."

"And you've just realised that?"

"Jean gave me some stuff. It's the first time I've had anything to compare with."

"When did your father leave?"

She hesitated. "Shortly after my mother killed herself."

"I thought your mother died in a drowning accident."

Kate stared at Lucy on her cushion at the fire working her way through a full body wash. "So did I. Until Jean told me otherwise."

"When did she tell you?"

"Three months ago." She could see him thinking back. "Just before Steve and I broke up," she confirmed for him.

"What did Steve say when you told him?"

"I didn't. Tell him, I mean."

"Why not?"

She shook her head. It was all starting to catch up with her. Her chest felt as if it would burst with the great ball of hurt and bewilderment it was trying to contain. But she was determined not to break down in front of him. She knew if she did he'd want to comfort her and she couldn't withstand that. She wanted nothing more than for him to put his arms around her and hold her close, her head against his chest, his hand stroking her hair. But she couldn't give in to it. And that left him feeling helpless. She could see that; could see him searching for something to offer that might make her feel better.

"Do you want me to get these checked out? Just to be sure." He tapped the cards and letters as he said this.

"By a handwriting expert you mean?"

He nodded.

"If you like."

"Can I ask you something?"

"Go on."

"How did Jean know that your mother committed suicide?"

"My father told her."

"Was there a note?"

"I don't know. Jean says she didn't see one. I think she and my father might have had an argument." But another thought had begun to formulate: one that she didn't want to entertain.

"I take it your father didn't say any of this to the police."

"I suppose he wouldn't want anyone to know my mother killed herself. It was easier if everybody believed it was an accident. If people knew she'd killed herself they'd want to know why wouldn't they?" She pondered on the implications of this as she watched Lucy again washing over, tummy full, curl up on her cushion: a warm, sleepy, contented night ahead.

"And you want to know why?"

She shrugged. A tear trickled down her face and she wiped it away with her hand.

John took a notebook from his inside jacket pocket. "What's your father's first name?"

"Alan, with one L."

"What about your mother?"

"Catherine, with a C. Her maiden name was Shaw."

"And she drowned when?"

"12ᵗʰ of November, 1987."

"In Greenock?"

"Port Glasgow. We lived in Port Glasgow then. It's just next to Greenock. I only moved there when I went to live with my grandmother." She watched him making a note of all this as if it was a proper police investigation.

"I know someone who works out of Greenock. I'll give him a ring to start with." He returned the notebook to his pocket and added the cards and one of the letters.

"Thanks."

"Anything else?"

She shook her head then said, "Could you ask your Greenock friend about the skeleton they found on the building site?"

"Do you think it might be someone you know?"

"I'm not sure what I think."

"I'll see what I can find out." He looked at his watch. "I have to go, Kate. Will you be all right?"

She stood up. "I'll be fine, John."

At the front door he turned to her and started to raise his arm as if to touch her then let it fall to his side. "Call me anytime, okay?"

She nodded and then he was gone. She leaned back against the door and closed her eyes, knowing he was standing on the other side. She almost heard him release his breath. Then she did hear him go down the stairs, slowly at first then faster, his footsteps echoing back to her until she heard the stair door close. She went into the sitting room and walked to the window. Her reflection stared back at her. She turned away and sat on the sofa. She gathered up the cards and letters from the coffee table. John had taken the only card written by her father. 'Let the past lie' it had said.

No, she would not let the past lie; not for a father who had buggered off and left her; nor even for a mother whose misery came before her child. She had to know.

# Monday

## 49

'Serial Killer Stalks Elderly'. The newspaper lay at the reception window like an accusation. The office was empty, the building quiet, though Betty Smyth's death had resurrected the media presence at the front door. Kate quickly glanced through the report noting how Maggie Keenan had been transformed by her murder from a blackmailing loan shark into a poor old pensioner and there was still that hint of more to come. So Betty wasn't the only source. She put the paper back where she'd found it and headed for Jean's flat.

She'd spent the morning putting together her report on the implementation of the records system. Installation was complete. The pilots had been successful. Security of the information had been rigorously tested. The tablets and palmtops which would allow access for workers on the move were waiting to be distributed. The mobile office was on its way. Social Work in Edinburgh, such as it was, was finally going hi-tech. And the I.T. company had increased its offer to entice her to join them. Oddly, the new offer was having the opposite effect of the one intended, welcome though the money would be. She kept remembering what she'd said to Steve about having a job she loved. The job she was referring to was not going round the country in her swish company car persuading other local authorities to buy this super-duper computer system. The job she loved was the one where she trawled the back-end of Edinburgh to persuade runaway kids that life had more to offer if they could just hang in there; where she spent sleepless nights worrying that trying to keep a family together was really the best option for the child; where she got the Natasha Farrells out of abusive homes to places of safety and, hopefully, the right kind of love.

"How's Marjorie?" she asked, following Jean into the sitting room.

"Much better," Jean said as she headed into the kitchen. "Do you want some coffee?" She reappeared at the door with a mug in her hand.

"Have I interrupted your lunch?"

"I was just reading the paper." Jean sat on the settee, nursing the steaming mug in her lap. "And Marjorie's not going to make a complaint. She thought giving Steve a black eye was enough. We had such a laugh about it this morning." Jean giggled then became serious. "Of course she's still upset about Betty's death."

Kate perched on the arm of a chair. "Have you seen Marjorie this morning?"

"I stayed the night in her flat. Slept on the settee."

She hesitated. Jean's brightness seemed more front than substance but even so Kate was reluctant to dent it. "I need to ask you something."

"What is it?"

"I found a Christmas card from my father in that shoebox you gave me."

Jean's face tightened.

"It said 'We're even. Let the past lie'. What did he mean? Was it to do with my mum?"

Jean sipped her coffee. "It was probably after one of our arguments. We were always arguing, that's why I didn't visit much."

"So you don't remember?"

Jean put her mug on the coffee table looking thoughtful. "It might have been just before your mum's funeral. I was saying how awful it was her drowning like that and how long had she been having these dizzy spells."

"Dizzy spells?"

"Your dad had told me that your mum had dizzy spells and that was how she fell into the water. They were caused by the tablets she took for the migraines."

"What was there to argue about in that?"

"Your dad just lost his temper with me, told me to shut the eff up about effing dizzy spells, only he said the actual f-words." Jean took a deep breath. "It was after that he told me your mum committed suicide. 'Let the past lie' was his way of telling me not to say anything." Jean looked up apologetically. "That was why I never told you, Kate. I was always a bit frightened of your dad."

"Why? You were older than him."

Jean fiddled with the cuff of her navy cardigan. "After I came back from America your dad was very cold to me. He said some things that really hurt me."

She could see the strain the memories were inflicting but needed to persevere just a bit longer. "I found something else I want to ask you about." She dug in her bag.

Jean sighed. "Go on, then."

"If this is too much bother for you just say so." She regretted the sharpness in her tone knowing it was likely to make Jean less forthcoming.

"It's not that. I want to put things behind me not dredge them up."

Like your son. The thought was in her head before she could stop it. When had she become so judgemental? She moved from the arm of the chair to sit on it properly and held out the wedding photo. "This was in the shoebox." She tried for a more conciliatory note.

Jean's face softened as she took the photo from Kate. "Your mum and dad were married in the registry office. I kept it with the card. They were the only things I had from your dad."

Jean's gaze remained focussed on the photo in her lap leaving Kate to talk to the top of her head. "Do you know who the other man and woman are?"

"I don't." Jean handed the photo back. "I wasn't at your dad's wedding. I couldn't get the time off work. That was another argument." She shook her head. "If I knew any more, I would tell you, Kate, but your dad and me just weren't close. There was a lot I didn't know about him."

"Okay." She tucked the photo away and stood up.

"Are you going?" Jean looked as if she didn't know whether to be disappointed or relieved.

"I've got a lot on today."

"Um…"

"What?"

"It's about Saturday." A tissue appeared from her pocket. "I was going for a walk and I heard somebody going into Betty Smyth's flat. It was just after you left." She hesitated. "I'm wondering if I should tell the police."

"Who was it?"

"I don't know."

"Not much point then."

Jean looked unconvinced.

"If you contact the police and have nothing much to tell them you're going to make them suspicious. And you don't want Mair crawling all over you again, do you?" She walked to the door. "I'll give you a ring later." As she left, she had the feeling that she'd said exactly what Jean had wanted to hear.

In the entrance hall Frances was ensconced in the reception office. The newspaper was nowhere to be seen. Kate got a weak smile as she passed. Outside, the police were doing a better job of keeping the media at bay and she walked round to the car park unmolested. She was getting into her car when her mobile rang.

"Are you still in Corstorphine?" Nick asked her.

"I'm just leaving Leapark."

"If you want to find out about Jessie Turner your best bet is the Corstorphine office. Her social worker's based there. Name's Mary Lappin."

"Thanks, Nick."

The attack by Eddie Ranford had been enough for Nick to tell her to take whatever time she needed. Betty Smyth's death was icing on the cake. Kate had taken advantage of Nick's uncharacteristic bout of sympathy to ask him about Jessie Turner and the allegations about Maggie Keenan. He'd promised to find out what he could. That was after he'd goaded her about why she couldn't find out herself on 'her' new system. 'Not an appropriate use' she'd said self-righteously, both of them knowing it was more to do with leaving a trail of her search behind. There was a limit to how much could be justified by a claim of 'testing the interconnectedness of the data'. Anyway, sometimes the human element was more useful. Personal impressions were more informative than bare facts.

She phoned Corstorphine only to be told that Mary Lappin didn't work on Mondays. She sat for a moment debating her next move. She found herself wiping her mouth, shaking off images from the night before. Her shoulders still ached from clinging to the railings. She made another phone call then set off for the Forth Road Bridge.

## 50

Greenlawns was a purpose-built complex on the outskirts of Dunfermline. It was a combination of redbrick sheltered flats and terraced bungalows alongside a forty-bed nursing home. CCTV cameras followed Kate's progress as she drove through the entrance gate and parked her car.

The three-storey block of flats squatted in front of a semi-circle formed by the bungalows and the brick wall that surrounded them. The ubiquitous cameras kept a wary eye out for unwanted visitors. Railings high enough to deter casual climbers sprouted at either side of the flats and extended to the boundary wall. Beyond the wall to her right the upper floors of the nursing home were visible. 'A continuum of care' was how it was described in the brochure she'd picked up in the reception hall that served the complex and acted as its only access.

She signed in and was directed to Nellie Pearce's 'cottage bungalow' by the young blonde receptionist but only after Nellie Pearce had confirmed by videophone that she was expecting a visitor. 'Safety and security are paramount' was another of the brochure's mantras.

Nellie Pearce materialised at the door of her bungalow as Kate made her way along the path. Shorter than Kate, with a trim figure and grey curls, she was dressed in a pink Fair Isle twinset and a neat grey skirt. The blue eyes were sharp above the appraising smile.

"Sorry I'm late."

Nellie Pearce nodded an acknowledgment of the apology and ushered her into a small sitting room off a hall the size of a police box. A two-seater cottage style settee sat in the middle of the room sharing a coffee table with a reclining chair. Opposite the chair was a television. An electric fire gave the effect of warmth, the real thing coming from a radiator under the window.

Nellie Pearce looked her up and down. "I'll take your coat." She held out her hand. Kate slipped off her navy coat and handed it over. "Sit down. I'll get the tea."

Kate did as she was told, settling on the settee. The sitting room was at the back of the bungalow with a view out to a patch of neatly fenced lawn. The small kitchen was off the sitting room to the front. She wondered if Nellie Pearce had done a special clean in preparation for her visitor or if the room was always pristine. She'd bet on the latter and was pleased she'd chosen to wear her Marks' grey pinstripe suit. She couldn't see jeans and trainers meeting with approval. A tinkling sound heralded the arrival of the tea, courtesy of a tea-trolley which Nellie Pearce was now wheeling to the coffee table.

"Here we are," she announced. She sat in her recliner chair and began a careful unloading of the trolley. A delicate, pink-flowered side plate was set on the table followed by a matching china cup and saucer. A pink napkin in a ring was placed next to them. The piece de resistance was the cake stand, complete with doilies, produced from the bottom shelf of the trolley. It was dotted about with a variety of multi-coloured cakes and biscuits. Kate could feel her teeth start to rot just looking at them.

Nellie Pearce poured the tea and sat looking expectantly at her.

"This is lovely, Mrs Pearce."

Nellie Pearce nodded and settled back in her chair. "You said it was Fraser who referred you to me." There was an attempt at refinement in the accent. It sounded well-rehearsed and not the one she was brought up with.

"He said you could tell me about Maggie."

"Fraser was a lovely boy, very polite, but if he knew what I could tell you he wouldn't have sent you to me."

"You know something about Maggie that Fraser doesn't know?" Kate reached for a fairy cake.

"The story Fraser wants me to tell you is about Maggie stopping a wee boy called Adam McNaughton from being abducted," Nellie Pearce began in her precise tones. "He was waiting at the school gates when a car pulled up and a man tried to drag him into it. Maggie grabbed Adam so there was a sort of tug of war between Maggie and this man, with the wee boy in the middle. Then some of the other mothers and I ran over and the man let go." Nellie Pearce sipped her tea. "So far so good, you might think. However, it turned out that the man was working for someone who had fallen out with Adam's father, Mark. To all intents and purposes it was a sort of gang war. Maggie let people think she'd saved Adam from a pervert but it wasn't like that at all." She settled a piece of shortbread on her plate and sat back.

"Does Fraser know all this?"

"He certainly knows about Adam McNaughtan because the pair of them owns this place. Some of the properties are rented out to good Council tenants and I got one of them. I think Fraser put in a word for me."

"I see," Kate said. Was the similarity to the arrangements that operated at Leapark coincidental? A.F. Holdings: could that be Adam and Fraser? It would certainly explain Maggie Keenan's two-bedroom garden flat. She became aware of Nellie Pearce frowning at her and re-focussed her attention.

"When you get too frail for here," Nellie Pearce continued, "you can move into the nursing home next door, as long as the beds aren't all filled with people from Edinburgh. Because I'm in this house I get priority. And they've got permission to build another nursing home next to that one."

Kate nodded, thinking about the £1 million plus sitting in some of the Leapark residents' bank accounts. Did they get the same priority as Nellie Pearce because they're in Leapark? "What's the story that Fraser doesn't know about?"

"Maggie and I used to live on the same estate. We brought our families up there. None of us had much money. I'd just been widowed, you see." Nellie Pearce paused to have a sip of tea. "We were all hard-working people, mind you, but a lot of the men had lost their jobs, and some of the stuff people had, especially their T.V.s and videos, came from Maggie." A pointed look was directed at Kate.

"Maggie sold on stolen goods?"

"And loaned people money to buy them, sometimes taking their benefit books as security. All illegal of course but nobody complained." Nellie Pearce nibbled on her shortbread. "Then a thirteen-year-old girl disappeared.

A rumour started that she'd run away because she was being interfered with by the insurance man."

"The insurance man?"

"He went round the houses collecting the insurance premiums." A pause.

"What did you think, Mrs Pearce?"

"Well, my daughter saw Scott Keenan with the girl before she ran away. Scott would have been about sixteen. Shortly after the girl went, Scott had a black eye." That pointed look again. "A few days later the girl was back."

"You think Scott had something to do with the girl's disappearance?"

Nellie Pearce's expression bordered on disappointment.

Kate added two and two and hoped for four. "Scott got her pregnant?"

An impatient nod.

"And Maggie gave him the black eye?"

A look of encouragement this time.

C'mon, Kate. The girl went away... "And arranged an abortion for the girl?"

Nellie Pearce sat back, cup and saucer in hand. "All surmise, of course, but it doesn't take a great imagination to work it out."

Suitably chastened, Kate wondered at the extent of Maggie Keenan's powers of persuasion, and the enemies it would have made her.

"Why would Maggie say it was the insurance man?"

"He was an easy target. He owned his own house in a nice area; he was always well dressed; and he was a widower. There was just him and his daughter, Sadie. She'd have been about twelve at the time." Nellie Pearce took time out to sip her tea and finish off her shortbread, dabbing at her mouth with the napkin which was then carefully rolled and tucked into its ring.

Kate hoped she wasn't in for another round of guess what happened next.

"The man had recently become an agent for the Provident." Nellie Pearce paused. "They were a loan company." Another pointed look.

"Maggie didn't want the competition." Go to the top of the class, Kate. "What did the girl who'd run away have to say?"

"Nothing. Nor did her mother."

Kate waited. Nellie Pearce liked her pauses.

"Shortly after all this they moved to a house on a new estate."

"Could Maggie have arranged that?"

"Mark McNaughtan could." A note of angry disapproval crept into Nellie Pearce's voice pushing her accent closer to its roots. "And Maggie was well in there."

So, Maggie and Mark McNaughtan and now Fraser and Adam McNaughtan. Was this another family tradition? And where did it leave Scott? "You're very well-informed, Mrs Pearce." Kate gave a placatory smile but Nellie Pearce was too caught up in her own narrative, bursting to tell more if Kate could find the trigger. "What happened to the insurance man?" she asked.

"He had to move away. Maggie Keenan made his life a misery. He lost everything, even his daughter. She went to live with her auntie." Nellie Pearce put her cup and saucer on the table and reached down beside her chair. "I've got a photo of them in here." She opened the album at a marked page and held it out to Kate. "That's me and my daughter with them." She switched on a standard lamp next to her chair before picking up her cup and saucer again. There'd been a hint of pride in her voice.

The photo showed a tall, thin man flanked by two grinning girls, his arms round their shoulders. A much younger Nellie Pearce stood smiling on the man's right, behind her daughter. A large, dour-looking woman stood off to the man's left.

"Your daughter's very like you. Who's the other woman?"

"That's the sister-in-law."

"Were there any more allegations after the man moved away?" Kate closed the album and laid it carefully on the coffee table.

"None." Nellie Pearce's cup rattled into its saucer as it landed on the table next to the album. She looked at Kate. "That man's life was ruined to save Scott Keenan. If there's a more useless waste of God's good earth I've yet to meet it."

Kate chewed on a pink fondant fancy, giving Nellie Pearce time to calm down, wondering if the insurance man had collected more than his premiums when he visited. "What about their father, where was he when all this was going on?"

Nellie Pearce sighed. "I never knew Scott's father. Jacky was Fraser's father. He died when Scott was thirteen and Fraser was five but he'd always left it up to Maggie to keep Scott in line."

"How did Scott and Fraser get on?"

"Fraser could get on with anybody but Scott used to hit him when he thought nobody was looking. Maggie caught him a few times and leathered him for it but it didn't stop him." Nellie Pearce topped up their cups, in full flow now. "Maggie always thought she could control

Scott and he was frightened of her right enough but he was sleekit."

"Was Tracy Spencer around at that time?"

"Now that was a good deed but it was Fraser got Maggie to do it."

"What do you mean?"

"Tracy's mother was a drug addict. So the granny looked after Tracy, if you could call it that 'cause she liked her drink but Tracy was fed and sent to school. Some of the bigger girls used to call her names. Till Fraser started walking home with her. He was only a wee boy at the time but he was Maggie Keenan's wee boy and a pal of Adam McNaughtan. Any time Tracy couldn't get into her granny's house Fraser took her to Maggie's. After a while she moved in permanently."

"Did her granny not mind?"

"The granny was glad to see the back of her."

"And Maggie didn't get anything out of it?"

"Not that I could see. Well, apart from the Child Benefit."

It was Kate's turn to pause. "Did you ever hear from the insurance man again?"

Nellie Pearce shook her head. "He could be dead for all I know, hen."

## 51

"What are you doing here?"

That's what Marjorie had really said, with the emphasis on the 'you', when she'd found Jean in her flat that morning. Jean had tried to explain about the doctor and his concern that Marjorie not be left on her own but Marjorie would have none of it. Even accused Jean of prying, looking in drawers and cupboards whilst

Marjorie slept. Or rather snored. Of course she was probably embarrassed about what had happened on Sunday. If John Nelson hadn't arrived when he did, Marjorie might still be lying there. It would have needed a crane to lift her. That was the real reason she decided not to complain about Steve. She'd have had to tell how she whacked him with her walking stick and punched him in the face before ending up lying across the coffee table with her backside in the air. Oh, and John Nelson turning on the charm might have had something to do with it.

And Marjorie wasn't her only misjudgement. She should have checked that bloody shoebox before she gave it to Kate. She'd thought it was just stuff from her mother and some cards from Kate that were in it, that she'd taken everything from her brother out. 'Let the past lie.' Jean shook her head. She hoped she didn't show the fright she felt when Kate said that. Their relationship was fraught enough as it was without any more revelations. Jean went into her kitchen. The doorbell rang as she switched the kettle on. She tiptoed into the hall and looked through the peephole. He was standing with his hands behind his back, head up, readily identifiable. She checked herself in the mirror, patting her hair and wishing she'd worn something more colourful than her grey and navy. Too late now. She sighed and opened the door.

"Sam. Come in." She turned away and led him to the sitting room not wanting him to know how pleased she was to see him. "Would you like a cup of coffee? I was just about to make some."

"That would be very nice, Jean. If it's not too much trouble."

Jean made the coffee in her percolator and set out her blue Spode. She carried the tray into the sitting room. "Here we are."

Sam MacEwen turned from the window. He looked very smart in a pale blue shirt under a royal blue 'Pringle' jumper. "Let me take that." He took the tray from her and laid it on the coffee table.

Jean busied herself with setting out the cups and saucers and pouring the coffee to hide the incipient blush. "Help yourself to milk and sugar."

"This is lovely, Jean." He sipped the coffee and sat back in the armchair, one flannelled leg draped over the other giving a glimpse of grey wool sock. "How are you feeling? It seems to have been one thing after another since you moved in here."

"It has been a bit unsettling." She tried for a brave smile.

"I think you're to be commended, the way you've taken all this in your stride. A weaker woman would have wilted. I hope your niece appreciates how strong you've had to be."

Jean fiddled with her cup. "You know how young people are. Not that I'm criticising her, but she has her own life to lead." She smiled again, aiming for magnanimity this time.

"You remember that little investment opportunity I was telling you about on Saturday?"

Jean nodded.

"I've had some more information about it. If you're still interested."

"Of course I am."

He leaned forward. "I don't know if you read about that situation in West Lothian."

Jean shook her head.

"Not to worry. The deal I'm trying to put together is similar to that. There's a small piece of land, I'm not at liberty to say where at the moment, but it will be crucial to a new upmarket housing development for access purposes and I can get us in on the purchase. However, we'd have to move quickly."

Jean opened her mouth to speak but Sam held up his hands.

"I know you'll want to know a lot more detail before you can commit yourself." He looked down at his coffee. "I wondered whether we might discuss it over dinner. There's a nice little restaurant not far from here." He gazed up at her, a hint of uncertainty in his expression.

"I'd like that. And it does sound as if it might be a very good deal." She hesitated. "How much money would I have to invest?"

"Keeping it between the two of us you understand. I reckon our joint contribution would be in the region of £75,000."

Jean struggled to keep her face from showing the shock she felt, aware of Sam MacEwen studying her.

"However, I'd be putting up the lion's share, as it were. So if you were able to contribute say 20%?"

"That would be £15,000."

"Bang on, Jean. Now don't feel you have to give me an answer right away. Have a think about it. We'll talk more over dinner. What say I book us a table for seven o'clock?"

"That would be lovely, Sam."

## 52

She sat in her car in the small car park in South Queensferry looking out across the water. The river tossed restlessly, waves flashing like 'white horses', as her gran used to call them. To her left, the road bridge she'd just crossed hung from its steel cables. On her right were the rust-red girders of the much older rail bridge. Between them a small boat approached the pier ahead of the murk that was closing in from the North Sea. It triggered something that hung on the edge of her brain, like the remnant of a dream you couldn't quite get back. But then water figured in her dreams a lot these days. She took a sip of the orange juice she'd bought before leaving Dunfermline, pondering what Nellie Pearce had told her, trying to see where it fitted with what she already knew.

Lost in her reverie, she was only half aware of the car pulling in alongside her, the sound of the door opening. She jumped at a tapping on her side window. An angry-looking man motioned for her to open it. She hesitated, noting a second man sitting in the driver's seat. She tried to remember if there'd been anything on her journey that could have resulted in road rage. The man became impatient, banging the window and gesticulating fiercely. She switched on the engine and reversed fast, forcing him to step back. Her phone rang as she shifted into first. She picked it up, watching her would-be assailant getting into a black Mercedes.

"Kate, Fraser Keenan here." The voice was smooth and confident. "I hear you're in my neck of the woods. Sorry if my employees have been a bit clumsy."

"What the hell are you playing at? Have you been following me?"

There was a sigh. "My apologies again, Kate. I'd really appreciate it if you'd come to the house. My men will lead you up."

She was about to argue but decided that she wouldn't mind a look at the Keenan homestead and demurely followed the Mercedes up into the wilds of South Queensferry.

The house was a mature, two-storey, double-fronted affair sitting in a couple of acres of ground: the sort of place you could only get in Edinburgh if you had a million or two to spare. She parked her car in the wide driveway and turned, anticipating a darkening vision of the river and the lights of its twin bridges. But the trees that screened the front garden blocked not just the view from the road but also the view from the house. Disappointed, she turned back to see Fraser at the front door.

"Come into the warm, Kate."

He led her into a large square hall where a staircase with a pale wood bannister curved its way to an upper floor. A door off the hall took them into a sitting room. It had been two rooms in an earlier incarnation but now stretched the length of the house, with a bay window to the front and French windows to the garden at the back. A large, squashy, cream sofa squatted in the middle of what had been the front room facing an open fireplace where the red and yellow flames exuded a comforting warmth. The floor looked to be the original boards stripped and polished to within an inch of their life. They were partially covered by two large and authentic-looking Persian carpets, maintaining the aura of mildly ostentatious wealth. A copy of 'Hello' magazine on the chunky, wooden coffee table completed the picture.

Tracy emerged from the sofa: all lady of the manor. The pinched, haunted look had disappeared under expertly applied make-up and clothes that owed more to Harvey Nicks than Marks and Sparks. "Hello, Kate." She smiled and held out her hand.

Kate took it, not sure whether she was expected to shake it or kiss it. She opted for the former. "Tracy."

"What would you like to drink, Kate?" Fraser asked, turning to a walnut cocktail cabinet.

"Nothing thanks." She sat down carefully on the sofa, not wanting to get too comfortable.

Tracy curled herself into a matching armchair. Fraser poured his drink and stood with his back to the large fireplace swirling an amber liquid in a cut glass tumbler.

"Nice place you've got. Seems a bit mean you living here and leaving Tracy in Scott's flat."

"I was getting the house ready for us," Fraser replied tightly. "So what did you think of Greenlawns?"

Was that what all this had been about? She wondered. Impressing her? Fraser Keenan, successful businessman and part-time philanthropist?

"A bit too institutional for me but I don't doubt its business potential with an ageing population and a shortage of nursing home places in Edinburgh."

"Exactly." He smiled.

"I might be more impressed if I knew where the money came from to set it up."

Fraser's smile held. "From the banks, of course. It's all legit."

"You and Adam McNaughtan? Legit?"

He smiled and took a sip from the tumbler. "I made sure of that."

"And that's what you wanted me to hear from Nellie Pearce?"

"That and a few other things."

"Like driving a man away from his home to save your brother?"

He frowned. "He was a pervert, a paedophile. As well as that he was going into business for himself. He was trying to get people to invest in his wee schemes, telling them how they could make a killing. These were people on benefit or very low wages and he wanted to get his hands on their endowment policies for his dubious investments. It was nothing to do with Scott."

"And Maggie was Dunfermline's answer to Robin Hood, dishing out her stolen goods and taking benefit books to pay herself for them."

"My mother gave people what they needed."

"That's what she told you?"

"It's what I know. I don't have any illusions about my family."

His comment knocked her off-balance. Was it directed at her or was she just being hypersensitive? There was no way Fraser could have found out anything about her mother was there? "So you know about Scott?"

"What do you mean?"

"That he's trying to blackmail Kirsten Cormack into having sex with him."

Fraser sighed. "I'll sort it."

She caught a sideways glance at Tracy. "What about his fondness for young teenage girls? Or is that something your mother didn't tell you?" She could hear the gears clicking in her brain. She looked at Tracy, her small, thin figure, the haunted expression, more than enough vulnerability to appeal to Scott. "Did Tracy move into Leapark with Maggie to keep her out of Scott's clutches?"

Tracy stood. "I'll start the tea." She shot an anxious glance at Fraser and hurried out of the room.

Kate watched her go then turned to Fraser. "Tracy stabbed Scott, didn't she? He tried it on and she stabbed him."

Fraser looked at her, smiles all gone. "Tracy and I were in our separate beds when Scott was stabbed. As your pet policeman has already been told." His eyes locked onto hers.

She smiled. "Aye right, Fraser," she said.

## 53

Kate dug around in her fridge and came up with the Marks and Spencer's 'Eve's Puddings she'd bought on Friday. She stuck them in the microwave. Lucy stretched out on her cushion at the radiator and rolled onto her back, tucking her front paws into her body. Kate put a saucer beside her plate. When the puddings were ready she spooned some of the custard onto the saucer and set it in front of Lucy, stroking the cat's soft fur. Lucy purred her appreciation. There was a lot to be said for being a pampered cat.

She ate the puddings leaning against the worktop, scraping the last of her custard onto Lucy's saucer. If, as it seemed, she'd decided against working for the I.T. company, she should do some work on her application for the team manager post. She'd been spending too much time on the deaths at Leapark. She poured herself a glass of wine and carried it to her kitchen table then booted up her laptop and opened the file containing her C.V. and sat staring at the wall. Should she tell John her suspicions about Scott Keenan and Tracy? Because that's all they were. She had no evidence, just gossip and other people's memories. She thought back to what Nellie Pearce had told her. Fraser seemed to be a legitimate and astute businessman. His complex in Dunfermline could be a goldmine, especially if he could persuade his Leapark residents to move to the nursing home when they were no longer fit enough for Leapark. She'd be interested to know how much his wealthier residents paid. Despite the Scottish Government's policy of free personal care, Fraser could still charge what he liked for the accommodation and the little extras like aromatherapy. 'Special care for special people' the Greenlawns brochure had said.

Her mind kept going back to Nellie Pearce's photo of the insurance man. There was something nagging at the back of her brain. Something she'd seen? Something Nellie Pearce said? She looked at her notes on Leapark, at her list of suspects and what she'd found out about each of them. Sam MacEwen, Marjorie Collins, Rose Toner, Frances Wordsworth and Kirsten Cormack were all old enough to have figured in Nellie Pearce's story in some form. If that was significant. She shook her head. If Nellie Pearce knew something that would shed light on the murder of Maggie Keenan surely Fraser would have got it out of her. As far as Nellie Pearce was concerned, Fraser was as pure as the driven snow. Or was the whole thing just a ruse to divert her attention from Scott, or even Fraser himself?

Her gaze drifted to her parents' wedding photo lying on the table. She picked it up. Was Jean telling her the truth when she said she didn't know who the witnesses were? Kate had thought so at the time but she wondered now. She looked at her mother smiling happily, genuinely. She smiled in response, tracing her mother's outline with her finger. An image clicked into place. Jean? Surely not. There was no reason. Unless she saw more on Saturday than she'd let on. She picked up her phone and keyed in Jean's number listening to it ring out. Didn't mean anything. Jean could be playing silly buggers and just not answering the phone. She disconnected and tried again with the same result. Oh, what the hell. She grabbed her keys and her mobile and rushed out the door.

On the way to Leapark she tried phoning Jean again but there was still no answer. Should she phone John Nelson? And say what? 'Hello, John, I think I know who murdered Maggie Keenan and I'm worried that Jean will be next.' Would he listen to her or would he just tell her to butt out of his investigation again? She debated this as she raced through Ravelston. Though if she kept up this speed, she wouldn't have to call the police, they'd be after her. When she stopped at the lights at Corstorphine Road, she speed-dialled John's number and left a message asking him to meet her at Leapark.

She abandoned her car at the front door and ran into the building. She took the stairs two at a time and pounded along the corridor to Jean's flat. The door was unlocked, the lights out. She stood in the hall, listening. A voice, low, soothing, not Jean's, drifted from the sitting room, its door slightly ajar. She pushed it wider. Her eyes took a few seconds to adjust to the meagre light trickling in through the window. When they did she saw Jean sitting on the settee. The figure beside her held out a mug, urging Jean to drink from it.

"No!" Kate rushed forward and swept the mug onto the floor.

Jean jumped. "Kate, what are you doing? That's a good cup of tea you've just wasted."

Frances Wordsworth looked at her in disbelief.

"What's going on?" Kate picked up the mug and sniffed at the residue of liquid in the bottom. It smelt like tea.

"I'd just sat down when my electricity went off. I didn't know what to do so I called the warden." Jean turned to the door as John Nelson came in. She pulled her dressing-gown round her, doing up the top button. "What are you doing here?"

He looked at the two women on the settee then at Kate. "So tell me, Kate, what am I doing here? And why are we all in the dark? Or is that just me?"

"Blown fuse," Kate mumbled and headed for the cupboard that housed the fuse box. When she came back in she flicked the light switch and four sets of eyes blinked blindly.

"I'll go and leave you to sort yourselves out." Frances Wordsworth leaned forward, hands on her thighs, to push herself up off the settee. The wedding ring swung freely on its chain.

"When did you know, Frances?" Kate asked.

"When did I know what?"

"That Maggie Keenan was the woman who drove your father away."

Frances looked at her, blinking. "I don't know what you mean."

"That wedding ring you wear, I assumed it was your own but it's your mother's isn't it? You've worn it since you were a child. I saw the photo. You've changed a lot since you lived in Dunfermline with your father but I think Nellie Pearce would still recognise you." She paused. "Sadie."

Frances held Kate's gaze for a few seconds more then she crumpled onto the settee as if her bones had melted.

"I'm sorry," she whispered, shaking her head. "I'm so sorry."

John Nelson moved forward to crouch in front of her. He cautioned her then said, "What are you sorry for, Mrs Wordsworth?"

She looked at him. "I've taken two lives." She shook her head. "May God forgive me."

## 54

"I spoke to Frances on Friday and she was wearing the ring on its chain then," Kate explained. She was curled up in one of Jean's armchairs cradling a mug of tea. John Nelson sat on the settee. Frances had been officially charged but deemed unfit for any further questioning until the morning. Jean had opted for her bed still shocked at the idea of Frances as a double murderer. "I assumed it was her own. It wasn't until I got home from Dunfermline and looked at my mum's wedding photo that it dawned on me that the little girl in the Nellie Pearce photo was wearing a wedding ring on a chain round her neck."

"And that was it?"

"Nellie Pearce called the girl Sadie. I knew Frances' middle name was Sarah. I wondered whether her auntie had swapped the names round when Frances went to live with her." She looked at him. "But even then I wasn't sure that it was Frances. That's why I hesitated to phone you. I didn't want to drag you here on a wild goose chase."

"I'd rather go on a wild goose chase than have you taking all sorts of risks on your own."

"You wouldn't like to put that in writing?" She smiled at him. "Did Frances say which two lives she took?"

"No, but assuming Maggie Keenan was one of them, it makes sense that Betty Smyth was the other on the basis that what Maggie knew Betty knew. We'll find out when we question her, or Steve will."

"Steve?"

"It's still his case."

"I thought Maggie was your case."

"Only in relation to her criminal contacts. The Leapark investigation is Steve's responsibility."

"Will he get the credit for the arrest?"

"Does it matter?"

She shrugged. Furthering Steve's career ambitions had not been part of her agenda. "What about Harriet Post?"

"We'll have to wait and see what Wordsworth admits to."

She looked at him long enough for him to ask, "What?"

"I was wondering about Scott Keenan, whether you're any closer to finding out who stabbed him."

"We're fairly sure it was Fraser or Tracy. Judging by the angle of the knife wound and its entry point, I'd bet on Tracy but we'll never prove it."

"What does Scott say?"

"He's now saying that he fell on it."

She looked at him in disbelief.

"It's not impossible just highly improbable."

"What about Kirsten Cormack?"

"What about Kirsten Cormack?" John returned her question.

They'd reached the 'drawing teeth' phase. "You're so bloody exasperating sometimes, do you know that?"

"Because I won't help you with your enquiries?" He was giving her the benefit of one of his sexy, superior smiles.

She felt like hitting him. Turned instead to a sound from the bedroom. She walked to the door. In the semi-dark Jean lay in bed, apparently asleep. She hadn't put her clothes away. The soft blue-green jumper was draped over the back of a chair. A black skirt lay on the seat. Low-heeled black shoes sat on the floor. Well, well, well. What had Jean been up to before the lights went out? Kate stood for a moment but Jean remained motionless.

John looked up at her as she returned to the sitting room. "Everything okay?"

She nodded, settling back into the armchair.

"Cormack's in the clear. For stabbing Scott, that is," John said.

"I'd managed to work that out myself. So is she suspected of something else?"

"Why would you think that?"

She sighed. "Just for tonight, John, could we stop playing these games of I'll show you mine if you show me yours?" She regretted the words as soon as they left her mouth, horrified to find herself blushing at the look he gave her. "I mean you wanting to find out how much I already know before you tell me anything."

"Oh, is that all you meant?" He faked disappointment then smiled at her. "We know Scott was trying to blackmail Cormack and that he went to her flat on Friday night probably with that intention. Both are now saying it was a social visit to clear up any misunderstanding between them about Maggie's murder, and Scott's decided he fell on the knife. It's got Fraser written all over it. He's turned out to be more his mother's son than Scott could dream about."

"So Kirsten did do something illegal that Scott knows about?"

"We suspect that Scott was involved in thefts of drugs from nursing homes a while back but we can't prove anything."

"Ah, right."

He leaned forward. "About these games…"

"Did you know Fraser has a house in South Queensferry?" she asked quickly.

He laughed and sat back. "Aye. And before you ask we also know about Greenlawns. How come you know?"

"Fraser invited me for a visit when was I on my way back from Dunfermline."

He shook his head. "You just can't leave it alone, can you?"

"It wasn't the sort of invitation I could refuse. Anyway, it gave me a chance to test out something Nellie Pearce told me."

"What was that?"

"That Scott had a fondness for young teenage girls."

He nodded. "And you think he saw Tracy as a substitute?"

"I think that was why she moved to Leapark with Maggie." She tried a pointed look Nellie Pearce style.

"You may well be right, Kate."

She sighed. "If you know about all this property Fraser has, how come you can't trace the money? Or is that something else you're not telling me?"

"The funding of both the house and the Greenlawns complex is legitimate. Fraser didn't hesitate to give permission for us to access his bank accounts. The only answer to the whereabouts of Maggie's money is cash."

"Do you know how much?"

"We calculate in the region of £250,000, probably in a safety deposit box but tracing it with nothing to go on is impossible. We don't even know what name it would be in. It's certainly not in any of the Keenans' names."

"You know there's another nursing home planned at Greenlawns?"

"And it would provide an excellent opportunity for a bit of money laundering."

Any further conversation was interrupted by the beeping of Kate's mobile phone. She listened to the caller, John watching her. When the call ended he looked questioningly at her.

"Frances Wordsworth is to be interviewed tomorrow morning. She's asked if I'll sit in with her."

John smiled, shaking his head. "That'll make Steve's day."

# Tuesday

## 55

The fluorescent light buzzed like a trapped insect. Tension crept up her neck threatening a headache. She wanted to flex her shoulders or do a neck roll but unclenched her hands instead. She'd already put her bag on the floor beside her chair to avoid clutching it. Once again sleep had been a long time coming last night and not particularly restful when it did. And she still didn't know what she was doing here. Why had Frances asked for her? She looked across at Heather setting up the recording system, all brisk and business-like then sneaked a glance at Steve, sifting through a folder, behaving as if she wasn't there. Beside her, Frances Wordsworth focussed on her hands placed neatly together on the black-topped table in front of her as if getting into character for her starring role, her big chance. Squeezed in at the corner of the table, the duty solicitor tried to look purposeful.

"Mrs Keenan called me into her flat when I arrived for my duty on Tuesday night," Frances began. "She made it clear that a paedophile incident she'd described earlier that day at the lunch club referred to my father."

"Do you remember the incident?" Steve asked.

"I remember what I now know was the aftermath which was my aunt coming to the house during the school summer holidays and taking me to stay with her in Musselburgh. My father told me that he had to go away on business and that I should stay with my aunt until he came for me. He didn't come back." She looked at Steve Oakley. "My father was a good man, Inspector. He would never have done the things that woman accused him of." Her gaze returned to her hands. "Mrs Keenan continued to say things about my father. I thought she wanted money or something else from me but she just seemed to want to torment me. I told her that I knew my father wasn't like that but..." Frances paused, gulping in air.

Kate touched her arm. "Do you need to stop for a while?"

"No, thank you." She focussed on Steve. "It was a tirade of filth and I had to stop it. I reached out my hand and found the angel. At the time it seemed to me that God had put it there for me." She took a deep breath. "I hit her with it."

"Why..." Steve began but was halted by Frances' raised hand.

"I didn't intend to kill Mrs Keenan. I simply wanted her to stop," she said then nodded her permission for Steve to continue.

"Why did you unlock the outer door, Mrs Wordsworth?" Steve was asking the questions mechanically, interested only in getting official confirmation of the confession already given to John Nelson.

"I knew that Harriet Post's door had been unlocked. I hoped that it would be assumed that Mrs Keenan had been a victim of a similar assault. That was also why I left the room in disarray."

"Did you search the flat?" This was from Heather.

"Only the sitting room. I thought there might be something about my father but I didn't find anything." Frances leaned forward, one hand stretching out as if for understanding, for some acknowledgement of her sense of loss. "All those years I waited for my father to come for me even though my aunt told me he didn't want me." She sat back, her gaze drifting to the table. "After she died I found the letters from him. He was in Canada and had wanted me to go there. He was waiting for me. I found out later that my aunt had told him I wanted to stay with her. Yet he'd kept writing. When I finally went to see him he was dying."

The light on the recording equipment glowed red, noting these outpourings with as much emotion as Steve.

Frances turned to Kate. "I looked after my father for the last months of his life." She was smiling as if the memory was still fresh. "I'd grown up believing he'd abandoned me but those last months gave him back to me." She tilted her chin. Her tone hardened. "Maggie Keenan changed that. She made me doubt my memories and my life with my father. I know you understand that. The job you do."

Kate gave an involuntary nod. The room felt close, the air cloying as if they'd all just come in from the rain and still had their wet clothes on. But there was no rain only that slate-grey cloud.

"Why did you kill Elizabeth Smyth?" Steve sounded bored with the whole thing now. Maybe all the credit wasn't coming his way.

Frances sighed. "At Harriet Post's funeral Mrs Smyth made certain remarks that suggested to me that not only did she know about my father but that she was prepared to disclose what she knew to the press. It was how Mrs Smyth worked when she wanted to imply that she knew something unpalatable. She more or less confirmed this when I went to see her on Saturday afternoon."

Kate jumped at a knock on the door. A W.P.C. entered and handed what looked like a pathology report to Steve. He took time to peruse it, a hint of a frown developing as he did so. Frances sat watching him, composed now, waiting for the opportunity to complete her story, on the road to her own form of absolution.

Steve slid the report into his folder and looked at Frances. "Continue."

Her hands tapped gently on the table as if marking the end of the pause. "Mrs Smyth's death was the consequence of a deliberate act on my part. I purloined two penicillin tablets from another resident and offered them to her. She was upset about an argument she'd had with Kirsten Cormack. I told her the tablets would help settle her down. She was always amenable to taking medication not prescribed for her. I knew that it would not be a pleasant way to die so I crushed some diazepam in her bedtime drink to ease her path."

Steve pushed his chair back and made as if to stand.

"I haven't finished." Frances' voice was firm.

He sat back. "Carry on."

"Maggie Keenan corrupted many of those she came in contact with and I allowed myself to fall under her malign influence. However, I had nothing whatsoever to do with the death of Harriet Post. I believe the culprit is now dead herself."

"You think Maggie Keenan killed Harriet Post?" Kate asked, receiving a glare from Steve.

"Yes I do."

"What evidence do you have for that belief?" Steve barked.

"I had remonstrated with Mrs Keenan to return the angel to Mrs Post and she refused. I threatened to report her to the management committee if the angel was not returned. The death of Mrs Post brought the matter to an end."

"How did Maggie Keenan get the angel?" Kate asked.

"She simply walked in and took it, along with a small clown. Mrs Post was most upset, especially about the angel. She'd managed to get the clown back herself."

Kate was about to ask more but Steve stopped her. "Is there anything else you want to tell us, Mrs Wordsworth?"

"Only that I do deeply regret causing Mrs Smyth's death but, as I saw it at the time, I had no choice." She stood up. "Now I've said all I have to say."

"Interview terminated at 9.57 am," Heather announced. She switched off the recorder and removed the tapes then handed one to Frances' solicitor.

Frances rested her hand on Kate's shoulder. "Thank you for sitting with me. I want you to know that I never intended any harm to your aunt," she said and allowed Heather to lead her from the room.

Steve gathered up his papers and tapes. "You can go," he said to Kate. "You're not needed here anymore."

"Did Frances say why she wanted me to sit in on the interview?"

"It's of no interest to me." He looked at her directly for the first time that morning. "Just like you, of no interest to me at all," he said and walked out.

"Wish they were all as easy as that one," the solicitor said as he followed Steve out of the room.

Kate stood for a moment listening to their voices and footsteps fade. A uniformed officer appeared at the door, a questioning look on his face. "Thought-gathering," she said smiling then slung her bag over her shoulder and left the room. Outside she got into to her car and headed for Leapark.

## 56

The dream had shaken Jean awake at six o'clock, shivering. She'd dressed and gone out, down the back stairs and along to the kitchen where she'd made herself a cup of tea. She sat defiantly at the window table in the dining room to drink it, watching the sky lighten in shades of grey, enjoying the peace and quiet of the building before the army of home helps and district nurses descended on it. And that would have been fine but for the three mugs of coffee she'd had since. Caffeine – her drug of choice.

She looked down at her clothes. Need to get changed. Kate would be here soon to take her to Maggie Keenan's funeral. Had received a proper invitation from Maggie's sons. How did Kate manage these things? Solving a murder for God's sake. Jean calmly, if unknowingly, taking tea with the murderer, appreciating Frances' kindness even if it was of the professional variety.

She found herself in her own kitchen and filled a glass with water needing to dilute the caffeine zinging through her veins. She'd cleaned and polished till her arms ached and her head throbbed with the smell from the polish and still she was buzzing.

Her hand trembled as she lifted the glass to her lips, sloshing water onto the cuff of her navy cardigan. Robert had been a genuinely kind man. In her old flat she would sometimes sit with her late night cup of tea in one of her Spode cups and remember his kindness, his gentleness, the romance. How he'd made her feel special, that secret knowledge that she was on someone's mind, in someone's heart. 'I think of you before I sleep,' he'd once said, 'whisper goodnight.' It had sustained her. Kate had said something once about people and mirrors, how we're attracted to those who reflect us back as we want to be seen. Robert had been the best mirror she'd ever had. His love had set her apart from that bunch of nondescript middle-aged women that nobody paid any attention to. Now she'd joined the club that nobody wanted, shunted off into the sidings and nothing to show for it. Seventy bloody years and none the wiser.

A sob choked her. In her dream Andrew and his father had been one. Like the day he came to her door. In that first moment she'd thought he'd come back for her before realising that the man standing in front of her was much too young. Only a moment but long enough for Andrew to think he wasn't welcome, to take against her. She'd tried to explain about his father but he wouldn't listen. Said he needed money to go to America to find him so she gave him her savings – all £300 of it. She'd withdrawn it for another purpose. That was why she had to go to Maggie Keenan. At forty-four she'd thought she was pregnant, the shameful result of a cold, comfortless coupling in a dingy hotel room. Only she wasn't; early menopause it turned out to be. So she took the money back, for all the good it did her.

She wondered if Andrew had gone to America and what he'd found there, who he'd found. Did he hate her for what she'd done? If only he'd let her explain. His hand reached out to her in her dreams, just as it had done that day. She always woke before she could touch him.

The sharp rap on the door made her jump, jolting her into the present. She set the glass firmly on the draining board, resisting the shudders pushing up from her diaphragm, and tiptoed into the hall. Through the peephole she saw Rose Toner looking right back at her. Jean pulled back but knew she would open the door.

Toner stalked past her to the sitting room as if she belonged, fat figure encased in a long-sleeved black dress. In the middle of the room she turned.

"Jean Markham." She looked Jean up and down. "I know about you." She picked up the photo on the sideboard. "That's your niece in that photo, isn't it?"

Jean gave an involuntary nod.

"Neat wee frame." She looked round the room. "No photo of the boy? That's odd, wouldn't you say?" She stared at Jean for a few seconds then handed her the photo of Kate and walked into the hall. "I'll see you later, Jean Markham." The door closed quietly behind her.

Jean sank into the nearest armchair. Kate had said that Rose Toner didn't know anything. Had she found out since? But what Maggie Keenan had known was about Jean having a son. And now that Kate knew, there was nothing Toner could threaten her with. Was there?

She slowed her breathing, focussing on the photograph in her lap. Kate smiled back at her, glowing with life and all its possibilities. Ready to take on the world if she had to. Easy when you looked like that. Even at university, she'd been full of herself, with her long, tangled hair and her torn jeans – the sort of look men would find sexy. Jules had seemed a steadying influence, if anybody could influence Kate. But there were things they got up to that Jean was not to know about, wouldn't want to know about. She could see it in the shared looks, the raised eyebrows, the secret smiles. They seemed so sure of themselves, so self-contained. Oh, Kate knew she was special alright, the bees' knees; didn't need a man to confirm it. Not like Jean. Awkward and angular, always apologising for who she was.

She left the photo on the chair and went into the bedroom. She slumped onto the bed, rubbing her face with the heels of her hands. Her black skirt still lay on the chair from last night. Her romantic night out. Today she'd wear it to a funeral. She took off her cardigan and slid her trousers down over her hips. When she bent to remove them the room spun gently. She sat up feeling tears gathering behind her eyes. Grief, guilt and more than a hint of self-pity. And a memory from last night to tip her over the edge. She'd been trying to overhear Kate's conversation with John Nelson but had dozed off. She'd jerked awake as a figure loomed over her.

"Sorry," a voice had said softly.

Jean had closed her eyes, aware of a hand gently stroking her face, just like her mother used to do when she'd had a bad dream.

"You're safe now," the voice had whispered. "Go back to sleep." A soft kiss on her cheek. "I'll see you tomorrow."

Jean gave in and let the tears come.

### 57

"Would you rather wait in the car, Jean?" Kate asked.

"If you don't mind. I'm feeling a bit tired."

They were standing outside the crematorium waiting for Fraser. Jean's pallor was accentuated by the black coat, its collar pulled up round her ears. The grey of the morning had lifted and light, fluffy clouds drifted across the sky, pushed along by the breeze. Occasionally, a promising patch of blue showed through.

The service had been a masterful exercise in masquerade. The orations spoke of Mrs Keenan's service to her community, her sense of social responsibility, her love for her family. There was no mention of intimidation, blackmail, or all-consuming self-interest. Kate wondered for a while if she'd come to the wrong service, but there had been Fraser and Tracy in the front row with Rose Toner alongside. Scott's fat bulk was parked in the aisle in a wheelchair. Apart from Annie and her friend, Renie, there was no one from Leapark. The rest of the church was likely filled with criminals, major and minor, and the police.

She was about to lead Jean over to the Yaris when Fraser and Tracy appeared arm in arm. "I'm going to take my auntie to the car," she said.

"Pete'll do that for you." At a nod from Fraser, Pete joined them. Jean took his proffered arm and, with a puzzled backward glance at Kate, allowed herself to be led to the car.

Pete returned with the car key then went back into the church. The breeze ruffled Fraser's hair and he smoothed it back into place. Tracy plucked a stray strand from his shoulder.

"You wanted to talk to me," Kate said.

"Aye. Tie up a few loose ends."

Pete reappeared with Rose Toner. He led her to a black limousine and helped her into the back seat. The limousine pulled away, off to the mansion in South Queensferry perhaps.

"Pete on elderly duty today?" Kate said.

"Rose was a good friend of my mother's. We take care of our friends." Fraser handed her a small package, neatly labelled.

"What's this?" she said, not wanting to be taking gifts from the likes of Fraser. Then she caught a glimpse of the label and tucked it into her handbag.

"That's one debt cleared but I still owe you, Kate."

"You don't owe me anything, Fraser. I didn't do any of this for you or your mother."

"I know that. The problem is you did do it. You caught the bitch that murdered Maggie Keenan. Like it or not, I'm forever in your debt."

"So tell me something."

"If I can."

"What have you done with Maggie's money?"

He forced a smile. "You need to learn when to leave well enough alone."

"What about Kirsten Cormack?"

"Kirsten Cormack is now the warden at Leapark. And before you ask, I'll be taking Scott to live with us in South Queensferry."

Kate smiled. "That'll be cosy, you and Tracy playing at love's young dream with Scott in the 'granny flat'. It was Tracy who stabbed him, wasn't it?"

Fraser's tone hardened. "We've done that one. Leave it alone."

"You can polish up your veneer of respectability as much as you like, Fraser, but you'll always be what you are, a wee wannabe gangster." His face tightened but anger pushed her on. "Well, I don't want that kind of debt owing to me. So keep your gratitude and keep out of my life."

"Or what?" Fraser sneered. "You'll set your pet policeman on me?"

Kate turned to see John Nelson standing by his car watching them. She looked at Fraser. "He's worth a thousand of you. If I can do anything that helps him put you away, I'll do it."

Fraser grabbed her arm pulling her towards him. "Don't you threaten me," he hissed into her face. Then he looked up and let her go.

"Problem?" John Nelson sauntered towards them, his black tie billowing in the breeze.

"No. We're all done, aren't we, Fraser?"

"We're done," Fraser said. Then he turned and walked away, Tracy firmly attached to his arm.

"I take it you and Fraser are no longer bosom pals," John said.

"Not while my pet policeman's hanging around." She smiled at him.

"That's me, is it? Do I get the same treatment as your cat?"

"She might share her scratching post but you'd need to fight her for her catnip mouse."

"I've got some information about your mother's death," he said gently.

She looked over at her car. "I need to get Jean home."

"I can drop it off later if you like."

"Any time after seven, if that's okay."

He nodded. "By the way, the skeleton on that building site in Greenock, his name was William James Makin."

She shook her head. "Doesn't mean anything to me."

"He was originally from Helensburgh. It's not clear how he ended up in Greenock, nor how he died. Why did you want to know who it was?"

"Clutching at straws probably." She turned to him. "I'll see you later?"

"You'll see me later." He smiled at her. It was one of his genuine smiles, warm with a hint of concern in his long-lashed eyes. She wondered what he had found out about her mother's death.

When she got to her car, she found Jean asleep. She gave her a nudge and handed her the package from Fraser Keenan.

Jean looked at the label with her name on it. "What is it?"

"See for yourself."

She fumbled with the wrapping then gasped. "It's my locket." She took it from the box and opened it. "And the wee lock of hair is still there and the photo. Oh, Kate." Tears shone in Jean's eyes. "I can't thank you enough for this."

"You don't need to thank me, Jean." Kate concentrated on her driving.

Jean sat back clutching the locket to her chest.

"Jessie Turner's vain: smart clothes, hair expensively coiffured, make-up perfect if a bit much for a woman her age. She really needs to be in a nursing home but the only Edinburgh places Jessie would consider are expensive. So the family are in a bit of a cleft stick. Jessie living with them is driving them up the wall but a nursing home would use up a lot of her money."

Kate had left Jean sitting on the sofa, mug of coffee untouched on the coffee table. Too busy gazing at the locket, fingering the little photo, stroking the dark lock of baby hair. Beaming gratitude till Kate couldn't stand it any more. Now she followed Mary Lappin round the Corstorphine office looking for Jessie Turner's file.

"Ah, here we are." Mary pulled a file from a cabinet. "I don't know all the details but money did seem to go astray and the blame was laid at Maggie Keenan's door. Maggie denied it. Said she was just making sure Jessie knew her place. Somewhere between that and Jessie moving out the allegations were dropped. Between you and me, Kate, I think Jessie gave her money to one of the men to invest for her. He's a bit of a Lothario apparently."

"His name wouldn't be Sam MacEwen by any chance?"

"How did you know that?"

"Educated guess, Mary. Was it just money or was there something else going on?"

"I don't know if there was a physical relationship. Knowing Jessie I'd say it was unlikely. She struck me as a woman who likes to put her goods in the window but isn't really interested in selling anything, if you know what I mean. But she could be flattered by the attentions of a presentable man."

"Did Jessie get her money back? Is that why the family didn't pursue it?"

"I don't know." Mary raised a finger in a sort of celebratory salute. "But I know how we can find out." She led Kate to another room that housed clerical staff and sat down at a computer. "This will be so much easier when your new system's up and running." Mary was saying. "Jessie had a financial assessment for nursing home care." She tapped a few keys and up came Jessie Turner's financial history. "There."

'There' showed a net reduction in Jessie's capital of nearly £6,000.

"So you're thinking at least some of that went to Sam MacEwen to be invested?" Kate asked.

"It's the most likely explanation. Jessie's got expensive tastes but £6,000 is a lot to spend in three months, especially with the amount of income she had from her late husband's occupational pension."

"How much did the family say was missing originally?"

Mary went back to her desk and checked the file. "£22,000."

"That's some investment. Do you think all of the £22,000 went to Sam MacEwen?"

"Are you thinking Maggie Keenan got some of it?"

"I'm thinking Sam MacEwen wouldn't want the police looking too closely at what he gets up to so he settled for maybe a couple of thousand and gave the rest back. Whereas Maggie..." She thought for a moment. "Would you call up Harriet Post's record?"

Mary Lappin looked at her. "Do you think Sam MacEwen was working on her as well?"

Kate shrugged.

Mary turned to the computer and tapped some keys. "You're out of luck."

Kate looked at the screen. 'Full charge – income not disclosed.' So much for that bright idea.

## 58

Kate stood looking down at the small cubic gravestones that marked the children's resting places. The names were listed on the headstone carved into the boundary wall of the Gallery of Modern Art's car park. The building that housed the artworks had once been a boarding school for fatherless children. From what she'd read the children were well cared for, their deaths attributable to diseases common at the time rather than any ill-treatment. The graves were tucked away in a quiet corner shielded by trees. The rest of the area was pretty much wilderness apart from the steps that led down to the Water of Leith and a Henry Moore sculpture courtesy of the gallery.

After leaving Mary Lappin, she'd gone back to Leapark to check on Jean. She was concerned that the joy and relief at the return of the locket would dissipate to be replaced with the depression of remembered loss, the photo and lock of hair all Jean had to show for a son she gave away.

The impromptu visit to the gallery grounds had been a delaying tactic. She didn't feel like hanging round her flat waiting for John to turn up, wondering what he'd found out. She'd debated detouring via Cramond and a walk along the seafront, she'd not been there since the deaths of Caroline and Emily Woodlands. She'd dithered long enough at the lights at Ravelston Dykes to earn an impatient honk from the car behind her before flicking her indicator to right, leaving him to head off towards Cramond on his own. She repeated her dithering performance at the lights at Belford Road, annoying even herself, before turning towards the gallery.

Beyond the wall, conversational voices preceded a car starting up and pulling away. Silence returned apart from a faint shushing sound from the Water of Leith down in the ravine, rushing past on its way to the North Sea. She let her head drop forward, rolled it round, feeling the cricks in her neck easing, then forward again letting the weight of her head do the work, feeling the stretch all the way down her spine. She straightened and stretched her arms up and out, exhaling as she watched soft, fluffy, cotton wool cloud drift across the sky. As a child she used to imagine it coming down to enfold her and carry her off to another land like in a fairy tale. A deep breath brought a smell of damp vegetation and a whiff of something like cat pee. She looked back at the headstone. At the bottom, below the list of names, was a quote from the Bible: 'Suffer the little children to come unto me' it began. She found herself hoping they had then turned away and walked back to her car not wanting to risk getting locked in when the gates were closed at dusk.

At home, after attending to Lucy, she went into her bedroom and stripped off the funeral outfit then ran a bath, pouring in a foaming oil that promised to be both restorative and energising. She eased her body into the hot water, sliding down until her shoulders were immersed, letting her head rest on the pillow Jean had given her one Christmas. Surrounded by the soothing, steamy warmth, she closed her eyes and let her thoughts drift.

A soft tap on her face jerked her awake. Lucy sat on the edge of the bath gazing down at her, paw raised for another tap. Disorientated, Kate looked round for a clock then, realising where she was, dragged herself out of the cool water, dislodging Lucy in the process. She grabbed the towel from the radiator and ran to the kitchen. Six o'clock. She leant against the door frame in relief. Greeting John Nelson wrapped only in a bath towel would absolutely not be a good idea.

By the time she buzzed John into the stair she was clad demurely in jeans and her oversized 'Ragamuffin' jumper, a reminder of a holiday on Skye. The blues and purples of the wool interwove to reflect the colours of the landscape. She left her door on the latch and returned to the kitchen. She hadn't felt like eating when she'd got home. After her bath she'd wandered restlessly from room to room, glass of wine in her hand, wondering, yet again, how much she really wanted to know about her mother's death. Now she hovered over the toaster needing to eat something to offset the effects of the wine.

John came in as the toast popped up. He was still wearing his suit from the morning but had swapped his tie for a dark red one.

"Want some tea and toast?" she asked him, frowning. "Or I've got wine."

He smiled at her. "Och, let's go for the toast."

Kate put another two slices of bread into the toaster and added a second teabag and more hot water to the teapot. "Any further forward on Maggie's money?"

"Running out of places to look." He leant against the worktop.

When it was ready, Kate set the buttered toast on a plate and handed it to John with two mugs. He carried them to the table. Kate followed with the teapot and milk jug.

Lucy rolled over to watch them pass then stretched her chubby back legs towards the radiator and curled up on her cushion for a sleep, catnip mouse tucked firmly between her paws.

"This is very civilised." John waited for Kate then sat on the chair at a right angle to hers and picked up a slice of the buttered toast. "I had a look at the transcripts from Eddie Ranford's interview. Were you in Ratho on Sunday night?"

"I drove out that way after I left Jules' flat. Did Ranford follow me from there?"

John nodded chewing on the toast. "He's saying he just wanted to talk to you but was worried you'd scream when you saw him and that's why he put his hand over your mouth." He glanced at the bread. "Like your butter, don't you?"

"So it was all a silly misunderstanding?" She began pouring the tea, the weight of the pot steadying her hand.

"Nobody believes him. And he's been remanded in custody."

"Good." She faffed about with the milk aware that he was watching her, waiting for her to ask what he'd found out. "Do you think Maggie Keenan killed Harriet Post?"

"Based on the circumstantial evidence, she's a better bet than Frances Wordsworth, but she can hardly be tried for it. And the pathologist is still hedging her bets as to whether it was a fall or a push."

"What'll happen now?"

"It'll be left on file in case any new information crops up. The bruises will be put down to Maggie throwing her weight about."

"Will Steve settle for that?"

"Not much choice. It would look better for him if Frances could be convicted for the three deaths but the combination of the pathology report and Frances' denial means that's not going to happen."

She nodded and looked at him expectantly.

He handed her an envelope. "You were right about the cards supposedly from your father, your grandmother wrote them."

She sighed as she removed the cards and letter from the envelope and laid them on the table. "I know she would have done it to make me feel better but I really wish she hadn't."

"Why?"

"In all of this my grandmother was the one person I thought I could trust not to lie to me. Now I find she'd been lying for years about my father."

"Would it have been better if you'd grown up believing that your father cut you out completely?"

"I don't know, John." She looked at the cards. Had she really never wondered about why her father had stayed away? Or, somewhere inside, had she decided that she preferred not to know?

"Do you want to see what I found about your mother's death?" John asked.

She turned to him. "Please."

"I got these from the National Library's archive." He pulled some sheets of paper from his inside pocket and handed two of them to her. They were copies of reports that had appeared in the Greenock Telegraph. The paper still held warmth from his body.

"I should have thought of that." She glanced over them. Her gaze picked up on 'Tragic Death of Local Woman' and 'Drowning Accidental'.

"I managed to speak to one of the police officers who had been involved in the case. He remembered the woman in the red coat."

"She was wearing her red coat?"

"Is that significant?"

"I sometimes dream I was responsible for her falling into the water. That was why Jean told me it was suicide. In the dream I pull away from her and she falls into the river. She's wearing her red coat. I watch it drifting away from me until I can't see it any more. Then I wake up."

She gazed at Joan Eardley's tumbledown cottages and that cold, hard moon, hanging on the creamy yellow wall. "I wondered if it was a memory."

"You weren't there, Kate."

"How do you know?"

"There was a witness"

She stared at him. "A witness?"

"A man on his way to work. He saw a tall, blonde woman in a red coat walking towards the quayside." He paused. "There was no one with her, not you, not your father. Your mum was alone."

She shook her head, struggling to keep control. The scene was too vivid: her mum in her best coat, walking towards the water's edge on that cold, dark November morning.

"Kate?" he said it softly, covering her hand with his own.

"For the first time I can see how desperate she must have been." She left her hand in his, feeling comfort in the warmth, wanting to leave it all there. "Sorry."

He let go of her hand, lifted a slice of toast and held it up to her mouth. "Eat," he said. She took a bite, chewed and swallowed. He pushed her mug of tea into her hands. "Drink."

She held the tea in her mouth for a moment before swallowing it, clasping her hands round her mug. "What else did you find out?"

He turned to the third sheet of paper. She glanced across at it: a one-page report on her mother's death. "Your mother's body was found at one o'clock on the shore at Newark Castle. Based on the tides, it was likely that she'd gone into the water at the Coronation Park around seven a.m. She was identified from a library ticket that was in a plastic purse in her pocket. Your father was checked out. He was at work from six-thirty." He looked at her. "You did wonder whether your father had something to do with your mother's death, didn't you?"

She shrugged. "It would have explained why he left."

"The fact that your mother was alone narrowed down the options to accident or suicide. The absence of a note wouldn't necessarily rule out suicide so the cause of death was classified as 'undetermined'."

"When my gran died I got some money my mother had left me. I assumed it was from an insurance policy. That could be why my father didn't say anything about suicide."

"Could have been. Though it doesn't explain why he left."

"No, it doesn't." She thought for a moment. "So I must have been with my grandmother."

"Is that what you were told?"

"Mm. My mother suffered from migraines. Apparently I stayed over quite a lot."

"Do you remember that?"

"I'm not sure what I remember. It gets mixed up with stuff my gran told me. I don't know whether I'm remembering something that really happened or just something I was told about."

"What about photos?"

Kate went into her bedroom and returned with the photo of herself and her mother in their red coats. She handed it to John.

"You've been looking at this for over twenty years and you wonder why you dream about your mother in her red coat?"

"But why would I dream about being with her when she killed herself?"

"I don't know, Kate. It's possible she took you there before and you've put the two incidents together. What isn't possible is that you were with her when she went into the river." He looked at the photo again. "Your mother was a beautiful woman. You're a lot like her but she looks more delicate, a bit fragile."

"But she looks happy there, doesn't she?"

"So do you." He smiled at her. "Who are you waving at?"

"I don't know. I don't remember the photo being taken." She shook her head. "I don't even recognise where we are."

"Is it all right if I take the frame off?"

She nodded and watched as his long fingers deftly dismantled the frame and removed the picture. He looked at the back then handed it to her. There was only one word, printed in a child-like hand in green ink.

"Helensburgh?" She found herself looking at John as if he would give her the answer to that as well. "I don't remember being in Helensburgh. I used to look at it across the river. It's right opposite Greenock. But I don't think I ever went there."

"The skeleton on the building site, William Makin, he came from Helensburgh," John reminded her.

"But I've never heard of him." She put her head in her hands. "None of this makes any sense."

"There doesn't have to be a connection, Kate." He stroked her hair, letting his hand rest on the back of her neck, massaging gently. "What else have you got?"

"This." She picked up the wedding photo and held it out to him. "I asked Jean if she knew who the two other people are but she said she didn't."

"And you don't know whether to believe her?"

"I think she'd have told me if she knew either of them. I don't think she wants to keep anything else secret."

"You'd get their names and addresses from the marriage certificate."

"I haven't got it."

"Get a copy."

She stared at him, feeling like the school dunce, knowing there was a simple answer.

"General Register of Scotland, opposite the Café Royale."

"I should have thought of that." She smiled at him. "Thanks, John."

His eyes held hers. "Any time, Kate. Any time."

She could feel the pull of him, the desire, to let him take over and sort it all out for her, comfort and protect her. An urgent trill from his mobile phone broke the spell. His demeanour changed as he stood listening to the caller, asking questions, giving orders, in full police mode now.

"Sorry, Kate, I've got to go."

She followed him into the hall. At the front door he turned to her, drawing her towards him. His lips touched hers, tentatively at first, then with assurance as she responded. She leaned into him, losing herself in the lovely sensations his kiss was generating, wanting more, so much more.

He pulled away reluctantly. "I'll call you," he said, his tone firm.

"Okay." She smiled at him and then he was gone.

# Wednesday

## 59

Kate focused on the traffic light on the opposite pavement, willing the red figure to turn green, hating this enforced delay. She'd walked fast, cutting through the cobbled lanes and side streets of the New Town. The newsagents and sandwich shops were already busy, the antique shops still to come to life. She'd half-jogged past the Georgian terraces of Heriot Row, where the trees in the gardens opposite drooped gloomily in the cold mist, before reverting to her fast walk uphill to the lights at Queen Street where she was forced to stop. She watched her breath hanging on the chilled air. A dark-haired man next to her was looking at her speculatively. Bundled as she was in coat and scarf there wasn't much to see except the blond hair poking out from under her woolly hat and a face flushed from her walk.

"Do you think they're stuck?" the man asked.

She glanced at him and shrugged though she'd begun to think the same thing.

"If they are we'll be here for the rest of the day," a woman said.

They stood watching the unrelenting flow of traffic, stepping back almost as one when an articulated lorry came too close to the pavement. In the distance, the red stone of the Scottish National Portrait Gallery was barely visible. The notorious North Sea haar had laid a shroud over the city. She stamped her boot-clad feet impatiently, watching for the merest break in the traffic to make a dash for it but none came. They were three deep by the time the lights changed. They surged across the road, going their separate ways. Kate headed up to George Street and St Andrew Square from where she cut off through yet another cobbled lane to the Office of the General Register of Scotland. The process was straightforward and a few minutes later she was back on the street, clutching a copy of her parents' marriage certificate.

She walked down to Princes Street and crossed to the gardens where she sat holding the piece of paper that might unlock the secret of her mother's suicide, wondering yet again how much she wanted to know. The mist hung like a curtain reducing familiar landmarks to shapes and shadows. Holyrood Park was invisible as were the buildings that hid Arthur's Seat from view. To her right, she could feel more than see the ghostly presence of the Castle atop its volcano. Yet, even on a day like this, when Edinburgh was showing its sinister side, the city's beauty was there. The mist would lift and people would sit here eating their lunchtime sandwiches, gazing at the higgledy-piggledy buildings of the old town with their jagged rooftops, and marvel at all the history laid out before them. The sun might put in an appearance and the Castle would grudgingly emerge from the shadows dripping contempt on the people below and their small, inconsequential lives. Whatever had happened in the past this beautiful, disdainful city was home now. Everything she wanted was here. 'Let the past lie'? She stood and headed back to her flat.

The woman listed on the marriage certificate as a witness was Winifred Shaw: Kate's mother's maiden name. Her mother's sister maybe. She took a sip of her coffee and set the mug back on the coffee table. As far as

Kate knew her mother hadn't had a sister. But what did that prove? There was a lot she didn't know. Winifred Shaw's address was given as Chapel Street, Helensburgh. That was over thirty years ago. What was the likelihood that the woman still lived there? She reached out to stroke Lucy, cuddled up on the sofa beside her. She could try the electoral register. There was bound to be a library in Helensburgh. She decided to stop off and see Jean before doing anything else. If Jean did know about Winifred Shaw she'd have no reason now to keep it a secret. And if she didn't, well, nothing was lost.

She went into the kitchen, made some more coffee and poured it into a flask. Then she took a couple of rolls from the bread bin, buttered them and filled them with sliced tomatoes. She didn't know why she was doing this; it was as if she was going on a picnic and it was never going to be that. But she could see herself sitting in her car in Helensburgh drinking her coffee and eating her rolls like she was on some sort of surveillance job. Too many policemen in her life.

She arrived at Leapark just before ten, having ensured that Lucy had enough food to see her through the day, uncertain what time she might get home, still undecided about going to Helensburgh. She didn't recognise the woman in the reception office but nodded a smile anyway. At Jean's flat she knocked before using her key.

"It's lovely to see you, Kate." Jean turned from the window. Back in grey mode she looked as if she'd just emerged from the mist behind her. She took a tissue from her cardigan pocket. "Are you all right now?"

"Why shouldn't I be?"

"The carry-on with Frances and then that wedding photo of your mum and dad."

"That's why I wanted to see you."

Jean's smile faded. "There isn't anything else I can tell you."

"The woman's name is Winifred Shaw. I think she's my mum's sister." She watched for Jean's reaction.

"Your mum had a sister?" The surprise looked genuine.

"She lived in Helensburgh."

Jean perched on the settee, clutching her tissue. "Your dad told me your mum came from Greenock."

Kate unbuttoned her coat and sat in one of the armchairs. "You didn't know any of this?"

"No, I didn't." Jean shook her head for added emphasis. "I've learned my lesson. When you walked out of my flat that day, I thought that was the last I would see of you. And let me tell you, I never want to feel like that again." She paused. "But there is something I've not told you."

Kate's eyes narrowed. "What?"

"I've been having funny turns. The doctor says it's a kind of vertigo. That's what happened on Monday night. I must have grabbed the emergency cord as I fell. Frances was beside me when I woke up. She'd just made me a cup of tea when the lights went out. Then you turned up." She hesitated. "That's why Sam MacEwen was here on Saturday afternoon."

"That's how you fell off the ladder?"

Jean nodded.

"Why didn't you tell me this before?"

"I didn't want to worry you."

Or saving it to deflect awkward questions. Nonetheless, she decided against a question about her next piece of information. "I found out who the skeleton on the building site was."

Jean's hand went to her mouth. "Who?"

"A man called William James Makin."

Jean sank back on the settee, sighing her relief. "How did you find that out?"

"John Nelson."

Jean looked down at her hands, folding and refolding the tissue.

Kate was trying to make sense of Jean's reaction. Who was she expecting the skeleton to be? "Were you worried it was my father?"

"I did wonder."

"You've never heard from him?"

Jean's head jerked up. "I didn't even know he was leaving. You've got to believe me, Kate."

"Okay." She gave Jean's hands a reassuring squeeze then stood and shouldered her bag.

"Are you going?"

She looked at the painting of the Scott-Lithgow crane, the River Clyde in the foreground. "Aye, I'm going to try to sort this once and for all."

"Can I ask you something?"

Kate nodded.

Jean continued to fiddle with her tissue.

"Sometime today would be good," Kate said.

"Do you know anything about those schemes where you can get money on your house and you don't have to pay it back till after you're dead." She blurted it out, attention firmly focussed on her paper hankie.

"Are you short of money?"

"Just be nice to have a bit more." She gave an unconvincing smile. "In case there's something I want to buy."

Kate studied her. "A bit of advice, Jean. Next time you see Sam MacEwen ask him what he had planned for Jessie Turner's £20,000."

Jean couldn't stop her jaw dropping in surprise.

## 60

The Yaris zipped through Glasgow in less then twenty minutes. The mist had gradually thinned after she left Edinburgh, the cloud with it. By the time she'd reached Glasgow the sun was shining. She shot past the slip road to the Erskine Bridge, anticipation building. As the car breasted the slope just before the Bishopton turn-off she slowed. The River Clyde opened out in front of her. On a clear day you could see, if not quite forever, at least all the way down to Gourock. Brake lights marked out unwary drivers stunned by the vista in front of them.

The river spread itself wide, fingers of water reaching into the narrow inlets, invading every space. On the north shore the hills reared up, solid, fixed, the rock shading from pale grey to purple in the sunlight. Today the farthest peaks were laced with a fretwork of snow. This was her own river, the one she'd grown up alongside, the one that had given her her bearings, the one that had taken her mother.

High tide at Langbank and the water seemed almost within touching distance, separated from the carriageway by a narrow, pebbled shore. Then the road swung inland to make way for the railway line, rejoining the river at the dual carriageway into Port Glasgow, Newark Castle in the distance next to the one remaining shipyard.

As she drove through a roundabout, the Coronation Park's green grass slid into her field of vision. Her mother's body hadn't travelled far before drifting into the shore. She turned into the town centre looking for somewhere to park, following the road as it curved snake-like past the Job Centre, the social work office and the Town Hall. A left turn took her onto Princes Street, busy with lunchtime shoppers. What had once been a supermarket was boarded up, but there was a bar, a baker's and a bookie's and, near the top, a funeral parlour.

When she'd first moved to Edinburgh, she used to delight in telling people that the place she'd been born in had a castle, a Princes Street and a festival every summer. It still did. Might soon have its own edge of town shopping centre, down on the shore, where the shipyards used to be.

At the railway station, she turned onto John Wood Street: newsagent's, chemist shop, big off-licence. The street was named in honour of the town's first shipbuilder. A final left turn almost completed the circle. She left her car in the health centre car park, walked to the traffic lights and crossed the dual carriageway.

The Coronation Park sat between the road and the river. It was mostly grass with a short esplanade and a play area with swings and roundabouts. She wondered if her mother had brought her here, pushed her on a swing, spun with her on the roundabout. According to the address on the marriage certificate the flat they'd lived in then was in the red sandstone building across the road. So this was an obvious choice for a mother to take her little girl to play.

The sounds of the traffic faded as she walked to the waterside. A railing edged the stone but there was an opening with steps leading down to the water. Was this the spot her mother had chosen? Today the river was calm, smooth as glass. The hills on the other side were sharply etched against the clear blue sky. This is not what her mother would have seen that cold November morning. The river would have been dark and forbidding. Did that deter her so that she stood here a while thinking of what she was about to do? Or had the decision already been fixed, no going back? Was whatever she was running from so bad that drowning in that cold, dark water was preferable to living with it? If so, she would have stepped straight down into the river. The tide had been on its way in so the water level would have been high. Was it a single deep breath or did she swim a bit, the thick, red coat hindering her movements, tiring her more quickly until it was easier to give in, to let go? Did her past life replay as she drowned? Was the daughter she was leaving behind in it?

She thought about Edinburgh and its 'thin places' and wondered if there was a 'thin place' here where she'd feel close to her mother. Had they ever been close? She picked up a pebble and dropped it into the river. It sank quickly, the few ripples it created soon dissipating. A light breeze skimmed the water, riffled through her hair and was gone. She turned away and walked back to her car.

She sat in the car park for a while, drinking some coffee and eating one of her rolls. Although she'd spent her early years in Port Glasgow she had no memory of the place. She watched an elderly woman battle with the library's revolving doors. Would there be an electoral register with Helensburgh electors on it in there? She thought not: different constituencies. And Shaw was not that uncommon a surname. Even if she found the register could she be sure of getting the right woman? What if the woman had married? She should have done more research at Register House but her brain didn't seem to function too well these days. She opened the car door and tipped the residue of her coffee onto the tarmac, screwed the cup back onto the flask and set it on the passenger seat next to her bag. She sat for a moment after closing the door then tucked a stray hair behind her ear and set off for the motorway.

At the slip road to the Erskine Bridge she turned off, heading once again towards the river. From her side window she could see all the way down to Gourock, Inverkip and beyond. She'd been to those places with her gran. Picnics at Lunderston Bay had been a favourite: Gran sitting on a blanket spread out on the grass, a flask of tea and tomato rolls for their dinner. And it was dinner. Lunch only came into her life when she moved to Edinburgh.

In Helensburgh, she left her car in the riverside car park and set off to find the library. She eventually located it in a side street some way from the car park but they had a copy of the electoral register and there was a Winifred Shaw listed at twenty-four Smith Street, a different address from the one on the marriage certificate. She decided to try it anyway. It was not unlikely that the woman might have moved house at least once in the last thirty or so years. Armed with directions to Smith Street from the librarian she headed back to her car.

Helensburgh was still one of Scotland's more affluent towns. The house prices on display in an estate agent's window bore witness to that. She stopped outside a restaurant in a small tree-lined square debating having something to eat but felt too restless so she walked down to the main street and the river. She wandered into a multi-purpose hardware store that sold everything you could ever want and a lot you'd never thought of. Her gran had loved shops like this. Kate had amassed a collection of souvenirs from Gran's day trips, like the slim, pocket clothes brush she still carried about with her.

She was smiling when she left the shop and crossed the road to the esplanade. The river sparkled in the sunlight, Greenock on its opposite shore. It felt strange being in the place that, as a child, she'd gazed at from her bedroom window. She sauntered along towards the car park, past the deserted pier, the swimming pool, stopped off at the public toilets, finally returned to her car. Her mobile phone held a number of messages. Tom Urquhart reminded her about the deadline for applications for the Team Manager post, as if she'd forget; Jules wanted to check some details of Kate's upcoming birthday party; and John said he had Michael on Saturday but was free on Sunday if she wanted to do something. Remembering that kiss she could think of quite a few things she wanted to do but that had probably been his intention. Nevertheless she texted a promise to call him then switched off the phone and started the engine.

Smith Street was lined with terraced bungalows on one side. In the park opposite, the swings and multi-coloured slide stood empty. The bungalows looked small, probably one-bedroom, possibly purpose-built for elderly people, with handrails at the steps leading up to the front doors. If she'd correctly estimated Winifred Shaw's age at the time of the wedding the woman would be in her sixties now, not elderly by today's standards. Number twenty-four was at the end of a terrace of four separated from the next row by a narrow strip of grass. She pulled into a space on the park side of the road and looked across at the only window that faced onto the street. A net curtain shielded the inhabitants from any nosey passers-by. Kate could see nothing beyond it. The only way to find out if this woman was her mother's sister was to knock on the door and ask her.

Before she could reconsider, she crossed the road and went up the two steps to the front door. The button for the bell was just above the peephole. Kate pressed it and waited. The ringtone echoed round the small house. She listened for the sounds of slippered feet shuffling to the door. When nothing happened she rang the bell again. Still nothing. She hadn't allowed for this. She'd psyched herself up for it being the wrong woman, even more for it being the right woman, but, stupidly, hadn't considered that whoever the woman was, she might not be in. She let go of the breath she'd been holding and went back to her car where she poured herself a cup of coffee and settled down with it and the last of her tomato rolls.

Forty-five minutes later she saw, in her wing mirror, a short, dumpy woman in a shapeless, brown coat and a green knitted hat coming along the street. Stumpy legs, encased in thick tights, disappeared into zipped brown ankle boots. A loaf of bread poked out of the grey shopping bag carried in her right hand. Kate watched her and wondered if this wee, fat woman could be the sister of her tall, blonde, slender mother.

The woman went up the steps at number twenty-four and disappeared inside. Kate decided she'd give her time to get her coat off and put her shopping away. So it was that fifteen minutes later, for the third time that day, she rang the bell of twenty-four Smith Street.

### 61

Jean looked at herself in the dressing table mirror. A pale face with dark-ringed eyes stared back. Her hair straggled over the collar of her beige blouse. Not the imposing figure she needed to be to put Rose Toner in her place. She dug in the top drawer for the few bits of make-up she had, wanting to confront Toner looking a bit less like death warmed up. She patted on the hard, sparse powder. No blusher so she pinched her cheeks, pleased with the enlivening effect. Next she threw off the cardigan and blouse and replaced them with the soft-hued blue-green jumper that Kate had bought for her. Much better, Jean.

Her newfound confidence faltered at a knock on her door. She stood quietly, debating with herself then she took a deep breath, walked into the hall and threw the door wide.

Sam MacEwen stepped back.

"Oh. Come in." Jean ushered him into the sitting room.

He turned to her. "You're looking very smart today, Jean."

She clasped her hands to resist the urge to reach for her tissue. "Would you like some coffee?"

"Only if it's not too much trouble."

"No trouble at all." She smiled as he followed her into the kitchen.

"I wanted to say how much I enjoyed Monday evening."

Jean concentrated on preparing the coffee, setting out her cups and saucers on the tray. "I enjoyed it too," she answered, remembering how he took her arm when they crossed the road, his hand on her back as he guided her to their table, holding her coat for her, the soft kiss on her cheek when he left her at her door. Romantic. Or playing her. She shook her head, annoyed at Kate for feeding her own doubt.

"Perhaps we could do it again sometime." There was the hint of a question in his voice.

She turned. "I'd like that."

He stood in the doorway, smiling. "Good." He stepped forward. "Now let me take that tray."

He laid the tray on the coffee table and sat in an armchair. Jean sat on the sofa facing him and set the cups and saucers on the table but when she reached for the percolator he put his hand on her arm.

"I'll do that. There's quite a weight in these things." He poured their coffee then sat back, adjusting the cuffs of his royal blue 'Pringle' jumper over those of his white shirt, leaving Jean to add milk to his cup – a soupçon.

Jean looked down at her coffee, smiling to herself.

"You make an excellent cup of coffee, Jean. I think you're something of a connoisseur, like myself." He set his cup down carefully in its saucer and smiled his charming smile. "I wondered whether you'd had time to consider our investment opportunity."

"Yes, well," she swallowed, noting his expectant look. "I'm not sure I can afford to take the risk."

"I can guarantee a good return." When she said nothing, he continued, "It could be a great venture for us."

"I'm sure it could." She paused. "To be honest with you I don't have the money."

For the first time he looked disconcerted. "Ah, I see." He examined his hands. "There's no way you can raise it?" He looked round the room ending with a glance at the Spode crockery, the delicate silver teaspoons.

"I'm afraid not." Jean could feel her heart pounding as she clung to her new-minted self -respect.

"That's a pity. Still, not to worry." He smiled and lifted his coffee.

She felt her hopes rise in spite of herself.

He drained the cup and stood. "Thank you for the coffee, Jean."

"You're going?"

"People to see. You know how it is."

"Of course." She walked with him to the door. "I'll see you again?"

"I'll be busy for the next few weeks. Final touches and all that." He held out his hand. "Goodbye, Jean"

She put her hand in his, feeling cool, dry skin. "Goodbye."

He dropped her hand and reached for the door handle.

"Sam."

He turned to her.

She hesitated. "Nothing."

She closed the door behind him and went into the sitting room. It had been on the tip of her tongue to throw Jessie Turner at him. For once in her life she'd had the perfect parting shot. But for what? He was just a sad, old man preying on even sadder, old women. Of course she'd always known it had been about money. Yet there'd been that moment when he'd let her hope. Her mother and Kate beamed at her from the photos on the sideboard. Oh, Jean, when will you ever learn?

She went into her bedroom and picked up the small, blue, velvet box just as Maggie Keenan had done all those years ago before walking out the door with it. She'd let Maggie Keenan take all she had left of Andrew, and Keenan had known that. Jean had pleaded with her, realising too late that the locket's importance simply made it more valuable. Afterwards, she'd accepted it as a punishment for abandoning her son, or so she told herself. But now, thanks to Kate, she had her one little part of Andrew back. She sat on her bed and opened the box. Once, she'd held him, just once; kissed his wee red face. When she'd stroked his baby fists a tiny finger had brushed her palm. She'd wanted to keep him then. But it was too late. All the arrangements had been made so she'd let the nurse take him away. Later the same nurse had come back and handed her an envelope. Inside lay a lock of dark, silky hair. The photo had come later to the nursing home she was staying in to recover from the birth. She couldn't lose him again.

She was about to stand when the knock came, three firm raps. She froze. Maybe Sam MacEwen had changed his mind. Though even as she thought this she knew who it really was; knew she couldn't face it, not right now. So she sat on, not moving, hardly breathing for fear Toner would sniff her out.

The knock came again. "I know you're in there, Jean Markham." The dull monotone was unmistakable.

Jean sat tight clutching her precious box. The door was locked. Wasn't it?

"I know you're in there." The words echoed round her head. Toner was laughing at her. She could hear it in that voice. She would sort it. But later. When she felt stronger.

## 62

Kate took an inventory while she waited. She was sitting on a green two-seater sofa with wooden arms and foam cushions still firm to the point of hard. The grey cord carpet showed signs of wear on the path from the door to the worn green armchair to her left. A small television sat on a bow-legged, mahogany table next to the fireplace. A trolley acted as a coffee table with slots for storage underneath its white top that held puzzle magazines. When she touched it, it spun easily on its castors. It was a haphazard collection, like a job lot from a charity shop. Despite that the room was spotless, smelling of polish and carpet freshener. It felt strange to be here in this small room waiting to hear the story of her mother's life from an auntie she hadn't known existed.

"Do you take milk and sugar in your tea?"

She turned to see Winnie smiling at her from the sitting room door. "Just milk."

She'd been surprised by the woman's reaction to her, hadn't been prepared to be so quickly recognised. After she rang the bell she heard the creak of a floorboard under the heavy tread of footsteps. She'd stepped back so that the peephole would give a view of her face rather than her chest. A key turned in the lock and the door opened as far as the chain would allow. She loosened her scarf and tucked her hair behind her ears. A round face framed by light brown hair streaked with grey peered out. Kate smiled whilst she prepared her speech to allay any concern the woman might have at finding a stranger on her doorstep but the door closed before she could say anything. Then the chain clattered off and the door was flung wide.

"Katie?" the woman gasped. "It is you, isn't it?"

Winnie had struggled to contain herself ever since. 'You're that like your mum,' she kept saying. Kate had explained about the wedding photo and tracing Winnie through the marriage certificate but wasn't sure that Winnie was listening.

She turned her attention to the fireplace. The two bars on the electric fire glowed brightly. Above them the chunks of plastic masquerading as coal did likewise. The fire sat in a wooden unit that housed a collection of ornaments in a variety of nooks and crannies. They were mostly teddy bears in unlikely poses including one in a pink tutu, poised to pirouette. Photos bedecked the unit's highly polished mantelshelf, all of Kate and her mother including the one in their red coats.

She'd thought the waiting and wondering would be the worst bit, that once she got to this stage it would be easier, the decision made, too late to back out. But a bit of her wanted to be back in her car, drinking her coffee and eating her roll before starting the engine and driving back to Edinburgh without finding out. Or walking up to the door of twenty-four Smith Street and ringing the bell to be greeted by a woman who didn't recognise her and had never heard of a Catherine Shaw. Then she could have given up and gone home to get on with her life. Would that have been better?

"Did you read the bits in the papers? I kept them for you." Winnie bustled in carrying a tin tray with tea and biscuits.

Kate took the tray from her and put it on the twirly table leaving Winnie to set it out. 'The bits in the papers' were more extracts from the Greenock Telegraph including some about the skeleton on the building site. She'd glanced through them wondering why Winnie expected her to find them significant. The final one read:-

'Skeleton Identified as Helensburgh Man

The skeleton of a man found on a building site in Greenock has been identified as William James Makin originally from Helensburgh. It's not been possible to determine a cause of death but the site has been notorious for flooding and it is believed this may have contributed to the man's death. Police are not looking for anyone in connection with the incident.'

The article was accompanied by a faded black and white photo that was too blurry now to see much beyond the fact that it was of a man.

After she set the mugs of tea on the table Winnie settled back in the green armchair, her hands in her lap. "I thought I'd never see you again."

"I only found out about you a while ago when I found this photo." She held it out.

Winnie looked down at it, smiling and shaking her head. "I've got lots of photos if you want to see them."

"Maybe later." She hesitated. "I came because I need to know about my mum."

"You're so like her."

Kate paused. "I mean why she killed herself."

Winnie's smile disappeared. "I thought you knew. I thought your dad would have told you now that it's all finished with."

"My dad?" She shook her head. "What do you mean? What's all finished with?"

Winnie was licking her lips, whimpering like a trapped animal.

"What is it?" Kate asked, struggling to prepare herself for whatever was coming. "Whatever it is, Winnie, I need to know," she said wondering if it was true.

"Hmm," Winnie said. She focussed on smoothing her skirt, patting it down over her knees then returned her hands to rest in her lap.

Kate picked up her mug and took a sip of the tea, giving Winnie some breathing space. Her gaze drifted to the photos, noting the smiles in every one.

"It was all my fault," Winnie said quickly.

Kate turned back to her.

"My mother took in lodgers." Her voice took on a defeated tone. "This was after my dad died." She nodded towards the newspapers. "Willie Makin was one of them. He used to go away to work and stay with us when he came back. I didn't like him. He had dirty fingernails." She paused, moistening her lips. "He took up with my mother." She glanced at Kate. "You know what I mean?"

Kate nodded.

"After a while he took up with me as well."

"How old were you?" the social worker in her asked.

"Six."

Kate closed her eyes briefly.

Winnie stared straight ahead, rocking back and forth, her words tumbling out. "My mother wasn't keeping well. Willie Makin said he'd take me for a picnic. He took me for a lot of picnics that year. Then my mother fell pregnant. She was in her bed a lot. Willie Makin could do what he liked." She smoothed her skirt again, soft, plump fingers patting it down. "Some days I couldn't go to school."

"Did you try to tell anybody?"

"He said if I told I'd be sent to a home. Anyway I didn't know how." Winnie shrugged, patted her skirt. "When the baby was born he went away. A health visitor came and we got a home help. Catherine was in and out of hospital for a while but she was a lovely baby. You were her image when you were wee." She gazed at Kate, her pale eyelashes blinking softly. The rocking had stopped. "You still are."

"So was Willie Makin my mum's father?"

Another shrug. "I suppose."

Kate looked again at the man in the photo. He was tall and skinny and even allowing for the fading, his hair might have once been a dirty fair.

"He was away for over a year." Winnie paused.

Kate turned back to her.

"I was nine when he came back. He picked up where he'd left off. He'd brought my mother a lot of drink from wherever he'd been."

"How long did it go on for?"

Winnie began rocking gently again, continuing as if she hadn't heard Kate's question. "Catherine was four when he took her for her first picnic."

Even though the social worker in her had known what was coming she felt her jaw drop, a scream of 'no' in her head.

"He didn't bother with me so much after that. Said I was too old for him that Catherine was his special girl." She looked at Kate. "I did try to stop him but my mother wouldn't believe me. So I took a knife to him." Winnie's gaze drifted downwards. "Got sent to a home just like he said." She nodded as if to herself.

"I was sixteen when I got back. Willie Makin had packed his bags. My mother said it was my fault and I'd have to look after Catherine. So I did. Did a better job than her."

She could hear the scowl in Winnie's voice, talking as if she'd said all this before, over and over, only herself to hear it, preparing for the day when she'd tell it for real? Or preserving her memory of what happened in a story that would give her a bit of distance from it all.

"Catherine was working in Greenock when she met your dad. I was pleased for her." She paused, nodding again. "But when you were born, oh, we were so happy. She used to bring you over on the wee Granny to see me."

Kate looked up to see Winnie beaming desperately at her. "The wee Granny?"

"The Granny Kempock: the ferry from Gourock. I would meet you at the café. That's where I took that picture." Winnie reached for the 'red coat' photo, words continuing to tumble out. "It's me you're waving at. It was a lovely time. Lovely." She looked down at the photo, stroking the two figures, holding onto that happy time. "Then one day Catherine thought she saw Willie Makin. She was terrified. She hurried down to the pier to catch the boat. I couldn't keep up with her and you got upset, kept trying to pull away from her.

"The next day he came to my door. He said he wanted to atone to me, to Catherine and where was she? He thought he saw her with a wee lassie. I told him I still had the knife." She looked at Kate, indignant now. "He shook his head. Him. Shaking his head at me like he'd never done anything wrong, like I was some kind of lost soul."

A scream from outside made them both turn to the window. Through the net curtain Kate saw a teenage girl in a school uniform swing up and back, legs kicking out on the upswing to push higher. She wanted to watch to see how high the girl would dare to go. Better than listening to what Winnie seemed determined now to tell her. She flailed around trying to find refuge in her professionalism but this was too close, too personal, too painful.

"They shouldn't be there. They're too big for that," Winnie said, scowling at the interruption. "I had to warn Catherine," she went on. "Are you listening to me?"

Kate turned to her taken aback by the angry impatience in Winnie's tone.

"I got the boat over. But she was frightened for you. So I went to get you from school to take you to your Granny McKinnery's."

"Did my gran know about Makin?"

"No." Winnie shook her head, calmer now. "They were in the kitchen when I got back. Catherine was huddled in a corner by the cooker. He was on the floor. There was a knife sticking out of his stomach." She sat silent, gazing into a space that Kate didn't want to see. Even her hands had stopped their interminable patting.

"Was he dead?" It came out as a croak.

"Not properly dead." Winnie frowned disapprovingly. "He was making noises like he was choking a bit."

Kate felt her head would burst. There was a buzzing in her ears, a sharp pain behind her eyes. She swallowed trying to make her ears pop, clear some of the pressure. When that didn't work, she tried to deepen her breathing, feeling her life unravel that bit more every time Winnie opened her mouth. She focussed on the photograph now back in its place on the mantelshelf. The two figures in their bright red coats seemed to dance in the shimmering heat from the electric fire. She shivered, feeling the small room close in around her. Winnie's words echoed like hammer blows.

"I helped Catherine into the sitting room and stayed with her till your dad came in from his work. He got a van from somewhere and took the body away. I put her to bed and sat with her till your dad came back." She sighed, a sob in her voice. "We thought she was getting better. She'd started going out again. But the migraines were worse and she was having to take stronger painkillers."

Kate stared down at her hands. "Did she leave a note?"

Winnie recited it like a prayer.

Kate flinched, struggling to keep tears at bay. A bang on the window made her jump and propelled Winnie from her chair. A girl's face seemed to materialise, ghost-like, beyond the net curtain. The pale skin contrasted with the black shadow that circled her eyes.

"Get you away from here," Winnie screamed.

The girl dropped down. "Auld witch," she yelled, her laughter drifting back to them.

"She's always doing that," Winnie said, stomping back to her chair. "Her and her pals. But I've warned them."

Kate paused to let Winnie calm down surprised by the sudden outburst. "Do you know why my father left?" she said.

"He thought it would be better if everybody believed Catherine died in an accident and he had to go away to work. He knew you'd be all right with your granny." Matter-of-fact now.

"Why wasn't I told about you?"

"Helensburgh was supposed to a secret. You weren't to tell anybody about coming here." She shrugged. "But I got the boat over every week and watched you coming out of school. Just to be sure you were all right."

"I never saw you. I think I would've remembered you then."

"You weren't supposed to see me. I just wanted to see you." Winnie's tone softened. "You were that like Catherine, it was as if she'd got another chance and she'd be happy this time."

Kate turned away, a sense of what she'd lost growing inside her, trying to focus on an incipient anger. "Do you know where my father is?"

"No." Winnie shook her head. "No, I don't know that."

### 63

Crosswinds on the bridge buffeted the small car. Behind her, pinpricks of light dotted the horizon. She wanted to leave Winnie's story behind in that small, respectable town, to return to her life in Edinburgh, to the person she used to be before she knew.

In front of her an enormous moon hung like a ghostly shadow behind a film of fractured cloud. Beneath her the river swirled and twisted, beckoning. Her arms twitched on the the steering wheel, making the car drift towards the guard rail. If she were to jump in now the water would close over her as if she were nothing at all. She pulled the car back to the centre of the lane and accelerated, drawn by that moon, relieved when the bridge finally came to its end and she was on the solid ground of the motorway.

After she'd left Winnie she'd driven into the town. Bought fish and chips and sat in the car picking at them. Winnie had nattered on, seeming to relax as if the worst was over. For her at least. Kate had tried to focus on the good bits. How her mum had taken her swimming, helped her build sand castles on the beach, played putting and crazy golf, Winnie always there in the background, laughing, laughing. Till Willie Makin returned.

Rain in Glasgow came as a relief, forcing her to concentrate on driving. Her mobile phone trilled an incoming call. She glanced at the screen – Jean. She ignored it. When it rang a second time she switched it to 'silent mode' but accelerated and moved to the outside lane. The remainder of her journey passed in a blur, on automatic pilot. With the professional bit of her brain she could see her mother's panic at the reappearance of her abuser; could understand her inability to speak about what had been done to her; the shame she would have carried throughout her life regardless of the number of times Winnie told her none of it had been her fault. And the guilt when she killed the man who had abused her, the man who was also her father. And Kate's grandfather.

She was on the slip road to the Newbridge roundabout when she noticed her mobile phone yet again demanding her attention. She ignored it unitl she reached St. John's Road when she pulled over and hit the answer button.

"Kate, Kate," Jean burbled breathlessly.

"What is it, Jean?"

"It's Rose Toner. Something awful's happened. You've got to come, Kate. Please."

She rested her head on the steering wheel wanting sleep and the oblivion it would bring however temporary.

"Kate? Are you still there?"

"I'm on my way."

"Where are you?"

She cut the connection. Five minutes later she turned into the small car park, exasperated with Jean but relieved to have something else to think about. She let herself into the building and went up the stairs. The emergency lighting left the corridor dim, throwing shadows ahead of her. She pushed through the fire door and strode on. At Rose Toner's flat she stopped. The door was slightly ajar. She nudged it further and stepped into the dark hallway. She heard a choking sound. "Jean," she called.

A figure rushed at her.

"For fuck's sake." She pulled clear of Jean's outstretched hands.

"Sorry. I'm sorry," Jean whispered, leading her into the sitting room. "It's in here."

Jean moved aside and Kate saw where the choking sound had come from. Rose Toner sat slumped in an armchair. A table lamp lying on the floor threw a deformed light on her predicament. Her right arm draped uselessly over the side of the chair. Drool hung from the right side of her chin.

"Chh," issued from Toner. The guttural sound seemed to come from the back of her throat, as if she was trying to hawk up years of gunge from her lungs.

Kate moved towards her. "Rose?"

Rose Toner mumbled something, raising her left hand.

"What?" Kate leaned closer.

Fingers caught and twisted the flesh of her upper arm.

"Aow. Bitch!" Kate jumped back resisting the urge to lash out. She turned her anger on Jean. "Have you called an ambulance?"

Jean seemed mesmerised by Rose Toner.

"Jean!"

Jean shook her head.

"For Christ's sake." She picked up the phone and hit the nine three times, noticing the wooden box on the coffee table as she did so. When the emergency operator answered, she described Toner's condition and said she'd wait for the ambulance to arrive.

"She was like this when I found her," Jean was saying.

Kate ignored her and turned to the box on the coffee table. The partitions from its days as a jewellery box remained. The left-hand section held a selection of keys, each with a plastic attachment indicating the flat it belonged to. There was one for Harriet Post's flat.

Toner growled.

The central section of the box was split in two, one held a key to Maggie Keenan's flat, tucked in its own little niche. The next-door niche was empty. Had that held the key to Maggie's money? 'Rose was a good friend of my mother's'. Wasn't that what Fraser had said? She looked at Toner. Strings of saliva extended onto the pale green jumper. Behind the round glasses the right eye drooped but in the left eye a glint remained.

"Chh," Toner protested as Kate turned back to the box.

In the right hand section, on a tissue bed, a small, candy-striped clown nestled. If this was Harriet Post's clown and if, as Frances Wordsworth had said, Harriet Post had got it back how come it was now sitting in Toner's jewellery box?

Kate thought about the bruises on Harriet Post's arms and legs. She'd bet there were similar bruises on Betty Smyth and now she had one of her own. She reached down to the jewellery box and used the tissues to pick up the clown.

"Chh." Toner was frowning furiously, left eye veering between Kate and the clown, fat body almost rocking.

"How did you get this back?"

"Chuh."

"Did you go to Harriet Post's flat to get it?" Kate looked down at the box. "You used the key you kept in the box for Maggie, didn't you?"

"Don't, Kate," Jean said.

"What happened when you went in? Was Harriet Post waiting for you? Or was it just her bad luck to come out of the bathroom when you were in the hall?"

"Chuh."

"Kate, stop it."

"What did you do, Rose? Push her back in?"

Toner growled.

"Did you hear the thump when she fell?"

"Kate!"

The intercom was buzzing, announcing the arrival of the ambulance crew. Kate pressed the button to release the front door. She realised Jean was staring at her.

"What did you do that for?" Jean said.

"To let them in."

"What?"

Kate turned away. She placed the clown back on its tissue bed aware of Toner's malevolent glare. She felt as if she was drunk, the world a bit skew-whiff.

"Are you all right?" Jean asked her.

She picked up the phone and called the police.

Jean took a tissue from her pocket and wiped the drool from Rose Toner's chin.

At Comely Bank Avenue she left her car on double yellow lines and went up to her flat. Inside she dropped her coat and bag on the floor. Lucy wound herself round her legs looking for food and reassurance. She provided the food; the reassurance was beyond her. On the kitchen table the detritus of her investigation lay scattered: the wedding photo, the letters and cards, the newspaper extracts and the notes John had made for her. She touched them, remembering when, just the night before, she'd been hopeful that she would finally know the truth about her mother's death. That maybe then she'd be able to trust enough to let John Nelson into her life. But now? How could she tell a police officer that her paedophile grandfather had been killed by her mother and the body buried by her father?

The photo of herself and her mother lay waiting to be returned to its frame. She remembered John's long fingers, with their short, clean nails, dismantling the frame and handing her the photo. She stood looking at it: her mum in her red coat, herself in her cut-down child's version smiling and waving at her auntie Winnie. She trailed her fingers down the tall, blonde, slender figure. 'Delicate, a bit fragile', John had said. And she was, much more so now. Kate extended her hand to touch the small, smiling red-coated child alongside. 'You were her image when you were wee'. In the photo she was about four. The age her mum had been when Willie Makin had taken her for a picnic and turned her small world upside down. And it still reverberated in Winnie's misery at losing both her sister and her niece, and in her own life, growing up without mother or father.

Kate picked up the photograph and saw her mum on that cold, dark November morning walking towards the river in her red coat and she wanted to hold her. She wanted to tell her that she loved her, always would. But most of all she wanted to put her arms around her. If she could reach back and hold her, just once. Her breathing rate increased, her heart began to pound, an adrenaline rush on the way: fight or flight. But there was nowhere to run. She slid down the wall, sinking to the floor.

"I can't take any more. I see him everywhere. Look after my darling Katie. Love her for me," she whispered.

She hugged the photo to her chest and curled herself into a ball. Burying her head as deep as it would go, she wept.

# Epilogue

## I

She walked up to the reception desk in the George Hotel and was about to ask for Alan McKinnery when she heard the voice.

"Katie?"

She turned and saw a well-dressed man coming towards her. He wore a blue polo shirt under an expensive-looking tweed jacket. He had cropped grey hair above a tanned face, craggy was the word that came to mind. He wasn't much taller than she was but he was broad, looked powerful despite his sixty-plus years. She stood where she was and let him come to her.

"It's Kate," she said sharply.

"Kate," he repeated, nodding.

He stood in front of her looking uncomfortable. She could see his problem. How did you greet a daughter you had ignored for twenty-five years? He settled for a smile and an invitation to afternoon tea.

"It's great to see you again, Kate," he said when they were seated at a table. "You're beautiful just like your mother." He smiled at her. "You must have a lot of questions. Where do you want to start?"

She shrugged off her coat. "Why don't we start with why you left me?"

He nodded maintaining eye contact. "You have to understand that I loved your mother more than life itself. I'd have done anything for her, to keep her safe." He paused as if considering his next words. "I had promised to take care of her, to protect her and I failed, not once but twice. I thought you'd be better off without me. But there wasn't a day, an hour when I didn't think about you."

"So you did it for me?" She kept her tone sharp letting the cynicism show through.

He nodded again – a single dip of his head.

"Why have you come back?"

He sighed then waited silently as 'tea' arrived. The waiter smiled as he set everything out. First came the pots of tea and coffee followed by a pot of hot water, a jug of cream and one with milk, and scones with cream and jam. The cups finally rattled into their saucers as if the waiter could feel the tension and was eager to get away.

Kate reached for the coffee pot, poured some into her cup and sat back. There was a hint of irritation in her father's quick, impatient pouring of his own coffee but when he looked up at her he was wearing his smile again.

"I came back because I thought that was what you would want, because there was nothing to hide from you anymore. And because you're my daughter and I missed you." He leaned forward looking at her face. "You've still got the scar." He touched it lightly with his pinkie, his finger barely brushing the spot just below her bottom lip.

She pulled back from him but couldn't stop herself reaching up to touch where his finger had been.

"You don't remember it, do you?" He shook his head, smiling. "You were running to meet me. You were only three at the time. I had my arms open ready to catch you but you tripped and fell before you reached me and you hit your face on the edge of the pavement. You let out such a scream. I think the whole street heard you. We had to take you to the hospital. They put a couple of stitches in the wound. You held onto me the whole time, wouldn't let go. 'Daddy, daddy', you kept saying."

She felt herself carried along by his story, wanting to smile with him, to share the memory, to be that child again.

"I loved you, Kate, but I didn't want your life to be tainted by what had happened. You were happy with your grandmother weren't you?"

She nodded.

"You've done something with your life. You went to university. You've got a good job, a nice flat. Would you have done all that if everybody had known how your mother died and why? I don't think so." He sat back looking much too pleased with himself, breaking the spell of remembrance.

"How do you know what I've done with my life? Who told you?"

"I set up a trust fund for you. Your grandmother drew on it when you needed something. The solicitor sent me reports on how the money was being used until you graduated then the balance of the money passed to you."

She remembered the letter from the solicitor, her whoops of joy at the amount. "I thought that came from the insurance policy on my mum."

"That's what your grandmother was told. But there never was an insurance policy."

She frowned. "That doesn't explain how you know about my job and my flat."

He hesitated. "I had someone in Edinburgh keep track of you for me: a private investigator."

"You've had somebody following me?" Her voice was loud enough to make heads turn.

He reached out a placatory hand. "It wasn't like that," he said quietly. "I just wanted to know that you were all right."

"And did this private investigator not tell you that your mother had died so that you could come to her funeral?"

He looked down. "I couldn't get a flight out in time to be there."

"Where were you?"

"I moved around but for the past fifteen years I've been living in South Africa." A note of impatience had crept into his voice.

"Doing what?"

"A variety of jobs, mostly in engineering. I've retired now. I can afford to."

She unclenched her hands, picked up her cup and took a sip. The coffee was lukewarm. She returned the cup to its saucer. "How long are you here for?"

"As long as you want me to be." He paused back in control now. "You're my daughter. Everything I've done has been for you." He shook his head. "I don't know, maybe I got it wrong. I can see you're angry with me and I can understand that but I'm here to make it up to you now in any way I can." He stretched out his hand to her.

She sat rigid, hands clasped in her lap. "Well, hail the conquering hero. You must really think my head buttons up the back if you expect me to believe all that." Her voice sounded shrill even to her, her Inverclyde roots there for all to hear in the accent.

There were looks of alarm on the faces turned in their direction. The waiter hovered in his neat little paisley-patterned waistcoat as if trying to get up the nerve to ask them to tone it down.

Alan McKinnery used his outstretched hand to lift his coffee cup. She watched his eyes narrow slightly as he sipped from it. He reached for the coffee pot, holding it over her cup. She shook her head still watching him. He wasn't used to this; he didn't like his motives being questioned. He signalled to the waiter to bring fresh coffee. When it came he topped up his own cup and carefully replaced the coffee pot.

"I can understand you being angry with me, Kate. You feel I deserted you, let you down." His tone was one of patient understanding. "But I've come back to make it up to you. Please, give me a chance to do that."

"Why should I do anything for you? I don't know you. I wouldn't have recognised you if I passed you in the street."

He sighed. "I realise that. That's why I've come back, do you not see that?"

"No, I don't see that." She had to give him points for perseverance but the dents in his armour were beginning to show. "If you want me to have anything to do with you, tell me the real reason you've come back." She watched as a range of expressions made fleeting appearances across his face, impatience, irritation, duplicity. "Or is it more to do with having to get out of South Africa?" That hit a nerve. "You've not come back for me at all, have you? You're running from something over there."

"I've never run away from anything in my life."

She raised her eyebrows at that one.

"I came back because I thought you might need me." His eyes narrowed. "Do you think I wanted you to find out about all this? If Jean had kept her mouth shut like I'd told her to do, none of this need ever have happened."

"Don't blame Jean. This is your doing. You're the one that buggered off." Heads turned towards them again.

Her father leaned forward. "Oh, no, we mustn't blame Jean for anything," he hissed. "She can keep her mouth shut when it suits her."

"What do you mean by that?"

"Tell you about her son, did she?"

"Aye, she did." She caught a hint of surprise in his face.

"What did she tell you about his father?"

She waited.

"I bet she told you how her life in the States was so miserable even Greenock was preferable?" He nodded at her unspoken acknowledgement of this. "She didn't tell you that she came back to Greenock because she'd been screwing her brother-in-law and his wife found out. That she didn't know who the boy's father was."

Throughout these revelations her father had continued studying her, watching for signs she was desperate not to give him.

"If you're wondering how I know all this it's because the guy she was screwing came looking for her. She was living in Glasgow at the time. I had to fob him off. Tell him I didn't know where she was."

"Did you tell him about the baby?" she asked in spite of herself.

There was a long pause. She tried to read his expression but his face had closed down.

"No." His tone softened. "I shouldn't have told you all that. Not in that way." He looked at her. "Kate, I …", he shook his head in a gesture of helplessness.

She met his exposed gaze with her own cold stare. "Why did you tell Winnie not to contact me? And don't tell me it was all for me. If you'd been that bothered about me, you would never have left me." She sensed his growing discomfort and went for the jugular. "You'd have done what my mum asked and looked after me."

"How do you know about that?"

"Winnie told me."

He turned away from her. "I couldn't look at you. You were so like your mum. I couldn't cope with my failure of her. If she'd done what I told her everything would have been fine."

"What do you mean?"

"I told her she'd be better cutting all her links with Helensburgh especially Winnie. It only reminded her of what had happened. But she wouldn't. And once you were old enough to go with her she was never away from the place. It was the only thing we argued about."

"You mean it was the only time she wouldn't do what you told her."

He shook his head, the smiles long gone. "You might look like your mother but the resemblance ends there. She was gentle."

"Winnie loved her, she took care of her."

"Aye," he snarled, "and the stupid bitch led Makin straight to her."

"Is that why you told her not to see me? To punish her?" She caught the admission in his face. "And you've just tried the same thing with Jean. 'I shouldn't have told you all that.'" She mimicked his comment. "You're a vindictive, controlling bastard. I'm glad it was my gran who brought me up. You were right about that at least. I was better off without you." She picked up her coat and bag and headed for the door.

"Wait," he called after her. "Come back here, Kate."

He caught up with her outside and grabbed her arm. "I'm still your father."

"You abandoned me," she was struggling to keep the sob from her voice. "What sort of father is that?" She pulled free and started to walk away.

"Kate," he called after her, making no attempt to disguise his anger. "We will talk. You will listen to me."

She began to run.

## II

She stood at her kitchen window sipping water from the glass in her hand. Frost silvered the roofs of the tenement blocks across the back gardens. Behind her, Springsteen whispered of faithless kisses on the streets of Philadelphia. It was dark, inside as well as out. Everything was in shadow, the only movement coming from the trees, their bare branches waving gently in the occasional breeze.

Since the meeting with her father she'd been wondering about the sort of life her mother had with him. Control masquerading as protection was how it had sounded, with Winnie the fly in the ointment. Even this flat had his metaphorical fingerprints all over it. Without the money from the trust fund he'd set up she would not have been able to afford it.

She had assumed her father had found the suicide note, that it had been left for him. But what if it had been meant for Winnie? Had Winnie seen the note because it had been sent to her? If so, it was Winnie to whom her mum had bequeathed Kate's care. 'Look after my darling Katie, love her for me.' That's what her mum had written. Was that what Winnie had been doing when she'd waited outside the school? Reassuring herself that little Katie was loved and cared for? Was it possible that it wasn't Willie Makin her mum was referring to when she'd written 'I see him everywhere' but her husband?

And what had Winnie's life been like with all those years of waiting: the journeys to Greenock to see Kate come out of school; the daily readings of the Greenock Telegraph in case there was a mention in it of Kate, or Willie Makin? Why hadn't Winnie ignored her brother-in-law's strictures and made contact with her? Guilt that she'd led Makin to her sister? Wanting to do what she was told was best for Kate? Did Winnie have reason to be afraid of Alan McKinnery? Before she left Winnie's house she'd taken the tray with their mugs into the kitchen having offered to wash up as her gran had brought her up to do. Winnie had shuffled after her saying 'no, no.' The small kitchen sparkled in the light from the fluorescent tube, all the surfaces clean and clear, except for the long-bladed knife lying on the draining board. Was that part of the warning to the school kids? Or was Winnie expecting another visitor?

Her father's decision not to tell Jean that her lover had come looking for her was yet more evidence of his vindictiveness. Jean had broken down and told him about her affair when she'd come back to Greenock but didn't want her mother to know. He'd agreed to keep it between the two of them. But not before he voiced his opinion of her stupidity, her lack of self-control. Self-righteous bastard. 'I know about the baby's father.' That was all she had to say and Jean's face had crumpled. They'd sat on the sofa, Kate holding her sobbing seventy-year old auntie like a child, seeing that younger Jean and her mad, passionate affair. At the end of it they had their understanding, their fresh start. And the Christmas card made sense. 'We're even. Let the past lie.' A pact to keep each other's secrets. But Jean's interest in the skeleton had a more sinister look. She had worried that it might be her lover or her husband. Killed by Alan McKinnery in a fit of temper. What sort of man was he that his sister could see him that way?

They'd not got round to Rose Toner and what Jean had been doing when Toner had her 'cerebral event'. Why she hadn't called an ambulance. How she came to find her in the first place. She'd convinced the police that it had been coincidence that she'd been passing Rose Toner's flat, heard noises and found the door unlocked. Fortunately for Jean, Toner obliged with a much more serious 'cerebral event' in the ambulance and was in no fit state to contradict her.

And in the end she hadn't told Jean that her lover had come looking for her. It was all too late and there was more than enough to regret.

Broken lives. That was what she dealt in. Now her own could fill a case file, a life-storybook brimming with second-hand memories. She'd told John about the meeting with her father but not everything he'd said. Just as she'd told him about Winnie but not any of the things she'd said. Secrets: her dominant family trait it seemed.

She set the glass carefully on the draining board, feeling the cold seep into her body. She switched off the hi-fi and returned to the bedroom.

Shivering, she slipped out of her dressing gown and slid under the duvet. John was still asleep. He lay on his back, head turned to the side, left arm stretched out where she'd been lying. Her pet policeman. She stroked his hair, letting her fingers trail down his neck to his chest. He stirred and turned towards her. Murmuring her name, he pulled her close, wrapping his arms around her. She snuggled against him, relishing his warmth, planting soft kisses on his neck and shoulder, thinking how easy it would be to love him.